OUR
FOREVER
PROMISE

BOOK THREE IN THE FOREVER SERIES

MARY A. WASOWSKI

Copyright © 2014 by Mary A. Wasowski
Cover Design by Okay Creations
Formatting by JT Formatting

Printed in the United States of America
First Edition: January 2015
Library of Congress Cataloging-in-Publication Data

http://authormaryawasowski.com/

Wasowski, Mary A.
  Our Forever Promise (*Book Three in The Forever Series*) / 1st ed
    ISBN-13: 978-0989623872

  1. Our Forever Promise—Fiction.   2. Fiction—Romance
        3. Fiction—Contemporary Romance:

DEDICATION

For my boys...
Three's a charm! In 2008, we welcomed our third son to our family.
Each of our children shines in their own special way, and they bring
us so much joy to our lives. This book is for them.

For Zachary:
Words cannot express how proud I am of you and the man you have
become. Your future is bright with a military career on the horizon.
You are focused and driven. I know you will make an amazing sol-
dier serving our country. I love you, son.

For Christopher:
You think being the middle child is tough at times, but I think it's
perfect for you. You have an amazing personality filled with laughter and wit. You are fearless and confident. Thank you for always
making me laugh. I love you, son.

For Cameron:
You are our miracle. I thank God for saving you and allowing me to
be your mom. For being only six years old, you seem to teach me
something new every day. I love your one-liners and never know
what you will say next, but it's always music to my ears. I love you,
son.

Being your mother has been my greatest achievement. I held your
hand when each of you were born, but it was you three who held my
heart. When I married your dad, we became a family, but when we
had you, we were complete.

Team Wasowski... Always and Forever.

A Note from the Author

THANK YOU, READERS, for taking time to purchase *Our Forever Promise*. Writing for Walker and Reese has taken me on many twists and turns. They were quite the challenge. In *Forever*, I had my moments where I was mad at Walker and wanted to shake Reese. In *Second Chance at Forever*, we see them reunite and rediscover they never stopped loving each other. Their pursuit of happily ever after is not an easy journey, but in the end, true love can never be denied.

So now, here we are! Get ready for another rollercoaster ride as Walker and Reese's love story comes to an exciting conclusion. …But wait, there's more! As we say goodbye to this amazing couple, we make room for the next generation, Jackson and Riley. I am happy to announce that I will be writing a fourth book in **The Forever Series**, where Jackson and Riley's story continues. The apple does not fall too far from the tree, and young Mr. Reed is truly his father's son. Title and details to come at a later date.

Happy Reading! I truly hope you enjoy where I have taken their love story, and all the exciting new adventures to come. Writing this series has been an amazing experience. I have grown so much as a writer, and I am looking forward to writing the next series with another super couple for you to love.

The best gift you can give an author is to leave a review. It doesn't have to be many words, a simple sentence if you can. Feedback is so important. I welcome each and every comment and message I receive, but I would also love to see them on the sites you purchased this title on.

With love,

Mary

Prologue

The road to happily ever after

Walker

IN ALL OF my wildest dreams, I never thought I would have this moment I have right now. But it wasn't always this blissful.

As I sat in my office with silence around me, I took a few minutes to reflect. I tried not to think of all the years of our problematic past, but my relationship with my father was complex, to say the least. Opening my bottom drawer, I pulled out the one picture of us that was taken on a good day, the day I took over as CEO of Reed Global. My father wore an expression of admiration for me. Our hands were entwined and raised high into the air. My mother could be seen in the background wiping her eyes. It was a rare moment of happiness for the Reed family.

My last conversation with my father didn't end so well, and one thing he said to me still resonated and was running through my head at the moment: *"For a man who has everything, I would think you would be happier."*

At the time, he hit the nail right on the head. The bastard was right. When my father said that, I really wasn't happy, not even close. Sure, I had my work, my amazing son, but what I didn't have was the one person I desired most. The one that simply walked out of my life one day to never to be heard of again. I wasn't living the life I always knew I wanted…with Reese. You would have thought I would have been able to move on from that kind of hurt, but I didn't. All I did was bury my feelings along with the pain of losing her deep down inside. I concealed it from everyone, including myself. I knew it was there, but I never allowed myself to feel it. To remember her would only bring back the hurt I felt when she left.

I became whole again, or as close as I could manage with the help from my friend, my best friend Elizabeth. She saved me in more ways than I could ever thank her for. One reckless decision after another, I was drowning until she threw me a life preserver to rejoin the land of the living.

"Walker, take my hand, and I will help you," she said. Elizabeth gave me hope when everything in my life was just hopeless. She stood by me when I lost Reese and the future that I intended to have with her. I always cared for Elizabeth, but I never could bring myself to love her the way she needed to be loved. She wanted me and never hid that fact.

When you lose everything that matters to you, it's easy to fall back into old patterns. I drank too much, fucked too much, and I did all of those things with Elizabeth. I was arrogant and took what I wanted. She deserved so much better. I only gave her small parts of me; it was all I was able to give her. I hated myself for using her, but she never felt like I was doing that. She would tell me over and over again that when I was ready, love would come for us.

Well, she was right: love did happen for us. It was an indescribable love. It was a love that could never be truly measured or even explained. I felt it all on the day she told me that she was carrying my child. For a brief second—less than a second—I thought it was the worst excuse for manners on my part. How could I be so irresponsible and careless with my friend? But she didn't see it that way. It was God's way of bringing two souls together and giving them a precious gift…our child.

Sounds like a beautiful story, doesn't it? So can you imagine how I felt when my world went dark on the day that I lost my best friend? How could the fates be so cruel to me for a second time? Our son survived, but I lost Elizabeth. She didn't leave me like Reese did…she left me for all eternity. I wanted to curse the heavens for taking my Elizabeth away from me, but how could I do that when I was holding the closest thing to perfection as one could have? All seven pounds and three ounces of him were perfect. He captured my heart with one look, and my life changed and undoubtedly changed me.

Now nearly two decades later, I'd been blessed with a rare and precious gift. The heavens were now smiling upon me. I was about marry Reese Mitchell, the one I thought I lost forever, but whom I was reunited with by a simple twist of fate. Our second chance, if you will. Our reunion was nothing short of a miracle.

We were only a few weeks to the moment where we would finally become husband and wife. Reese always had a way of knocking me off my feet. Well, she certainly managed that when she told me her amazing news. I was going to be a father again! Reese telling me that she was pregnant was a feeling I could not explain. It was pure joy penetrating my heart down to my soul. Here I was with a grown son about to go off to college and then Reese told me her news. I never thought I would be experiencing this again, but it became very real when I held the Ultrasound picture of our baby in my hands. My eyes filled with tears as Reese told me more happy news. We would be welcoming to our family a daughter of our very own. My legs weakened and I nearly fell over. After countless times making love to her in front of the fireplace, I held my angel in my arms while marking her soft skin with kisses. I couldn't stop touching her. She gave herself to me openly with no barriers between us. I had never felt freer in all of my life.

All of our years spent apart and separated by the unknown had led us here. We were about to finally get our happily ever after, and I was beyond ready to begin my new life with Reese. I didn't even recognize the man that I used to be. I laugh when I remember the words that Jenny, my assistant, used on me when I left for the trip that would change my life forever. She told me to live a little and get a life. How right she was when my past collided with my present, and became my future. That was the moment Reese Mitchell walked back into my life, and I vowed never to let her go. Well, I haven't, and Reese was back where she belonged. She was here with me and now carrying our child.

I was the luckiest man in the world to be given such a gift. All the money in the world could never give you these precious moments that I'd been able to have in my life. I thanked God every night for returning Reese to me.

I picked up a photograph from my desk of my beautiful Reese. My heart beat a bit faster, even looking at a picture. I was so in love with her. I had everything a man could ever want in ten lifetimes. I had Reese, our family, and a new baby on the way. New promises of forever had sealed us together, and we were truly blessed. This time around, no one would ever come between us, and we would spend the rest of our lives in complete bliss.

Looking back at the photo of my father, I was ready to answer his question, even though he wasn't there to hear it.

"I'm happy, father. I've never been happier in all of my life." Placing the picture back in its place, I head home to my heart...my Reese.

Chapter One

It gets worse at night...

NO MATTER HOW happy I was at this moment, I couldn't seem to shake the uneasy feeling that had strangled me through my dreams the last few nights. My recurring nightmare was rearing its ugly head again in the form of Phillip Reed. He was haunting me. I felt my mind fighting through the nightmare, only seeing grainy images of my father, until tonight when he completely materialized in my dream.

It felt real. Real enough that I heard his voice as if he was still alive and in front of me. I screamed at him to leave me alone and to rot in hell. He wouldn't leave, and even in my dreams he was willing me to talk to him, just like the day in my office when I rejected the olive branch he was trying so hard to give. All I had to do was accept it, but I refused him.

Was this my punishment for not listening to him then? If he truly wanted to confess his sins to me on that day, he shouldn't have hesitated, but he did. He may have thought he wanted to finally reveal the truth to me but that would have meant that he was remorseful, and I will never believe that he was sorry for all he had done to us. Yes, he left letters, letters filled with words that he didn't have the courage to say to me in person, so it doesn't change anything. He's gone now, and I've made my peace with the past that he controlled. *Why do my dreams keep revisiting this?*

In my dream, I was in my office, just like the day my father visited me. It was the anniversary of Elizabeth's death, and my son's eighteenth birthday. This time around, my father wasn't talking in circles, he looked confident, as if he knew something I didn't and taunted me with it.

I kept myself in control this time, and didn't succumb to his prodding. He once again fixed himself a drink, and then he turned to me and said something that completely made me catch my breath. His voice was calm and controlled, but yet I also heard defeat. He took a sip of his drink and said, "Every story has a villain. In your story son, I'm yours." He repeated this, over and over again.

There was no freedom from this nightmare, I fought against it. Seeking strength I didn't know I possessed. I could not wake from it, and I was literally caught with no means of escaping it, or him. *How can this even be possible?* He was dead, but yet standing right in front of me. *Was he here to drive me insane? Or was he trying to convey a deeper message to me?*

"Get out of my head!" I screamed at him, but he stood there with a stoic expression and didn't blink.

"You may be with your Reese Mitchell again, but you will never have your happily ever after."

"You're wrong father, I already have it, and I will continue to have it for the rest of my life. You can't hurt me anymore, so get the hell out of my head and go back to hell where you belong."

"I was in Hell, Walker. All those years ago when I hurt you and continued to hurt you. You will never know how sorry I truly am. I wanted to tell you so many times, but my guilt scared me. I didn't want to lose you completely, and I knew once all my deceptions were revealed, I would have. I was a selfish bastard, this I know, but I always loved you. I'm sorry I failed you as a father, but now all I seek is your mercy. I have no place. I have no sides to cross until you decide my fate."

"What the hell are you talking about?"

"You need to forgive me. You are still carrying your deep rooted hatred for me, and it will destroy you in the end if you don't let it go. Forgive me, son. Free me from these chains that now bind me. Only you can decide my fate. Forgive me, Walker. Forgive me... son."

"I will never forgive you for what you did to me and to Reese. I lost her because of you and Henry. You do not deserve forgiveness, even in death. I will never give it to you. Now get the hell out of my head!"

"Every story has a villain. You will never know how sorry I am that I'm yours. Forgive me. Forgive me. Forgive me." As his voice faded out into the unknown, I finally broke free of him.

"Shut up! Shut up! Shut up!" I shouted out in our darkened bedroom.

"Walker, wake up!" Reese softly speaks over and over again until my eyes blink open. The most beautiful brown eyes stared back at me, as she continued to calm me with her sweet voice and soft kisses on my face.

"Baby, are you okay? You were screaming in your sleep. You're soaked in sweat."

There was no way I was going to tell Reese about my dream. I simply would not put her through any unnecessary pain, especially at the hands of my father again. I wasn't about to analyze why I was dreaming about him. I closed that chapter of my life the day I left his home for the final time, making promises never to return. I wanted a clean slate, and it was never to be had holding on to the sad memories of my past.

I wrapped my arms around Reese and made love to her, burying myself deep inside her. I loved her like I needed my next breath.

Reese was my Forever, and I wasn't going to let these nightmares get in the way of that. All would be right with my world in a matter of a few weeks from now. I would be marrying Reese, surrounded by our family and friends. I couldn't wait to see her walk down the aisle and into my waiting arms.

My girl was in a deep sleep. I wore her out with our middle-of-the-night sexathon, but it was what I needed to rid my mind of the bullshit that occupied it. She never questioned or held back the same need of desire that made us both fit like missing pieces to a puzzle. We were always connected in every way that mattered.

She was lying here next to me, and all I wanted to do was wrap myself around her and never let her go. She shifted just slightly and her stomach was now exposed. I showered her tiny baby bump with gentle kisses and spoke to my child growing inside of her. "Daddy loves you, little one. Stay nestled inside where you are safe. Daddy and mommy love you so much."

I kissed her stomach a few more times, and I swore I thought I saw Reese smile, but who knows? She tends to do that when she dreams. I didn't know how much I missed that until I saw her do it on one of the first nights we shared this bed in our home. I would lay awake for hours just watching her. If she only knew how much peace it brought me to see her sleep so soundly.

The waking hours weren't as stressful for me. We were weeks away from our wedding, and so many plans still needed to be finalized. My office was now turned into Wedding Central.

I put all of my projects in the capable hands of my right hand man, Donovan Tate. I knew he was up to task. I had him finishing up a very important request, one that required complete discretion. He would be back here soon, and I could finally move on from a mistake that should have never happened. As important as it was for me to run my company and maintain complete control over it, I had other matters that needed my attention. Marrying Reese was all I could think of, and I couldn't wait to make her mine…forever.

She had been home resting in between dress fittings and cake tasting. She'd been ferociously sick lately with morning sickness that never really seemed to go away. I called Freddy in from New York to spend time with her and help her with anything she might need.

Reese didn't want a big wedding with all of the trimmings. This was where we disagreed. This was Reese's day, and I wanted it to be perfect for her. The dress Freddy designed for her was something that belonged on the cover of *Vogue*. She was already contacted to do some pre-wedding publicity photos, but she refused. My Georgia Peach was still the same simple girl I fell in love with the first time many years ago. She exuded confidence, beauty, and grace. She may have modeled for years and still looked like one, but she was most comfortable wrapped in simplicity.

How could I refuse her one request: A small wedding with only our closest family and friends? Her side was considerably small, where my list was going into the hundreds. I knew I was out of control with my planning, but I wanted to show the world what I was denied all of those years ago. As much as this was for my girl, it was also for me.

Reeling myself in was no easy task, but I couldn't help myself. I actually enjoyed the break I was taking from my usual ten hour + work days. I wanted to lavish my girl with all that I had. I needed to show the world she was finally mine, and that took help from Rosalyn Davenport-Baker. She was the best wedding planner in her field, and the waiting list to be a client was two years long. When Jenny placed the call to her office, all other clients took a back seat to me. She was dreaming up ideas and had them on my desk two days later. I liked Rosalyn very much. But convincing Lila to accept her help? Well, that was another challenge!

Reese didn't want Lila to feel left out, so she asked her grandmother to be in charge of the rehearsal dinner. As much as I loved Lila, and especially her cooking, I wanted a particular menu that consisted of what Lila calls "snobbery at its finest." I tried not to be insulted. I was no snob. I just wanted the very best for our wedding, and Reese not participating in the day-to-day made me the bad guy. I hated to disappoint Lila, so I compromised and suggested two parties instead.

Lila and Thomas would be here the week of the wedding. They didn't fly because of Thomas's heart, so I had arranged for them and several of their closest friends to be driven out to California by a luxury mobile home on wheels. The trip would take approximately thirty-three hours without stopping. I hired four drivers over the course of the trip. This was the best solution I could come up with, and it seemed to satisfy the grandparents and Reese.

All was falling into place until I received a call from Rosalyn. She had reached an impasse with the final menu. That impasse was Lila Mitchell. She had insisted to include some of Reese's favorites on the wedding reception menu. It included Peach Cobbler, Sweet Potato Pie, and Fried Okra? *What the heck is that?* And a wide assortment of appetizers from their home country of Ireland. My stomach retched after hearing some of it, and I stopped her mid-sentence. Reese was also pregnant, and the kids nor the grandparents weren't told of our good news yet. We had decided that as a wedding present to our family we would tell them the night of the rehearsal dinner.

Reese couldn't wait to tell Lila. I was more concerned with Thomas and his shotgun. Obviously we were adults, but Reese was their only granddaughter, and we weren't married yet... legally anyway, but always in our hearts first.

I assured Rosalyn that I would work everything out and would be in touch with her when I could. I held my head in my hands and took in some calming breaths. Jenny stood at the entrance of my door and simply laughed at me.

Raising my head up at her, I said, "What's the joke? Care to let me in on it?"

"Oh, Mr. Reed, no joke, I am simply overjoyed for you. What a sight to take in to see you this happy, but you would think a man of your stature who controls billion dollar deals from behind his desk can easily handle planning a wedding? You seem a bit overwhelmed."

"Am I that obvious?"

"A little bit, sir. Forgive me for overstepping, but wasn't it your sweet Ms. Mitchell that wanted something small and intimate? This is turning into a circus, if you ask me."

"Well, I didn't ask you, Jenny, but thank you for stating the obvious. What do I do now? Rosalyn had warned me that Lila was upset and planned on calling Reese today. They video chat every week. I have the bus completely online, so I have to imagine their call will happen today."

"Are you afraid to go home?" she asked.

"Truth?"

"Yes, that would be nice."

"Yes, I am," I said. "If Lila gets to Reese before I do, I think I may be sleeping on the couch tonight." Once again, Jenny laughed at my expense.

"Everything will be fine sir. I think you need to take a break from all of this wedding planning and relax. You are turning into a Groomzilla, and it's not a very flattering look on you. Can you please remember that this is supposed to be a happy day? The biggest moment of your life. Now go home, and start enjoying it."

I relaxed my shoulders and hugged Jenny. Wiser words were never spoken. Thank goodness for her and her words of wisdom. I couldn't wait until she met Lila. They were definitely going to be the best of friends.

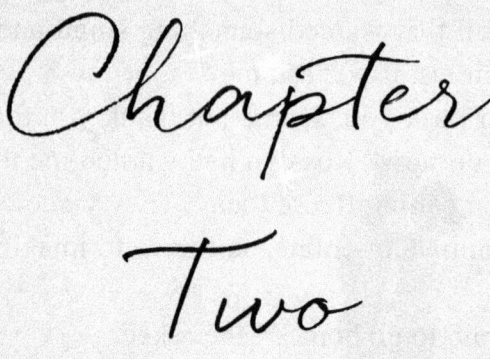

Chapter Two

The voice of reason

Reese

AFTER SOME TOUGH rounds of throwing up, I was pretty much done for the day. Freddy wanted to do some shopping on Rodeo drive, but I was just not up for it. I had so much to do and little time to accomplish it all. Freddy and Fabrizio, along with Marsha, promised to take care of anything I still had to complete. My wish: To manage walking down the aisle without tossing my cookies all over the beautiful decorations and rose petals.

Freddy, never one to miss an opportunity to tease me, threw rose petals at my feet the other day. I looked at him strangely until he busted out laughing. Of course I knew what he was referencing. Freddy and I shared the same taste in movies, so he rented as many as he could that contained a wedding theme. One of the choices was *Coming to America*. He bowed at my feet and covered my floors with rose petals as I walked behind him. What a mess! Our house manager, Priscilla, loved him at first sight but made him grab a broom and return my home to its pristine manner. We laughed out loud. That was a great night with my best friend.

I was nearing the end of my first trimester and praying for the end of my morning sickness. It was never this bad with Riley. I had taken all the necessary tests that we were required to have. With my high risk pregnancy past, Walker wasn't taking any chances with my health. Shortly after we returned home from Georgia, talking with him about my headaches didn't go over so well. Knowing what happened to Elizabeth, Walker immediately turned ten shades of red. He was beyond angry that I didn't tell him about my migraine history. Once I found out I was pregnant, he was even more concerned. I hardly ever needed to take medicine for the migraines, least of all a prescription. I would just simply do some relaxing exercises or rest in a quiet, darkened room until it would pass. Pregnancy hormones were known to bring on worsened headaches, and it was just something that Walker would have to come to terms with. What happened to Elizabeth was tragic, but our two cases are different. Explaining this to Walker? Almost impossible.

Thank goodness Jackson hadn't had any headaches since New York. He was young and very healthy. Jackson told me that he was secretly happy that he wasn't the center of attention at the moment. He welcomed the reprieve from his father's incessant worrying. I scolded him a bit on that remark, because his father's concern came purely from love. To understand Walker was to accept him in all areas, even the ones that drive you crazy.

Having Priscilla, our house manager, help me was a breath of fresh air. We immediately hit it off and she seemed to read me like a book. She spent all of her time taking care of me throughout the day, and once I was over this morning sickness, she would get treated to a spa weekend.

I was about to fall asleep after my chamomile tea when my iPad alert was ringing. I looked down to my watch and realized I nearly missed my afternoon chat with Nana. It rang several times, but I needed to fix my appearance first. Nana didn't know about the pregnancy yet, and today I didn't look so hot with my flushed cheeks. I was red and blotchy from straining my face muscles. I looked awful. Walker didn't like to hear me put myself down, but men truly don't seem to grasp what a woman goes through while pregnant.

I opened up the screen and was welcomed to not just Nana, but Granddaddy, Mabel, Beatrice, Clara, and of course two very loud puppies. Yes, Socks and Pockets also made the trip. *Oh my goodness, the poor drivers.* I laughed to myself.

This bus they were traveling on offered every bit of luxury you could imagine. It had everything from soup to nuts, and it sure did look like Granddaddy was enjoying himself, but today? Not Nana. She looked like a bee just landed in her bonnet.

"Hi, Nana how's the trip so far?" I smiled and pleasantly asked. My fingers were crossed behind my back.

"Hello, sweet girl. I miss you more than a million jelly beans, but to answer your question, the trip is fine, but my mood is not."

"Now Nana, what's wrong? It's not like you to be upset over anything. What can I do to help?"

"You can start by telling that soon-to-be husband of yours to stop interfering with my menu! You know I love him, Reese to the moon and back, but he don't know nothing about southern cuisine. Now, you wanted your favorites, didn't you? No one has ever complained about my pastries, and that goes for my cooking too!"

I was about to answer Nana, when I heard footsteps outside the door. I told Nana that I was stepping away for a moment to drink some water, and to wait for me to return. She said she had all the time in the world to do so. *Oh boy! What has he done?* I thought, as I stepped away.

Sure enough, my instincts were correct. It was Walker arriving home, and no doubt overhearing his name mentioned by Nana.

"Why, hello there, my handsome fiancé." I said to my love. "Care to know who I'm speaking with now? Or have you figured it out?"

"Baby, I am so sorry you have to deal with this. Do you want me to talk with her? I could smooth things over, I promise."

"Oh honey, I think you and your wedding planner have done way too much already. You stay back and just listen."

"Yes, my love," he replied.

"If I survive this call, then you owe me a full body massage that includes multiple orgasms."

"Then I hope you survive it, because I am definitely up to the task of fulfilling your request. I love you."

"I love you more," I said back to him.

"Impossible, but thank you."

I STAYED OUT of sight while Reese continued with her call with Lila. Before sitting back down in front of her laptop, she gave me the sexiest wink. Oh I knew what my girl was thinking about. And I knew what we would be doing later.

"Okay Nana, I'm back. So as you were saying…"

"Reese, I am trying to remember that I am a Christian, but that horrid wedding planner has got to go! She doesn't know anything, let alone can't appreciate our southern dishes. I think she may have liked my pastry choices, but when it came down to the appetizers, well she wasn't silent with her opinions. If you ask me, she was a bit too forthcoming for my taste, and I wanted to wash her mouth out with soap."

"Nana, please calm down and tell me what Ms. Davenport-Baker said."

"And that's another thing! What kind of woman has two last names like that?"

As I continued to listen to Reese and Nana's discussion, I became very apprehensive waiting in silence. I definitely noticed the change of the tone Nana was using with Reese. *This can't be good.* I was beginning to sweat. I couldn't believe how nervous I was. Being on Nana Lila's bad side was not a good place to be, especially when

I was weeks away from marrying Reese. I got myself into check and let out a few breaths. *This is Lila we are talking about. She's the sweetest person I have ever met. I'm sure she's exaggerating about Rosalyn. I hope.*

I was wrong, it was worse than I thought.

"She said that my food choices should come with a warning label that should read 'Proceed with caution. Would you like a heart attack on the side with your salt?'"

"She said that? Are you sure, Nana? She is a professional wedding planner. I can't imagine she would use that type of language with a client."

"Oh, she most certainly did." Clara chimed in.

"What a rude woman!" Mabel shouted.

"You see, Reese? I am not imagining what I heard. She was downright disrespectful, and I will not coordinate a menu with that woman. We have been through this, Reese. You said you wanted a simple menu that included your favorites, and because I was doing the cooking, you would let me handle it all. Now to add more *salt* to my open wounds, she said that your *Walker* has final approval and instructed her to run this by him first. He also said that he wanted a pure organic menu to be included. What the heck is a pure organic menu? So some haughty uptight woman who can't keep her tummy in check has to have a specialized menu? Oh my! I would rather hang up my apron than to cook something that will probably contain more letters in it than the alphabet."

Nana continued her rant. "Come on, Reese! This is your special day, and it seems to be turning into a circus. I'm sorry, honey, that I'm raising my tone with you, but I'm just offended. I can't believe your sweet Walker doesn't want my Peach Cobbler or my Fried Sweet Potato Casserole. Was he fibbing to me when he ate all those dishes at my table?"

Reese needed to calm her down, "Of course not, Nana. Walker loves your cooking. Unfortunately this probably has more to do with me than him. Nana, I believe the reason why Walker has been so strict with the menu guidelines is because of me and my sensitivity issues to certain foods and smells at the moment."

"What? The only time you have ever turned my food down was when you were pregnant with my Riley girl. Now Reese, we can always compromise on… Oh, my sweet lord! Reese, are you expecting?"

"Yes Nana, we are. I am three months along and about to begin my second trimester."

"Thomas, Mabel, Clara, Beatrice, come on out here. Reese has wonderful news to share."

Reese held her hands over her ears from all the loud cries of joy when Nana heard our news. I couldn't help but smile. Her mood changed in seconds, and the fight over the menu was now over.

Watching Reese move the iPad screen away, and out of Nana's direct view, all I heard was the happy cheers going on in the background. It was time to be with Reese. I had waited in the shadows long enough, and now that Lila had heard our good news, it was time to join the party. I was hoping all would be forgiven on the wedding planner disaster now that she knew she was going to be a great-grandmother again. I hoped with fingers crossed behind my back.

"*Now*, you come out and face the music?" she smiled. I leaned down to kiss my soon-to-be beautiful wife.

"I'm sorry, baby." I replied. "If it means anything at all, your Nana scares the shit out of me." Now we both busted out laughing. "Your sweet Nana is a force to be reckoned with. I have no doubt she could serve as a worthy adversary against any business associate of mine. I love you, Reese, so very much."

"I love you too. Let's finish up with Nana, and then you and I are going to have a long talk."

What does that mean? A long talk? Reese can't be mad at me, is she? We were just laughing a minute ago. I silently nodded at her and kissed the top of her head. Reese turned the screen back around to see Nana wiping the tears from her eyes.

"Oh Nana, please don't cry. I don't think my heart could take it."

"I'm sorry, sweet girl, but you have truly made me the happiest grandmother on the face of the planet. Now don't you go sneaking off, Walker! I see your shadow off to the side. Come on, son, show yourself."

I couldn't help but let out the laugh I was holding inside. Reese's grandmother always had her own unique style of bringing out the good feelings in people, even me. Nana wasn't taking no for an answer, and then I finally joined Reese on the sofa. I sat behind her and protectively wrapped my arms around my girl. This was my move I tend to do when I'm nervous. Reese knows me all too well, and she knows exactly what to do to calm me. She placed her hands on top of mine and leaned back into my chest. I inhaled her beautiful scent and let out the breath I was holding. Nana was deliriously happy at this point.

"Hi, Lila," I said quietly through my smile.

"Hello to you, Walker. Boy! You are one handsome man."

OH MY GOODNESS! I don't think Walker ever expected this when he first arrived home. Nana is so amazing. But that didn't stop me from scolding her for being a big flirt that she is.

"Nana!" I was a bit shocked with her flirting with Walker. He visibly relaxed after that. This was Nana's way of always lightening the mood when we were in a heavy conversation, like this one right now.

Walker loved the compliment. "Why thank you Lila, but don't let Thomas hear you say that. He owns many shotguns and I want to be around to see my baby be born."

"Don't you worry about Thomas. He loves you, and so do I. I am so happy for you Walker. You and my sweet girl are expecting a baby of your very own. You have been blessed with such an incredible gift from God himself. We couldn't be happier for you. Now I want to jump in the driver's seat and move along this bus even quicker to California. I can't wait to hug you all."

"We can't wait to see you too, Lila. I'm sorry about Rosalyn. I guess I've been going overboard with all of the wedding plans. I'm sorry if your feelings were hurt. Please forgive me? I shall not hurt your feelings again."

"Oh Walker dear, you didn't. You see, son, Reese is incredibly special to us, and I just wanted to put all my personal touches on her special day. It comes from love, I sure hope you know that. I feel terrible for losing my temper with your...what do you call her? Wedding planner? Anyway, it's your day too, and you can have whatever you want."

"Thank you, Lila. Nothing would make us happier than your delicious Peach Cobbler, Apple Pie, and please don't forget your homemade Vanilla Ice Cream."

"How on earth could I forget that son? You can't eat pie without ice cream. Now that would be a crime. We love you so much, and we will see you soon."

"We love you too." We both said at the same time.

As I watched the screen go black, I let out a deep breath. I fell back into Walker's chest and began to cry. These damn hormones. I can't help myself these days. I'm unbelievably happy, truly happy for the first time in years, but something still feels off. Walker is now wiping away my tears.

"Oh baby, I'm so sorry," he says to me. "Please forgive me for driving you and your family crazy."

"Walker, we need to talk."

JUST THAT STATEMENT alone made me freeze. I felt my heart drop down into my stomach. I was suddenly afraid about what she would say next. Reese dried her eyes on my sleeve. I steadied myself and waited for her to start talking.

"Are you okay?" she whispered as she looked into my eyes. "I want you to tell me the truth. You're not sleeping well, and when I ask you about your dreams, you silence me with sex. Now usually that's not a bad thing, but I sense that you are troubled and you are shutting me out. Would you please talk to me and allow me to help you?"

"I'm fine, Reese. You needn't worry about me. All I'm trying to do is give you everything your heart desires." She reached for my face and pulled me in for a kiss. Our tongues were dancing as she took me deeper into her mouth.

Resting her forehead against my own, she whispered, "Oh baby! How can you possibly top what you have already given me?"

What does that mean? I thought to myself.

"Walker, I already have everything. I have YOU, and that's all that I want. I don't need this big fancy wedding to have everything."

"What if I need it?"

"Then I guess the bigger question, is why?"

"Reese, what do you want me to say? This is who I am. When you are born into wealth, you have this sense of entitlement that comes along with it. It's almost expected. I take that back, in my world it's *required*."

"Well, that's not how it is in mine, and I will not partake in this overblown grandiose wedding."

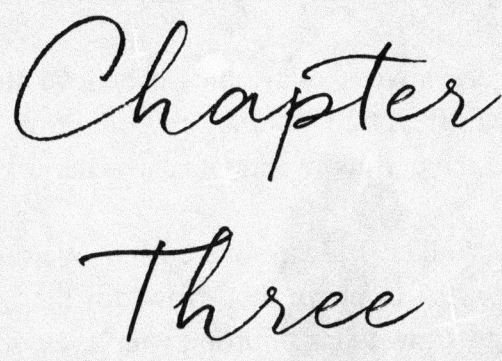

Chapter Three

Torn

Walker

"**W**HAT ARE YOU saying?"

"I think you know, Walker. Until we get to the bottom of what is troubling you, the wedding is off."

No, no, no! No way in hell am I going to lose her now.

"Reese, please baby, you don't mean that."

"I'm sorry, but I do. After everything we have been through to be together, a wedding could make or break us? Or is it something that you're afraid to tell me? I'm going with the second choice. You don't always have to take on the weight of the world on your shoulders. Trust me to listen and help you when you need it. We are supposed to be partners. I will not begin another marriage standing on the outside, looking in. I've been down that road before with Samuel, and I will not do that with you."

"Do you honestly feel that's what I'm doing?"

"In some ways, yes. Please talk to me, and convince me that what I'm feeling is just crazy pregnancy hormones, and we are okay."

"Reese, we are always okay, please believe that. I love you more than my own life, and would lay my life down for you. I trust you with all that I have. I just wanted to show the world that you are finally mine."

"I am yours, Walker. I always have been. We don't need a five hundred plus guest list to prove that. Now, for the last time, please let me in? I want to know what's hurting you."

Reese never looked so determined. She was right. I was shutting her out, while she was trying to break down my walls of resistance. I was keeping her at a safe distance to protect her, but I'm doing the opposite and hurting her feelings. I just didn't want to freak her out about my nightmares, my visions of my father, and now even my thoughts of regret involving my history with Elizabeth. I was afraid it would be too much for her to bear, but my girl was so much stronger and was now fighting for us.

"I love you, Reese. You know me so well, and I'm sorry if my distance has hurt you."

"I love you too, but you need to trust me to help you. Are you ready to tell me what's been bothering you?"

"Yes, I am." I took a deep breath and told her the truth. "I've been having a recurring nightmare starring my father. He comes to me almost every night and asking me for forgiveness, no begging. I refuse him each and every time. I'm still so angry with him for what he did to us. Even with his death, I can't bring myself to move be-yond his malicious attempts to keep us apart. I didn't want to tell you any of this because he caused you enough pain, and I couldn't bear it if you were hurt again."

"Oh Walker, that's impossible! Your father will never be able to hurt me again. Do you want to know why that is? Because I won't let him. I made so many mistakes back then, I lost count. The reason why your father was able to do what he did to me, to us, is because I gave him permission to do so. He claimed my fear of him, and the love I had for my family, and used it against me. It's time I take responsibility for the part I played in our break-up."

"What do you mean? It was mine and Elizabeth's fathers that did this to us, not you."

"Walker, I am partially responsible for this, and let me tell you why. A few months ago when you told me he was dead, I won't lie to you, I didn't shed a tear over it. I blamed him for everything, but then Nana enlightened me when I was finally able to reveal the truth to her. She was disappointed in me because I didn't have enough faith in our family to reach out to them so they could help me fight your father. That goes for you as well. I accepted my fate, and it was these legs that walked out your door that morning. The only thing I'm thankful for was that you weren't there to see it. You would have known that I was lying. All you ever asked of me was to trust you, and I didn't, not where it should have mattered and counted the most."

Reese continued explaining herself. "I wasted so many years being angry and blaming him. I should have been stronger and leaned on those who loved me and those who would have helped me if given the chance. With you back in my life, and our baby growing inside of me, all I can do is forgive. I have forgiven him, and I urge you to do the same. Love and hate go hand in hand, these feelings can make or break you. I choose love to be the driving force behind anything I do from this moment on. I'm done living in the past, and for your own peace of mind, you should too. I love you. I choose you…forever."

WEARING MY HEART on my sleeve, my imploring pleas fell on to his fallen expression. Walker was silent and wasn't responding to me. I pushed him enough, so I decided that I was done talking about this, at least for now. My man needed to be comforted, and of course, I was still marrying him.

He still wore the look of apprehension all over his beautiful face. I couldn't hold back any longer and took him in my arms. This time, I was the one that was holding him tightly to my body. We held on to each other until he released his arms from my waist and stroked my cheeks with his fingers. Gazing into each other's eyes, I was lost. I closed mine for a brief second until he commanded me to open them.

"Look at me, Reese, and don't turn away." He requested with a strong undertone to his voice.

His eyes were dominant. Walker was completely drawing me in, and I willingly submitted. Lifting me easily into his arms and carrying me up to our bedroom, he kicked the door shut behind him and locked the rest of the world out. My anticipation level was rising as he remained silent. Never taking his eyes off of me, he began to remove me from my clothing. I lay there in our huge California King sized bed completely bare and exposed to him. He shrugged off his suit and climbed his way up to me.

"You are so beautiful, Reese Mitchell. You have my heart... forever."

His words were my undoing as he plunged two fingers inside my wet clit and began working me over with his skillful and sensual touch. Holding my arms above my head as he worked me over, I was surrendering more and more to Walker. He was a physical lover, showing me every erotic and carnal desire for me. He expected no less in return.

"Let me hear you, baby. Come for me."

Oh, I did! I screamed out his name as I hit my release. Walker wasted no time and entered me with a force that had my hips rising to meet his powerful thrusts. He was pounding into my sensitive flesh. I could barely hold on when he pulled out of me and flipped me onto my stomach. This time a bit more gentle, he raised me up onto my hands and knees and took me from behind. I could feel my wetness tightening around him as we came together. Never releasing me from his hold as he poured into me, he stayed connected with my body until every last drop of his release was now inside of me. I was wrapped in his cocoon with no means of escape. How I wanted to remain here forever. I loved this man unconditionally with everything that I had.

"Are you okay, baby? Did I hurt you?" he asked.

"No sir! I loved everything we just did."

"I'm sorry for today. I know I'm a beast, but I promise we will come to an understanding about the wedding. Whatever you want, Reese, I want to give you. Your happiness is all that matters to me. You let me know when to show up, and I will be there."

"Promise me something?" I kept my eyes trained on him as I asked my question.

"Anything." He responded quickly and kissed me.

"Stop apologizing for being you. You are perfect. I love you for all that you want to do to make me happy. I also want you to relax and know that you have already made all my dreams come true."

MY BODY ANSWERED "yes" for me, and I made love to Reese again. I had to forever show her that she was all I would ever need to feel completely whole again. Too many years spent apart from her, and both of us just existing in our separate worlds. We are together now and for the rest of our lives. I don't need to have a fancy wedding or a thousand press releases to prove anything. Reese was here with me right now and in our bed. She's been mine since the minute our eyes met that day in the NYU library.

Our past is in the past. I have to try to come to terms with it and not let it come between us again. She nearly gave me a heart attack when she said she wouldn't marry me, but that was her subtle way of proving a point. I know I'm stubborn and can be controlling, but I would never control her. She has a beautiful mind, and she has no problem ever voicing how she feels. I heard everything she said to me today.

I held her in my arms, as she soundly slept. She was falling deeper and deeper into a contented sleep. A small smile now appeared as her eyelashes began to flutter. *Oh I will love her until I take my final breath.* I silently prayed to the heavens that tonight, I would find the same peace.

Chapter Four

Wrapped in love

Reese

I WASN'T SURE what time it was. The clock had been turned around, and the drapes were shutting out the rest of the world. No doubt, Walker did this on purpose. Whenever we were at odds, he always seemed to lock us in our own private bubble and keep all others out. To be with him yesterday was all that I wanted. It was no sacrifice on my part. He had been carrying the weight of the world on his shoulders when he didn't need to be. I meant everything I said to him. I loved him, I would stand by him, and his love alone was all that I would ever need. *Oh, my stubborn man! Just get that through your head and we will be fine.*

My muscles were sore from all the positions he had moved me in. Who needed Yoga classes when Walker Reed was your personal Kama Sutra instructor? Giving my body a good stretch, I made my way into our bathroom to shower and then off to find my man. The hot spray from the multi showerheads felt like heaven on my body and massaged my sore muscles. I put on a cotton tank dress with sandals to match. I had no plans to go anywhere today, so I thought I would be as comfortable as possible. A breakfast tray filled with my favorites was now waiting for me. My eyes scanned the room to find vases of wild flowers mixed with roses placed on each side of our bed. My dressing table also had flowers placed on it, and of course Walker's signature move: one long stemmed rose on my food tray accompanied with a note.

Good Morning Angel,

Hope you slept well. I did, with you wrapped around me. Enjoy your breakfast, and then come find me. I have a surprise waiting for you in the garden.

I love you, beautiful girl.

Walker

Oh, my crazy man, how I love you so much. What are you up to? With my curiosity now piqued, I wanted to snoop to find out what my surprise was. Our baby had other ideas. My belly was beginning to growl, so I followed Walker's orders and enjoyed my delicious breakfast. Glancing at the clock, it was only nine thirty, but it felt much later than that. I finished off my tea, and then looked for Walker.

"Good morning, Ms. Mitchell," I heard as I walked down the stairs.

"Good morning, Priscilla. I'm looking for Mr. Reed."

"He's waiting for you in the rose garden. He asked me to walk with you until we reached the entrance. I have instructions to place this blindfold on your eyes and then you will wait for Mr. Reed to continue on with your surprise."

"Are you serious? Blindfold me? Come on, Priscilla, what's going on?"

"Oh Ms. Mitchell, you know I am not permitted to say, but I can assure you that you will be pleased."

"Okay, Priscilla, I will play along. Lead the way." I giggled practically the entire way to the rose garden. I couldn't imagine what Walker was doing out there, but didn't care to question it. I already loved it and didn't care what it was.

"Okay, Ms. Mitchell, this is where you have to put on the blindfold."

While Priscilla placed the covering on my eyes, I took in the smell of the fabric. It was laced with his cologne. Oh my goodness, he certainly knows how to draw me in. I felt the anticipation rising, as I waited patiently for Walker. I was beginning to climb out of my skin when strong arms engulfed me. My panties were already drenched and dripping with desire. My arousal was evident with this little game we were playing. Goosebumps were lining my arms as he drew closer to me.

"You smell like me," he whispered in my ear as he tasted my earlobe, and then moved on to licking my neck.

"Wasn't that the idea of the blindfold?" I shyly asked.

"It was, but I always want my personal mark and smell on you. Don't you know that by now? Take my hand, my love, and let me show you your surprise."

With our hands entwined in one another, he gracefully guided me to where I wasn't sure. Although I couldn't see him, I knew he was happy.

"We're here Reese. I'm going to remove your blindfold now, but don't open your eyes until I tell you, okay?"

"Okay. You know you are driving me crazy, right? Are we alone out here? Because I need you inside me, like right now."

"Be careful, my love, on what you wish for. I may just have to fulfill that request." He nipped my shoulder as I let out a small yelp.

"Open your eyes, baby," he whispered into my ear as I slowly opened my eyes.

"Oh my goodness, Walker! How did you do this?"

I knew we were in California, but our garden had now been transformed into an exact replica of our meadow in Georgia. Rows and rows of wildflowers lined the back stretch of the garden. New trees were planted where there were none yesterday. A gazebo now stood at the end of a rose-lined aisle. Intricate lights and flowers were covering the breathtaking altar. The first thought that came to mind was marrying Walker under it. This had been my dream all along, and now it was here before my very eyes. I had never seen anything so beautiful in all my life, and my beautiful soon-to-be husband had once again made me the happiest woman in the world.

"Say something, Reese. Do you like it?"

"I love it, Walker. How can I not? It's our meadow. Thank you so much. I love you. How did you do this in so little time?"

"You know I love the spotlight, but I can't take all the credit. I had a team to help me pull this off for you. After you fell asleep last night, I expedited all the plans that I had in place for the wedding. I designed the gazebo myself and had it built a month ago. I planned to have this placed in our garden, and it would just be a special place for you and I to share, but then the idea hit me. We could get married under it. I thought this would be much better than a big stuffy reception room, don't you agree?"

"I agree!" I screamed aloud with so much joy in my heart. "And there is nothing I want more than to marry you right here in our new garden. I love you, Walker."

"I love you too baby, so much. I also plan to revise the guest list as soon as I get into the office today. I was out of my head with the planning, and you were right. All we need is our closest family and

26

friends around us. At the end of the day, as long as you marry me, that's all I need, baby."

Walker continued, "I also have more good news for you. No need to worry about the wrath of Nana. I spoke to her this morning, and she will make anything your heart and stomach desires. She is over the moon with our news, so anything beyond that is not even on her radar. Rosalyn will still oversee the final touches, but she has assured me that your wish is her command, and she will behave herself around Lila."

"Oh, my sweet man! Anything else I need to know before I kiss you madly?"

"Actually, there is one thing," he smiled coyly.

"Name it, baby."

"I believe you said you wanted a certain request fulfilled. I am a man of my word and will always grant your wishes, my love. I do believe you survived your call with Nana. So, just to make sure I am clear on this matter: I am to give you a full body massage that includes multiple orgasms? Am I correct on this?"

"You are," I giggled. "When do you plan on fulfilling that brief?" I nearly combusted, I was incredibly horny at this point.

"Right now, my love."

He placed my hand in his, and we stepped up and onto the landing of the gazebo. Walker hit a button on a small keychain he was carrying. I watched as the walls came up, locking us in and shutting the world out. Once again we were in our private bubble. He hit another button on the remote control, and we were surrounded by sparkling white lights. Another button made the moon appear on the high arched ceiling of the rounded gazebo. It was as if we were under the Georgia night sky. It took my breath away. He got every little detail just right.

"So, my love, ready to be taken in the moonlight?"

I was silent and let my body answer for me. He knelt down in front of me and breathed in my arousal.

"Hmm…you smell delicious, but how do you taste?"

Gliding his hands up my thighs, he easily separated me from my soaked panties. Entering my swollen bud with his skillful tongue, he worked me over until I screamed his name. I held his face and drew him in, as he took me deeper and deeper. I nearly collapsed with my orgasm. He gently placed me down onto the blanket I hardly noticed was there. Crashing his lips onto mine, I tasted my slick wetness on his tongue. He was sucking on mine, as he commanded me to open my eyes.

"Please, baby, look at me, as I take you and make you forever mine."

This wasn't a hard taking. I went willingly over and over again. Walker was ever so gentle with me as his body covered mine. We entwined our hands together as he slowly and tenderly made love to me. We matched each other's moves and then came together in total bliss. Our rhythm was perfect. We were two perfectly matched pieces of a puzzle.

"Thank you for my surprise. And thank you for my orgasms, my body thoroughly enjoyed them," I said, out of breath.

"You are welcome my love, but I'm just a man who loves his woman with all that he has. No request is out of my reach to fulfill. You'd do well to remember that. How do you feel? How's our little one today?"

"She must be content with the sound of her daddy's voice. I haven't been sick since yesterday morning."

"I can't wait to see her on screen. The picture doesn't even come close," he said.

"I'm so sorry I found out on my own. You should have been with me to share our good news, but it was something that I needed to do alone."

"No need to explain baby. You and our daughter are healthy, and that's all I care about. From this moment on, I will be at every appointment, I promise you."

"I don't doubt that."

"I hate to leave you baby, but I do need to get to the office and plan on speaking with Jackson today. I can't believe they have been away for nearly two months now. I miss that boy more than I can say."

"I miss Riley too, but she really needed this time with Jackson. She's still not speaking with Samuel, and as much as I have encouraged her to move on from her anger, she's not ready to do so."

"I know and understand that all too well. I am the last person that needs to lecture someone on anger. Have you spoken to Samuel?"

I OBSERVED REESE very carefully after I mentioned her ex's name. She dropped her head down in silence, igniting the insecurities I possess.

"Reese, what are you not telling me?"

"It's nothing, Walker. I didn't want to mention anything to you, especially after the last run in we had with him. Samuel is still grieving over the loss of our marriage, and he is trying to work through his feelings."

Why is she defending him? I hated where my mind was going right now, but I had to know. "I can't believe you still feel sorry for him. He called you the vilest words. He's lucky I didn't deliver a bigger beating to him. Reese, yesterday you asked me to share my feelings with you, and to not shut you out. In order for that to work, you have to give me the same respect. How can you still come to the defense of this man? I don't understand it."

"Walker, I really don't care to get into this right now. We had a beautiful morning. Please let's not spoil it."

"I have to get to the office anyway, but this conversation is not over."

"I didn't think it was."

HIS GRIP TIGHTENED around my upper arm as he led me away from the garden and back into the house. Walker was trying to contain his anxiety over my past with Samuel, but I knew he was struggling with his feelings. He only had a short amount of time with Elizabeth, where I had nearly eighteen years with my husband. My past was more in depth, and he wanted to know all about my time with Samuel, but what was the point? How many times can you agree to keep the past where it belongs when it is constantly being brought up and dragged into the present?

When he finally broke his silence, Walker took me in his arms and held my face in his hands. I leaned in to his palm, igniting the flames that were already burning between us. His deftly fingers were wrapped up in my long mane of hair. He pulled me closer. I couldn't get any closer if I tried.

"I love you, Reese. You. Are. Mine. And...I. Am. Yours. Always and forever, my love: my forever promise to you."

He left for the office, but not without leaving me with a bruising kiss. One that was hard and rough, before finishing up gently.

"I'll miss you today, baby," I said to him.

"I'll call you later." He replied.

Holding on to the counter for support, I needed to catch my breath. *Oh, my mercurial man, master of the universe, master of my heart.*

Still trying to catch my breath after Walker left, I was too oblivious to notice my best friend standing in the doorway.

"Now that was a hot kiss! Damn, Peaches, what has gotten your hot man into such a frenzy?"

"Freddy!" I shrieked with excitement as my best friend scooped me up for a big hug. "What are you doing here? I didn't expect to see you until tomorrow."

"Now, Peaches, how could I stay away when my beautiful girl needs me? Okay, your man called me and asked me to come sooner, but I already had planned on it anyway. So it's already dinnertime in Milan. Show me to your wine selection. Pour me a glass, and let's talk Walker!"

"Freddy, you've been living in New York, so according to the clock, it's still morning in New York. How about a mimosa?"

"Oh you know me so well, but I want Cristal, 2002 to be exact. Don't hold out on me, Peaches. I know your man stocks his wine vault with only the best selections of wine and champagne."

"What is it with you today? Are you high? Or just happy to see me?"

"Peaches, Peaches, Peaches... Of course I'm happy to see you, my sweet girl, but yes I am high. I am completely, madly, and deeply addicted to my hot Italian man that I left unconscious in our bed just an hour ago. So yes, my sweet girl, I am high. My drug of choice: Fabrizio. Now bring on the mimosas, lady, and let's talk about our men. I bet my guy tops yours?"

"Oh my goodness! What a dirty mouth on you? You are still my no filter, dirty mouth BFF."

"You love me, Peaches, and my dirty mouth!"

"Yes I do, and I wouldn't change you for all the gold in the world."

After Freddy made a large pitcher of mimosas with Walker's best Cristal, we made ourselves comfortable in the living room. Priscilla had served us some snacks that Freddy devoured in minutes.

I loved having him here with me in our home. This house was huge. Walker had redecorated the entire estate before I moved in. Although he had made changes over the years since Elizabeth died, he didn't want me to feel uncomfortable in a home that was originally meant for Elizabeth and him to share. Walker raised his son in this home, and when he suggested that he could build a new home for us, I just cried my eyes out. Of course the sight of me breaking down on his suggestion concerned him, but he let me have my moment.

I explained to Walker that this home also belonged to Jackson, and I wouldn't feel right just dismissing it as if it the last eighteen years didn't happen. I do feel at home here. It's a beautiful home filled with happy memories. Walker had already made it so unbelievably special for me. Our wedding would be here and shared with our family and friends. Our baby would be born here, and I could already hear her laughter resonating through the house, as her daddy played hide and seek with her. Yes, this was a beautiful house...our home.

"Hey Peaches, snap, snap! Come back to me, and join in on the conversation. My buzz is beginning to kick in, and I'm sad it's not from hearing all about Mr. Hot Walker Wall Sex."

"Freddy! Okay, you caught me daydreaming. It's easy to do when it comes to Walker. He makes me believe in the fairytale of our story and all the good things to look forward to in our future."

"Aww, baby girl. You have it all now. You never have to dream about the fairytale part again. Your life with Walker is very real, and it's about time you both get your happily ever after. Your story can go no other way."

"Thank you, my best friend, but something is off, I can feel it. He's holding something back from me, and I can't help him if he doesn't talk to me. We had a beautiful morning, then Samuel was brought up into our conversation, and all the air got sucked out of the room."

"Sounds kinky. You sure it was the air that got sucked and not something else?"

"Freddy, can you for a minute be serious, please?"

"Oh I'll try, but you don't make it easy on a guy. You mention your hot man and sucking in the same sentence, I can barely contain my erection after that. And besides, you don't play fair, Reese. I already told you my hot man is passed out in bed where I left him."

"First of all, gross, and second of all, if you miss Fabrizio so much, why don't you join him in bed instead of not listening to me."

"Scratch, scratch. Kitten has claws this morning."

"Freddy, come on and be serious for a minute please."

"Okay, okay. You want my advice on Walker Reed?" he asked.

"I do."

"You really don't need me to tell you, but I will try my best to put it in perspective for you. That man loves you. You know this, you feel this, and it's his love that completes you. Sorry I'm quoting movie lines again, but truth is truth. You are each other's half, and now you are connected again in every way that matters."

Freddy continued, "Give him time, Peaches. If I know anything, the one thing about Walker Reed is that he can only be challenged so much. Don't push him into something he's not ready for."

"What does that mean Freddy?" I asked. "Am I doing that?"

"No, Reese, I don't think you have to push Walker at all. You own him body and soul. You have the power to disarm him with just batting your beautiful eyelashes at him. You have to give each other time to feel out and get used to all the crazy quirks you both have. The love you have for each other can probably be seen by the space station, for crying out loud. It's an amazing thing to witness. You two are my heroes for heterosexual love. Just enjoy each other, and don't sweat the small stuff."

He continued, "Now, if you wish to ignore my sage advice, by all means push him, Peaches. Let the fireworks begin, but can you give me a heads up first? I want to have my popcorn ready for the show. Bring on the wall sex! You better be ready for that."

"Oh Freddy! You do have a way with words. I can't tell you how much I wish I could drink right now. "

"Oh, my sweet Georgia Peach, I love you too!"

As crazy as his no filter mouth was, Freddy knew exactly what to say to make me smile. I felt so much better after our very animated talk. Walker knew he could tell me anything. He had never held back any emotion from me before, and there was no reason why he would start now. He trusted me completely, even when I didn't deserve it. I spent too many years without him. Freddy was absolutely right. A man like Walker probably had a million things on his mind all going at the same time. I loved and trusted him completely. I had to believe he would share with me whatever was troubling him, and together we would work it out. Together...our forever promise.

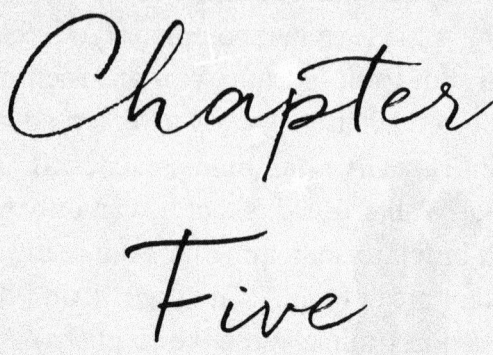

Chapter Five

Romance tested

Riley

HE PROMISED ME the summer of our lives, and by all accounts, it was. When we said goodbye to our parents, our adventure began. Our first stop was camping under the stars in Big Sur. Jackson promised to show me all of his favorite spots in California. We were surrounded by the tallest trees I had ever seen in my life. We hiked for hours with my leg muscles burning. Jackson's energy never faltered, and at times, he was dragging me along.

I never hiked a day in my life, but he knew that, so he was very patient. Jackson and his father did things like this all the time, where that wasn't the case for me. I shared many things with my father, but outdoor recreation was not one of them. He preferred to take me to museums of art and history, to opera performances and regatta races. I didn't know how many girls did those sorts of things with their fathers, but for me, the gesture was always welcomed and appreciated.

I always felt that I was very close to my father, a daddy's girl, but he shattered that image the last few months and I see him differently now. My heart hurt to remember the state of affairs I found myself in with him. He was angry and spewed ugly at my mother every chance he had. It took Jackson's father punching him out to shut him up. This was not who Samuel Briggs was. My father was a respected surgeon at one of the best hospitals in the world. He saved lives every day, performed miracles on the cases where they were deemed hopeless by others.

I'd been ignoring his calls and e-mails. My mother told me to forgive him and to move on. I wasn't ready to have the conversation I needed to have with him, so I chose to remain silent until I was ready.

All I wanted was to enjoy the last couple of weeks of my time with Jackson. We were in our own private and secluded world. I loved every minute sharing many firsts with Jackson. He had become the center of my universe. No wonder why my mother fell so hard for his father, Walker. The Reed men had charm dripping from their pores. I was so in love with Jackson Reed.

He told me he loved me every chance he had. All he ever asked of me was to trust him, believe in his love for me, and look forward to the future we were going to have. His father, from the beginning of meeting my mom back at college, always used those exact words on her. *What did I tell you? It's that irresistible Reed charm, and I have fallen hopelessly under its spell.*

It sounded amazing every time I heard it. You could imagine how taken back I was when I caught Jackson in a lie, and sadly that lie chipped away at our trust. As strong as I thought I was, I could be insecure. I was only eighteen years old and had much to learn about the ways of the world and about love. I turned my heart over to him so easily. I could only trust how I felt in my heart, so it broke a little when Jackson kept something from me. Little did I know at the time, that lie of omission would change the course of our life together.

After traveling through California, Seattle, and several amazing state parks, we were finally back in New York. We were staying at the Reed's penthouse, of course under the supervision of Jackson's bodyguard, Richard. He was never too far behind, but respected our privacy and gave us our time.

Our entire itinerary was controlled by Mr. Reed; any change of plans had to go through him first. He always kept his son on a short leash, but that's because he was so protective of Jackson. I knew this from the beginning, but it didn't bother me at all. For Jackson, he seemed to get frustrated at times, but as long as we didn't veer too far from our plans, Richard didn't seem to mind...*and what Mr. Reed didn't know wouldn't hurt him.*

But that's where I was wrong. Mr. Reed did know all, and I soon would find that out and learn a hard lesson.

Jackson was tired the last few days since arriving in New York. It was no wonder with all of our traveling. He knew New York better than I did, so he was my personal tour guide. We met up with friends from New York and Connecticut that would be going to school with us. We saw the Broadway show *Rocky*...oh yeah, Jackson's choice.

We took in a few museums all in under a week. My favorite one was the American Museum of Natural History. Jackson knew that museum from top to bottom. I teased him about it, because he loved the movie with Ben Stiller. He reenacted some of his favorite scenes. Jackson can be so funny. One of the many traits I love so much about him.

Brandon and Clay also had the chance to visit with us before returning home to California. They had been on a cruise with a bunch of friends who all mutually knew Jackson. Their ship met its final destination in New Jersey. I was happy they took time to spend time with us before their flight. These three guys were thick as thieves in high school, but were disappointed about their friend's school choice. Both Brandon and Clay were attending UCLA. I think they were hoping Jackson would see the light and reconsider, but with me loving New York as much as I did, I didn't think so.

Yes, this trip was amazing. I was one lucky girl, and our parents trusted us, which was even more of a blessing. Mom was in wedding heaven right now, so I probably could get away with a lot if I wanted to, but I was happy just being with Jackson.

I wanted to pick up a few gifts for mom and Mr. Reed. I would have loved for Jackson to join me, but he sent me on my own in the company and protection of Richard. The poor guy was weighed down with my bags, I couldn't help but laugh. Richard was a good sport about it. He even helped me pick out a present for Jackson.

Having been gone for most of the morning already, I didn't want to miss another moment with my amazing boyfriend. I called out for him as I walked through his outrageously big apartment. At first, I thought he wasn't there, until I heard his voice coming from his father's office. I was about to sneak up and attack him with kisses, but what I heard next stopped me at the door.

Jackson was yelling, "I don't care what your policy states, nor do I care what you have in your instructions. I'm the patient here, not my father, and I want a copy of my file. I have already signed all the consent forms. What is the issue with the delay? I will be there within the hour, when I expect to receive my files without any more delay."

The sound of the phone crashing down into the cradle made me jump. I had never heard Jackson raise his voice before. *Who was he yelling at?* It was time to stop eavesdropping and find out what was going on. I entered his father's office quietly to see Jackson holding his head in his hands.

"Jackson," I called out to him just barely above a whisper. He lifted his head and his eyes found mine. He smiled, and I instantly calmed.

"Hey baby, how was shopping?" he asked me as he extended his arms out for me. I accepted his invitation for a hug, and he folded me into his warm chest. "I missed you so much," he continued. "No more outings without me. I will even endure the shopping." I could feel his smile against my neck as he kissed me.

"I missed you too," I said. "Are you okay? Who were you on the phone with? You didn't sound like yourself."

"Don't worry about it, Riley. Everything is fine."

He held my face in his hands and kissed me again, but this time on my lips. Staring into his beautiful hypnotizing eyes, I saw something shift. Whatever was troubling my boyfriend, I was the last person he wanted to share his secret with. His eyes dismissed me.

I shrugged my shoulders as if I didn't care that I was a little hurt. He didn't seem himself, and I wanted to help him.

"I wasn't worried," I said to him. I lied. "I was just simply asking a question. Jackson, you can talk to me. Who were you on the phone with?"

"Riley, drop it okay? It was no one of importance. I have a few errands I need to run by myself. Why don't you relax, maybe take a bath, and by the time I return, we can go to dinner."

Now putting some distance between us, I was getting frustrated with the fact that he wouldn't answer a simple question. He began rubbing his head again. Clearly he was in pain. *Does he think I am blind not to notice?*

"Jackson, please talk to me. Are you getting another headache?"

"How many times do I have to say it? I'm fine, Riley. You're my girlfriend, not my mother. I don't need another keeper, I already have enough of them in my life."

Wow! That hurt. This was not like Jackson to erupt like this and lose his temper with me. It was obvious that something was bothering him and this tantrum he was having wasn't really about me.

I gave him the most dignified response I could. "Okay Jackson, shut me out. When you're ready to talk to me, I'll be upstairs."

I didn't want to overreact and was quite proud of myself for not slamming my way out of his father's office. He didn't follow me, probably knowing that I needed a few minutes to vent on my own. Jackson looked like he was in pain. *Why not just tell me?*

I went into his bathroom to get him some pain reliever, but didn't find any in the cabinet. I looked around and still didn't find what I was looking for, so the last place was his dopp kit. I immediately found his migraine medicine, only to find the bottle nearly empty. When we left Montana, this bottle was nearly full. *How is this possible? And how did I not notice this before now?*

"Riley! What are you doing?" His angered voice made me jump.

Not knowing how long he was standing behind me, I was startled at the sound of his voice and dropped the pill bottle. The remaining pills scattered all over the granite floor. I felt like the child that just got her hand caught in the cookie jar. *But what did I do wrong? I'm trying to help my boyfriend, but here he stands in the doorway yelling at me...Why?*

"Why are you in here?" he questioned me. I kept myself in check. I wasn't about to overreact and make the situation worse.

"Jackson, I was in here getting your medicine because it's clear to me that you have a headache. I didn't think your bathroom was off limits to me. Now, here's a question for you. How long have you been hiding your headaches from me? This pill bottle was filled over a week ago, and now it's nearly empty. Care to explain? Or are you going to throw another hissy fit?"

Without answering my question, Jackson picked up his empty pill bottle and grabbed his bag from me. Clearly frustrated, he threw it back onto the counter. *Take a deep breath, Riley,* I silently recited to myself.

"I'm waiting, Jackson. Either you tell me why this pill bottle is almost empty, or I'm calling your father." *Well, that got his attention.* I wasn't really going to do that, but he was pissing me off with his silence.

"Riley, the last thing I want is for you to call my father. It's no secret that I take migraine medicine. The last few weeks I've been getting a few headaches, and I needed it to take the edge off."

"Twenty-four pills, Jackson? This is how many you need to take the edge off? Talk to me right now, or I am out of here." I wasn't really going to leave him, but I was willing to try any scare tactic to get him to talk to me. Counting slowly in my head, I gave him to thirty to talk to me… *Well, time's up*. I turned to leave the bathroom, and he pulled me back into him.

"Let me go, Jackson. I am not going to stand here and be ignored." I tried with my best efforts to be strong and not overreact. I already learned that lesson all too well, but fighting with Jackson was not something I was used to. At the moment, he was behaving strangely and was obstinate.

I was slowly losing my fight, as my tears began to fall. I wanted to run, but I was caught up in Jackson's proximity. I couldn't resist Jackson if I wanted to. *The Reed charm gets me every time.* He held my face in his hands, as he wiped away my tears with his thumbs and began to kiss me softly.

He said, "I'm sorry, baby, please don't cry. I was hoping that this conversation could have been avoided, but now I am out of time. Will you lie down with me, so I can hold you?"

"Jackson, you're scaring me. What's wrong?"

He led me to his king-sized bed, where we both climbed in and held each other. We laid there for a few minutes without any words spoken between us, until he let out a breath and once again took hold of my face so I could look at him.

"Riley, I'm sorry for being an ass back there. I never want to upset you, not ever. You heard me yelling at Dr. O'Larien's nurse. I requested my medical file after signing all the consent forms, and I still haven't received them yet."

"Why do you need them?" I asked through my sniffles.

"I need my records to seek another medical opinion. I'm in all rights to have them in my possession, but I need your help, Riley, and it involves your father."

"What does my father have to do with this?"

"My headaches have been getting worse and coming on more frequently. The medicine helps, but I am probably taking more than I should, which leads me to believe I may have a bigger problem. I can't bring this to Dr. O'Larien. He will tell my father and all hell will break loose."

I was so confused and needed clarification. "Start from the beginning, Jackson. How long have you been getting the headaches?" His expression changed with uncertainty and apprehension clearly showing all over his face. I wanted to just hold him, comfort him, but I need him to talk to me. He couldn't shut down now. I needed to know everything. "Please, Jackson, how long?"

"They started in New York the last time we were here with our parents, when you went missing and were taken away by your father. I was out of my mind with worry. I didn't know where you were. I was upset. It began as a headache, and it got increasingly worse. My father immediately called Dr. O'Larien to our home to examine me. My father wanted me to go to the ER for an MRI, blood work, etc. He was plagued with worry, so I played it off and told him it wasn't bad. Once I calmed myself, it did get better. He talked with Dr. O'Larien, and I simply went to sleep. I chalked it up to stress over not knowing where you were. Then with my father being preoccupied with finding your mom, the focus was off of me for the time being. Stress usually tends to bring them on, but lately they are becoming a regular occurrence."

"You had one in Georgia after our fight. Oh my goodness, I am so stupid! Why didn't I see what was right in front of me. I'm so sorry, Jackson. This is my fault."

"Riley, stupid is not a word I would ever use to describe you. Baby, this is not your fault, and we did not fight in Georgia. If anything, I sealed my soul with yours in Georgia. I love you so much." *Why didn't I see the signs earlier? My boyfriend, who I should know pretty well by now, has been hiding a major secret from me. Why? I have been so caught up with my parent's drama, and my own anger with my father, only to be avoiding the obvious issue right in front of my face.* I felt foolish as he held me in his arms. I was crying like a silly girl. *He's my first love, and I hope him to be my forever love, but am I worthy of him?*

I didn't know if I was angry with him for lying to me, or at myself for not being stronger. My nana always told me that the Mitchell women came from strong Irish stock. I laughed every time she said that. I'm a person, not cattle, but with Nana, there was always a hidden message. *We are not to fear anything because no matter what it is, we have our family to lean on for support.* That piece of advice was lost on my mom, and Nana was upset that she never came to her when she needed her the most. I couldn't repeat that mistake with Jackson. He was my boyfriend, and I loved him very much. He had to know that he could share anything with me, no matter what it was. *I have to be better for him. Now if only these stupid tears would stop falling.*

Chapter Six

Truth

Jackson

SHE BEHAVED THIS way in Georgia. She blamed herself then too. Couples fight; we are not immune to this. She had the power to completely break me down with just seeing one tear on her beautiful face.

I never wanted her to know about this, but now it seems I had to tell her everything. I should have never lost my temper with her, but I was taken off guard and did the one thing I never do. I let my fear of her knowing about my headaches cloud my judgment, and I just lost it. For that alone, I felt sick.

It broke my heart, her lying in my arms and crying. She was fighting against her tears. I could feel her trying to stop, but her tears still flowed. Her body was trembling. I knew she was scared and that it was my fault for making her feel this way. Still holding her and not wanting to break our connection, I let her cry it out until I could explain everything to her.

"Riley, I need you to stop crying. Please, baby, my heart can't take it. I'm sorry I yelled at you."

"I'm sorry too. I hate it when we fight."

"Riley, we're not fighting. We're communicating with each other. I'm not doing a great job at it right now, but please don't make it worse than it is. I was just trying to protect you, but my plan didn't quite work out that way."

"Jackson, you swore to me that you would never keep anything from me. We talked about this is Georgia. I promised you that I would always talk with you first before becoming reactive, so when the shoe is on the other foot, you completely shut me out. A lie is a lie even when it's a lie by omission. If something is bothering you, then you must tell me, no matter what it is. Together, we can work out anything... You do know that?"

"I do, but Riley this was something I was hoping I would never have to tell you. I have no choice now, but to be completely honest. I need my file, because I want to take my records to your father and seek his advice. Dr. O'Larien is a great doctor, but he's on my father's payroll, and I know he would tell him."

"What about patient confidentiality? He just can't disclose what you tell him to your father."

"You don't know Walker Reed. He has no boundaries when it comes to me. If he knew I was experiencing these headaches now, our summer adventure would be over."

I continued, "Riley, he would drag me back to California and place me on lockdown. It is a miracle he hasn't shown up yet. Thank goodness for your mom, or we would be home already. Being on my own is not something that I am used to, nor my father. He has never allowed me this much freedom in my life. I may have traveled all over the world and have seen some major sights in my life, but never ever on my own. Who do you know in our circle that requires a security detail?"

"No one," she quietly answered.

"Exactly. Welcome to my world, and the strong arm of Walker Reed. Listen, baby, we only have a few days left before we fly back home for the wedding. I don't want to spend those days arguing with you. This trip has meant everything to me, and I will always remember it. I love that I had you to share it with."

Riley looked at me and replied, "I love you too, boyfriend, but Jackson, he's your father. He loves you and only wants you to be okay. Do you think you might be exaggerating a bit?"

"Riley, he is completely obsessed with my health, he always has been. Watching my mother die in front of him and me barely surviving as a newborn changed my father and how he reacts to things that are beyond his control. Losing my mother was a failure that he has never gotten over. I know it sounds crazy, but that's how he feels. You can't even begin to understand what I had to do to convince him to allow me to go to school in New York. He wants me in California, and it took months of convincing to change his mind. Even then, I had to agree to certain concessions."

I continued, "We are only on this trip because of your mom. She has got my father completely focused on their happy reunion, and with the wedding approaching, they are probably on cloud nine right now. This is probably my only chance to do this. My father will soon remember that I have an appointment coming up, and then it will truly be out of my hands."

I explained to Riley, "I need to go over to Dr. O'Larien's office to pick up my flash drive with my records on it, and then I want to bring it to your father. I tried calling his office, but the wait to get in for a consult is over six months long. Riley, I don't have that kind of time. I probably could pull strings to see him with just my last name being what it is, but I don't want that either. I can't risk it getting back to my father. I know you are still very upset with him, but I need you to put that aside for now and reach out to him. I would like to see him tomorrow if possible."

"Jackson, how am I going to arrange this consult for you? He is going to have all sorts of questions and will probably say no."

"Riley, he's not going to say no to you. He loves you, and all he wants to do is talk with you. All you have to do is ask him to meet you for lunch tomorrow, and once he shows, I will take it from there. Even if I could get an appointment to see him on my own, he probably would say no because of who my father is. I need to try, Riley. Please help me."

"Jackson, I haven't spoken to my father in months, and after how he treated my mother, I don't want to. He is not the loving father I always looked up to. My father has changed, and is not someone that I respect right now especially after the hurtful words he said to my mother."

"I agree, but I think he learned his lesson after my father set him straight. You have to cut him some slack and meet him halfway. Look at what he's been through. I'm not condoning his actions, but if I were in his shoes or even my father's, I would have a problem with this shitty situation too. His marriage is over, his wife has returned to her past lover, his daughter is with the past lover's son... Oh my goodness Riley! This is the making of a movie. I know we joked about this, but you can't make this up if you wanted to. My loyalties are with my father, but I can't help but feel bad for yours. Come on, baby, can't you soften a little?"

Riley got off the bed and started pacing the room. *Oh, my girl is stubborn.* I could see the wheels turning in her head, but she still remained silent.

I tried again. "Riley, he loves you. He has been calling you nonstop. I'm not saying you have to forgive him, but please talk and meet with him. He's your father, but he is also a doctor, one that I especially need. Will you please call him for me?" *Please let me get through to her.*

"If I do this, Jackson, I will only be doing it for you, not him. I'm just not ready to forgive him yet. What are you hoping for after talking with my father?"

"I'm hoping this is nothing, but it has never been proven that what happened to my mom won't happen to me. Dr. O'Larien has told this to my father a thousand times, but even 'A headache is just a headache' theory doesn't sit well with my father. Riley, if my father finds out about this, my chances on attending NYU are slim to none. He will make me return to California. And all of my dreams—our dreams—will be over."

"Jackson, I can't believe your father would force you home. He knows how important NYU is to you, and to us. I can't believe he would take that away from you."

"He won't care, Riley. My health is his number one priority. You don't know what it was like growing up with him. If he feels that it is compromised, I'm fucked. If I can get the answers I need, then at least I may have an advantage. My father relies on facts, knowledge of every situation he finds himself in. I can't surprise him with this. I need to know and understand every option before he does. I am praying that my anxiety is just getting the better of me and I'm really fine. Riley, this is a happy time in all of our lives. Our parents are finally going to be together the way they always wanted to be. You and I will be together here in New York and attending college with our friends. I'm confident that everything will be okay, but I need you to be on board with this. I won't keep anything else from you, I promise. Please trust me on this? I know what I am doing, Riley. I know my father better than anyone, and I have to try to be one step ahead of him, maybe several."

"Jackson, you sound like you'd been living under this dictatorship your entire life, and you are ready to jump the wall to your freedom. The way you are describing your father is different from the man that I've come to know. Is this how he will treat my mother?"

"Riley, you misunderstand what I'm saying to you. It's my fault that I suck at trying to get my point across to you. Let me break it down the best way I can. My father is an amazing man. He has a heart, a good one. He loves hard, works hard, and when you are loved by Walker Reed, he puts you above anything else that matters. I have never come in second when it comes to my father. His dominant side comes from a time in his life that he simply didn't have control of."

"You mean your mother?"

"Yes, my mother. Since reuniting with your mom, he has shared some parts of his past with me, but certainly not all of it. He had a very volatile relationship with my grandfather, a relationship with my mom that was never supposed to go beyond friendship, and to top all that, he lost the love of his life…Reese, and he never understood why. All my father had in his life was his work and me. He didn't have anything in between. It never occurred to me how lonely he was until your mother walked back into his life. As young as I am, I have so much in my life, whereas my father didn't, until he fell in love with your mom. I know him well enough to know that all his protectiveness comes from a good place, and he has never used that to hold me back. He's just scared for me. I get it, so I'm trying to be patient and respectful of his feelings."

"Jackson, with all that you just told me about your father, how can you sit here so calmly and keep the one thing from him that will hurt him the most? I don't understand this at all."

"It's complicated, Riley, and it does hurt me to keep things from my father. I don't want to, but I feel I have to for now. Let them get married and be happy for one freaking minute before…"

"Before what? Before you get sick? What the hell, Jackson? Do you want that to happen? Where is the positive and confident guy that I love and respect? I know I'm an emotional, crazy girl sometimes, but I don't change my colors that much. You are all over the place right now, and I feel I can't keep up."

My girl looked like she was going to throw up. I knew I threw everything at her all at once, but she had to know. *How do I get through to her? If this is Riley's reaction, I can't even imagine how my father would be.*

The tension was so thick in our room, you could slice it with a knife. That's an accurate description on how I felt. I knew I was wrong on so many levels. I'd been lying to Riley and my father. I loved this crazy, over-reacting, full of life girl who was now crying

48

inconsolably over me. I needed to close the distance between us. I leaped off the bed and walked toward her. She held up her hands to me, stopping me.

Ouch. Now I feel like I can throw up. She's never rejected me. I'm at a loss. My back is up against the wall. *What do I do now?* I've pushed her too hard, when I should have given her time to process all that I've told her.

I watched despairingly as Riley exited the bedroom. She turned back and half smiled back at me. She said, "I need a few minutes alone, please give me that."

I silently nodded and watched her walk out. My heart dropped down into my stomach. I felt awful for hurting her. *What the hell am I doing here? I'm trying to be so independent and live my life without the long arm of Walker Reed, but hell!! I fucking needed him so much right now, and he along with Riley are the two people that I should have been able to trust above anyone else.*

My head was again pounding. I sat down and said my silent prayers to the one person I prayed was listening. "Please mom, help me. I thought I was strong enough to do this on my own. Am I just fooling myself? Please show me the way, and if you can, help Riley too. She's amazing, mom. She's like lightning in a summer storm. She gets all fired up with a thousand sparks lighting up the room, and then she smiles. Her face is the sun that parts the clouds on a cloudy day. Her smile makes me forget my own name, and all is right in my world."

Chapter

Seven

All in with you

Jackson

FEELING LIKE TIME has stopped and not knowing what to do next, I splashed some cold water on my face to wash away the few tears I couldn't stop from falling. Here I was, crying like a fucking pansy, and all I wanted was her. I looked at my cell, and it only had been ten minutes, when it felt like hours since she walked out. I knew she was near, I could feel her presence. She's struggling with this and all I can do is wait for her answer. *I hate this! How can I fix it?*

We were completely happy until she discovered my medicine bottle almost empty. I was careless to keep it out in the open for her to find. She was only trying to help me. And I behaved like an ass. I walked out of my bathroom, and there was my beautiful girl waiting for me. I said nothing. She came back to me. It was now my turn to listen.

"Okay, Jackson, I will call my father, but you have to do something for me first."

"Anything, all you have to do is ask."

"Do you promise me?" she asked.

"Riley, I promise. Anything you want, I want to give you."

"I hope that's true, Jackson, because I've been thinking a lot about this, and every fiber of my being says this is the absolute right thing for us to do." She paused, slowly cracked a smile, and looked into my eyes. "I want to get married. Jackson Walker Reed, will you marry me?"

"What did you just say?"

"Come on, baby, do I really need to ask it again?

"Riley, I want nothing more than to marry you, but this is not the time."

"Jackson, you're wrong. This is the perfect time to get married. If you ever want to break free from the control your father has on you, then this is the perfect time to do so. We are of legal age, and no one can stop us from being together, not even Walker Reed."

"Riley, I can't marry you for the sole purpose of getting out from under my father's thumb. He will always be an influence in my life; getting married is not going to change that."

She was starting to look flustered. She said, "Back in Georgia, we made promises to each other, our forever promises, did you forget? Or was that just talk?"

"How can you even question that? You know I meant every word spoken to you. I love you with all my heart and want to marry you, but to do it now would be wrong. You deserve a magical day surrounded by our family and friends. I know you're angry with him, but haven't you always pictured your father walking you down the aisle? Lifting your veil with tears in his eyes, as he takes in the beauty of the woman you've become? Riley, it would be incredibly selfish of me to take that away from you."

"Jackson, let me decide on what is best for me. As beautiful as that sounds, I don't need it. If we have learned anything from our parents love story is this: *Live in the moment.* I want this moment with you and everything that will follow. Please say yes."

"Riley, oh baby, my heart says yes, but my mind is a different story. I can't have history repeating itself. That wouldn't be fair to you. I love you too much to hurt you that way. Please believe me that I would marry you a thousand times if I could predict the positive outcome I'm praying for."

"Jackson, we have no absolutes in life. If you truly believe in fate and all that the universe has aligned for us, then you should know our destinies have already been planned out for us. You said it yourself that meeting me at your mother's dedication ceremony was fate. We found each other almost a year ago to the date, and now here we are in love and together. Our love story has been nothing but guided by fate, and I will never question it. I depend on it, trust it, and believe in it, and I believe in us."

She had completely broken me with her declaration of love for me. *Who was I kidding to ever fight this force between us? Riley loves hard. She goes in with her full heart, and she uses that amazing heart to guide her through every decision she makes. She is fearless, my girl. If she is scared, she's not showing it to me.* She was willing to throw caution to the wind and not let my fear hold us back, or define our future for whatever it will be.

I held her hand and said to my girl, "I have never loved you more than at this very moment. I know we are young, but it feels like I've been connected with you all my life. I'm not going to lie to you Riley, I'm scared. But you're right. Everything is telling us that we belong together, and this is the best thing for us. Let's get married!"

With her tears gone, she crashed her lips onto mine, sealing our commitment to each other. Our tongues swirled together in perfect unison; we only disconnected to catch our breaths.

"I love you, Jackson, and I will be with you for as long as you want me to be."

"I want forever with you, Riley, and I won't settle for anything less."

We held onto each other as if we were each other's lifeline. We just got through a major moment that other couples may have given up on. Not us, we were stronger together than apart, and I should have trusted Riley from the beginning.

No one will understand the decisions we made here today, especially my father. He is going to go ballistic when he finds out about this. I promised my father that I would never keep things from him, and I always intended to keep my word. He'd been through so much over the years and had sacrificed everything for my happiness. To tell him now would only cause him to worry. I had to try my best to shield him from the unknown, until I don't have any options left. He deserved this time with Reese. They waited long enough to be together. And with their wedding only a few weeks away, I wouldn't be the one to cause them one minute of unhappiness. My father would not see it the same way I do, I was sure of it. I would deal with his wrath when the time came.

Chapter Eight

The first step is always the hardest

Riley

JACKSON AND I fell asleep entwined with each other. It was only a short nap, but very much needed. I composed myself to make the call to my father. He had phoned already twice today, and I ignored both calls. He was going to wonder about my sudden change of heart, but this was for Jackson, not him. I called his private line, and my father answered on the second ring. His tone was professional, but curt and right to the point. He softened once hearing my voice on the other end.

"Hi daddy" was all I could say at first. He was surprised to finally hear from me, but encouraged me to continue talking with him. I told him that I would be in Maryland with Jackson tomorrow and invited him to have lunch with us. My father said he would cancel his entire day to have his chance to apologize and clear the air with me.

Jackson wanted us to meet him at the hospital. If my father agreed with our request, we would be able to move forward with the consult. It was a huge gamble, but I was willing to try for my boyfriend and soon-to-be husband. Everything was riding on his agreement. I feared this would be a challenge given his feelings toward Mr. Reed, but my father never held any resentment toward Jackson. I was praying that his feelings had not changed and he would rise above and keep the personal feelings out of it.

Jackson made his daily call to his father, this time by phone and not video chat. He looked a bit pale today and didn't want to raise any alarms with his father. After our fight—or what Jackson calls 'communicating'—he was exhausted. I spoke to my mom as well. She was going on about the wedding plans and final dress fittings. Freddy arrived early to California, another surprise by Mr. Reed. I was happy he was there to help her when I couldn't be. They were so close, I couldn't wait to see him again.

On our last phone call, Freddy promised me that my eyes would pop out of my head when I saw my dress. All designed by him, of course. I would love to wear a Freddy Mac original when I marry Jackson, but he's all I need. I was also getting excited to see Fabrizio again. The only person I hadn't met yet was their friend, Marsha, my mom's former agent. Mom and Freddy have told me countless stories about her, but they always said nothing compares to meeting Marsha Malin in person.

My great grandparents would also be making the trip out to California for the wedding. I wish I had Nana Lila here with me. She always knew what to do, no matter how small or big a problem was. I could use one of her pep talks right about now, and a hug or two couldn't hurt.

With our phone calls now out of the way, it was time to go down to Dr. O'Larien's office to retrieve Jackson's file. He was hoping we could be quick about it and leave without raising any suspicions. Richard was our constant shadow. He drove us to the Upper West Side where Dr. O'Larien's office was located. We knew he would recognize the building immediately, so we called a friend to meet us at the local Starbucks a block over.

Jackson asked Richard to stay with the car while we went inside to meet up with our friends. He didn't have any issues with it since we were all seated at a front table where he could have clear access to us. Richard was only following orders. I think he actually felt bad for us at times but never voiced any opinions that would cost him his job.

Phase one was already in motion. I needed to cause a diversion for Jackson, so he could sneak off to his doctor's office. After about twenty minutes, I walked outside, when Richard immediately approached me. An actress I wasn't, but after my performance, I didn't think I did half bad at convincing him that I was suddenly ill.

I had Richard drive me to a local pharmacy where I told him I needed to pick up a few things for my upset stomach. He wanted to get Jackson, but I explained that Jackson would simply wait for me and stay back with our friends. As soon as we pulled away, I saw Jackson slip out the door. My fingers were crossed that we could pull this off and not get caught.

WITH MY FRIENDS being my lookout, I made it to Dr. O'Larien's office in a few minutes. I entered his upscale office and greeted his office manager, Mindy. She knew me well and was always kind to me. I didn't see his bitchy nurse lurking around. My last conversation with her was not pleasant, and I was hoping to get out of there as quickly as possible.

"Jackson Reed, how are you, son?"

"I'm well, Mindy. Thank you for asking."

"What brings you here today? I don't see you on the doctor's schedule."

"I'm here to pick up my records. I spoke to Wanda earlier. She should have left it for me."

"Jackson, all requests go through me first. The nurses only log the messages into the computer. Let me take a look here and see what we have." She began clicking away on her keyboard.

This was not going right, according to my plan. Looking down at my phone, I already had been there for more than ten minutes already. I had to get back to the coffee house before Richard figured out that I was missing.

"Mindy, I'm kind of in a hurry. Can I just have my file?"

"I'm sorry, Jackson, but all I see here is that you requested a copy of your records, but they would have to be released by Dr. O'Larien himself. It's clearly stated here in the doctor's notes.

"Fucking bitch of a nurse!" I mumbled under my breath. I hoped Mindy didn't hear me, but I wanted to strangle Wanda. *Hell! I want Wanda's ass fired.* Mindy frowned at me. She heard my disgust for the incompetent nurse, but she was cool and didn't call me out on it.

"Jackson, please have a seat, and I'll be with you in a few minutes," Mindy said, as she got up from her desk. I had no choice but to wait.

My phone beeped twice while waiting on Mindy to return. I read the "Where are you" messages from Riley. I was so screwed. How long could she hold off Richard before he found me? Not ten seconds later, Dr. O'Larien greeted me. *Yup, I'm screwed.*

"Hello, Jackson. What brings you here today? Is your father with you?'

Liam O'Larien and my father go all the way back to prep school. They had been friends since they were teenagers, and my father completely trusted him with my care. Their close friendship was one of the reasons why I couldn't trust him with this. I didn't believe that the patient confidentiality agreement would be respected here, not with my father always calling the shots.

"Hi, Dr. O'Larien. No, my father is not with me today. I'm here in New York on vacation with my girlfriend. I just stopped by to pick up my medical records."

"Is there a reason why you need them? I already provided your father with the most updated notes, and your next appointment is not until September. Why would you need them now?"

"I would think that would be obvious. I am the patient, after all, and I'll be living here in New York on my own. I just wanted to hold onto something that is rightfully mine. Can I please have my records?" I couldn't help the anger in my voice. This was not Dr. O'Larien's fault. I meant no disrespect toward him. I knew he was just asking out of concern.

"You may have your file, Jackson. You are right. You are my patient first, and I have to respect your wishes. Have you signed over a consent form yet?"

"I have, sir. I sent over the signed consent electronically to Wanda."

"Okay, Jackson, give Mindy a few minutes to transfer everything over, and you can be on your way. Before I go, how are you feeling? Is there anything else I can help you with? Are you experiencing any issues that I need to be made aware of?"

"I'm fine, Dr. O'Larien. I just want my files." *Liar!* My conscience was screaming at me. "Would it be too much for me to ask you to keep this quiet and not mention my visit here to my father?"

"I won't mention it, Jackson, but I hope you know that if you are dealing with anything, you could always come to me. You are my patient. I will always put you first, contrary to what you might believe."

I simply nodded my head and watched him go and speak with his office manager. She gave me a hand signal to wait a few minutes. I called Riley, and she told me that they were on their way back to Starbucks. I only had a small window of time to get back. Mindy came over as I hung up, and she handed me a flash drive. She gave me a quick hug, and I literally ran back to the coffee shop.

I just made it inside when my phone beeped again. Riley and Richard were back and waiting on me. I said goodbye to our friends and walked back outside. Riley's eyes widened at the sight of me, and so did Richard's. I ran all the way from Dr. O'Larien's office. It was summer after all, and I was dripping in sweat. There was no way

Richard was going to believe that Starbucks didn't have air conditioning. Riley quickly greeted me and tried to wipe my face down, but I knew I already aroused suspicion by the looks Richard directed at me.

"Are you ready to head back to the apartment, sir?"

"Richard, I still have a few errands to run. You can drop Riley and me off downtown. I will call you when we're ready to be picked up."

"I'm afraid I can't do that, Jackson. You may have diverted my attention back at the coffee house, a mistake I will not be making again. Now where do you need to go?"

"Richard, I'm not trying be a jerk here, but I'm an adult and I am more than capable of finding my way around the city. Riley and I will get off here. Please pull the car over."

"Jackson, I work for your father. I have my orders, orders that need to be carried out as he has directed me to do so," he replied, and then refocused his attention on the traffic in front of us.

I was beyond angry and couldn't care less if he called my father. I pulled my girl closer to me and made it look like we were hugging. I whispered in her ear, "When the car comes to a stop, we are going to make a run for it. Keep going, and don't look back. We will lose him in the shopping district."

Although she was nervous, she followed my lead. Richard stopped at the next light. The car was basically boxed in due to the late afternoon traffic. This was our opportunity to make our move. I grabbed Riley's hand and flung open the door. We ran as fast as our feet could take us while listening to Richard scream out for us. *Oh man, I knew he would be angry, but enough was enough already. I needed a moment to breathe.* If Riley and I wanted to get our marriage license, I couldn't have Richard reporting back to my father.

Satisfied that we lost him, Riley and I slowed down to take a breath. She wrapped her arms around my neck and pushed me up against an alley wall to kiss me. What we just did excited her, and I had to admit turned me on too. Having tried other things first, we hadn't made love yet, but we knew we would soon. This wasn't the place to have my first time with Riley. She was making my dick throb against my zipper the way she was rubbing against it.

"Stop," I barely managed to get out. "Come on, we have things to do." I said as I circled my arm around her waist.

An hour later, we had our marriage license. Palming hands with hundred dollar bills can move things along for you in City Hall. This was suddenly becoming very real. I looked for uncertainty in her eyes, but found none. In a few days, I would be marrying Riley Taylor Briggs, the love of my life and my future wife. *Holy shit!* I know I was acting on pure adrenaline and leading with my heart. If I took time to question it, today would be completely different. *I just want this moment with Riley. Right here and now, I'll worry about the rest later.*

We grabbed dinner and walked hand in hand back to my apartment. As soon as we entered the building, I saw my doorman on the phone. I already knew he was probably notifying our return to Richard. He didn't need to, because the building was under twenty-four hour surveillance and I was sure my bodyguard already knew the minute we walked through the door. What was strange was that I hadn't received a phone call from my father yet. The elevator opened up to my floor, and there stood Richard waiting for us. I whispered into Riley's ear to wait for me upstairs in the bedroom while I had a conversation with Richard.

I couldn't judge by his expression if he was angry or disappointed, but I was about to find out. We sat down in the living room, and he crossed his arms over his broad chest.

"Jackson, I haven't called your father, if that is what you are wondering."

I let out the breath I was holding and let him continue. "I don't know what that was back there, but if you ever pull a stunt like that again, I most certainly will call your father, and you will find yourself on the next plane back to California. My job is to protect you and care for your well-being. I am medically trained to assist you in case of an emergency. I know you are of age and want to be treated as an adult, but that also comes with respect. You did not respect me today by running off like children. What if you would have had a seizure? Riley is not trained to know what to do if that should ever occur. This could have happened anywhere. Please tell me that you will not be this irresponsible again?"

He had a valid point, several of them actually. Richard has witnessed me having a seizure, and he took care of me throughout the entire ordeal. I have to remember to talk to Riley about this.

"I'm very sorry, Richard. I now know I was wrong to ditch you, but I was suffocating and needed to be on my own for a while. I know you have your orders from my father, but there should also be boundaries too. I want my privacy respected. No, I demand it."

"I can do that for you, Jackson, as long as you show the same respect for me. You have my word. Are you okay? Is there anything I need to know?"

"I'm fine, Richard. Tomorrow we will be leaving here at eight a.m. We are going to Maryland to visit with Riley's father. Before you say anything, I plan on calling my father in a little while. I'm going up to bed now, and I will see you in the morning."

I was clearly done with this conversation and dismissed him. I made my way upstairs to hear Riley taking a shower. I took the opportunity to phone my father. He would still be at the office, and I was hoping to make this conversation go as quickly as possible. It didn't matter what my father was working on, my calls were always put through. If he talked to me while at Reed Global, I knew we wouldn't have any time for heavy conversations. This would be my saving grace. I called his private line, and Jenny answered for him.

"Hi, Jenny, it's Jackson."

"Hello, handsome. When are you coming home? We miss you."

"I miss you too, Jenny. I'll be home soon. Just enjoying my summer vacation with Riley, who is having an amazing time."

"That's wonderful to hear, Jackson. Enjoy the rest of your trip and I will see you when you come home. I'll connect you now with your father." I took a breath and counted to five. I knew I had to choose my words wisely when speaking with my father.

"Hello, son, how are you?"

"I'm fine, dad, and Riley is too. I just wanted to check in with you and let you know that I will be in Maryland tomorrow with Riley. We plan to visit with Dr. Briggs, and hopefully Riley and her dad can work some things out." The line was silent. I knew he wouldn't be happy about it.

"Jackson, I am not comfortable with this. That man has shown me nothing but animosity and has hurt Reese too many times. He may even hate you just on principle. I prefer you to stay behind. Riley can fly over to Maryland by herself and have her visit with her father. Once she is finished, she can then return back to you in New York." He made it sound so simple.

"Dad, she's not going to Maryland by herself. She's my girlfriend, and I should be with her. Please don't try to talk me out of this or make demands of me. You have to trust me, dad."

"I do trust you, son, emphatically, but not him. I want you to keep Richard close by. Can you at least agree to that?"

"I can and will, dad. We're going to meet him at his hospital, grab some lunch, and like I said, hopefully they can reconcile. It would make things a lot easier on Riley. I know it bothers Reese that they are estranged."

"I will take care of Reese, and believe me son, Samuel is the last thing on her mind. Okay, I don't want to talk about him anymore. How are you feeling? The pharmacy called me at the office yesterday. Why didn't you mention that you ordered another refill of your migraine medicine?"

He knows! Here I am about to once again lie to my father. I surprised myself how my lies so easily rolled off my tongue. "I meant to tell you about that, dad. I'm sorry it slipped my mind, but I accidently spilled my pills down the bathroom sink. It was totally my fault. I had a headache coming on, no big deal, but when I was about to take a pill, my hand slipped and I dropped my medicine." *Please*

God...let him believe me.

"Jackson, are you feeling okay son? If you felt that you needed your migraine medicine, then your headache must have been pretty bad. I'm going to call Dr. O'Larien, and he can run a few tests."

"NO! Please don't call him, dad. It was just a headache, and I'm fine now. Please don't make this more than it is." *The way I just shouted into the phone receiver, if I get away with this, it will be a miracle.*

"Jackson, I will never take anything lightly when it comes to you. We've been down this road before. Do I need to remind you again? Just a few months ago I had to witness one of your headaches incapacitate you. Now you're three thousand miles away from me, and I am powerless to help you. Let me call Dr. O'Larien. This way my mind will be at ease."

He stopped talking with me, as I heard him buzz Jenny. He asked her to get Dr. O'Larien on the line. My heart just sunk. I had to convince him that I was more than capable of taking care of myself. I tried to get his attention until I had to shout into the phone once again.

"Dad, for the last time, I am fine. I will see him at my next appointment in September, as scheduled. Please do not call him." Trying to calm my already out of control anxiety, I waited on his answer.

He sighed. "I hate this separation, son. You are making me feel helpless, and it doesn't sit well with me. If something is wrong, you need to tell me...now. This is not a request," he curtly said.

I knew just the mention of the headache would set him off. Now with the pharmacy calling him, I was sinking deeper in my lies.

"Dad, please don't see it that way. I am fine, and there is nothing wrong. I'm growing up, and I have to begin taking care of myself. This should not make you feel weak or insignificant. If anything, it should show you that you have done a great job raising me, and you can trust me to make my own decisions. Dad, we have been over this a thousand times already. Please focus on marrying Reese, and just take a chill pill."

He laughed out loud, *thank God*. It wasn't too often I could win an argument with Walker Reed, and who knew if I could claim victory with this one.

"Okay son, you have made some very strong talking points. I do trust you very much and love you. I can't just turn it off and not worry about you. You may be of age, but you will always be my child. Please just promise me that if you continue to get your headaches, you will call me immediately?"

"I will dad, I promise. Riley and I will be home soon. We miss you both and can't wait for the wedding."

"We miss you too, Jackson. I have so much to catch you up on, but I would rather be in the same room when I do. I have to run now, I'm late for a meeting. Be sure to call me tomorrow. And one more thing, be careful with that Samuel Briggs."

"I will, dad. Please give our love to Reese. Good night, and I'll talk to you soon."

"Tomorrow, Jackson. I will hear from you tomorrow."

"Yes sir, you will."

The line clicked off, and I let out my held breath. I felt sick to my stomach over lying to my father again. He had come so far with me. Once he discovers that I have been lying to him, that progress will be shattered.

I keep thinking back to Reese's explanation as to why she left my father all those years ago, and why she did what she did to protect her family. *What I'm doing right now with my father is like the same thing, right?* I've been playing it out in my head over and over again with the same outcome.

I will get my consult and everything will be fine. I never have to mention this to him and no one will be the wiser, right? I keep telling myself this and pray he will never know my lies.

My father had always put my needs above anything or anyone else my entire life. I almost felt bad for him. He should have been living his life and opening his heart to someone that could care for him all those years ago. He silently mourned my mother and ached for his lost love, Reese. His entire adult life had been two things: Reed Global and me.

He always explained to me that *the decisions a man makes in his life, he has to stand behind and own them. Live up to your convictions and stand tall. Never bow down to anyone, for this will show your weakness.* Now I know the last part pertained to his professional world, but probably his personal life as well.

I may be young, but I am a man…my own man. A Reed through and through. *No! I won't cause him even one day of unwanted worry.* Reese and my father deserved this time to be happy and to focus only on each other. I just had to remain positive that whatever was happening with me was miniscule and could be easily fixed. Everything had to be okay. With Riley by my side, we will go to NYU in September and begin our college days, but as husband and wife.

Wow, oh wow! I still can't even wrap my head around that. Husband and wife. How in the hell will I ever be able to explain my duplicity to my father? Will he see it as an act of betrayal by his own son? The thought of my father seeing it that way makes my stomach hurt. Will he freak out and make us get it annulled? God, I hope not. My father always said that my relationship with Riley was history repeating itself.

We are Walker & Reese, the newer models. He laughed at me when I referenced this to him once, but how true it is. I had to try to make him understand my reasons behind the choices I made. I just prayed for all our future happiness that he would give me the time to explain it all to him.

I had to believe that he would. He was my father. He loved me. His love always protected and guided me, along with my mother's in heaven. A few months ago when I told him that I had kept my true identity from Riley, he wasn't angry. He listened then and promised me that were okay…we always were. I prayed that vow still held true.

We have to be okay.

I know no other way.
And neither does my father.

Chapter Nine

Get out of my head

Walker

AFTER MY PHONE call with my son, I had one last meeting to attend before leaving for home. I couldn't help the nagging feeling that something wasn't right with Jackson. He asked me to trust him and for the most part I did, but this was Jackson we were talking about. I didn't usually sway on anything when it came to him. He was adamant about me not calling Dr. O'Larien. I could always make an unscheduled trip out to New York, but that would probably backfire on me.

I could use work as the reason, but I don't want to leave Reese either. She could come with me and she could visit with Riley, but they will be home soon enough for the wedding, so this plan wouldn't work. *I'm frustrated because something is off with my son. I feel it. I just don't know what it is yet.*

Entering my office and taking a seat in front of me, Jenny called out to get my attention.

"Sir, are you ready?" she asked while holding her tablet.

I snapped my head up. "Ready for what?"

"Your schedule," she simply replied and blindly ignored my tone.

I usually do this with her at the beginning of my day, but I was swamped with work that I needed to catch up on, along with revising the wedding plans. I promised Reese that we would downsize the guest list and make our wedding more intimate.

After work, I arrived home to find Reese already asleep. She had been experiencing severe morning sickness the last week or so. She kept me at bay with this, only telling me the littlest information. Reese should have known by now that she couldn't keep anything from me, especially when it came to her well-being. My staff here at the house kept me updated throughout the day. I asked her to slow down on the wedding plans and allow the planners to do their jobs.

Now that Freddy had arrived in California, they were spending their time catching up. I could relax knowing he was helping her. They were so close again. I couldn't be happier for their friendship. All I wanted Reese to worry about was getting from the beginning of the aisle to meeting me at the altar, and I would take care of the rest.

I ate the dinner that had been prepared for me. I hated to eat alone, but I knew she needed to sleep. After my meal, I quietly checked on my beautiful sleeping angel. Reese was out like a light. I softly kissed her on her lips and made my way out of our bedroom. She let out a soft moan from her very delectable mouth.

Those sweet sounds were my undoing. She had the power to completely decimate me. All I desired was to make love to her. I needed to feel skin on skin and listen to her heartbeat, as I buried myself deep inside her body. Yes, I was a man in love, but also felt like a horny teenager. Splashing some cold water on my face to bring down my wanton desire to wake her, I left her sleeping and continued to do some work in my study.

I was exhausted. I hadn't been sleeping at night. I should have been over the moon right now, but as soon as I closed my eyes, he would appear in my dreams: my dead father, Phillip Reed. With each nightmare that came to pass, his image became clearer and clearer. His voice was unmistakably recognizable. I had awakened one time screaming and covered in sweat. I knew I had scared Reese, but she never said it. She was worried for me, and I lied through my teeth. She knew how hard I worked and the hours I put in.

After the first nightmare, I began to have them more frequently, and I just said it was work related stress. Reese knew that Reed Global was currently involved in an international deal. We were designing a new building in Germany, and this had been in the works for over two years now. She easily believed me and did her best to console me. We always ended up making love. It was the one act that completely sated me, and my nightmares were erased from my memory…until tonight.

I don't even remember how much time had gone by, but I must have fallen asleep. Once again, I found myself caught in another violent nightmare, and he was back.

"Hello, Walker" was all he said. I opened my eyes to have him staring right at me. I was again at my desk at Reed Global. It was always the same dream. I was back here on the day he last visited me, Jackson's birthday, the anniversary of Elizabeth's death.

"Please go away, father. Leave me alone, and go back to Hell where you belong."

"Walker, I told you, I'm not in Hell. I'm everywhere. Every story has a villain. I'm sorry that I'm yours."

"Stop saying that!" I screamed to him. "Get out of my head and leave me alone. Why do you keep doing this to me? You're dead! Be dead, and leave me alone." I began to hold my head and close my eyes. I begged him to go away, counting to fifty in hopes that when I opened my eyes, he would be gone. Well, no such luck, because he was still there.

"Forgive me, son."

I suddenly awakened from my dream, knocking over objects that were on my desk. I never made it back to our bedroom. I had been here all night in my study. I looked over to the clock and tried to get my eyes into focus. It read five a.m. I scrubbed my face and tried to wake up to gather my bearings.

Reese? Has she been asleep this entire time? Usually if she were to wake in the middle of the night, she would have searched for me. I quietly opened our bedroom door, and there she was, still very much asleep and almost in the same position I had left her in.

I quietly entered our closet and changed into running clothes. I needed to run, and run for many miles to clear my head. *Too early to call Tyler for a workout. I'll be better on my own anyway. These nightmares are bullshit, and I want them to stop.* I leave a note for Reese and kiss her lips. Brushing away the hair that had fallen on her face, I ran my fingers along her jaw line. She was exquisite to stare at, especially when she was sleeping.

She must know that I practically did this each and every night. She was the only vision I wanted in my dreams, not Phillip. Kissing her one last time, I made my way out to begin the run that would hopefully help me find some peace and resolution to my sleeping problem once and for all.

My run started out aggressive, and once I reached eight miles, I began to slow down. I ran nearly thirteen miles when I had reached an unexpected destination. I was at the cemetery. *Who would have thought when I began my run that my legs would bring me here?*

I hadn't been here for more than a year now. I was ashamed that I stayed away this long, but it's not a place I liked to visit. Who does when it's a final resting place of someone that you cared about? This place was quiet, but it also haunted me. Elizabeth was here, and she should not be. My heart began to ache as I got closer to her grave. The grass seemed to be a bit overgrown and her current flower arrangement had wilted. Leaves were scattered all around her stone.

I had a bench installed in front of her grave as soon as I was able to. Her parents used to visit her frequently. I didn't want Gail to be uncomfortable while she was here mourning her daughter. I always took care of her parents, but not anymore. After discovering what

Henry did to me, and to Reese, his needs did not matter to me at all. I would always love Gail, but her loyalties were with her husband, just like my mother to Phillip. Gail would never know what a bastard Henry was, and the crimes he committed. I wouldn't hurt her or dishonor Elizabeth. That act would only hurt our son.

I took a seat in front of her memorial. I loved what I had chosen for her. Her memorial stone was made of solid granite in a dusty rose color. She had angel wings sprouting out from the top of it and an inscription well-suited for the woman Elizabeth Townsend Reed was.

"What we have once enjoyed, we can never lose.
All that we love deeply becomes part of us."
Elizabeth Townsend Reed
1974 – 1997
Rest in eternal peace, my friend

I can't even remember how I came to choosing this fitting quote, but I found it scribbled in one of her journals. It was from Helen Keller. Elizabeth liked to write down inspirational quotes, sometimes using them on me when I was being a stubborn ass. Who knew that a quote she loved would end up on her gravestone. I hope she liked what I had chosen for her.

My legs were weak from the high endurance run I had just unexpectedly taken. I usually didn't push my body this hard, but they led me here. I didn't come here as often as I should, but when I did, I couldn't help but talk out loud to her in hopes that she could hear me.

"Hi, friend, I'm sorry I haven't been here in a while, and without flowers. I will send you roses today…the yellow ones that you love so much. I'll add some lilies too."

"Remember to tell the florist that I like the calla lilies," I heard a voice say behind me.

"What the hell?" I whipped my head up, not believing what I

71

just heard. *I thought I was alone here. I just heard Elizabeth's voice loud and clear, but how?*

"Fuck! Now on top of having nightmares, I'm losing my mind," I say aloud.

"Watch your language, Walker. This is a place to find peace, not sound like a potty mouth. Open your eyes, Walker. By the way, you are not losing your mind."

I slowly lifted my head and saw Elizabeth standing before me. She was beautiful and young, just like I remembered her to be. Her eyes were shining and piercing mine as I took in the beauty before me.

"You're not real! This is just my imagination playing tricks on me, or I have a tumor that I don't know about. Go away!"

I closed my eyes again and took in deep breaths in hopes when I open them, the vision of Elizabeth would be gone. I opened them slowly and she was still standing before me, but laughing. *Laughing, like the joke is on me. What the fuck?*

"I can see you still have your temper. Calm down, Walker, and breathe," she said.

"How are you here, Elizabeth?"

"I'm here, because you needed me."

"I've needed you since the day you left me, Elizabeth. Of all the times I prayed for a sign from heaven, finally now you appear before me? Why? I don't understand this at all."

"I don't know how much time I have here with you, so are you going to argue with me, or will you let me help you?"

"I don't need any help, Elizabeth. I can't even believe what I'm saying right now, this is not real. You are a product of my overactive stressed out subconscious, and I want you gone."

Slap!

"Is that real enough for you? God! You are still the same obstinate man you always were. I am real, Walker, and whether you are willing to believe it or not, I am here to help you. Now shut up and listen to me."

"Oh my God, you *are* here! I can see you still have skills in the slapping department."

"Yes I do, and you deserved it. Walk with me, and we can talk."

As much as my brain screamed at me not to believe what was happening in front of me, my heart led me to take her hand. I felt her hand in mine as we walked through the grounds of the semi-darkened cemetery.

"Walker, like I said, I don't know how much time I have with you, so I will try to make you understand as much as I can."

"First, I want you to breathe and try to relax. I'm here because you seem to be struggling with a darkness that is strangling you night after night. It breaks my heart to witness it. For a man who is about to finally get all that he has desired and ever wanted, you should be happier than what is standing in front of me now."

I stopped and dropped to my knees. Her words just sliced me wide open, and all the pain I'd been holding on to for years came pouring out.

"I'm so sorry, Elizabeth. I should have known earlier that you were sick. I worked way too much when I should have been home with you. I missed the signs, and it was a time where you needed me the most. Please, Elizabeth, forgive me? You died. You fucking died! And you left me alone to raise our son. Do you even know what I went through, living this life without you?"

"Yeah, that sucked by the way. It was never my choice to leave you or Jackson. Believe me, Walker, I would have done anything to stay. I love you, and I've never stopped. I've always been here watching over you and Jackson. You don't have anything to be sorry for. You have been an amazing father and role model for our son. I couldn't have asked for anything more. Our son has grown into an amazing human being. That's all because of you and the love you bestowed upon him every day of his life. If I had a choice, Walker, I would have always chosen our son to survive."

"It's not fair, Elizabeth. You should be here with us."

"Yeah, you're right, it didn't work out that way, but besides, you have all that you need. Your one true love has returned to you. You now have your chance to make it right this time. Don't let the sad memories of the past stop you from having that."

"Why do you say it that way? My one true love? Elizabeth, it feels like it dismisses everything you and I had shared, and I never wanted to dishonor your memory by loving Reese."

"Oh Walker, what am I going to do with you? You could never hurt me. I know you loved me, but it was a different type of love. We always knew that, and I was okay with it."

"It was real, Elizabeth. Please believe that. I meant every promise I ever made to you."

"I know you did, and now it's time to make some new ones with Reese. You have mourned me long enough. I want you to be happy again. I want to hear you laugh and see your smile as much as I can. But in order for all of those things to happen, you need to do something for me first."

"What? I'll do anything you ask of me."

"Forgive our fathers."

"No!"

"Forgive our fathers, Walker."

"Never!"

"It's the only way for you to move on and find peace, my friend. Release your anger, Walker, and forgive our fathers."

"Ask me anything else, Elizabeth. I will never give forgiveness to those bastards…ever!"

"And to think I thought this would be easy. Please hear me, best friend. For once let your anger fall away, and open your heart to forgiveness."

"Walker, loving Reese will never erase the love you had for me. Forgiving your father will not make you weak. It will make you stronger. You are losing yourself night after night in your nightmares because somewhere deep inside, you have guilt. You never gave your father the chance to make amends to you, and now he's gone. He and Henry were so wrong for what they did to you, and to Reese.

It's not impossible for you to do this. If not for them, forgive them for *you*. Let this go, Walker. …And by the way, please stop punching people."

I laughed for the first time since this crazy hallucination took over my brain. I suddenly felt lighter.

"I didn't technically punch Henry, but you know he damn well deserved it."

"Thanks for that, by the way. He certainly did, but it would have only hurt our son and my mother. You did the right thing that day."

"I hate him, Elizabeth. I hate them all for what they did. I will never understand why they played God with our lives."

She looked into my eyes and said, "Losing me was punishment enough for my father. How do you get absolution when you lose the one person that matters most to you? It was the same for your poor Reese losing your unborn son. You were cheated from being a father to him, and I think that was Phillip's undoing."

Elizabeth continued, "They are not soulless men. They do hurt, Walker, and we may never know the real truth why they did what they did to you. Why does it even matter at this point? All I know is that part of your life needs to close and really be finished. You will never heal those wounds you carry deep within you if you don't try. You may think you have accomplished this, but if that were true, then why the nightmares? Phillip is dead and will never hurt you again, but he is very real in your dreams. His blood runs through your veins, as yours does in our son. We are all connected in this life. And because I'm here with you now, this should show you without a doubt that we will forever be connected in this life and the next."

"Forgive him?" I asked. "That's impossible, my friend."

"Let his spirit rest, and free yourself."

"How do I do that, Elizabeth? How will I ever be able to voice the words that my father needs to hear for his absolution?"

"The words will come when you are ready, but first you need to open your mind and heart. You have a past. A painful one filled with loss, but it's not something that can't be overcome. I love you, Walker. I will always be with you."

"I miss you, friend." I could hear the brokenness in my voice, as her beautiful image slowly faded before me. I reached out to grab her, as my hand flew through thin air.

"Elizabeth!" I called out, but she disappeared.

I could still hear her voice. It said, "I'll always be with you, Walker, and with Jackson. He's going to need you now, more than ever before. Remember…I'm always with you."

"Wait! What does that mean? Elizabeth, come back!" I shouted as loud as I could. My vocal cords were burning as I continued to yell out into the early morning dawn. "Elizabeth! "She was gone, drifted away like a shimmering light that had now darkened. *What the fuck? I feel like I can't even breathe. I feel lost and confused, and now I'm left with more questions than I had before. My face is soaked with tears. I don't believe I have ever cried more for Elizabeth, as I am doing right now. I'm exhausted and rooted to the ground. I'm in front of her gravestone. Did I imagine it all? Was Elizabeth really here with me? It felt so real, real enough to feel my face sting where she slapped me.*

The sun was coming up, and I had to get out of here but couldn't make the run back home. I practically ran the length of a half marathon to get here. I phoned Stephen to pick me up and drive me to my office. *I will phone Reese from the car. I can't have her seeing me like this, it will only scare and worry her. I know she is stronger than I give her credit for, but she's pregnant, and I will not risk her health or our daughter that she is carrying.*

I was walking out of the cemetery when bright lights blinded my vision. When my eyes adjusted, I saw Stephen walk over to me. I suddenly felt my legs give way, and I fell down on to my knees. He came rushing over to me at a rapid speed.

"Mr. Reed, are you ill?"

He easily hoisted me up from the ground and wrapped his bear-like arms around my shoulders. I was lifted into the backseat of my car before I even realized what was happening.

"Here sir, drink this," Stephen said while handing me a small carton. "You seem to be dehydrated. You need electrolytes. The orange juice will help. Eat this protein bar until I can get you a proper breakfast."

"I'm okay, Stephen, so stop hovering. Get me to the office where I can shower and dress. Call Jenny to come in early. I need her."

"Yes sir."

My voice was still hoarse and dry. Texting Reese was a better option at this point. I briefly explained to her why I wasn't there this morning. I simply said that I left the house early for a workout and had an early meeting, hoping she would believe me.

As I waited for her reply, I couldn't begin to even process what I experienced this morning. I still don't know if I had imagined it all or it was in fact real? Was I hallucinating due to dehydration?

Reese: *Good Morning! Missed you and waking up to your arms holding me. I love you baby and wish you an amazing day. Call me when you can. Xoxo...your loving fiancé.*

A simple text message had the ability to bring me to my knees. *God! I hated to be without her for even a minute, but I am in no shape to face her right now.* My head was spinning from overexertion on my run and lack of water and food. Talking to my dead wife this morning didn't help either.

We pulled up through the underground entrance to Reed Global. This entrance allowed me to come and go without being visible. I was very grateful that I had this today.

After a very long hot shower, I dressed and sat in the quiet of my office. Jenny was expected to arrive at any moment, and I could start my day. *The routine of work and business should be all I need to get my mind off of nightmares and ghosts.*

Nightmares and ghosts...Oh God...Why me?

Stephen had breakfast ordered in for me. As hungry as I was, everything seemed to taste like sawdust. Knowing I would get a glare or two from Jenny, I did try to eat. She hovered like Stephen but in a more maternal way. Jenny could read all of my moods and pick the battles she knows she can win.

As I began to relax, my mind took me back to seeing Elizabeth. *Did that conversation really happen? Did I actually touch and speak to my dead ex-wife?*

Elizabeth wants me to forgive our fathers, but how do I do that? I want to believe that I closed the door to that painful chapter of my life, but apparently not if I'm being haunted in my dreams. Isn't it enough that I spent all those years without Reese? Suffering over the pain of Elizabeth dying? Yeah, I've had enough of the suffering part, that's for sure.

Now my father who created this whole mess wants forgiveness? If he hadn't interfered in the first place, than I wouldn't need to forgive him. How can I say that? That would mean I wouldn't have had Jackson, and I always said he was the one true thing in my life that I would never regret. None of this makes sense to me.

And what did Elizabeth mean by saying that Jackson will need me? Jackson knows he can come to me with anything. Have I been neglecting him? I don't see how? He's on his trip with his girl and it wasn't easy agreeing to that, but college is next for them. They should be able to enjoy their last summer of fun before things get serious in their lives.

A timid knock at the door broke me out of my deep thoughts.

"Good morning, sir." Jenny entered my office with a tray of fresh coffee and muffins. She had the sixth sense of a Jedi knight. I never had to utter a word to Jenny. She always seemed to know exactly what I needed and when.

"So what wedding plans are we doing today?" she shyly gives me a smile.

"Good morning, Jenny, and thank you for coming in so early. No wedding talk today. I have different matters that require my attention."

She poured my coffee and plated a muffin for me. Grabbing her tablet, she awaited my instructions.

"Jenny, call Miles Jacobson and tell him that his presence is required here at Reed Global immediately. Secondly, find out where Henry Townsend is and his schedule for the week. Thirdly, have my plane prepared and ready for departure by noon. Am I clear?"

"Yes sir, on all counts. Where am I filing your flight plan to?"

"New York City."

It easily rolls off my tongue. After speaking with Jackson, and now after seeing a vision of Elizabeth, I knew what I had to do. I never questioned myself...not ever. My heart was leading me to the direction of my son.

"Sir, if I may ask, will I be accompanying you on this trip?"

"No, Jenny, not this time. This trip to New York is solely based on personal reasons. I will need you here to run the office. As soon as Donovan checks in this morning, put him through immediately for me."

"Will there be anything else?"

"Not at this time, Jenny. I'll reconnect with you in a couple of hours. I don't wish to be disturbed by anything or anyone, other than what I have requested."

"Yes sir."

Jenny quickly departed my office with her eyes focused on the door. I knew I'd been curt with her this morning and would make a note to apologize to her later. My head was spinning right now with the turn of events this morning. I couldn't seem to shake the uneasy feeling that was putting me on edge.

Elizabeth said, *"For a man that has everything, I should be happier."* Those were the same words that my father recited to me months ago. *I'm already there, I do have everything.* The ghosts of my past keep reminding me of painful memories. It's almost comical at this point. *Are the fates laughing at me? What am I not seeing? Was my father's prediction a prophecy? Well, whatever it may be will not prevent me from having a future with Reese.*

With all our near misses that Reese and I had to endure over the years, I felt that I was waiting for the bottom to fall out from under me. *No! I have to put these negative thoughts out of my head. We are going to be okay, we have to be. Fate would not be so cruel again. It's our time. I believe. And so does Reese.* The happily ever after is right in front of me, but yet so far away. Reese will be completely mine once we take each other as husband and wife.

Everything happens for a reason. Maybe we had to go through what we did to get to this point now. All I knew is that if I was ever truly to forgive Phillip Reed, I needed to delve deeper into his web of lies. Could there be more that I don't know? His letters spoke otherwise. He promised that he disclosed everything to me in his letters. His time left was limited. There was no point to keep anything else from me.

Sitting and fighting my inner monologue right now was not helping me at all. *Focus, Reed! Do what you do best.* I took my own advice and got right back into my work.

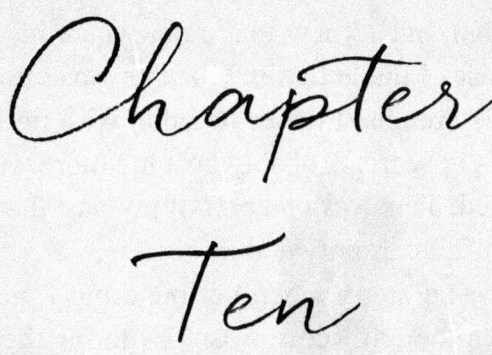

Chapter Ten

Discovered secrets

Walker

I WAS FINISHING up a conference call with the Reinhart brothers when Jenny stepped into my office. Designing and building the new hub for Sebastian and Viktor Reinhart has been the focus for more than two years now. We worked endless hours on this deal and were about to reach the finish line. I thought the memorial wing at Johns Hopkins was the signature piece for my work, but the Reinhart building was international and will keep Reed Global on the front lines for many years to come.

It was my design that they wanted most. I almost did the happy dance the day we signed the contracts. My father never wanted me to pursue this side of the business, but I couldn't help myself. As much as I loved commanding my ship from behind my desk, I also loved being in the middle of the creative process. This was my passion, my true passion: To create something in your mind and then build it from the ground up. It still gave me chills.

I saw the same drive in Jackson when he was working on a film project. Nothing would make me prouder if he joined me here by my side at Reed Global, but I knew that's not where his heart was. One of the early promises I made to him when he was little was to always support him in his dreams. I never had that with my own father. To pursue my dreams in secret probably cost me more ways than I could have ever predicted. This was one part of my past that I knew I could leave behind with full certainty and no regrets.

My father was so angry when he found out I pursued degree in Architecture. Even though Reese wasn't with me the day we should have graduated together, knowing she was the only person that knew my secret warmed my heart. In our short time together, we shared everything with each other. Now we had the rest of our lives to see our dreams come to life.

I ended my call and looked up to see Jenny. She appeared to be nervous, but she never needed a reason to interrupt me.

"What is it Jenny?" I asked as I began to pick up the receiver to make another call.

"You have an unexpected visitor waiting for you outside."

"Whoever it is, send them away."

She raised her eyebrows at me. With my curiosity piqued, I asked who the mystery visitor was.

"Jenny…" I said, "I'm not in the mood for games right now."

She replied, "Walker Phillip Reed, forgive me, sir, but you are way too serious for your own good. I will send in your visitor, and you can find out for yourself."

Jenny had let out a huff and turned away from my door.

I scrubbed my hands over my face and didn't even attempt to figure out Jenny's obvious take on my personality traits. I was this way for as long as I could remember, so why change now? Not making my call, I looked back at my computer and began typing an e-mail when my guest walked in.

"She's right, you know. You are way too serious."

Just what I needed…my Reese. The sound of her soft velvet

voice cloaked me like a protective shield. She was exactly what I needed right now. I wasted no time getting up from behind my desk and rushing over to her. I swept my beautiful girl up in my arms, and she wrapped her long slender arms around my neck and began kissing me, deepening every stroke of her tongue with mine.

"I missed you, Walker. I know you're busy, but I couldn't stay away."

"Oh baby, I missed you too! More than you know. Did you drive here on your own?"

"No, I was driven in. I wasn't feeling too hot this morning, and it didn't help that I woke up with you already gone, so I phoned Stephen to pick me up. I hope that's okay."

"Of course it's okay," I said to her. "I've been so busy this morning, I didn't even know Stephen was absent from the building. What's going on? How are you feeling right now?"

I take Reese's hand and lead her over to my plush sofa. I want to be as close as I can, so I sit first then pull Reese onto my lap.

"I'm better now," she said. "I woke up feeling sick and was experiencing some dizziness. Priscilla helped me, and I was able to keep some broth down."

"Did you phone your doctor? It seems like you are sick not only in the mornings, but throughout the entire day."

"Walker, it's all due to the hormone change in my body. It's perfectly normal to be having morning sickness, and as long as I stay hydrated, I should be okay. I promise you if I feel anything out of the normal bounds of the pregnancy, I will tell you immediately."

Her words gave me little comfort, but I believed her. Reese wouldn't keep anything from me now. So I gave her the same respect.

I held her tightly to my body and breathed in her beautiful scent. The perfume she wore was pulling me in like a moth to the flame. Reese was intoxicating. Her scent alone was thrilling me. I could never get enough of her. I wanted to just peel her out of her clothes and have my wicked way with her, but I held back. My mind was all over the place. I didn't want to be rough with her. She calmed me with her touch. Her body was my temple to worship in, and it cured all that was plaguing me. *I need her so much...she's my home.*

Her hand was caressing her small baby bump, leaving me with chills throughout my entire body. She was unbelievably sexy, and my resolve not to take her was breaking down.

"You are so beautiful, you know that, right?" I said to her.

Gazing into my eyes, she placed a chaste kiss on my lips.

"If I am beautiful, it is only because you make me feel that way. I love you so much, Walker."

"Reese, you are so precious to me. I thank God every single day for reuniting us again. Now that you're carrying my child, I can't help but fall in love with you more and more each day. I just wish I could have been there when you found out the sex of our baby."

"I wanted you there, Walker, believe me I did. Having lost two babies before, I was so scared to hear a negative outcome. I'm older now, so I will face more risks."

"You're healthy, right? Everything is good with the baby?"

"Everything is absolutely wonderful. You have no need to worry about us. My next appointment is in two weeks, and you can see for yourself."

"Thank God! I don't think I could bear it if anything happened to either one of you. As happy as I am Reese, I'm a little scared."

"I understand that feeling, Walker. How could you not? I did this alone last time. I promise you will be involved every step of the way from here on out."

"Thank you, baby, I needed to hear that. Now I have a few things I need to discuss with you."

"Okay," she replied. "What's wrong? Does this have anything to do with your sleepless nights? After our talk, I had thought you were feeling better, but I'm guessing they returned again?"

"They have, and I'm doing a piss poor job at hiding them from you."

"Walker, I don't want you to keep anything from me. We talked about this. We need to always be honest and forthcoming with each other."

"Like you've been honest with me? What about Samuel? Were you ever going to tell me that he reached out to you? And what was said?"

Why did I say that? Fuck! The look that Reese is giving me right now tells me that I opened my mouth and inserted my foot...big time! I couldn't help it. He was still a trigger for me. Here she was comforting me, and I once again let my jealousy over her ex spoil our tender moment. My head is once again spinning in directions. *Was it out of control? Out of fear? Or from the unknown? I refuse to allow this to happen. I was behaving like him, my father. Stubborn. Closed-minded. It's the stress of all this bullshit that has me crazy and acting out. Samuel is nothing to me. Reese is everything.*

"You have to stop this, Walker. Whatever battle you have raging through your mind right now is going to break you, and then it will break us. We have already been down this road too many times before. It is not one I wish to travel down again. Do you want to know what happened with Samuel? Will this satisfy you?"

"Yes," I quickly answered her.

"Not much happened. He phoned me several weeks ago and apologized for his behavior toward me back at the house. He said he was trying to work through his anger and bitterness about our divorce. What could I say? Throw his apology back in his face? You know that's not me, and it was never my intention to hurt him by loving you. I was a fool thinking that walking away from my marriage would be so easy. Riley was right about one thing. I left a trail of hurt feelings behind me. Once I left, I really never looked back. Was that fair to Samuel? He tried his best to be all that I needed, but I made him pay for it over the years for not being you."

"I'm sorry, Reese. I guess I never really took into account how you spent your life without me in it. All I know is that when I saw you in that restaurant, I knew I had to have you, and to hell with the rest of the world."

"It's not your fault that my marriage ended. It was over for me and Samuel, and long before you ever came back into my life. Samuel knew this deep down where it mattered and so did I, but neither one of us ever had the courage to voice the words out loud. It took a conversation with Nana to finally convince me to leave and to drum up enough courage to find me again. I never thought that would lead me back to you. Although I know I hurt Samuel, I can't regret how everything has turned out for us. Look at us, Walker. We are about to get married and have a baby of our very own. We are blessed."

At that moment, I was so caught up in my emotions, I literally dropped to my knees and wrapped my arms around Reese, laying my cheek against her stomach, listening to the beat of her heart, and sending love to my child growing inside of her. I willed myself to talk and finally get it all out.

"Yes. I've been having a few nightmares," I said, "But something else happened. I'm not sure what to make of it, or least of all, understand it."

Reese kissed the top of my head and ran her fingers through my hair. She knew me so well and understood that I needed to take a breath before beginning my explanation. She waited patiently for me to continue. Her smooth strokes through my hair and along my face were slowly calming me. I loved the feel of her caress. I craved it, and I never wanted to be without it.

"Reese, I've been having the same recurring nightmare since you told me about the baby. My father keeps visiting me in my dreams. He tells me that I will never get my happily ever after with you, as long as I continue to not forgive him. He begs me for it, and I always refuse him. Last night was the worse one yet. After waking up, I fled our home to clear my head of that nightmare. I was led to the cemetery to visit Elizabeth, and—are you ready—she appeared right in front of me. As real as you are with me now, I actually felt her presence on my skin. Can you say something Reese? Anything that tells me I'm not crazy."

"I believe you, Walker, and you are not crazy. No matter what is said here, it's okay…we are always okay. Talk to me, I want to know everything."

Taking in a few deep breaths, I continued. "I didn't know I would end up at the cemetery, it was like I was being drawn there. I found myself directly in front of her grave, and I broke down for the first time in years. I have never felt her loss more, and I didn't even know what I was hoping to find. I began talking with Elizabeth, and then that's when I heard her voice call out to me. I thought I was having a hallucination, not believing for one second that she was real."

"What happened next?" she asked. Reese was now at full attention and sitting up to look at me.

"I yelled at her and told her to go away."

"You yelled at her? Why would you do that?"

"Um…seeing a vision of someone that you know is dead would make anyone shout out loud. Yes, I did yell at her. I felt as if I was having an outer body experience."

"What happened next?" Reese asked as if she was anxiously watching a movie play out in front of her.

"Well, when she didn't disappear, we argued and then she slapped me. I swear I believed it after that. I literally felt the sting on my cheek."

Reese's expression is very hard to read right now. Does she think I lost my mind? Or is it the shock over hearing about Elizabeth? I can't blame her if she is surprised. Look how I behave when she mentions Samuel. I see no reason, nor do I care to hear it. Now I'm asking her to believe something I still doubt myself.

"Say something baby, are you okay?" I asked.

"I'm okay, I guess," she replied. I have never experienced anything close to what you are describing. Not even when my parents died. I always wished to see them again, but Nana always had told me that if I ever needed them, they would come to me in my dreams. Walker, they never once came to me. I was a little girl of ten years old. I wanted them to return to me every single day. And still, I never experienced what you did today with Elizabeth. I'm almost jealous of you. I'm sorry if that sounds wrong, but I can't help it. I miss my parents so much, and I would have liked for this type of revelation to happen to me."

"Don't be sorry, baby, and please don't feel bad. I'm not sure this was such a precious gift to be given. It almost felt like a punishment. I never got the closure I needed when Elizabeth died, and I wished for a sign to know that she was at peace. Today after many years of hoping, I was given my answer, but for me I didn't feel at peace. I felt guilt over moving on from her and reuniting with you."

Reese was now moving away from me. I hadn't planned on saying it that way. I could see the hurt in her eyes.

"Is that how you feel? Guilty because we're together now?"

She is a bit shaken now. I reach out to touch her, but she put her hands up to me. It felt like her rejection was piercing my soul. *How could she ever doubt my love for her?* I attempted to speak, and my intercom buzzed.

"What is it?" I yelled rather loudly.

It was Jenny. She said, "Sir, I have Mr. Tate on line three for you."

"I'll have to call him back, Jenny."

"Sir, if you don't speak with him now, he may be out of touch for a while. He said he will be traveling for the rest of the day in dead cell zones."

"Okay! Put him through. Reese, please don't leave. I have to take this call."

She now has several tears falling down her beautiful face. *Dammit! I fucked up again and hurt her.* Walking over to my desk, I took my call, but not before witnessing my beautiful girl crying. I turned away when all I wanted to do was hold her. *Fuck!*

"Donovan, I need an update. What did you find out?"

"I've located the family of the three workers that were killed in the accident. They all live together but deep in the jungle out here. The town is desolate and hidden deep within the mountains. I will be lucky if I come out alive. This area is so backwards. They haven't caught up with modern times yet, and I don't think they ever will."

"Well that doesn't surprise me. My father always tried to cut costs. No wonder he hired migrant workers like these men. What about the family?"

"From what I can gather, they are a tight knit group, consisting of probably twenty or so. They live very poorly, but their basic needs seem to be met."

"Did you make contact with our man Salvatore over there?" I asked.

"Yes sir, I did. I already arranged for the money to be secured into an account. They will never know where it came from. Per your instructions, sir, all monetary help with be distributed from the mission that oversees the village. Many families will prosper from your help, and the quality of their lives will improve."

I wasn't looking for pleasantries or a pat on the back from Donovan, just simply righting a wrong. These weren't my sins, but I carried them for my father. It was the least I could do.

"Excellent," I said to him. "I need you to get back here right away. I have to go out of town for a few days, and I don't want to leave the day-to-day to just Jenny."

Mentioning my trip out of town now put Reese on high alert. She stared at me with questioning eyes.

Donovan replied, "I should be able to get on a flight later tonight, hopefully direct with no connections. Walker, believe me, everything is settled here."

"I do believe you, Donovan. You are one of the few people I trust. I can't replace what they lost, but I can certainly help make their future easier. Call me when you are back in California, and safe travels."

I hung up with Donovan and looked over to Reese. My beautiful girl looked like she was ready to run from my office. *I have to get myself in check, and right now before I fuck up anymore with her. It's these damn nightmares screwing with my mind!* I was about to speak when she beat me to it.

"When were you going to tell me that you were leaving? And where to? You know when I woke up yesterday morning, I never expected to be treated to the surprise you had for me. It was truly beautiful. The euphoric moment that we shared made me feel so loved and wanted. The entire time driving here to your office, I smiled with you solely on my mind. How did we go from making love under the stars in our gazebo, to you suddenly leaving? Now you tell me you are having visions of your dead wife. Are you questioning us? Are we getting married, Walker? Or do you still want that?"

Her words were razor-edged swords slicing me through and through. I had to take a few calming breaths before answering her questions. Reese was gutting me right now. And I had no one to blame but myself. She looked visibly shaken. I kept my distance and didn't push her anymore. I stayed propped up against my desk and as calmly as I could manage to do, I began to speak.

"Reese, if you believe anything I say from this moment on, please believe that I want to marry you more than anything else in this world right now. To walk away from you now is just abhorrent to me. I would rather cut off all my limbs than do that. You are mine. We will make it known to the world very soon."

Somehow my words didn't bring any comfort to her doubting eyes, which were now filled with tears again. I stayed where I was and extended my arms to her.

"Please, baby, can I hold you?" I asked. "Let me touch and feel you against me. I promise I will explain everything to you."

She quietly accepted my request and folded herself into the safety of my arms. *I don't ever want to let her go. She's scared and doubting me. I fucking hate this. This is why I never wanted to tell her about my nightmares. Phillip Reed is like the bad penny that keeps turning up, and I have allowed him to get to me and fuck with my emotions. I have to make this right. I will never allow my father to come between us again.*

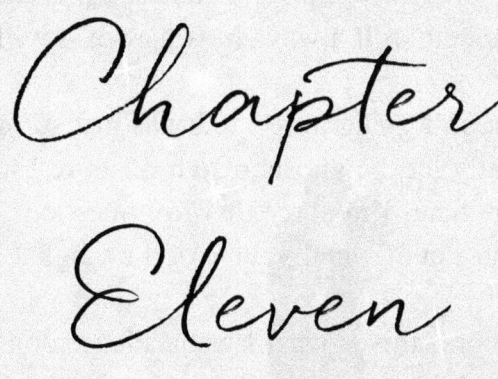

Chapter Eleven

Here with you

Reese

HE WAS HOLDING me so tightly. I had to pinch him to loosen his grip. Remembering this simple gesture I always did to him when he wouldn't let me go, he smiled and looked up at me.

"I'm sorry, baby. I guess I'm still a bit nervous that I will blink and you will disappear."

"Walker, I'm in this for life with you. Don't you know that by now?"

"I'm trying."

"Well, try harder," I responded. "I will never leave you again. The days of running and hiding are over. If anything, I will be running toward you…never away."

"Reese, I'm sorry if I hurt you when I mentioned Elizabeth, it was not my intention. I need you like I need my next breath, but your reaction scared the hell out of me. How can I not think you would turn away from me? You completely shut down at the mere mention of her name. Elizabeth will always be a part of my life. She is Jackson's mother."

"Walker, I wasn't going to leave. I was just surprised, that's all. I thought we finally let the ghosts of our pasts rest and were beginning with a clean slate. I'm sorry that my questions hurt you, but I can't help but feel doubt when your mood swings tell me differently."

"Reese, of course this is what I want. Please don't ever question my love for you. I have never loved you more, and I will move heaven and earth to keep you here with me."

"It's exactly what I want. So if we both want the same thing, then we have to move forward and stop living in the past. Please tell me what's wrong? What is it with these nightmares? Tell me how we can fix this. I love you, Walker. Let me in to help you"

"You are in," he said. "I trust you completely. I love you with every beat of my heart. I will never keep anything from you. This is so incredibly hard to explain to you in detail without making me look like a lunatic. Are you okay? I want you to calm down and drink some water."

"Walker, I'm fine. I just want to hear the rest of the story. Please go on."

"Witnessing Elizabeth appear out of thin air was like a supernatural feeling taking over my body and mind. I actually felt her. I could hear her voice. And for a few precious moments, she was real. Do you remember telling me when you finally felt peace after dreaming about our son? You saw Elizabeth caring for him."

"I do. It was the first time ever that I actually believed he was safe."

"That's exactly how I felt. When I saw and talked with Elizabeth, I knew she was at peace. She wants me to move on and stop mourning her death. She wants me to be happy with you and the family we are going to have. She wants me to stop feeling guilty and move on with you."

"That doesn't sound too scary. It sounds pretty wonderful," I said, as I began to smile.

"It does, because that's who Elizabeth was in life. She always put my needs before her own happiness. She thanked me for becoming the father I am to Jackson. She said she couldn't be more proud. She also asked me to do something for her."

"Which was?" I asked.

"Elizabeth wants me to forgive our fathers and truly move on from the painful parts of my past. She believes this is why Phillip is consistently haunting me in my nightmares. He is seeking forgiveness…my forgiveness. As long as I refuse to give it, he will keep coming back."

"Walker, you don't really believe that? Do you?"

"I'm beginning to. Reese, my dreams are so vivid. You would think he was still alive too. Now I know how this must sound, but we agreed to believe in the universe, right? Well, I believe this is its way of telling me something. I want to talk to Miles Jacobson again, make sure I truly know it all. A few months ago, I thought I did, but now I'm questioning everything. Also there's Henry Townsend. I've completely shut him out. I don't really care if I ever see him again, but I have to think about Jackson and what it's costing him."

He continued, "Reese, I know we talked about our time when we were separated, and how we can't hold each other accountable to how we lived our lives, but I need to know something."

"Okay. You know I will tell you anything."

He sunk his head down. "Reese, I was so foolish back then. When I couldn't find you and every lead turned up dead, I gave up. I just gave up. When Elizabeth passed, I never searched for you again. I had the means to do so and I should have looked for you, but I was just numb. I just lost my wife and was left to raise our baby on my own. I was starting from scratch. All while being without you. I tried with everything I had to block you out of my thoughts. That alone hurt like hell. How can you forget someone that you handed your soul over to? It was something I struggled with every day. When I did allow myself to remember you, and the future we were supposed to have, I shut down again."

Walker continued. "I felt like I was losing you all over again, a pain that was constantly pecking away at me when I gave it power to do so. Months turned into years, and well, you know the rest. Seventeen years later, we found our way back to each other. I forced myself back into your life like a speeding train with no brakes. You left your husband and the only life you had known to come back to me. Am I crazy to believe that I wasn't being this obsessive and arrogant asshole that took his control back? I never gave you a choice. I saw you, wanted you, and ultimately removed you from the life you were living. I reeked of Phillip Reed. I simply didn't care who the casualties were and the damage I left in my wake. Did you see it the whole time? Did you feel manipulated? Am I becoming...my father?"

THERE I'VE SAID it. I just gave Reese a full disclosure of all the bullshit in my past. I loathed this with a passion. This made me feel weak, and I don't do weak. I wanted this over. I didn't want to talk about this anymore. Judging by the way she was looking at me, it told me this conversation was far from over. At least her eyes are filled with love and not pity.

"Walker, where is this coming from? Baby, you didn't take back anything that didn't belong to you first. You are not your father. Please don't ever reference him again. Those words alone make my skin crawl. You are more a man than he ever was. I have always loved you for who you are, all parts that make up who you are. I am not blind, nor naïve, but I was foolish back then. I kept telling myself that I was doing the right thing by accepting all your father did to me, and to us."

She continued, "He scared the hell out of me time after time, and when I finally had the courage to fight him, I lost more than I could ever imagine. I was lost and broken, just like you. I never planned on meeting Samuel; he just kind of appeared out of nowhere and slowly pushed his way into my life. I had lost everything that meant anything to me."

She held my hand and went on. "Yes, I still had my family intact, but you know I kept them at bay. I gave up Freddy. I basically gave up. I could have looked for you as well, but I loved you from a safe distance and accepted my fate. I'm surprised I stayed married to Samuel for as long as I did, but once you convince yourself that you have nothing else, then it's an easy conclusion. Once I had Riley, and then my teaching, they filled the voids of loneliness."

"Samuel was more a friend than a lover," she continued. "My life with him was safe and predictable. I played my part well as the doctor's wife. I promised myself that once Riley was ready to leave home and begin her new life, I would be right behind her. I never expected that traveling that road would lead me back to you, but it did. And I couldn't be happier."

"Walker, our past is our past. We can never change it, and I don't want to. I want to concentrate on the present and our future. We can never get back what we lost, and maybe your vision is correct. Continuing to blame your father will never move us forward. It's over. We are stronger now. I will never push you to forgive him; that has to be on you. I can only speak for myself. The moment we committed our new promises of forever, I was done being angry. I am so in love with you, obsessiveness and all. I loved you then. I love you now. Thank God you forced your way in. My Walker: the only man I have ever truly loved, place your hand on my heart. Do you feel it?"

"Yes," I replied, staring into her eyes.

"Good. It's the same beat that matches yours. This is where you are and exactly where I want you to be. You are with me. In my heart. In my mind. In my soul. Forever…with me."

"I love you Reese, I always have. You are my forever. I want nothing more than our life together. I want to pour my heart out to you. I never want to shut you out. Keeping you close to me is a full time job. I guess I need to work on communicating without scaring the hell out of you. Baby, I never want to see doubt or fear in your eyes when you look at me. I'll walk on glass if I have to before causing you one minute of pain."

I knew I had more to say, but I let my body and desire finish up our conversation. Reese felt it too. I could feel her heartbeat racing up against mine. Two hearts…one love. I didn't know which one was faster, but we matched beat for beat. I locked my door and told Jenny not to disturb us. I carried Reese into my private suite. I had never taken a woman to this bed, not even Elizabeth. Reese would be the only one that I would forever make love to.

Reese stood there, appearing before me like a goddess. She untied her dress, letting it fall down to her feet. Stepping out of it, she then unclasped her bra and let it fall away to join her dress on the floor. Lastly, she slowly skimmed the rim of her barely there thong panties, teasing me. The scrap of material she called panties then slid down her legs. I loved to see her desires for me. She played out every part for me. She was a blossoming flower coming to life. I was beyond excited. Before I could say it, she knew what I was thinking. *Leave the stockings on.* My girl knew how I loved them on her long, slender legs. She reached out her arms and invited me in. I never undressed so quickly, discarding all of my clothing into a heap on the floor next to hers.

With one swift move, I had Reese under me. I began to make the sweetest love to her over and over again until we were sated. I was patting myself on the back for soundproofing this private suite. Her cries of pleasure were resonating throughout the room. I wanted to be the only one to hear my woman. After the multiple orgasms that racked our bodies, we were exhausted. I held onto Reese with all I had and listened to my angel as sleep took over her. She was right where she belonged. And nightmares or not, I wasn't going to ever question our love again.

I tried with my best effort to untangle myself from my sleeping angel. She looked peaceful as she slept, especially after we weathered another storm together. I gathered up my clothing off the floor and quickly dressed. Glancing at the clock, it was way past noon. After unlocking the door, I ducked my head out to call Jenny in. Despite the soundproofing, she had to know what we were doing, but of course she discreetly kept her conclusions to herself.

It was close to two o'clock. My plane had been ready for hours now. Stephen had my pilot and co-pilot on stand-by with also Elise, my flight attendant, ready to go at a minute's notice. I felt a bit foolish for having them wait this long, but I hadn't anticipated Reese would stop by, nor my telling her about the day's events. Jenny sat patiently across from me as she handed me a cup of coffee and a prepared fruit and cheese plate. I hadn't eaten since seven a.m., and once again my assistant was taking care of me. I mouthed "Thank you" to her as I sipped my very hot espresso. I needed this jolt of caffeine if I was going to get through the rest of this trying day.

"Where are we with what I asked for?" I asked as I nibbled on some grapes.

Jenny shifted in her chair and opened up her tablet to peruse her notes.

"Mr. Jacobson is currently on holiday in the south of France. He is with his family. He is expected back in the states ten days from now. Henry Townsend is currently at his home in Arizona. His office confirms he hasn't been back in New York since your father's funeral."

I didn't understand why I was requesting any information about my former father-in-law. With my recurring nightmares taking up space in my head, I trusted my instincts to be on guard for anything. Henry was and still remained a calculating bastard. He used his daughter's memory to persuade me to absolve him of the crimes he committed against me. No way in hell would he ever convince me that he was full of remorse. He certainly let his feelings be known when I confronted him about the part he played in separating me from Reese so many years ago.

I shunned him at Jackson's graduation. I didn't allow his grandparents to be seated with us. My security detail kept them at a safe distance from us. When they were escorted to another area, Gail had given me a look of sadness, but dutifully followed her husband. Reese squeezed my hand, and once again her touch comforted me. She had only seen Henry and Gail once when she was first introduced to them at my family's home when we were first dating. I had to remind her who they were. I doubt she would have remembered them. My promise still stood on what I would do if he dared to interfere with my life again. Henry Townsend would suffer a great deal if he chose to cross the arbitrary line that I had drawn out for him. *No mercy will be shown. This I promise without any doubt.*

"Mr. Reed, as you know, your plane is still on stand-by for take-off. Your pilot is waiting for your instructions on when you would like to depart. Sir, will there be anything else?" Jenny asked me.

"I need a location on Stephen."

"Stephen is currently with security and also awaiting your instructions regarding your flight."

"Have Stephen call the pilots and inform them I shall be at the airport within the next hour. I will be traveling with my fiancé, Ms. Reese Mitchell. I will also need you to phone over to Cedars-Sinai Hospital and connect me with Dr. Rachel Lemay. She is Ms. Mitchell's physician. I am requesting her services for an emergency appointment. Have her come and meet us on my plane. Tell her that I will make it worth her while. I want to leave in the next hour. Make this happen, Jenny. Call me if we run into any complications. If not, then I will meet the good doctor at the airport."

I had no doubt Jenny could pull this off. I paid her very well to be at my beck and call, with no task too difficult. I'm sure I sounded like a crazy man, but I would not leave Reese behind. Bringing her with me was the only option, and I wasn't risking anything to chance. She said she was dizzy today and the morning sickness was rough on her. A quick check from her doctor will ease my nerves, especially when we were about to travel across the country.

I walked back into the private suite to check on Reese, who was now awake and on her feet. I closed the door behind me so Jenny couldn't hear us.

"Hi," she said barely above a whisper. Her hair was a completely tangled mess. Her lips were swollen, cheeks a rosy pink. She was holding up a sheet to cover herself. Asleep or awake, unkempt or primped, I loved the sight of her and wish I had more time to devour her again, but we needed to leave before I changed my mind.

"Come here, baby," I called to her.

She teasingly took her time walking over to me. I loved that. When she was close enough, I pulled her into my arms, and she let out a giggle. *Oh I love to hear her simple laugh. I love everything about Reese.*

"How did you sleep? Can I get you anything?"

"I slept well, and I can use a snack. Some sex fiend really worked me over, and now I'm simply ravenous for food."

"Sex fiend? Well, we can't have you starving now. He may want to have his way with you again." She blushed, as I fed her a piece of sweet melon. I kissed the sweetness off her lips and fed her some more.

"From what I heard you mention to Jenny, I gather you decided to still leave for your trip? Where are you going anyway? And when should I expect you back?"

"Not just me, my love. *We* are going somewhere, as a matter of fact, and *our* destination is New York. You need to get your very bitable ass off of my lap, before I take you again right on my desk, or do you prefer the bed? You know how I love multiple surfaces." I wickedly grinned.

"Walker, we can't go to New York. What about all the wedding arrangements that still need to be completed? I have the grandparents arriving soon, and Freddy is in town for me. I can't leave now. What will the kids think? We can't just drop in on them during their vacation. I think that would be a violation of the kid's trust, and we said they can have their time together on this trip."

"Reese, they have been gone for weeks now. I believe they

spent more than enough time together. It's time for them to come home. We're not crashing their party. I was hoping to spend some time with them and finally share our good news. I know you are dying to tell Riley, and I really want to tell Jackson. You are out of your first trimester, and no one even knows yet."

"Wrong! Freddy and Fabrizio know our news, so does Priscilla, and don't forget Jenny."

"Okay, smartass, don't be so cute. Freddy is always the exception, and our staff does not count. I want our children to know. As for the other details: One, I have paid an obscene amount of money to hire the best planner to complete every last detail for our wedding. I have the utmost confidence in Rosalyn. Secondly, I spoke to Lila and Thomas this morning. They have decided to stop at the Grand Canyon and take a few days for sightseeing. Lila assured me that she will have plenty of time to pull off the best rehearsal dinner California has ever seen. Thirdly, Freddy and Fabrizio are now at our home and I'm sure are enjoying *another* very expensive bottle of my vintage champagne and lounging by our pool, probably wearing *nothing*. By the way, my love, thank you for giving Freddy the combination to our wine vault. It may be empty by the time we return."

"Oh baby, you know I crack under the best friend power of persuasion tactics."

"Don't worry. He makes you smile. All I want is for you to be happy. Let them enjoy and have their fun."

"You seem to have all your T's crossed and I's dotted, Mr. Reed. So fine, I will go to New York, but you have to answer some questions first, agreed?"

"I endeavor to always be honest with you, my love."

"Are we leaving because you heard that they plan on seeing Samuel tomorrow? Walker, Riley needs to work things out with her father, and Jackson will be right by her side."

"I know that, Reese. I trust them both. I don't trust that bastard of an ex-husband, but I do trust our kids."

"Walker, you need to get past this with Samuel. I have."

"You are too good. I am not as forgiving, and I never forget. Why do you think I am struggling with moving forward from my past with my father? It's an internal power struggle that I face daily to not have my past define me."

I took a deep breath and said to her, "The truth is, my son has never been this far away from me, and for this length of time. I am trying very hard to come to terms with his independence, but some days are harder than others, like today. Before disappearing this morning, Elizabeth's ghost said that she would always be looking over us, and Jackson would need me more than ever. I called out to her, but she faded away into thin air. Reese, I know I should probably be getting a brain scan after what I experienced, but it felt very real, and I know what I heard. Something deep inside is telling me that I need to check on my son. I have to know that he is okay. Reports from Richard and a few short phone calls will not reassure me until I see for myself. Please tell me you understand?"

"I do, Walker. Thank you for telling me the truth. I love you. I'm sure the kids are fine. I'm actually excited to travel to New York. It will do us both some good. One more thing…"

"Anything, baby."

"Did I hear you right? Are you actually summoning Dr. Lemay to your plane? I'm fine, Walker, I promise."

"Oh how your memory is short. Are we seriously going to revisit the conversation about you accepting all the parts of me?"

I now deliver her one of my smiles that she loved so much. I saw her deeply concentrating on what she wanted to say, which was probably calling me crazy, but she didn't. Reese loved everything about me and knew I would never change.

"I'll see Dr. Lemay and hold my tongue while you keep grinning at me. You're lucky you're so hot." She winked at me and pinched my butt.

"That's my girl. I love you too."

"Do we have time for a shower?" She fluttered her eyelashes at me.

Oh, she is such a tease. I scooped her up into my arms, as she let out a very girlish squeal. I carried her into the bathroom in the private suite.

"Oh baby! I love how you think and know me so well," I said, excitedly.

Letting the sheet fall away to her feet, I was once again treated to her beauty. This was one vision that I would never shy away from. Soon after, the warm spray of water showered over us as I lathered her body with her favorite body wash. Her breast swelled beneath my touch. Her nipples pebbled, inviting my mouth to suck on them. Reese let out a whimper of pleasure, as I continued to bite, pinch, and suck away at her tender flesh.

Opening up wider for me as my hands parted her legs, Reese was on the edge. I took my time with my sensual assault on her body. My tongue made its way down to her swollen clit. Plunging my tongue deeper and deeper into her folds, her hands found my hair and pulled me in. It was beyond erotic, listening to her moans and feeling her body shake with the orgasms that she was having.

"I can't take anymore! Please, Walker, I need you inside me...now."

"All in good time, baby. I'm not finished with you yet. You need to be completely open for what I have planned for you."

With one more flick of my tongue and a loud piercing cry from Reese, we reached a level of pure ecstasy between us. She was wrecked by my sensual assaults on her body. I knew she was craving more from me, but how I loved to tease her and drive her mad. It was my insatiable need for her that drove me to the edge of my control. Her eyes alone ignited the feral desire that raged through my body and needed to take her at any given moment. *She rights all things in my world. My heart holds her and her alone.*

"Wrap your legs around my waist, baby. Hold on to the bar above your head and don't let go," I said to her.

"I can't, Walker. I have no strength left."

"Yes, you can, baby, and you will. This is for the both of us. I'm going to fuck you now and hard. Eyes on me. Be here with me. Right now."

That's all she needed to hear because once her eyes found mine, her legs tightened around my waist, and I took her to new heights of pleasure.

"Hold on baby, and don't let go. This is going to be quick," I whispered.

As we reached our climax together, Reese bit down on my shoulder, and fucking hard. For once, I whimpered in pain.

"Baby, what the hell? I love that you leave marks on me, but that was even rough for you."

My Georgia Peach was in vixen mode and smiled at me with glimmer in her eyes.

"Oh sorry, baby, couldn't help myself," she said.

"You're forgiven, and you can bite me anytime. I love it all, from our hard fucking to our sweet love making. Every time with you Reese is amazing. You own my ass."

"Good to know, baby, and what an amazing ass you have. I love you so much. You do know you own mine as well."

"Oh baby, that is one fact I am most certain of. You. Are. Mine. Forever."

She gave me one of her sexy winks that earned her a slap on her delectable derriere as she skipped off to dress. Without a doubt, Reese Mitchell—soon-to-be Reese Mitchell Reed—owned all parts of me. Parts of me that were so closed off until we reunited. As much as I was in bliss with Reese, I don't doubt we would hit a stumble or two along the way.

As long as we were together and our two hearts beat as one, I knew I could handle anything with Reese by my side. Her love and commitments of forever made the impossible become possible. Our love was strong enough to conquer anything, even the ghosts of my past.

Chapter Twelve

Love is my guide

Riley

I COULDN'T BELIEVE how nervous I was. It had been nearly two months since I had seen or talked with my father. I had never been away from him for more than a few days, let alone two months. My heart missed him, but my brain was having difficulty catching up. I was still so angry with him and his treatment of my mother. He played victim so well, but I now saw him as a bully. He physically hurt her not once, but twice—that I know of—and the verbal abuse was endless. Even after our Bahamas trip disaster, my mother forgave him, and he still behaved like an ass, instead of the loving father I always knew him to be.

The rational side of my brain was telling me to move on from this. My father made a mistake driven by his hurt and loss over his marriage. I knew this deep in my heart, but the difficult part of all of this was trying to forget. My mother was blissfully happy, probably the happiest I had ever seen her. I took a breath and crossed my heart I would try. I remembered that no matter how emotional this day would be for me, I was doing this for Jackson, and Jackson only.

He'd been feeling so much better since he came clean with me and explained his headaches. He just wanted a second opinion without raising any alarms with his father. He felt my father was the best choice to help him. For me, the jury was still out. I had played out every scenario in my head and most of them ended up badly. I had a very short temper lately, and I wanted my father to say yes. Jackson repeatedly told me that if he said no, then we maturely say "Thank you for your time" and leave. *Jackson has the patience of a saint. Me...Not so much.*

I thanked the travel gods for our form of transportation...Mr. Reed, that is. He didn't want us driving the four hour plus car ride to Maryland, so he chartered a private plane for us. Forty five minutes is better than four hours. I let Jackson sleep in this morning since we were up way too late the night before. I kept him up by talking about everything that popped into my head.

The topic of marriage came up again. He kept dropping hints of waiting for a better time. He told me he loved me a hundred times, but he didn't want me to make a rash decision that I could regret later on. Was Jackson crazy? I loved him more than anything else in the world, other than my mother and of course Mr. Yankees Bear that he gave me, a token of his love to try to persuade me to love the New York Yankees.

He even reminded me last night that our marriage would be doomed if I didn't accept my fate and love Derek Jeter. I took the wind out of his sails when I reminded him that this was Derek's last year as the beloved Yankee captain, as he would soon retire. Oh, my poor future husband. He pouted for an hour after that. Although Jackson was born and raised in California, he is a die-hard Yankees fan.

We never really settled the marriage argument. It was tabled for now until our visit was finished with my father. I loved Jackson, he knew that. It wouldn't matter to me if we got married now while dressed in sweatpants or years from now dressed to the nines.

He also hinted that he knew the perfect spot where he wanted to make me his bride. I had an idea, but I wasn't telling him what I suspected. *One thing at a time Riley! Let's get through a visit with Dr. Samuel Briggs first.*

PLEASE GOD, LET me get through today. I'd been feeling sick since early this morning. My head began to throb to the point where I needed to take a pill. I didn't want to, but it was stupid to suffer through a headache when I had the medicine to help me. I tried to do some yoga and work on my breathing, but nothing helped until I took my migraine medicine.

I said a silent prayer to my mother in heaven asking for strength to get through today. I hadn't heard from my father, and I failed to call him like I said I would. He was unpredictable, to say the least.

I truly felt today was my only chance to convince Dr. Briggs to give me a consult. I was due to see Dr. O'Larien next month, and I would have no choice but to keep the appointment. My father always accompanied me through my check-ups and testing. I knew why he did what he did, and that's why this was so hard to do. I was going behind his back and keeping him purposely out of the loop in the name of sparing him any worry. He would never understand my reasoning. He would most likely be deeply hurt if he found out, another request I asked of my mother today.

The pill was beginning to take effect. Once I ate breakfast, I was feeling much better and steadier on my feet. Riley popped her head in a few times to hurry me along. The fight in her quickly tampered down with one smile from me. I knew she was anxious to leave, no more than I was. Richard was getting antsy as well. He wasn't looking forward to the trip, but he had his orders to be my shadow.

The flight was easygoing, and we made it to Johns Hopkins Hospital by ten. Hand in hand with Richard following close behind, we entered her father's expansive wing…courtesy of my father. We paid respect to my mother's memorial. Riley had given me a moment alone and that's when I said more prayers. Dad always said I could talk to my mother anytime, and it wouldn't matter where I was, she would always hear me. I always felt comfort while admiring this portrait of her that graced the entry way of the building. She was beautiful. Her eyes were Irish Green, and you could almost see your reflection in them, or so I was told. I looked just like my father, but I had my mother's eyes.

Continuing to walk the path that would lead us to Dr. Briggs' new wing, I stopped to pull Riley aside and talk with her. Richard had raised his eyebrows at me in confusion, but then figured I needed a minute alone with my girl. He gave us the privacy I requested, while Riley was apprehensive all of a sudden. I guess that was my fault for giving her all my crazy mixed signals, but I needed to get a few things off my chest before going in to meet with her father.

"Jackson, what's wrong? My father is waiting for us. I want to get this over with it as quickly as we can. We have a date with a minister today." She sheepishly smiled.

Oh, my girl! I have no chance when she looks at me that way.

"Riley, that's what I want to talk to you about. Please don't be upset, but I cancelled that meeting." By the look on her face, I wasn't sure if she was going to scream or cry. With Riley, any reaction was possible.

"Why would you do that? Jackson, I told you that I don't care about having a big wedding, or my father walking me down the aisle. I thought we were only messing around earlier. I never thought you would cancel the minister."

"It just doesn't feel right. This entire plan of mine doesn't feel right. I had another headache earlier, and it was bad enough where I needed to take my medicine for it."

"Dammit, Jackson! You can't keep doing this. Do not shut me out. Is this the way we roll? You're this Alpha male, and I'm what, the quiet little mouse that submits? I don't think so. Do you trust me or not?"

"Riley, keep your voice down. Richard is watching and no doubt listening. Of course, I trust you. I trust you emphatically with everything I have, but this shit is scary. I'm fucking scared! You can't even begin to understand what is running through my mind right now. And to top it off, I'm lying to my father. I feel terrible that I am deceiving him like this. Believe and trust me on this. When he finds out what I've been up to, his reaction is not going to be pretty. I almost want to leave you here so you can reconcile with your dad, while I do the same with mine."

"Jackson, you're not at odds with your dad, and you have nothing to feel guilty about. So you got a copy of your medical file, so what? We are planning to get a head start on our future by marrying now. Again, so what? I don't see any crimes here, do you?"

"You are impossible, Riley. Please stop trying to move me off course to what the real issue is. The moment I began to have the headaches, I should have been honest with you, more importantly, my father. I chose to deliberately keep this from everyone who cares about me. Riley, right there is the crux of my problem, and I feel sick about it. Our entire lives changed from the minute our parents reunited in that restaurant. I feel like I've been on this nonstop roller coaster ride with no end in sight."

"So what are you trying to say? Do you regret all this? Do you want out, Jackson? Because if you do, don't be a dick about it. Excuse my tone, but I have a heart to protect here and you are about to crush it."

Does she even know me at all? She actually believes because I'm hesitating on getting married, that I wish to end things with her? She's got me spinning in every direction. I don't even know how to set her straight. I could almost shake her, because she is that stubborn. She has her arms crossed over her chest, fighting to hold back her tears. This is a disaster. It was a mistake to come here.

Richard was stoic in his corner, watching us and the rest of the room from a safe distance. I took a breath, and instead of engaging in this crazy conversation, I let my body do the talking. Wrapping my arms around her, with her back to my chest, I just held and breathed her in. Riley fought against my hold and tried to put up a brave fight.

"Please baby, listen to me," I said calmly to her. "I love you so much. You know you have my heart. I have given it to you freely from the minute we met. Those promises we made to each other back in Pottersville were very real. Our commitment to each other has changed my life. I have not regretted one minute spent with you, no matter what we were doing. I'll fight with you all day long, if I know I'll get to hold you in my arms at night."

The fight had now left her. She placed her head back to me so I could place kisses on the side of her cheek.

"I love you, Riley. Please don't ever doubt me or my love for you. I don't know what else I can do to convince you that what I say is true. I'm sorry if I hurt you. It was never my intention. You demand honesty from me. You can't shut me out every time I give it to you."

I loosened my hold on her and turned her around to face me. She didn't look away. If anything, her stare had me almost hypnotized.

"Talk to me, Riley. Please?"

"I'm an idiot! Why are you even with me, Jackson? I am crazy. You should be with someone more like you. Not a girl that is always questioning why you're with her. I want to be deserving of your love. Your love is a gift. My thoughts are all over the place. I jump head first without ever thinking about the consequences of my actions. You're right. I do demand so much from you, and when I disagree, I shut you out. I hate feeling so insecure. This is not me, Jackson."

"No it's not, Riley. You are incredibly strong. You have a pure heart filled with a thousand emotions, all that I love by the way. You do deserve me, and I you. I love you, crazy girl...even your crazy mood swings. You can't just pick parts of a person to love. You are my chosen soul mate. I freely gave my heart over to you without any conditions. You accepted that love, and now here we are. I love you. I promise to always remind you of that love each and every day."

I held her tightly as I continued, "You are kind and loving, but never ever stupid, and certainly not an idiot. I'm actually getting pretty pissed off every time you belittle yourself. This is my final warning, so stop it. We will be married, Riley, just not today. The day you become mine, and really mine will be the happiest day of our lives. We will be surrounded by every single person that loves us and believes in our story. We deserve our moment, just like our parents do. Our love is forever, and it's not going anywhere. Please believe me, baby. I have never ever lied to you when it comes to my feelings for you, Riley Taylor Briggs. You are part of me. And I am part of you."

"That sounds like a line you would use in saying your wedding vows," she said.

"It could be. I'll make sure to remember it when we get to that part of the program. Are you okay now?"

"Yes, I'm fine. I may be the one that needs her head examined after this."

"That's my girl. Let's go and talk with your father. I will broach the subject of the consult. If he says no to my request, then we will leave it at that. I don't want to come between you and your father. You have fences to mend today, not break them down even more. Okay, sweet girl?"

"Jackson, if he loves me like he says he does, then he won't say no. How could he? He is a doctor, the best in his field. He won't be that closed-minded especially when it comes to the well-being of his patient."

"That's just it, baby, I'm not his patient. I am the son of the man that he believes destroyed his life. Once we cross that threshold, my mere presence will remind him of everything he lost. I don't want to make you any more nervous than you already are, but Riley, you need to understand that he may not be receptive to me. He loves *you* and will welcome *you* with open arms, but I have to be prepared for a less than kind reception."

"Jackson, let me handle my father. You asked me to give him a chance. Well, today is his chance. I'm extending the olive branch out to him, and it will be his choice to take it or not. I'm betting my father will take it. He loves me. I know our estrangement can't be easy on him. Let's go and find out."

"One more thing, Riley," I called out.

"What is it?" she answered with anxiety to her tone.

"You didn't answer my question. Once again, you skated right over it."

"Jackson, what more do you want me to say?"

"The one answer I need to hear."

"Which is what?"

"Promise me you will truly *try* to mend these fences. You need your father in your life. He loves you, and I'm asking you to remember all those good feelings and memories you have with each other when you finally come face to face with him. That's the answer I am looking for."

She looked down to the floor and shuffled her foot back and forth. I had fallen in love with the most obstinate girl on the planet. She was full of fire and fight. Looking back up at me with a smile finally breaking through, she whispered, "I'll try."

I swept her up into a body crushing hug. I said to her, "Thank you! I love you, crazy girl...so very much. Don't look now, but you're a grown-up. Don't worry, I won't tell anyone."

"Gee! Thanks, boyfriend, for the vote of confidence. Maybe I won't keep you after all."

"Oh yeah? Try getting rid of me, smartass!"

"Okay, since you put it that way. You do have a great ass. Okay, I'll keep you. I guess I will marry you and love you crazy hard for the rest of my life."

"I wouldn't want it any other way. Love you, baby."

I took her hand and led her to Richard, who was holding the elevator. We had been talking for nearly an hour, but I was thankful that we didn't officially agree to a time with her father. He told Riley that he cleared his entire schedule for the day. That alone should have proven to her that he was serious about their meeting.

Chapter Thirteen

The first step is always the hardest

Riley

MY FATHER'S WAITING area looked as if it was featured in an interior design magazine. He had soft Italian leather couches in place of chairs. Exotic flowers and plants were all around the room. Fine artwork hung on the walls, and a huge fish tank lined one entire wall. A beverage center was set-up, along with an assortment of healthy snacks.

My father was aiming for his patients to be comfortable while here. He always said it was hard enough just dealing with the reason. He wanted to lift the sanitized feeling that people usually get when visiting a hospital. He put his personal touch on every surface in this room. He always did put his patients first. I already had a few tears forming in my eyes.

"Hello, Riley." A familiar voice brought me out of my daydreaming. It was Gretchen, my father's personal assistant.

"Hi, Gretchen! I would like you to meet my boyfriend, Jackson Reed. Jackson, this is Gretchen. She keeps my father on track. Without her mad skills, my father's ship would sink."

"Please make yourselves comfortable. I'm afraid it's going to be a little while. A post-op patient of your father's had a complication this morning, and your father had to perform an emergency procedure. I was just updated about ten minutes ago. He should be here shortly after he does his post-surgery monitoring."

"I guess I shouldn't be surprised, duty calls. Would you mind if we waited for him in his office?"

"I don't see why you can't do that. Go make yourselves at home, and I can bring you in some drinks while you wait. What can I get for you?"

We both answered at the same time that we were okay and thanked her for her hospitality. We left Richard out in the hall of my father's office. He was content and out of the way. We didn't want to call out attention to him. If we needed Richard, he would be at our side in seconds.

"Jackson, you look a bit pale. Has your headache returned?" I nervously asked him.

"I'm fine babe, just nervous. I'm going to shoot my father a text, letting him know that we are safe and sound. I'm surprised he hasn't called me ten times already."

"He could have already spoken to Richard, and he would have updated him."

"You're right, he could have, but I still should reach out to him."

Me: *Dad. Arrived in Maryland. No worries. Waiting on Dr. Briggs. Lunch to follow. I will call you later. Jackson.*

I hit the send button and not a minute later, my phone pinged with his response.

Walker: *Sounds good, son. Richard has already updated me, but thank you for keeping in touch. Love, Dad.*

Just reading his text made my heart hurt. I was racked with guilt. *I should just bite the bullet and be honest with him.* I was about to send him another text when the door pushed open. Dr. Briggs arrived with a full smile on his face, until his eyes found mine. *Was my father right? Did he hate me on sight because of who I am? I guess I was about to find out.*

I didn't show my apprehension to Riley. She was already a bundle of nerves and didn't need to worry about me too. No matter what happened here today, they needed to sort their problems out first and foremost.

"Hi, Daddy," she managed to get out before her tears began to fall. I knew how much she missed her father. No matter what she had said to me up to now, I knew better. I saw the love they had for one another, and her reaction didn't come as a surprise. Scooping his daughter up in his arms, he wasted no time hugging her back.

"Oh my sweet girl! I have missed you so much. Let me look at you. You look beautiful."

"Thank you, daddy, you look good too. Aren't you going to say hello to Jackson?"

"Of course I am, I just wanted to take you in and commit you to memory. It has been way too long since I have laid eyes on you. All my fault, by the way. I am so sorry, honey."

"Daddy, we will get to all of that. Please say hello to Jackson."

Oh, please don't punch me sir. I know I look like my father, but I'm definitely not Walker Reed!

WITH HIS MANNERS back in check, my father extended his hand out to my boyfriend. They shook hands and exchanged smiles. *Well that's progress, let's hope it gets better.*

"How are you, Jackson?"

"I'm good sir. Thank you for asking."

"Forgive me, son, but I thought it was just going to be Riley and me for lunch."

"Daddy! You knew I was in New York with Jackson, and I told you that he would be joining me today."

"No, I didn't know anything Riley, and you want to know why? Because you have shut me out for months, and with not even offering a simple text in return. So please, give me a break."

Taking the higher ground and remembering what Jackson told me, I took a breath and simply moved on from this hostility.

"Well, we are both here now," I said, trying to maintain a calm demeanor and hold a smile. "So let's go to lunch, and we can all catch up."

Just as we were about to leave, Dr. Christopher McGovern entered my father's office. He headed the Board of Directors at Johns Hopkins. He was the one that commissioned Jackson's father to build my father's wing. He also loved money. He could smell it a mile away like sharks do when blood is present in the water. He was smiling from ear to ear when he saw Jackson.

Dr. McGovern said to Jackson, "I heard the chatter that Mr. Reed was in the building. I hadn't known it was the younger Reed but am happy just the same. How are you, son? What brings you here today?" He shook Jackson's hand as if he was royalty or something. My father stood silent and was annoyed with his intrusion.

"I'm good, sir. I'm just here for a social call. Riley and I are having lunch with her father."

"Is your father here in town?"

"Um…no sir. Just me."

"That's a shame, son. I would have enjoyed a conversation with him. Oh well, maybe next time. Anything you need while you are here, Jackson, you just let me know."

"Will do, Dr. McGovern. Thank you."

"Always a pleasure, Jackson. And please pass on my hello to your father."

"I will sir."

Oh my goodness! He didn't even acknowledge my father. He just brown nosed my boyfriend. As if Jackson would fall for his fake pleasantries. Oh the hospital politics! What a bunch of bullshit. You have to hand it to Jackson. He has impeccable manners and has been around many McGovern's in his life. He handled him like the pro.

As awkward as that was, my father took my hand and led me out of his office with Jackson following close behind. I looked over my shoulder to him, and Jackson just winked and assured me he was okay. Richard was keeping a safe distance behind us. I don't think my father even noticed him. It was Richard's job to be discreet and invisible. We didn't need any new problems today.

My father chose Henningers Tavern. It was his home away from home with the long nights he spent at his hospital. I would have been okay with a burger place, but my father wanted to spoil me today. Henningers was fine dining with an eclectic mix of arty décor. It had amazing seafood to choose from.

We were seated at a secluded table at the far back of the restaurant. It was quieter here, as my father wanted to talk with me without any interruption. We ordered drinks and made ourselves comfortable. My right hand was linked with Jackson's, a gesture my father did not miss. He cleared his throat and looked directly at me, ignoring Jackson completely.

"Riley, no matter how I begin my apology, this conversation will be a hard one to have. I am so very sorry for missing you when you left on your summer vacation. I broke my promise to you. That is one regret I will always carry with me. I also missed my baby girl's prom. Another mistake that I still feel sick over. I guess I should be thankful to your mother for sending me pictures. Time away from you has given me the chance to reflect on many things. I can promise you that I am working on my anger. I'm embarrassed to admit that it took a right hook to my jaw to set me straight. I was on a destructive path, one I deeply regret. I am now on the right path and have begun the process of healing."

He looked over at Jackson as he said his last sentence. I didn't react to his comment. This was me listening, giving him a chance. I remained quiet, with Jackson holding my hand for support. Little did Jackson know, but this was exactly what I needed.

My father continued, "I should have never sold the house without discussing it with you first. All I can say is that I was allowing anger to lead me. I just couldn't bear to live one more day in a house that I no longer considered our home."

"Daddy, I don't think we need to rehash everything. This meeting today is not about that. I have moved on from the house and you not being there when I left for my trip. What upsets me is the way you treated mom. The hurtful words you had said to her were cruel. How could you? You say that you are sorry? Well, apologize to my mother. Once you do that, I can begin to believe your apologies."

"Riley, my relationship with your mother is complicated, to say the least, and I will not discuss it with you, especially not in front of him."

So much for extending the olive branch. Jackson visibly shifted in his seat. My boyfriend looked like he was sitting on nails.

"Him? Really daddy? He has a name. His name is Jackson Walker Reed. Oops! I said the very name that is never to be mentioned. Kind of like Voldemort from Harry Potter. Note to self: Do not say the name 'Walker.' Oh man, there I go running my mouth again! Where are my manners? I guess I'm taking my cues from you today. Clearly, you forgot yours as well."

"Now that's enough out of you, little girl. I am your father. You will not disrespect me, especially in public. I understand you are angry with me, but this is not the place to show it. Show some restraint, Riley, and grow up."

"Believe me, daddy, I am showing restraint. Sorry if I'm embarrassing you, but I thought we could have been civil with one another today, but clearly that is not the case. You want respect? I will gladly give it to you, but you also need to show respect to my boyfriend.

Better get comfortable with it, daddy, because he's not going any-where."

I refocused my attention back to Jackson, who clearly looked uncomfortable. *Is he getting angry with me?*

"Are you okay?" I asked him. "I'm sorry, Jackson."

"Riley, can I speak to you in private?" my boyfriend said to me.

I take his offered hand and walk with him to a more private area of the restaurant.

"What the hell was that back there?" Jackson asked me. "Riley, what happened to hearing each other out? You two are like stubborn bulls colliding with each other at full speed. I can't believe your be-havior toward your father. He's trying, Riley. I thought you would too. You promised me."

"No. I said I *would* try. And I did. Jackson, please don't be an-gry with me. I can't bear it. I'm sorry. I told you this was a bad idea. I'm clearly not ready for this conversation to happen."

"You think? At this point babe, I'm not even going ask him about a consult."

"Well, if that's what you want, then let's leave right now."

"No! You don't get off that easy, I will not let you. You are go-ing back to that table. You will try, and this time, succeed. Work it out with your father. I mean it, Riley. No more tantrums. You are so much more than that girl who just spewed ugly insults at the one man she *claims* to love."

"I do love my father. How can you say that to me?"

"Prove it. End of discussion. We're here, and you're going to talk with him."

I was going to continue to plead my case when Jackson sudden-ly appeared unsteady on his feet. He quickly grabbed onto a chair for support.

"Jackson! Are you okay? Oh my God! I'm going to get Rich-ard."

"Relax. I'm fine. Just got dizzy for a second. Come. Let's rejoin your father."

We walked hand in hand back to our table. My instinct was to run and return to New York, but Jackson wasn't having it. My father was sitting there, waiting with no expression on his face. I just wanted to scream at the top of my lungs right now. Jackson was too calm. It was almost making me nervous. He pulled out my chair and placed my linen napkin onto my lap. I looked at him lovingly, thinking all the while that I don't deserve him.

He leaned into me and whispered in my ear, "Why don't I give you and your father some time alone? My presence here is not helping at all."

"Jackson, please don't leave. I need you here. I'm sorry." I tried to object, but he dismissed me. I was crushed.

He whispered in my ear again, "And I need you to exercise patience. This is not easy for him. Get out of your head right now and listen with your heart. Open yourself to listen to your father. Allow your heart to lead you on the path of forgiveness. I love you."

"I love you, too."

Jackson nodded at my father in a respectful manner and left me with a chaste kiss to my cheek. I knew deep down he was right. *Jackson is always right.* Once Jackson disappeared from my sight, I turned back to my father.

"Happy now, daddy? You just ran off Jackson."

My father rubbed his temples and was clearly annoyed with me. *I don't know anymore. I feel like I'm at the table with a stranger. He is far from the man that I once considered my hero.*

"*I* ran off your boyfriend? Wow! You just love passing the blame. You ran off Jackson with your emotional and adolescent behavior. He even tried to make you see reason. I could hear him the whole time he was whispering to you. And here you sit, still blaming me. How can I make this right? Riley, I feel like I have been tried and convicted in your eyes. When you finally agreed to meet with me, I truly thought it would be you and you alone. I have so much to make up for, and I am doing everything wrong. I'm sorry for being rude. I am not mad at Jackson. I just can't stand to look at him. I know how that sounds, but it's how I feel. All I see when I look at him is his father."

He continued, "You are so young and so inexperienced on how love works. You invest all you have into the person you choose to stand beside you. You love hard. You trust even harder and completely hand over your life's happiness to the other person. I had all of that with your mother, nearly two decades of loving her, giving her all that I had. What took me years to build was lost in the blink of an eye."

"I believe my anger is justified Riley, and that hurt just doesn't magically go away. It feels like I am going through the stages of grief. I'll admit every part is harder than the first. I don't feel better. I actually feel worse. If I didn't have my work, the pain would swallow me up. Can you even try to see my side?"

I had tears in my eyes, but was still feeling hostile. "Daddy, believe it or not, I can. I may be young, but I do know and understand what love is. All that you had with mother is different to what I have with Jackson. I have true love with him. We connected from the start. We have an all-consuming type of love. It's very real. Please don't scoff at me. I do have it, and I will have it for the rest of my life. If he would agree to it, I would marry him today. He wants our wedding day to be magical with you walking me down the aisle, with tears in your eyes. His words, not mine. You're right about one thing, I don't know how you feel, because I have never been hurt that way, and I pray I never am."

I continued, "I was blind for so long when it came to your marriage with mother. I remember so many nights listening to mom cry herself to sleep when you didn't come home for days at a time. Of course, mom never knew that I listened by her door, but I did daddy, and I still had my head in the clouds. Little girls want to believe in their fathers and believe in love. I'm not saying that you didn't have that with mom, but as I grew older, I began to see the cracks in your foundation."

"Mom shielded me from so much of it. On the outside, we were the picture perfect family, but I can see now we weren't. I never even considered my choice of colleges when I chose New York. With me gone miles away from home, mom would truly be alone. Knowing that hurt me, daddy. I never knew her plans of the divorce, but after coming to terms with it all, I understand it so much better now. Forget about Mr. Reed coming back into her life. She was planning to leave way before they found each other again. She was giving you an out, a chance to move on and be with someone that could truly be your match. She always put you first, and that was before Mr. Reed came waltzing back. And how did you repay her for her kindness? You took what she offered and threw it back in her face. How am I expected to feel about that?"

"Are you done yet? For a young woman, you certainly have the martyr act down."

"For a smart man, you sure act incredibly stupid. Daddy, are we done hurting each other yet? Because I am, and I'm about five seconds away from walking out of this restaurant."

He said nothing. I got up and shoved back my chair. As I turned, my father grabbed my wrist.

"Please Riley, don't go. I need you." He released me, and I returned to my seat.

"I guess I should increase my therapy sessions because I completely failed here today," he said.

"Are you seeing a therapist?" I asked. This revelation shocked me.

"Yes, I am in therapy. I only go once a week, but after today, I will increase my visits. I know I'm full of anger and resentment. I thought our time apart was actually helping me get a better handle on it, but clearly I was wrong."

His head and shoulders sunk, and he said, "I know I was a bastard toward your mother. I am not ready to cross that precipice with her yet. I'll have you know that under the encouragement of my therapist, I have spoken with Reese. The first step was to apologize for my actions. Once again, she took kindness on me, and accepted my apology. Riley, from this moment on, anything I say to you or your mother will always be heartfelt, but this is all that I'm capable of right now. I will not pretend to you that all is bright in my world. I had many years with your mom. Those feelings are not easily erased, nor forgotten. Please tell me you understand this?"

"I'm trying daddy, but you are not making it easy on any of us. The first thing you need to do is accept my relationship with Jackson. I love him, daddy, and he's going to be in my life. This means he will also be in yours. Please meet me halfway here. If you can promise to try, then we will figure it out together."

I couldn't help the tears that began to fall down my cheeks. He was quick to wipe them away, but more fell. He leaped out of his seat and took me in his arms. I shut my eyes and tried to shove the hurt away.

Samuel Briggs may be a superstar at his hospital, but here, he was just my father. I loved him with all of my heart. Our relationship was stronger than this. I had to believe that we could move past our hurt and be father and daughter again. I dried my eyes in a not-so-ladylike manner on his Armani dress shirt. He didn't even try to stop me. He held me against him until he was assured I was okay. Stroking my hair and whispering "I love you's" calmed me. I was a daddy's girl through and through. And right now, all I felt was his love…not anger.

"Can we start over?" he asked with hope.

"I would like that, but can I check on Jackson, first?"

"Of course! Please have him return to the table, so I can offer my apologies to him."

I excused myself from the table. I searched the entire restaurant. No sign of Jackson. *Where is he?* I dialed his cell number, and it went straight to voicemail. I dialed Richard's cell number, again going straight to voicemail. *What on earth? Where are they?*

I walked outside to look around, and several patrons were lingering about. I heard a woman say to another that she hoped the young man would be okay. I immediately gasped and pain shot through my heart. *It's not Jackson. It's not Jackson.* I kept repeating those three words over and over again, until I had the courage to ask who they were referring to. Fighting against the tears, I apprehensively approached the women.

"Excuse me, ladies. I don't mean to listen in on your conversation, but who do you hope will be okay?"

They looked at me with confusion, but answered me anyway.

"A handsome young man was walking along the waterfront and collapsed. We were outside chatting and ran over to try to help. A bigger fellow was at his side. He asked us to dial 911, so we did."

I froze after the woman finished explaining what happened here. Her expression was sad. I could only imagine how I looked right now. My head felt fuzzy, and my stomach no better.

I just lost it. I already knew it was Jackson, but pulled out my phone anyway to pull up a picture.

"Is this him?" I asked the women.

They both answered "yes" at the same time.

"Hope your friend is okay." They wished me well as they turned to walk away.

My friend? I whispered to myself. *How about my life? The reason I smile a hundred times a day? Please God, let him be okay.*

How did I not hear the ambulance sirens? The restaurant was always a bit loud with music playing over the sound system. I guess because we were in the back, I wasn't focused on outside noises. I ran back into the restaurant. I called out to my father for help. He was out of his seat and by my side in a flash.

"Riley, my God! You are white as a ghost. Are you ill? What's wrong? And where's Jackson?"

I could barely speak through my tears, but I managed to quickly explain. My father took my hand, and we sprinted to his car. He called the hospital and was told that Jackson was in the Emergency Room. Over the phone, he clearly issued his instructions on what tests should be performed on Jackson. He then gave our ETA and hit the gas. He was in Doctor Mode right now. I was thanking the heavens for my father. If anyone could help Jackson, it would be Samuel Briggs. My father is a healer and the best in his field.

"Please God, take care of Jackson for me." I was praying out loud. My father just held my hand, as I continued to beg God for a miracle.

We arrived at the hospital with the valet taking our car. We moved fast through the Emergency Room. My father was updated and brought up to speed on Jackson's condition. He wanted him moved to his wing immediately. Staff jumped at the request. I watched my father command the room. I saw Richard off to the side, on the phone.

"Richard! What happened?"

He shut his phone and looked down to me with his tear-filled eyes. He had known and taken care of Jackson for many years. He treated him as a son. Richard was clearly upset.

"Miss Riley, I am so sorry I didn't call you, but I had to act quickly."

"Just tell me what happened?"

"Jackson had me meet him in front of the restaurant. He said he wasn't feeling all too well and wanted to get some air. We walked across the street, and not even five minutes later, he collapsed. He was having a seizure. I've seen them before, but this one was different. Five minutes felt like an hour. That's when I knew he needed help. An ambulance was called right away. I didn't know if he hit his head when he fell to the ground."

"Why didn't you come and get my father? You know he could have helped him." I almost sounded angry.

"I'm sorry. I just reacted the best way I knew how."

"Did you call his father?"

"I was about to when you walked up to me."

"Please, Richard. Can you go be with Jackson? I'll call my mom."

"Mr. Reed will want to hear from me."

"Please, Richard. I need to be the one to make the call."

"Very well, miss. I'll be with Jackson."

"Thank you, Richard. I won't be long."

My legs felt like jelly. I sat and shakily called my mom. Her cell went directly to voicemail. *Dammit!* I found myself praying again. I knew I had to be strong for Jackson, but calling his father would probably take all the strength I had left.

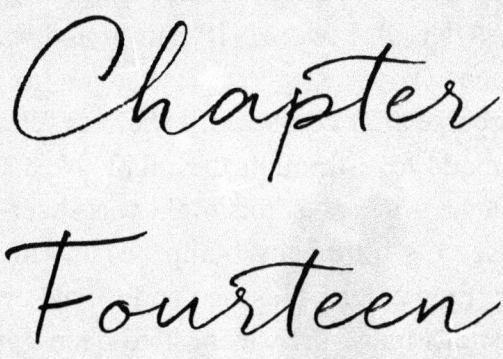

Chapter Fourteen

Temporary bliss

Walker

"**B**ABY! I THINK we helped New York's economy to-day," I called out to her.

I carried ten filled shopping bags with everything our little baby girl would need. Reese asked me to help out our doorman after he made two trips. Reese was glowing. She was so happy.

The minute we arrived in the city, we wasted no time at all. Having taken a suite at the Four Seasons the day before allowed us to have some private time. We had been planning to surprise the kids, but we knew they were in Maryland, so we did our own thing.

We dined back at Brasserie Les Halles, but this time with less drama. Andre's expression was very illuminating. His eyes were dancing as he took in my arrival, along with my escort. We declined wine on account of Reese's pregnancy. Andre pouted, but served us sparkling water instead. He asked me several times if I wanted to try anything from the private collection, but I finally raised my hand to him, clearly ready to dismiss him. Reese giggled at his overattentiveness with us. After all, I was a VIP patron and was always given the golden treatment.

I fed Reese course after course until she was full. We danced off our dessert and made love through the night. Next to proposing to Reese at all of our favorite spots, this night was sheer heaven.

Overnight, Reese's little baby bump became more visible. She was breathtaking. I gave her a massage and kissed every inch of her stomach. My precious baby girl was nestled deep within her womb, and so protected from the big bad world. I sang to her and told her our love story. As she would get older, our little one would love hearing it again and again, I imagined. I remembered every detail of Reese, and my little princess would certainly believe in love.

"For centuries," I spoke to Reese's baby bump, "books had been written with stories of the *Happily Ever After's*. For Reese and me, our story was like no other tale told before. It didn't have to be in a book; we lived it and survived it. We didn't have an evil queen casting a spell on us, but we had something similar to it: an evil king. He and the other trolls did their worst by keeping us apart. They thought they had written our ending for us, but then a miracle happened, and love did prevail. We found each other again, and our love became stronger. It's the same love that made you little one…our daughter."

As I rubbed Reese's belly, I spoke again to our princess. "Do you hear your daddy? Believe in *Happily Ever After*. Believe in *Forever*. I love you so much. I can't wait to hold you in my arms. You, my precious little girl, will remind me of your beautiful mother, the smallest version of her. My heart will not only beat for mommy, but you too, my princess. I'm already imagining you running through the meadow with bouncy brown curls. You have pink ribbons in your hair, and your laugh is the sweetest melody. Daddy loves you, princess, and I can't wait to hold you in my arms."

All my talking had lulled Reese into a deep sleep. Oh my poor angel. I definitely wore her out yesterday, but she never complained.

We were making new memories together.

I probably could have stayed asleep with Reese, but I was never one to require no more than four hours at a time. I left my angel nestled under the plush blankets with her mane of gorgeous hair flowing over our pillows. She was safe, and I knew this time when I returned to our room, she would still be there waiting for me. Every once in a while, my mind drifted back to that morning where my world fell apart, but I quickly shoved it away.

I was working my way through the tough chapters of our story. Elizabeth wanted me to forgive, well easier said than done. I still hadn't explained all to Reese, but I layered so much on her already. I wouldn't risk another fight between us. I loved the making up part, but it pained both our hearts to hurt each other.

I needed to sort this out on my own. I believed that day in the cemetery was real. Even if I shouted it from the tallest buildings, would my father hear me forgive him? Saying the words is one thing, but to believe them is another altogether. *I'm not ready yet, this much I know.*

My run this morning through Central Park was invigorating. My workout with Reese, even better, but my stomach was growling something fierce. The day had flown by with all we did today, and I was beginning to wonder what could be taking Jackson and Riley so long to return back to the city.

After receiving my son's text message, my worry was gone. I was concerned with my son being so close to Samuel Briggs. I know he is Riley's father, but he hated me, and I certainly didn't want him to show my son any animosity. I wasn't going to worry, not yet. Richard would call me if anything was wrong.

I busied myself in the kitchen and made some sandwiches. I left instructions with the staff to keep the refrigerator and pantry fully stocked while Jackson and Riley were here.

I wasn't sure if Reese could handle Pastrami and Swiss, her favorite New York sandwich, so I went with grilled cheese and tomato. It was a safer bet for now. I accompanied it with soup and fruit for dessert. I carried the tray into our bedroom where my sleeping angel was now awake, clearly waiting for me.

"Hey, baby, how was your sleep?" I asked her.

"It was heaven, but lonely without you." She flashed her eyelashes at me." *Tease!*

"Oh really? Well how about you eat this amazing meal I prepared for us. Our daughter is hungry, and she needs to keep growing. Once you are nice and full, we can discuss how lonely you were without me. Deal?"

"I love you. You are such a flirt."

"This is true, but I only have eyes for you…Now eat!"

I gave her a stern look. Reese just smiled and ate every last bite on her plate, very much pleasing me. Quickly clearing the tray, I had her wrapped up in my arms afterwards.

"So tell me? How can I satisfy your cravings? What are you in the mood for?"

"Can I get back to you on that? Nature is calling," she replied.

She kissed me soundly and bounced off our bed. I was going to follow her when I was interrupted by the sound of my cell phone.

Not checking the number, I simply answered, "Reed."

"Mr. Reed?" *Riley,* I thought. *Something is wrong.* I could hear her crying on the other end.

"Riley, what's wrong honey? Are you okay?"

She didn't answer my question. I asked her again, as she continued to cry.

"Please, Riley?" I now was off the bed and getting dressed.

"It's Jackson!" she screamed. My heart plummeted in my chest. *Oh God, no!*

"Come quickly, Mr. Reed, he needs you." She doesn't know that we're in New York. I took a breath and asked her where they were. She said at Johns Hopkins. I told her that her mother and I would join her as quickly as we could. I hung up with Riley and phoned my pilot.

Reese came out of the bathroom, her smile now gone.

"What's happened?" she asked with worry in her voice.

"That was Riley on the phone. Something has happened to Jackson, and he's at Johns Hopkins. Baby, we need to go…right now."

She never moved so fast. She quickly dressed and grabbed her bag. We were in the car in a matter of minutes and on our way to the airport.

I phoned Richard on the way, and he told me that Jackson had suffered a seizure. The seizure was not like one he had before, and it lasted beyond five minutes. Jackson was taken to the hospital by ambulance and was being seen by doctors.

What stopped my breathing was what Richard had said next: The attending physician was no other than Dr. Samuel Briggs. I clenched my fist so tight that I could feel wetness on my palm. Blood was trickling down my hand, as I released my nails from my skin. Reese gasped and grabbed a tissue to wipe my small little slices that lined my palm.

"What is it? Talk to me, Walker."

My head was spinning. *How the hell is this happening?* With my best efforts, I tried to remain calm, especially in front of Reese. *He is the best in his field. Right now, that's all I want for my son. I can't let myself go to dark places right now where he's concerned. I know Briggs doesn't care a flying fuck about me, but he's a doctor first. I have no choice, but to trust him right now.*

"I'm sorry baby. I'm fine, this is nothing." I waved off my hand. "That was Richard. Jackson has been moved to Samuel's wing, and he's the doctor overseeing his care right now. From what I gathered, Riley and Jackson were having lunch with Samuel. He walked outside for some air, and collapsed. We will know more once we get there…I hope."

"Walker, listen to me. If I know anything about Samuel, it's that he is the best. He will do everything in his power to help Jackson, I know it." She pleaded with worry eyes to convince me that everything she was saying was true.

All I could do was hold her and pray. We boarded my plane, and my pilot had us in the air within ten minutes of fastening our seat-belts. I phoned Stephen before we took off. He would have to take a separate plane to Maryland and meet us at the hospital.

Chapter Fifteen

Not again...not my son

Walker

KEEPING MYSELF IN check was no easy feat, especially around Reese. She was watching me intently, gauging every move I would make. She entwined her hand within my own and rubbed small circles over my knuckles, a move I would normally use on her without even knowing I was doing it. Touching Reese was so natural, I knew no other way.

We experienced a slight delay over Washington D.C. due to a storm. I instructed my pilot to do everything he could to fly around it. I didn't want to delay one more minute away from Jackson. I excused myself from Reese and made some calls in my office. I knew Stephen was already in the air and would join me later on tonight. I hadn't received any more updates from Richard, so I called the one person I could get answers from.

In my right to the point voice, I asked for Dr. Christopher McGovern, who not only was a Cardiothoracic Surgeon, but who also was in charge of the Board of Directors for Johns Hopkins Hospital. I was put through immediately and skipped over the pleasantries.

I made it clear to the point of my call. "I need a status on my son, Dr. McGovern."

"Mr. Reed, all we know at the moment is that he is still unconscious and is undergoing testing. I assure you we are doing everything we can for you son."

"Which is what, exactly? Why is he still unconscious? Is Briggs with him?"

"Yes sir, he is. Dr. Samuel Briggs is the best Neurosurgeon we have here on staff."

"I didn't ask for his credentials, McGovern, I simply want a status on my son. It's clear to me that you know more than I do at the moment. I will be arriving in about thirty minutes, so make sure you have something more comprehensive to tell me when I get there."

I ended my call before he had the opportunity to say goodbye.

WHILE JACKSON WAS being triaged and prepped for his CAT scan and MRI, I stepped out to check on my daughter. As I approached my daughter, a man whom I had never met before stepped in front of her. *Was he acting as her personal bodyguard?* Riley, who bypassed him to get to me, told him "It's okay." *Okay? I am her father, and to have restricted access to her is completely ludicrous to me.*

"Daddy, how's Jackson? When can I see him?" Riley was asking me through her tears.

Right here, right now, I was a father, and nothing more. I wanted to do anything in my power to comfort her, to reassure her that everything would be okay, but I didn't know myself.

"Riley, Jackson is still unconscious and is being transported for testing. You will not be able to see him for a while. I have a few minutes, if I may ask you some questions?" She quietly nodded her head.

"This was in Jackson's pant pocket," I said as I showed her the flash drive. She recognized it immediately. "Can you tell me what's on this?"

"That flash drive contains all of Jackson's medical records."

"Why was he carrying this around?"

"Daddy, there is something I need to tell you. I had another reason why I wanted to see you."

"From the look on your face, honey, I figured you might. Was Jackson seeking my help? Is that the reason why he was carrying around a flash drive with his medical records on it?"

"Yes."

"Why didn't you just tell me this when you first arrived?"

"Would that have made a difference? Would you have helped him, if I asked you? Before I even knew what was going on, he had already reached out to your office. The wait to see you was over six months. Jackson thought that if I asked you personally, then you might treat him. I'm so sorry I didn't tell you the truth, daddy. This is my fault. I am always causing him stress. If I hadn't argued with you, then he wouldn't have left the restaurant, and we wouldn't be in this hospital."

My daughter just broke down in my arms, letting go of the wall that was between us. All I could do was hold her. My heart was breaking for her.

Our moment was interrupted by Dr. McGovern.

"I need a word, Briggs, in private."

He clasped his pudgy hand on my shoulder and directed me to a private corridor.

I said to my daughter, "Riley, please drink some water and take some calming breaths. I need to speak with Dr. McGovern. I will be right back. I love you, sweetheart."

"I love you, too."

Dr. McGovern took me down the hall for a private conversation.

"What is it, Christopher?" I asked him. "I need to get back to check on my patient."

"Yes, you do Briggs, and immediately. You should have never left his side to tend to your daughter here. Your attention and priority should solely be focused on Jackson Reed."

"Christopher, when I treat a patient, their well-being is everything to me. He is undergoing some tests right now. What the hell are you driving at?"

"Are you kidding me, Briggs? You are going to stand here and play dumb with me? That boy in there will be your number one priority from this minute moving forward. He is your only patient at the time, and you will not leave his side again. Do I make myself clear?"

"Who the hell do you think you are speaking to? Don't you dare walk your condescending ass into my building and believe you can order me around. You are wasting my time."

"And you are playing with fire. Don't fool yourself into believing that boy is *just* another patient. He is the son of Walker Reed, the same man that built this building. And the same man whose money funds your research. God help us all if anything happens to that boy while under your care. You better believe it will be all of our collective asses on the line. Now get the hell back in there! His father just phoned me from his plane, and he is due here at any moment. He wants to be updated immediately, so you better have something to tell him."

I took a breath as I watched McGovern disappear from sight. I couldn't waste a minute worrying about him right now and rejoined Riley, who was wringing her hands in her lap.

"Riley, I have to go and check on Jackson. If I can't update you right away, I will send out Francesca, my head nurse, to come find you. Okay honey?"

"Daddy, please help him. He didn't trust Dr. O'Larien. This is why he asked for his medical records to see you."

"He did what!?" I heard a familiar voice scream a few feet away.

That voice was unmistakable and laced with anger. The sole

reason for my months of pain just bellowed in through my doors: Walker Reed, in the flesh, and not alone. My beautiful *ex-wife* was by his side. There he stood, already breathing fire at me.

"Mr. Reed. Mommy! Thank God you're here." And just like that, my daughter flew out of my arms, and into his. I felt my stomach drop as I took in their reunion. He stroked her hair to comfort her, and my stomach coiled into spasms. I thought I would be sick. *She's my daughter and she's in his arms.*

"Riley, we're here now. Please calm down honey and tell me about Dr. O'Larien. What did you mean by Jackson not trusting him?"

I broke up their moment, and excused myself to check on Jackson. Without waiting on Riley's answer, Reed shouted over to me.

"Briggs," he called out. "What do we know? How's my son?"

"He's up in Radiology. He's having a CAT scan, and then an MRI to follow. I will know more once I get the films back. Please excuse me."

He didn't question anything else, making my escape that much easier. As I stepped onto the elevator, I watched helplessly as another man comforted my daughter. As Reed held my daughter, my ex-wife held him. It felt like a knife piercing my heart and served as a reminder that I have truly lost them both.

ASSURED THAT RILEY was now calmer with her mother and me here, I wanted to speak with her about Jackson. I gave her another moment with Reese, before doing so.

"Reese, I'll leave you with Riley for a few minutes while I speak with Richard, okay?"

"We're fine, Walker. Don't worry." She gave me her best smile. I leaned in to kiss the top of her head and breathe in her sweet smelling scent of flowery shampoo. It was like a drug calming all my nerves. We walked down to a private conference room, courtesy of Dr. McGovern.

Richard had been nothing but a loyal and trustworthy employee for many years now, but he has a soft spot where Jackson was concerned. I feared he may had been falling behind in his detail for my son, and I was about to find out.

"I want to know what the hell has been going on with Jackson and Riley. I heard Riley tell her father about Jackson not trusting Dr. O'Larien. How is that possible? Has Jackson been to see him recently? If he has, Richard, this is news to me, and it will not sit well with me not knowing this important piece of information."

"Sir, for the most part of this entire trip, Jackson and Riley have been exceptionally behaved. I have had no issues whatsoever."

"But?"

"No issues until a few days ago. I took them to a local Starbucks, so they could meet with some of their friends. Jackson did not want me to join them inside, so I had them placed at a table in front of the window where I could still observe. A few minutes later, Riley exited the restaurant complaining that she was ill and needed to be taken to a local pharmacy for some stomach aides. I wanted to bring them both home, but she convinced me that it would only take a few minutes. I agreed and took her to the store, leaving Jackson unattended. She was taking longer than she should have. I insisted we return to the restaurant immediately. Upon arrival, I observed something suspicious."

"Which was?"

"Well, sir, Jackson was clearly perspiring, so much that it could be seen through his shirt. I know we are in the middle of summer, but they had air conditioning inside."

"Richard, was my son ill? Is that the reason why he looked sweaty?"

"Sir, what I have failed to mention is the location of the restaurant. We were only a couple blocks from Dr. O'Larien's office. While I was attending to Riley, your son made his exit to go to Dr. O'Larien's office, for whatever reason I do not know. He must have ran all the way back, that is the only logical reasoning why he looked the way he did. We were en route back to the apartment, when Jackson said they wanted to run errands. I refused his request, insisting they both return to the apartment. When I was stopped at a traffic light, they both ran out of the limo, and I could not catch them. They didn't return home for hours. I was very alarmed at the fact that Jackson would pull a stunt like this, he never did before. I chastised him about putting his health at risk by doing such an irresponsible act. He apologized to me, and I decided to keep it between us. I vowed to tell you immediately if he ever did something like that again."

I could feel my jaw beginning to tick, my skin beginning to heat, as I listened to Richard's detailed account about Jackson. His bodyguard was now crestfallen and waiting on me to speak.

"Why wasn't I told about this immediately? It is your job to report back to me with every last detail about my son, no matter how insignificant you think it might be. It has been very taxing on me already, knowing he was on the other side of the country, but now this? He's pulling stunts of disappearing acts? I don't understand this at all. Was Jackson carrying anything on him when he collapsed at the restaurant?"

"Yes, sir. I have his wallet, along with his small backpack."

He handed me the items, and no longer caring about his privacy, I immediately began to search his things. What I found next completely floored me. It was a State of New York Marriage License issued to Jackson Walker Reed and Riley Taylor Briggs. *No! This can't be real. My son did not marry his girlfriend, without my knowledge of it.* I shoved the paper back into the pack and sat down to catch my breath.

Richard handed me a glass of water, but I shoved it away. I was almost in a catatonic state. *If they are married, then Riley has a legal say in my son's medical care. As his wife, she can make decisions on his behalf. Hell no! I will not fucking abide by this.*

I don't even know how much time passed before I came out of my initial shock. I kept hearing over and over again someone calling out, "Mr. Reed."

I finally whipped around and shouted, "What!"

"Excuse me, sir, but my name is Francesca, and I am Dr. Briggs' nurse. He asked me to come find you."

No pleasantries to greet her, I just bolted from my seat.

"Where is my son?" I practically screamed at her.

"Your son is on his way down from Radiology and is being taken to the I.C.U. within Dr. Briggs' wing. He hasn't regained consciousness yet, but all will be explained to you shortly." With that, she turned and exited the office.

Now accepting a bottle of water, I drank it down in several quick gulps, wishing it was scotch. I felt as if I was spinning out of control and needed to get a better handle on it. I turned to Richard, who was nervously quiet.

"I need to check on my son. You take care of Reese and her daughter. Do not let them out of your sight, and especially make sure Reese is comfortable. If you fail me again, you are fired. Do I make myself clear?"

"I understand, Mr. Reed, and I am very sorry."

"I don't want your apologies, nor do I need them."

We walked out together. Reese was waiting for me. My eyes found hers, as I took in her beautiful features. She was holding Riley's hand, and with the other was stroking her belly with our growing daughter inside. Riley was oblivious to what Reese was doing. Just the sight of her calmed me. As I got closer to where they were sitting, Reese got up to greet me, wrapping her arms around my waist and reassuring me. I wanted to believe that she was right, and my son would be okay.

"Jackson will be in his room in the I.C.U. in a few minutes, so we can see him then. Reese, baby, I want you to go with Richard and take Riley. I need to see Jackson alone." She clearly looked hurt by my words of dismissal. It was never my intention, but I knew what I needed. I wanted her to rest and be safe.

"I also need you to find out something for me," I said. I hooked her arm within mine and walked over where no one could hear us. "I found this in Jackson's backpack, and this never came up in one of my daily calls with my son" I showed her the marriage license, and she was clearly shocked as well.

She gasped. "What the hell does this mean? Did the kids get secretly married and not tell either of us?"

"That's what I need you to find out for me. I don't trust myself around Riley right now. I am too upset, and I don't want to be curt with her. Please get to the bottom of this right away, and then send me a text with what you know. I will join you in a little while."

"Okay, I'll take care of it. I love you."

"I love you too, baby, so much." I couldn't kiss her again, knowing I wouldn't be able to stop. Reese was the only reason I wasn't losing my mind right now. She was keeping me in check. With Reese being pregnant, I wasn't going to cause her any unnecessary worry.

I came upon Jackson's room and watched through the glass, as the nurse checked his vitals. My legs locked. I couldn't bring myself to enter his room. I was beyond frightened on what I would be told. Briggs came up behind me and invited me in.

"He's stable and should awaken soon. His blood pressure was extremely elevated upon arrival. His scans show no visible injuries to his head when he collapsed. I will give you a few minutes with him, and then you can join me in my office where I can speak with you in private."

"You can tell me now, Briggs."

"It's *Doctor* Briggs to you, and I thought you might want to have a few minutes with your son before we talk. It's up to you."

I gritted my teeth and nodded at him. He took that as a sign to leave. I never thought I would be taking in this image of my son in this state. He looked pale and with no light on his face. I pulled up a chair as quietly as I could and gripped his hand in mine. I rubbed my fingers over his, silently praying for him to wake-up. My tears began to fall, and I got as close as his wires would allow me to.

Please God. Please. Don't take him from me. I won't survive it.

I kissed his forehead and made my way to Dr. Briggs' office. Reese was waiting for me there in his waiting room. I immediately noticed Richard's absence. *Where could he be?* I wondered.

"Where are Richard and Riley?" I asked Reese.

"I sent them out to get some air. Riley was so upset to the point of getting sick. After our conversation, she could take no more. How's Jackson? Do we know anything else?"

"He's still unconscious. His blood pressure was very high when he was brought in. He's stable now, but I would feel a whole hell of lot better once he wakes up. So, what did you find out?"

"Come sit with me. It's quite the story. I will give you the short version until we can talk as a family. They didn't officially get married, but the marriage license is real."

"I don't understand this at all. Why would they do this? To keep something so important from us is beyond anything I ever had to deal with when it comes to Jackson. Reese, do you even know what this could have meant if they had gotten married? It would have meant that Riley would now legally be his medical advocate and could make decisions on his behalf. Of course, I would fight it, but the law is the law."

I continued, throwing my hands in the air, "What the hell were they even thinking? My son lied to me, not only about this reckless decision, but also about his health. He deceived Liam, and withheld the real reason to why he needed his medical file. To top it off, he was seeking medical advice from your ex-husband. That man hates me and my son. My son reached out to him for help. My son! What the hell? I am so angry right now, I can't even see straight."

Riley and Richard came into the waiting room shortly after. She nearly dropped the tray of drinks she was carrying after seeing me. Clearly, she heard my rant. Richard took the tray from her, and she made her way over to her mother and me.

"Mr. Reed!" Nearly knocking me over, Riley lunged herself into my arms. "How's Jackson? Can I see him now?"

"I'm afraid not, sweetheart. He's still unconscious."

"Please, Mr. Reed, I need to see him. I will be quiet as a church mouse. I just need to be near him."

"Riley, he knows you're here. Come sit down and talk with me, please?"

"Mr. Reed, I already know what you are going to ask me. I told mother everything. Now, I have to see Jackson."

"You will sit down, young lady, and talk with us," Reese said to her daughter. "I will not say it twice."

Always the reserved one, Reese had found her voice, surprising us both. Riley took her seat again and wrung out her hands in her lap. She was beside herself. We all were.

Chapter Sixteen

Riley

AS I SAT there in my father's waiting room, all eyes were on me. Mr. Reed was angry. My mother was worried. Richard looked defeated, and my father's assistant just shook her head at me. If I had the gift of reading minds, she was probably judging me on my adolescent behavior. Jackson was right. I didn't try very hard with my father today. I actually made matters worse by arguing with him.

If I would have stuck to our original plan and just allowed Jackson to speak, the situation we were now facing could have been avoided. My mother would argue that conclusion with me. She would always tell me that there are no absolutes in this world. Life is unpredictable like the stormy seas. You can have sunshine one minute and then the next a damaging Tsunami wave could wreak havoc and change your life in an instant.

I could never be accused of being too over melodramatic, but this was how I felt. Mr. Reed was my Tsunami, and I was about to take him on. I calmed myself the best I could and watched him sit beside me.

"RILEY, WHY THE marriage license? Were you and Jackson seriously planning on getting married? And without our knowledge?"

"It was my idea, Mr. Reed. He tried to talk me out of it, but I convinced him that we could marry, and then just simply tell you and mom when we returned to California."

"*Simply* tell us? Riley, are you out of your mind? What the hell were you and my son thinking? And, might I add, how could you think that I would ever be okay with this?"

I knew my tone was louder than I wanted it to be, but after her revelation, how could it not? Of course, the voice of reason stepped in.

"Walker. Let's take a minute to calm," Reese said, placing her hand on mine.

"This is calm. I want an answer to my question. Riley?"

Taking me by the elbow, Reese whispered quietly in my ear, finishing me off with a soft kiss to my neck. I let out my breath and gave her the look she needed to see. My eyes promised her that I would not lose my temper with Riley. She was Reese's daughter, but also the love of my son's life, who was so young and innocent. As angry as I am, I held back. I gave Riley a minute to calm down. I needed to hear it all, no matter what it cost me.

"Please, Riley, start from the beginning."

I held on to Reese's hand as if my life depended on it. Every once in a while, she would stroke me gently with her fingers to keep me steady.

"Mr. Reed, all I know is that when we arrived in New York, Jackson was experiencing some headaches. I discovered that he only had four pills left in a thirty pill prescription. I'm sorry Mr. Reed, but he lied to you, and to me. He had taken nearly the entire bottle within a week."

How could my son go through this and not tell me?"

NOW IT WAS Mr. Reed's turn to hold his head. He got up and paced my father's waiting room for a minute or two until he faced me again. I was expecting to be hit with many questions, but all he asked me to do was to continue with my explanation. I did with no hesitation.

"Jackson caught me with his pills and grabbed them away from me, once again scaring me. We argued. He completely shut down on me. I threatened to call you if he didn't tell me what was going on. He still stood there in silence and called my bluff. I was angry with him, and that's when I walked out of the room. I only made it as far as the bedroom where he found me. I was beside myself at that moment. I wasn't really going to call you, but I needed for him to start talking to me."

"He apologized. I cried. And then he held me in his arms. He finally told me that he had been experiencing headaches for a while now. He didn't want to worry you, Mr. Reed, not when you and mom were so happy. He thought that if he could side step Dr. O'Larien and seek out my father, you would never know. He told me that he didn't trust Dr. O'Larien to keep his confidence."

"Is this why you planned the ruse of deceiving Richard?"

"I wouldn't use the word deceive, that word sounds so much worse than it really was."

"Riley, no matter which way you spin it, you and Jackson both lied, and your lies have cost him his health. I should have been called immediately once you discovered he was having headaches."

"Mr. Reed, I couldn't do that, and I should hope you would understand why. He's my boyfriend, and I couldn't betray him like that."

"No, Riley, I guess you couldn't. But you could pretend to

threaten him and use *me* as a way to get him to talk to you, right? Does that sound fair to me and your mother? As his father, I had a right to know. Answer another question for me, where does getting married fit into all of this?"

"We knew marriage was going to be in our future, so I asked him to marry me. I didn't see why we had to wait. It would be a way to break free of the hold you have on him."

"My *what*!? What did you just say?"

GAUGING FROM MR. REED'S reaction, I knew I crossed a line. He wanted the truth, but I could have held back. The words just fell right from my mouth without any power to stop it.

I had never seen him so angry. I began to shake. My mother immediately tried to coax him out of the room, but he would not follow. His cold eyes bored into mine. Jackson was spot on about his father's reaction. I prayed that his bark was worse than his bite, but it was way worse. He broke away from my mother and stepped right up to me.

"My what?" he demanded again.

His jaw muscles were pulsating, clearly visible through his skin. I wanted to run straight into Jackson's arms, but he could not help me now. I was the one that was taking the verbal tongue lashing from his father. I tried to be strong and understand he was scared for his son. Mr. Reed had been nothing short of amazing to me. I should have listened to Jackson when he changed his mind. I pushed him, and because he loves me so much, he allowed me to do it. Mr. Reed raged on and directed all of his anger toward me. How much longer would this go on? The room was silent and filled with cold tension. He turned around and directly faced me now.

"Jackson is my son. I will always be a presence in his life. It doesn't matter how old he is, or who he is in love with. Don't you ever forget that. I resent it to hell that you are trying to come between us. He and I are connected for life. You had no right to persuade him to follow through with this ridiculous act of irresponsibility. You were right the first time. You should have followed through with the threat of calling me the minute you discovered he was sick. To make matters worse, you convinced him to marry you? You are both only eighteen years old! What a *grand* plan to break free from me, his father. Let me remind you of one simple fact…"

His words were chilling. Goosebumps lined my skin, and not the good kind.

"Over my dead, cold body that will ever happen! Do you understand me? Is that clear enough for your young, eighteen year old mind to understand? Or do I need to explain it in a simpler manner?"

Mr. Reed remained standing in front of me, never once blinking his eyes. All I could do was let my tears fall as my body trembled in fear. I thought I was going to wet my pants.

"Walker!" mom shouted. He ignored her completely. He was still staring me down. I was frozen and could not move.

"Walker!" her voice now louder. My mother was about to take on Mr. Reed in my defense.

"What!" He finally broke his stare and shouted back his response. When his eyes found hers, he softened, but my mother didn't. The battle lines had been clearly drawn out in the sand between the two of them, and it was my fault.

"I need to speak with you outside…now." She slowly enunciated every word and walked out.

As Mr. Reed turned away from me and followed my mother out of the room, I collapsed back onto the sofa. My tears fell and fell hard. All Richard could do was offer me a box of Kleenex, and Gretchen gave me water.

I had to pull myself together and take a few minutes for myself. I walked into my father's private office, locking it behind me. I was safe in here from the wrath of Mr. Reed. Sliding down his door with my arms wrapped around my knees, I cried and prayed to anyone that would hear me. *Please, God, take care of Jackson.*

Chapter Seventeen

Reese

B REATHE, JUST BREATHE. *He's out of his mind right now with worry, and not thinking clearly. Walker would never hurt my daughter, he's just sick with worry over his son. I know I have seen many sides to Walker Reed, but his actions today with Riley is something new and definitely not welcomed by me.*

"Reese, I—"

"Stop!" I scream, as I put both my hands up to him. "It is my turn to talk now! And you will damn well listen to me. What were you thinking speaking to Riley that way? She is my daughter! And she is scared to death. Your actions are not helping any of us, especially Jackson who needs you the most right now."

HER WORDS GUTTED me. Those were the same ones that Elizabeth had said to me.

"Are you going to stand there in silence? Or are you going to acknowledge what I just said? Aren't you the one always accusing me of shutting down? When can we get off this merry go around? I need you to talk with me and not lash out on any of us, especially my daughter."

I found the nearest chair and sat down before my legs gave out. Fighting with Reese is the last thing I want to be doing now, but she's angry...so angry with me.

"REESE, PLEASE SIT down. I know you're angry, but you getting upset like this cannot be good for the baby. Please...if not for me, then for our daughter?"

"What about my other daughter, Walker?" I asked him. "Doesn't Riley count too? She loves Jackson so much. She would never do anything to hurt him. What do expect from them? They are young and in love. When you love someone, you protect them at all costs. You keep their secrets without ever questioning as to why. You do whatever it takes to shelter them from any kind of pain or disappointment. Does that sound familiar to you? She is behaving no differently than how I was all those years ago with you. All I did was in the name of love for you and my family. In the moment, you see no other way out. All you want is to protect the one that you love. You sacrifice your own heart and happiness for the other."

I continued, "Riley is a dreamer. She leads with her heart. She sometimes acts before she thinks, but that's not for you to judge. Jackson is the one that has chosen to love all parts of her, including her spontaneity and zest for life. Those two young adults are exactly how we were. I know we joke about it, but they are, Walker, through and through. Don't you see it? The difference is that they will not repeat our mistakes. They will stick it out no matter what challenges life presents to them.

Say something, Walker. Give me a sign that you heard what I said."

"Only if you sit and get off your feet. I see the exhaustion on your face, Reese, please."

"I'm fine, Walker. Going round and round with you only fuels my energy, it doesn't exhaust me. Please don't shut me out. I'm sorry for coming down so hard on you, but you have to see what is happening here. I know you are upset over Jackson, but lashing out on those around you will not help anyone, especially your son."

I said all I could at the moment. I wasn't angry with him, I was just as worried. I pushed him far enough. I saw the pain in his eyes, as he stared at me. It was time to give him comfort and reassurance. He wore many masks to hide his emotions and to keep me at bay, I knew this.

I got up from my seat, and his eyes followed me, but not for long. I sat on his inviting lap and held my love close to me. He wrapped his arms around my waist, pulling me tighter against him. He was breaking my heart with his sadness. I ran my fingers through his hair and sheltered him the best way I knew how.

"I'm sorry, baby," he said to me. "Please forgive me. Don't leave me when I need you to breathe."

He needs me? Oh my goodness! If he only knew how much I needed him as well. Leaving Walker now would just destroy me. It would be like living in a constant state of darkness with no light on the horizon. This was his fear talking for him, and he was reaching out for anything to hold onto.

"I love you, Walker Reed. You have my heart…forever. Now stop this right now and look at me."

I cupped his beautiful face and kissed his lips, closing my eyes and letting his love wash over me. His strong arms caressed up and down my back. His tension slowly eased with each touch he placed on me.

"I love you, Reese. I love you, I love you, I love you. I'm sorry for my behavior back there. I just feel so fucking betrayed and hurt by Jackson. He lied to me, Reese, and it's been going on for I don't know how long. He can potentially have something seriously wrong with him, and he just shuts me out? How could he do this? This is what I can't come to terms with. Please, Reese, help me understand."

"Oh baby, I wish I could, but the only person that can answer these questions is Jackson himself. When he wakes, you can ask him, but, baby, you need to give him the time to tell you. Trust him to tell you the truth. It's there, believe me. Give him time to explain his reasons to you. The way you handle hearing those reasons will make the world of difference for the both of you."

No more words were needed to be spoken. Holding him in my arms was all I needed.

"Excuse me, Mr. Reed?" the nurse said as she came up to us.

Walker remained where he was. He didn't move and didn't talk. I nudged him, but his arms remained around my waist. I greeted the nurse. I could feel Walker's heart rapidly beating against my chest while I talked for him.

"I'm Francesca, Dr. Briggs' O.R. nurse. Dr. Briggs is still in Radiology but asked me to come find you. Your son has completely awakened now and knows you're here. You can visit with him now, and Dr. Briggs will be up here shortly."

Walker just remained silent, while I thanked Francesca for the update on Jackson. He didn't let go of me, so I tried again to nudge him to move.

"Walker, go see your son. I'll be here waiting for you when you get back."

"I can't. I'm not ready. What if I lose my temper in there? I can't do that, Reese."

"Listen to me. You will not lose your temper. You love that boy with every fiber of your being. You are an amazing father and would never hurt him. You need to listen to Jackson, no matter how much it hurts you. You need to move beyond what you think is betrayal. Once you truly understand his reasons, I know you will feel differently. I can join you if you wish, but I think you should go in on your own."

Walker looked at me for what felt like a minute without speaking. Then he said, "How do you do it, Reese?"

"Do what?"

"Look beyond all my flaws."

"It's because I love you, remember? I love all parts of you. Wasn't that our agreement?"

"It is and so much more. Thank you, Reese."

I was going to say something more, but then Walker knelt down in front of me and held his cheek to my stomach.

"Princess, it's your daddy. Forgive me for being an ass today. I love you, baby girl."

He slowly lifted my blouse and chastely kissed my baby bump until he completely marked me. I held onto his shoulders as he so openly loved me and his child. When he was ready, he slowly rose from the floor and continued to hug me.

With a final kiss to my forehead, I asked him, "Are you ready?"

"Yes."

We walked hand in hand on the path that would lead to Jackson's room. He took a breath before entering the private suite. I gave him one last reassuring smile for his confidence. Our hands detached, and he walked inside. I'd never seen Walker so bereft before, but then again, I wasn't around for those years he needed me the most. I wasn't going to allow my fear to revert back to our loneliest time when we were separated.

Leaning up against the wall, I took a few deep breaths. The reality of this crisis that we were all facing has just hit me. My shoulders felt heavy, and my head was spinning. I prayed I did my very best to help Walker. He still kept many parts of himself closed off. He was a creature of habit, and a hard one to break. I wasn't sure if I was dizzy because of the pregnancy, or the seriousness of the crisis we were now dealing with.

I silently prayed to the heavens that I wouldn't throw up. My plate was overflowing at the moment, and I couldn't pile on anymore. I rubbed my bump and talked to my little girl, but she had other ideas. Letting go of the wall, I began to walk slowly back to Riley, and that's when I felt my legs give way. I was on my way down to the floor, only to be caught by Samuel.

"Hey, are you okay? Talk to me."

For the first time in months, I once again saw the man that lovingly held my hand the first time we met. His eyes were soft, but filled with concern. I had no voice, and tears began to fall. *Damn hormones!* This put him on more alert. He picked me up in his arms and carried me to a spare room. I instinctively held onto him and was praying that no one saw my exchange with my ex-husband.

"Reese, your pulse is racing, and you appear to be a bit dehydrated. When was the last time you ate something substantial? If memory serves correctly, I'm sure you still think a bag of almonds or granola bar is a meal."

His lips slightly turned up, and I couldn't help smiling back at him. Standing before me was the Samuel I had always known, not the angry man of late. I couldn't blame him though. I was the one that left.

"I'm fine, Samuel. I have eaten today, but it was hours ago. I should eat now before I get nauseous. Let me just catch my breath, and I'm sure it will pass."

"Let me be a doctor and check your vitals. Your pulse should not be this high, and your blood pressure is reading 140/90. I want you to lie down here for a while and rest. I can check it again in twenty minutes."

"Samuel, I'm fine. I need to get back to Riley. Please just take care of Jackson. Do we know anything yet?"

"Reese, I *am* taking care of Jackson, and I was on my way in to speak with him when I saw you collapse. Riley is with Reed's two bodyguards, or whatever he considers them to be. She clearly is not ready for my comfort. I'm a doctor first, right? Wasn't that always our problem?"

He said his words sarcastically, but I knew the hidden meaning.

I always accused him of putting his hospital and patients before his family. To Samuel, I must have sounded like a hypocrite, because I was begging him to tend to Jackson, when he should also be a father to our daughter.

I remembered that I should position myself on my left, but my blouse raised and didn't go unnoticed by Samuel. His eyes went directly to my baby bump. I saw the obvious hurt lining his face, but he said nothing. He jotted down some notes on his tablet.

"Reese, I'm going to put you on an I.V. Drip with nutrients. It will help you get hydrated quicker, and your blood pressure should return to normal soon. Stay here, and I'll send a nurse in to get you hooked up."

"Samuel, wait…"

"Congratulations, Reese. You truly do have everything you've always wanted. And with the one man who has never left your heart. Too bad I wasn't that man. What is the old adage? 'To come full circle is God's way of returning your heart to its rightful place.'"

With pained eyes, he turned and walked away from me. He was clearly hurt upon discovering my pregnancy. After having a second miscarriage, to experience that loss was just unbearable for me. He was loving and supportive. He said we could try again, but I always said no more. I convinced him that I was done having babies and wouldn't risk another loss. He unselfishly got a vasectomy for my benefit. I truly loved and respected him for that decision.

To see me now pregnant with another man's child? Walker's child? He's got to be devastated. I can't come up with one reason why he should be okay with it. I rubbed my belly and tried to calm myself.

"It's going to be okay, baby girl. We've seen worse…much worse. Mama will not allow anything to happen to you. I love you, princess."

My eyelids grew heavy and began to close. I drifted off into sleep and dreamed of Walker holding our daughter.

Chapter Eighteen

I will not lose you

Walker

JACKSON HAD BEEN moved to a room located in the I.C.U. of Samuel's wing. The corridor I walked through contained only four rooms, with Jackson's being the last on the left. As I approached his room, I heard voices coming from inside. It was Riley. She must have sneaked in while I was with Reese. As much as I wanted to see my son, my feet felt heavy, and I was unable to move forward. I knew he was waiting on me, but I wasn't ready. I knew it was best to let him have time with his girl, so I willed my body to move away from Jackson's room. Once I was in the open hallway, I knew where I needed to be.

I entered the dimly lit chapel filled with the overwhelming pungent smell of burning incense. Candles were flickering all around me, no doubt from worshipers praying for the sick. I was about to do the same. I was alone and sat down in the pew. My eyes found His, and all I could do was stare up at the man on the cross, the one man whose followers flocked to when they needed help, implored him to take away their burdens, and made all the wrongs right in their lives. He would heal the sick and grant them the miracles they were praying for. If your prayers were answered, then he was a hero. If they weren't, then he was to blame.

I wasn't a religious man, never pretended to be. I always believed in what I could see, not what I couldn't. The universe had a way of really fucking with my psyche. How could I not believe when I was given the most amazing gift a man could ever receive…My son? My eyes found His again, and I said my words out loud this time.

"You did it, didn't you? You gave me my son, but took my wife. A life for a life?"

This room was meant for solace. What was I expecting to find here? Comfort or devastation? All I felt was anger at the moment. I'm angry with my son for lying to me when he should have been reaching out for my help. I'm his father! The one person he should always be able to trust and know will help him in any way I could. I would die for my son on any given day, and twice on Sunday.

"Why Jackson? Why him?"

I shouted at the man on the cross. Sinking lower down into the pew, I felt helpless and weak. *I am not familiar with these emotions. Having the utmost control is what I know, and yet it is nowhere to be found right now.* All I felt was a chokehold of something that I had no connection with at all, but I had to believe in it for the sake of my son's survival.

I stepped out of the pew and dropped down onto my knees to the hard floor. I laid it all out for the God before me and the two spirits that had been in my dreams: Elizabeth, who came to try to help and guide me, and my father, the dark one who haunted me from beyond the grave and demanded absolution for his sins.

"Elizabeth, are you here? Can you hear me? Please hear me. Don't take our son. He's mine! Do you hear me? He's mine, and I need him with me. Please don't take Jackson. I won't survive it, not this time. Losing you was hard enough. How can this be happening again? He's only eighteen years old. He has his entire life filled with an amazing future to look forward to. You were cheated. We were cheated. Our boy was cheated from knowing and loving his mother. We should have had more time. I'm so sorry, Elizabeth, that we didn't."

"He has loved you through the stories I have told him. You've always been where it counted the most, in our hearts. You were my best friend, my only true friend. The time we were able to share with one another is a time I will never forget. It can't be measured…just treasured. It gave us our son, our own piece of heaven, all seven pounds of him, swaddled in blue. Jackson is an extraordinary young man now. The best parts of us, Elizabeth, live on in our son. He still has so much to offer to this world. Please, my friend, I'm begging you. Give him the chance to prove it. Please, Elizabeth, don't take him from me."

"Please. Please."

"I beg for no one, but I will for my son. I will give up everything I own for our son. Please don't take him from me."

I was face down on the cold, hard marbled floor, reaching out for a sign from the heavens above, not expecting what I heard next. *Can fate be that cruel? Even at my darkest hour?*

I heard a voice. A man's voice. A familiar one that I despised. "What makes you think it will be Elizabeth that takes him from you?"

No! Please, not now. I don't think I can bear it. I clenched my eyes shut as hard as I could, willing him to go away, but I knew better. He was here…my father.

"Open your eyes, Walker," he calmly asked me.

I kept them shut. I refused to submit to him. *I am stronger than him, and I will break his hold on me.*

"Open your eyes, Walker. Every story has a villain, I'm sorry that I'm yours. Why are you in here? You should be with your son for the time he has left."

"No! Don't you dare say that to me! He's your grandson. How could you be so cold and cruel? I could take just about anything you do to me, but this is your grandson. You will not take another son from me, you fucking bastard!"

I was screaming at the top of my lungs, alone in God's house with a form of the devil challenging me to fall before him. *No way in hell! I'm stronger than that and so is my son.*

"Jackson will survive this, and he will live a full life, despite your prophecies about him."

"Not my prophecies, Walker. It's just his destiny."

"The hell it is. The hell it is. I will not let this happen. My son will survive."

"Forgive me, Walker. Free yourself from the chains that bind you. Free yourself of the pain and guilt you feel. Free me, please. Jackson needs you. Don't waste any more time hating me. Your son needs you more than ever right now, and so will your daughter."

His voice faded away from me, and once again I was alone in my despair. My knees and legs were numb from kneeling on the floor. My eyes found His again, and once again I was at His mercy.

"Is that what it will take? Forgive my father? I said I would do anything, so yes, I forgive you, Phillip Walker Reed. I forgive you for taking Reese away from me. I forgive you for the lies you told and the people you hurt. I forgive you. Is this what you want to hear? Because I will say it a thousand times a day if it means saving my Jackson. I forgive you!"

I was planted to the floor, screaming up to the cross with balled fists in the air.

"I forgive you! I forgive you! Here before God, I set us both free. Do you hear me father? You are free. Be in peace."

I dropped my head and hands to the floor, begging God to hear me…*Please hear me.*

I felt someone's presence behind me, as I slowly got up from the floor. My knees were shaky as I tried to regain my balance.

"Forgive me, sir, for intruding on your private time, but there is something you need to know." It was Richard standing at the entrance of the chapel's door.

"What is it? Is it my son? Is he…"

"No sir. It's Ms. Mitchell. She collapsed."

"What? Where is she?"

"She's on the same floor as young Mr. Reed, but on the other side. Dr. Briggs put her on an I.V. drip for dehydration. The nurse who found me told me that her blood pressure was escalated and needed to be monitored. That's all I know, sir."

"Take me to her right now."

"Yes sir, I'll show you the way."

First Jackson, and now Reese. I can't take much more today. *Please let our baby be okay,* I silently prayed to myself as we made our way to her room. I haven't done this much praying in all of my life. I was definitely one of the hypocrites that beg for divine intervention when needed the most.

"Richard, have you checked on Jackson?"

"I have, sir. He's comfortable and with Ms. Riley. He asked for you, but I said you were busy with the doctors and would see him soon."

"Okay. Thank you. Please go to his room and wait for me there. I'll be along soon."

Once I sent Richard off, I glanced at my watch. I had been hiding in that chapel for more than an hour, away from my family who needed me the most. I should have been with Jackson and Reese. I leaned against the door and took in a calming breath before entering.

Man the fuck up, Reed! Your family needs you.

"HI. WELCOME BACK." A familiar voice greeted me as my eyes fluttered open. It was Samuel's nurse, she was very kind.

"Hi. Fran, right?" I asked her.

"I prefer Francesca, but either one is fine. You don't remember me, do you?"

"Should I?"

"I guess not. We met under unfortunate circumstances many years ago. I was just beginning my career back then."

"I'm sorry Fran...Francesca, but I'm confused. How do we know each other?"

"I was working the E.R. the night you were brought in and lost your baby, and now I'm here with you again."

"What the hell?" I cried out. "Are you trying to tell me that I lost another child? Oh my god! You heartless bitch!"

"No, Ms. Mitchell, please calm down. Your baby is fine. I'm sorry I frightened you. I was just pointing out the coincidence of it all. I feel foolish."

"As you should be. How the hell can you sit here and reminisce with me about something that was so painful from my past? Get the hell out! Or I will have my security throw you out."

"Ms. Mitchell, I am so sorry. It wasn't my intention, please."

"I said...get out!"

I HEARD HER screaming as I entered her room.

"Reese, are you okay?" I bypassed the nurse and took Reese into my arms.

"Thank God you're here, Walker. I was so scared. I thought something was wrong with our baby."

"Is she okay? What got you so scared?"

Reese was shaking and her beautiful face was now tear stained.

"It was me Mr. Reed. I said something out of line, and Ms. Mitchell misunderstood."

"And you are?"

"I'm Francesca, I work with Dr. Briggs. I'm so very sorry. I didn't mean to scare Ms. Mitchell."

"Leave now. Do not bother us again, or I will have you removed from this building. Do I make myself clear? Or do I have to write it down for you? Get the hell out! You incompetent fool!"

I watched her quickly leave the room. I didn't give a shit about her feelings. She nearly collided with Dr. Briggs, who was standing on the threshold, as she made her exit. He appeared to be shocked at the scene he just witnessed and stood at the door, silent.

"Baby, just breathe. You're safe now," I said to Reese, caressing her arm.

"Walker, I'm fine. Don't worry about me. I just got scared for a minute. How's Jackson?"

"I haven't been in to see him yet."

"Why ever not?"

"I was about to, and then I heard Riley in there with him. He was stable, and I just wasn't ready to face him. Can you believe that? I was hiding from my own son. I've been in the chapel of all places."

"I believe you are just a father that is worried for his son, and nothing more. I'm better now and will go with you to see Jackson."

"Why are you in this bed to begin with? When I left you, you were fine. Please tell me that was true."

"Walker, I was fine. I guess the shock of today finally kicked in, and I was just worn out. I had no idea that I was dehydrated."

"I think I can answer some of your questions," Samuel said, as he popped into the room.

"Samuel. Is Reese okay? What happened?"

"She had a spike in her blood pressure and, along with being dehydrated, her body weakened. With the nutrients she has received, her levels are all back in normal range. Your baby's heartbeat is steady and very healthy."

I closed my eyes and thanked God for watching over my girls. I wasn't sure how to feel about Samuel knowing such intimate details about Reese, but was thankful for him for caring for them both. I wasn't ready to say that out loud, but I was thankful all the same.

"Reese, as long as you get rest and eat properly from this moment on, you should be fine. The stress of today was certainly a trigger for the effects to your system that followed. Now, I also have Jackson's test results. I'm ready to talk to him about it."

"Why don't you tell me first, and then we will see Jackson," I said.

"I'm afraid I can't do that. Jackson is of legal age, and I must disclose all my findings to him first. It will be his choice for you to stay."

"Like I will ever allow that to happen," I said. "You are out of your mind if you think I will be shut out of any conversation you have with my son."

"Calm down, Reed, I was just stating the law."

"Don't you know by now, *Briggs*, there is always a loophole when it comes to any law?"

We just stood there eyeing the other down. I knew I had just spent the last hour begging God for help, but when it came to Briggs, I just couldn't help myself. By the way he was looking at me, he knew exactly what I was referring to. He said nothing and walked out.

Reese spoke out. "Was that really necessary, Walker? Haven't we caused each other enough pain already? This is not the time to dredge up old wounds that are still healing. Let's go and see Jackson."

Reese placed my hand in hers and led me out of the room. I easily followed her. I would do just about anything for Reese. She was right. I shouldn't be doing pissing contests with her ex-husband. He wasn't the only one that still had open wounds.

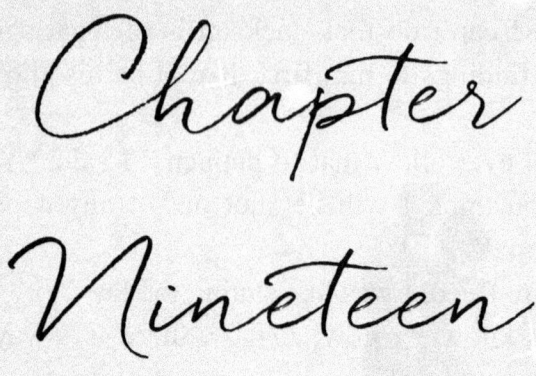

Chapter Nineteen

This changes everything

Jackson

AFTER FINALLY CALMING Riley down, she fell asleep beside my bed curled up on the recliner. Holding my hand in a tight grip, even in her sleep, she's strong. My father unleashed his wrath on her because he was angry with me. I wish he hadn't done that, but I knew deep down it was the calm before the storm. I should have never kept my worsening condition from him. *Did I actually believe I could pull this off without him ever finding out? I was fooling myself into thinking I could.*

Now I laid here in this bed and waited for him to walk through my door…

Ten minutes later, Riley's father, Dr. Samuel Briggs, entered with my father and Reese following close behind. I nudged Riley awake, and she immediately sat up. I gave her a reassuring look that I'm okay and not to worry. She tightened her grasp on my hand and turned to greet the others.

It's showtime! All I could do was wait for my father's reaction, but when my eyes found his, all I saw was pain and fear. His eyes were red and puffy, and he just looked beaten down. Reese was holding his hand and lovingly giving him support. He said nothing, just kept his eyes fixed on me. As tired as he appeared, I had never seen him this calm before. *Like I said...calm before the storm.*

They all had taken a seat, and Dr. Briggs addressed me first.

"How are you feeling, Jackson?" The obvious first question all doctors seem to ask.

"I'm good." With my father listening intently, I kept my answers short and to the point.

"I have your test results here, but before I begin, I need to make you aware of a few things. First of all, you are of legal age, and it is solely up to you if you wish for the others to remain in here while I give you your results. Do you wish for them to stay?" he asked in his most professional manner. I heard no malice in his tone.

My father didn't even blink. His eyes remained focused on me.

"Yes, Dr. Briggs, my family can stay."

"Very well. Okay, Jackson, let's start from the beginning. I have spoken to Dr. O'Larien, who is on his way here to consult your case with me. Your last scan was done September 2013. All your images came back clean. It says here in his notes from April of this year that you suffered a grade ten migraine. Is this correct?"

"Yes."

I looked toward my father. He knew now that I lied then and kept the severity of my headache from him. The first lie of many that I told.

"You were prescribed the drug called Fioricet to take orally for any future migraines. Is this correct?"

"Yes sir."

"This is a very strong medication. You should experience relief from your migraine within an hour of taking it. I see here you recently finished and filled another prescription for this medicine, Jackson.

Like I said, this medicine is quite strong, and it could pose risks to your liver and lead to other stomach issues. Were you aware of these risks?"

"Yes."

"Knowing this, you still frequently took it?"

"Yes, I did. Dr. Briggs, I have never felt any side effects from taking my migraine medicine or my anti-seizure meds. I'm fine. It's not as if I'm addicted to them. I take it because when my headaches are that bad, why suffer through the pain?"

My father still remained silent. His silence was beginning to freak me out. *Why isn't he saying anything?*

Dr. Briggs continued interrogating me. "This is exactly my point, Jackson: 'Why suffer through the pain?' Is this what you have been doing? Medicine will only mask the real underlying issue, and it is only a temporary solution. The scans we performed on you today show what you probably already expect. You have an AVM. It is what we call a grade one malformation between arteries and veins, and it is approximately three centimeters in size. We consider that to be small, but of course it comes with risk. You can see here on your films that it is located right above your Occipital lobe, which controls your vision. I can only guess when your migraines are at a pain level of ten, you have experienced blurred vision and surrounding pain around your sinuses. Am I correct?"

"Yes. It's more on my right side."

"As I thought, but now you have confirmed it."

"Okay. Now the AVM is intact. You have no others in your entire brain. This is good news. We can approach this from several different angles. Let me assure you on one very important detail. This is treatable. Once I explain all of your options, we can choose the best line of defense for this AVM. Now, we can treat it with drug therapy and radiation. The radiation will slowly shrink the AVM to almost being undetectable. You have no bleeds at this time. My only concern is your high blood pressure at the time you were brought in to the ER. Now your readings could have been elevated because of the seizure you endured, but, Jackson, this wasn't a seizure you are used to experiencing. This one debilitated you for more than the average five minutes or less. I chose to put you in a dream-like state at the time so your brain function could rest. The seizure you experienced could have made the AVM rupture, but because of its size, we were lucky that didn't occur."

"Dr. Briggs, what are the other options?" I nervously asked him.

"Surgery."

Riley gasped and her tears began to fall. She finally let go of my hand and rushed over to her mother, who comforted her. My father remained silent. *It's killing me to have him say nothing when all I expected from him was to flip out and be angry. I truly don't know what is worse.* We all take a minute with Dr. Briggs also consoling his daughter. For the first time since we have been here, I actually see Riley moving past her anger toward him and needing her father. Dr. Briggs kissed Riley on top of her head and came back over to continue speaking with me.

"Jackson, as of right now you are stable. All your vitals are back in normal range. Your blood work came back clean. You are young and strong. I see no immediate danger with this AVM, and we can take the time to decide your best treatment plan."

"What if I want the surgery? Can it be done right away?"

"Of course it can, but you must understand, it also comes with risk. This surgery requires going directly to the source, and in your case this AVM is located in a very intricate and delicate position. I would recommend performing a micro-surgical resection to remove the AVM. Once it is removed, it will not come back. We are very optimistic that once the AVM is removed, you will make a full re-covery and can return to your normal routine. You will have to be monitored in the future, but it will be no different than what you do now. Like I said, you are young and that is working in your favor. The only risk to speak of is loss of peripheral vision either on your right side or both. Time will tell through your recovery post-surgery progress if that occurs."

"You mentioned the other risk. What is that?"

"In case of a rupture, we would have to immediately operate on your brain to remove the bleed and prevent any other bleeds from occurring. As of right now, your scans present no immediate danger of that happening. I will also put you on a more proactive regimen for taking your prescribed medication. This will not be something you can just take when you feel the need, it will be regimented from here on out. Drug therapy only works when taken properly. You have time to think about this. I'm going to leave you with your family now to discuss it privately. I will be in my office to answer any additional questions you may have."

"Dr. Briggs, can I ask a question now?"

"Of course, Jackson, what is it?"

"If I decide on the surgery, can it be you who performs it?"

From the minute the words spilled from my mouth, I watched two very different men react to my question. Dr. Briggs looked over at me, then to my father, who was breathing fire. Dr. Briggs took a breath and focused on me once again.

"Jackson, you must understand this is a huge conflict of interest here. I would recommend that Dr. O'Larien perform your surgery. He is more than qualified to do so."

"What if I want you? You are the best, Dr. Briggs. I want the surgery. You are my only choice to do it."

"Let's just take some time, son. We can discuss it after you speak with your family."

He quietly stepped out of my room without saying another word. I looked over to my father, who remained silent. Reese let out a deep breath, as if she was holding it until Dr. Briggs was finished explaining his findings. I welcomed a warm hug from her. Pushing my hair away from my forehead, she kissed me and told me how happy she was that I was okay. I am not to scare her again. I simply just smiled at her. Richard patted my back.

I wanted nothing more than to hold Riley and comfort her. I know seeing me here scared her, but it scared me too. She knew I needed time with my father. She kissed me and promised she would be back soon. They didn't need to say any words. They all knew what was coming, and one by one exited my room. Reese was the last to go. She kissed my father and whispered something quietly in his ear. He nodded, and she winked at me as she left with the others.

My father was combing his fingers through his hair and finally took a seat next to me. He said nothing but held my hand and placed his head on top of it. I could feel his warm breath on my skin. I knew he was trying to calm himself before speaking to me. He wasn't the only one trying to keep it together. I was scared for his reaction. All I could do was guess until he actually began to use his voice. I broke first.

"Dad, please say something. I can't take it anymore. You need to talk to me. Yell at me. Throw a chair. Do something! Do anything, but no more silence. I would rather be screamed at than to sit here in this bed and face your silence for another minute. Please, dad, talk to me?"

His grip tightened on my hand, and now I knew what was coming next.

"Why, Jackson?"

The two words I knew he would say. These two words hold so much pain and disappointment behind them. I knew he wanted my answer, but what could I actually say that wouldn't hurt him anymore than I already have. My father always demanded honesty from me, and I never kept anything from him, until now. I felt sickened by the lies that I told. I convinced myself that I was actually doing something good by keeping him in the dark, but I was wrong, so very wrong. My actions have cost him, hurt him, and it was completely my fault.

HOW DID I get here? How did we get here? I'm sitting beside my son who is in a hospital being treated for the same thing that killed his mother. I am using every single disciplined tactic to regain control over my rapid breathing. To be here in this moment with Jackson is resurrecting all the memories that bring me back to the night I lost Elizabeth.

I stood watching my beautiful boy just look back at me with his glazed over eyes. His tears were threatening to spill over and down on to his face. I heard nothing but our two heartbeats and the sound of the machine controlling the medicine he was being given. His chest was rising and falling with every breath. I wanted to take him in my arms and just hold him, but I was afraid to. I never felt this way in all of my life, not even on the night Elizabeth died. To witness your child in this state was heartwrenching on a parent's soul. It is an indescribable pain that no parent should ever have to feel. It is the fear of losing him or her with no power to prevent it. It is the unknown fear that every parent possesses, but keeps their fear hidden quietly away from their child.

"I'm sorry, dad."

He blinked back his tears as he said it. I could barely hear my son's words above the whispering tone he used.

Swallowing hard before I answered him. I brought his hand to my lips and placed a chaste kiss on it. Closing my eyes, I asked him.

"Sorry for what, son? What exactly are you sorry for?"

"Dad. I…"

"How long, Jackson? How long have you been lying to me about your headaches? Why, son? I just don't understand."

"You know why. I'm so unbelievably sorry, dad. I can't even begin to explain how sorry I am for hurting you. I swear I thought I had a better handle on it."

"If that were true, you wouldn't be lying here in this bed right now, would you, son? After all the conversations we had about honesty, especially when it came to your health, you completely disregard my feelings and keep the one thing I asked you never to do. This is what I need to know and understand. Did you think of me at all? What it would have done to me to lose you without ever knowing why? How could you be so selfish? I've raised you better than this. In all the time I have had the honor of being your father, I am so hurt and disappointed in you right now. You have irrevocably broken my trust. I feel sick to my core that I feel this way, let alone saying the words to you. I'm your father. The one and only, who always has your back. How could you not trust me enough to come to me with this? I love you so much, son. To lose you would destroy me. I know I can say without question, I would not survive it."

I continued, "I would move heaven and earth for you, Jackson. You are my child. It doesn't matter how old you are. That promise of love and protection never ends. I will always put you first, above anything else. This is what parents do for their children."

"That's just it, dad. For once, I was putting you first. I can say this over and over again, and I know you won't believe me, but I am truly sorry. I never meant to lie or hurt you."

"Then why, Jackson? You never meant to hurt me? But you did! You, my son, hurt me in the most unimaginable way…You lied! Not just any fucking lie, but the one omission that would destroy me. I could take just about anything, but not this.

"I was protecting you, dad."

"Protecting me? From what? What are you not saying? For God sakes! Don't lie to me now."

"Pain, dad. From Pain! The look that you have in your eyes right now is what I was trying to protect you from ever having. I love you, dad, and I will say it again and again. It was to protect you, not hurt you. You already lost mom, and I didn't want you to be afraid to lose me. I may have not known her, but I love her just the same. She gave me life, and lost her own. How can I not understand what you went through? I lived it with you from the minute I was born. I'm still living it, dad. It's like the song that is constantly on repeat mode. From you, to the grandparents, to all who knew and loved mom: You all treat me like I'm made of glass. I am not fragile! I'm a man! I deserve to be treated like one, and not this helpless little thing that could break at any moment.

Jackson went on, "We're in the building that you designed and built for her. Sometimes I feel that I will never escape her tragic sto-ry…my fucking story. I want to write a new chapter in my story, dad. One that includes me marrying Riley. She's it for me, dad. She's mine, and I'm hers. I'm going to marry Riley Taylor Briggs under our tree in Big Sur, the same tree we carved our names in. I want babies with her. I can't wait to see her pregnant with my child. I want a career making movies. The wish list is very long dad, but I am determined to check off every wish one by one. You may think I'm way too young to even be entertaining all of these dreams, but I'm not. Age is just a number, and no one can tell me what I have in my heart and what I believe in."

"Do you want to know what I want most, dad?" Jackson contin-ued, "What I have always wanted? My wish is for you to be happy, to finally be free from your past. Free from the sad memories…just free. That's my story. All I was trying to do was change the outcome of what happened to mom, and not let that happen to me. You think I don't know or understand the potential dangers of having history re-peat itself? Like I said, I've played the starring role in this story all of my life."

My son went on, "I know you're upset because I lied, but dad, please try to see this from my point of view. It's the love I have for you that drove me to make the decisions I made. Call it selfish, call it anything you want, but it is the truth. And before you ask, every sin-gle day that I continued to lie, it ate me up inside. Even knowing that my secrets and lies of omission have led us here, I don't regret them. You've been through enough. I didn't want to be the one to cause you anymore sadness, especially when you are the happiest I have ever seen you. I need something from you, dad, more than anything I have ever asked for."

"Anything, son, you know this."

"Please, dad, I need your forgiveness just in case…"

That was it. My breaking point with Jackson. As much as I was fearful of losing him, he was fearful of losing me. Carefully and avoiding his I.V., I took him in my arms, and we cried together. As father and son, we never experienced this kind of connection until now. We were both clinging to each other for comfort.

"Shhh," I said to him. "Stop it, and stop it right now. I don't ever want to hear you ever say anything like that again."

Taking my son's face in my hands, I kissed the top of his head and looked directly into his beautiful eyes that matched his mother's.

"You are a Reed. Reeds are like no other. You are strong in mind and body. You will beat this. As your father, I promise to never leave your side. We will get through this like we do everything else in our life, together as a family. We are not alone anymore. Our family is growing, and you have a little sister on the way that will need you too."

"What did you say?"

"I don't mind repeating it, son. I said you have a sister on the way. Reese is pregnant and it's a girl. This news was meant to be a surprise for you and Riley, and this is why we made the trip out here."

"That's amazing news. I can't believe I'm going to be a big brother!" His happy smile soon faded, and I quickly squashed it.

"Jackson, look at me son. You are going to be here to see her be born. No more talk of 'what if' scenarios. I'm here, and we will get through this. We have people that love us so much. We will lean on each other for support. I promise to give you respect and put your feelings first. We have been a team for a long time now, remember?"

Answering me through his tears, he says "Yes, I do, dad. We are always a team."

"Good. Don't ever forget it. With your sister on the way, we are outnumbered with the women in our life, so stick it out with me, okay?"

"Okay. I love you, dad. I will never keep anything from you again, I promise.

"I love you more," I whispered, holding him once more and thanking God I still had him with me.

I think we both felt the weight of the world slowly fall off our shoulders. He should have never had to carry this burden on his own. *I'm here now, and I meant everything I promised. We will get through this together.*

"Dad, please don't be angry with Riley. She didn't know. When I told her, it was only a few days ago. She's pretty torn up that you don't like her anymore."

"Jackson, I was angry and I lost my temper, but how can I not love her? She's Reese's daughter, and the love of your life. I was just taken by surprise. When I found out about the marriage license, I just lost it. Son, I'm not going to sit here and lecture you about being young and question your feelings for Riley. You're in love, and it's a beautiful thing to see. But to make a decision to marry Riley now was just plain reckless. You have to look at all sides and what it would have meant, especially when it comes down to your health."

"My health?"

"Yes, your health. Legally, Riley would have been your next of kin, because in the eyes of the law, she was now your wife. She could speak on your behalf and become your medical advocate. If anything would have happened to you, and you were not able to make a conscious medical decision, that responsibility would have fallen upon Riley. This is what I meant about being reckless. Does she even know everything about your medical past? Judging by your silence and the way you are looking at me, I will take that as a no. We all need to have a long discussion about this, but right now you need your rest. I need to check on Reese. She wasn't feeling well before."

"Dad, I'm not finished talking yet. Can you answer a few more questions, please?"

I let out a long extended breath, and braced myself for what was next. "Okay, what's on your mind?"

"If Dr. Briggs agrees to perform my surgery, will you fight against my decision? You were uncharacteristically quiet throughout his entire explanation, and it was kind of freaking me out. I have never seen you so calm and reserved. Do you dislike him so much that you wouldn't want him to help me?"

"Jackson, my history with Dr. Briggs is complicated, as you well know. He's too close to the situation, and he still holds a strong personal grudge against me. I know he is probably the best in his field, but knowing all that, I am not convinced that he can so easily put his personal feelings aside. You are the patient, obviously, but I am the man his wife left him for, and you look just like me. Okay, there's more to it than that, but it pretty much sums it up. I can't take the risk. I'm sorry, Jackson, but yes, I will have a problem with your choice. Dr. O'Larien is more than qualified to handle your surgery."

"What if Dr. O'Larien assists? Will that change your mind?"

"Why are you championing Dr. Briggs? Is this because of Riley?"

"No, of course not. I want the best, and a Reed only gets the best. For me, my choice is Dr. Briggs. If I am truly to beat this ticking time bomb in my brain, then it's him. I will not settle for second choice. I have choices where mother didn't. I feel this is the best option for me, dad. You said you would respect my choices, so now here's your chance to prove it."

"You sure are a Reed, but I can't decide if you are me or sounding more like your grandfather at the moment. Jackson, let me be clear. Do not mistake my moment of grief and worry for weakness. I will not be topped. Respect goes both ways. When I received Riley's call about you being here, I thought my heart stopped beating. I was back to a very dark place in my life, and it scared the shit out of me. Until you are a parent, you truly will not be able to understand how I felt seeing you here, and in this hospital bed. It is an image I will not soon forget, if ever. Please give me time to process all of this and allow me to speak with Dr. O'Larien. Together, we will come up with an answer, okay?"

"Okay."

"Good. It's late, and you need your rest. Please close your eyes, and get some sleep. I love you, son. I won't be far away."

"I love you too, and I didn't think you would."

"Smart ass."

In light of all that happened here today, my son still managed to make me smile. As I exited his room, I looked to the chapel and considered going back in. They say prayers are always welcomed and you can never have enough. I would scream from the tallest buildings if I knew they would be answered. I had to trust the medical science of it all and have faith that my son would be okay. No room for doubts here, just positive affirmations to get him through this. I had never broken a promise to my son, and I would not start today.

I guess the hardest part of this entire mindfuck of a situation was that I knew deep down that Briggs was the best. *Can he truly put aside his feelings for me and focus solely on my son as his patient?* No matter what had happened between us all, even Reese still championed his surgical skills. He was a well-renowned doctor, an innovator in his field. Patients came from all over the world to seek his help when all others have failed.

Can I do it? Can I actually ask Samuel Briggs for help to save my son? I heard the words in my head, but to say them out loud would be like swallowing gasoline. He hated me. Knowing his feelings toward me didn't give me the assurance I needed to make this decision.

I was exhausted and desperate to be with Reese, but I needed to do something first. I quietly walked back into Jackson's room just wanting to take one last look before I left, and that's when I heard him praying and talking with his mother. I stepped out before he knew I was there. I had my answer and knew where I was headed next. *Please let this be the right thing.*

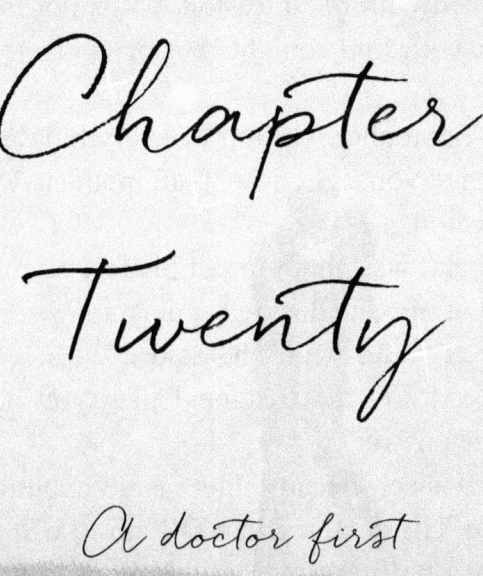

Chapter Twenty

A doctor first

Samuel

I HELD MY head in my hands in my semi-darkened office. Surrounding me were AVM case files covering my usually meticulous, custom Italian made desk. I was not used to disarray of any kind. It was abhorrent to me.

When I woke up this morning, I played out in my mind how the day would go: I would reconcile my differences with my daughter and once we were able to talk maturely, all would be righted between us. But I never imagined the turn of events that actually happened.

"How did today happen?" I asked myself, not realizing I spoke the words out loud.

"I'll tell you what happened. The golden apple doesn't fall far from the tree. He's here, and expecting you to fix him, which is exactly what you will do." Dr. Christopher McGovern said, as he popped his head into my office unannounced, enunciating each word he spoke.

Clearly agitated with his intrusion, I was not in the mood to go round and round with him tonight, but of course McGovern never took the hint.

"Not now, Christopher. On top of everything else I have going on, I will not engage you right now. I am inundated with papers here that I need to research."

He sat down and was about to put his feet on my desk. With the death glare I shot at him, he decided against it.

"That research could wait," he said. "We need to have a talk about Jackson Reed and the treatment plan you have in place for him. So what's the answer?"

"There is no answer, because there is no treatment plan for him, at least not by me. His doctor, Liam O'Larien, will arrive tomorrow morning at seven. I will turn over my findings to him, and I will be effectively removing myself from this case."

"The hell you will."

"Excuse me? You don't get to decide what cases I take on."

"Yes I do, especially when it comes to this one. As far as me and this hospital are concerned, you are his doctor now. If your patient wants this surgery, then you, Dr. Briggs, will perform it. Do I make myself clear?"

"Fuck you. Do I make myself clear? Who the hell do you think you are, speaking to me like that, Christopher? You barge in to my private office and make unrealistic demands of me. If I operate on this boy, it presents a major conflict of interest. And what about the ethics code?"

"That's a load of bullshit, and you know it. No code is being violated here. You just have a rod up your ass, because you are making it personal and using that to say no. You can't do that Samuel. Be the damn professional I know you to be, and do this surgery."

Running my hands through my usually perfectly in place hair, I sighed in frustration. "I just can't do it, Christopher. It has to be someone else. What if…"

"You're fucking with me now, right? You, Dr. Samuel Briggs, are actually doubting yourself? As long as I draw breath, I never thought I would hear those words come from your mouth."

"I didn't say anything, Dr. Exaggeration. You did. I'm too close to the players that are involved in this case. He is in love with my daughter…. my daughter, Christopher! Right there is conflict of interest number one. My ex-wife is pregnant and marrying his father. Right there, conflict number two. Do you even know how this feels for me? Or are you too busy suckling on the power teat of the millions of dollars that Walker Reed donates to this hospital? Fuck! You don't know shit, and you certainly don't care how it affects me. Get out of my office before I throw you out!"

I pushed away from my desk and went over to my cabinet where the hidden bar was kept.

"What are you so worried about?" Dr. McGovern asked me. "AVM's to you are like tinker toys for mechanics. You can operate on them in your sleep. You've got this. Hell, these papers you have strewn all over your desk here, half of them were written and published by you. What are you searching for that you don't already know? Do what's best for your patient, and fix him. He wants the best…You are the best."

"Stroking my ego is not what I need right now." I sighed at the fact that I had to explain myself to my friend. "Christopher, you just don't understand. And my friend, you are too obstinate to even try."

Swallowing my drink with one fast gulp, I sat back down into my chair, feeling defeated.

"I understand more than you know, Samuel. You have this boulder sized chip on your shoulder that you can't seem to knock off. It's weighing you down, layer by layer, and if you don't cut it the fuck loose and let it go, it will bury and consume you. I'm afraid it already has. I'm not your boss right now. I'm your friend, and I'm asking you to let *her* go. Find yourself again. He's in there somewhere, and I miss my friend. You got a raw deal. We both know it, but you are better off now in the grand scheme of it all. What is the saying, how does it go? 'It is better to have loved and lost, than never to have loved...?' Well my friend, screw that! I'll take being loved by the right person that loves and accepts me whole, and not just a part or two. Take all of me, or none of me. If I can't have that, then love can take a hike, because I deserve better. You my friend, deserve better."

"Christopher, are we still talking about me, or did we shift this conversation to you?"

"Fuck you. We are talking about you, and the pile of shit that you are carrying around. You dare call *me* obstinate? Hell, you invented that trait, not me. If you want to talk about my story, then I think we need to find an open bar that has no closing time."

"You know, McGovern, just when I thought I knew everything about you, you actually show me your human side. It's quite the revelation, if you ask me."

"Well, Briggs, I didn't ask, so shut the hell up. Don't go and blow sunshine up my ass. I do that enough for the both of us, and sadly, I do it well. Taking over as the hospital's lead on the board, I never thought it would be this way."

"Then give it up. Concentrate on being a surgeon again, if that is your true passion. Don't you ever grow tired of wining and dining the power players that fund your ambition?"

"Let's not forget, Samuel, the power players fund yours as well. Don't forget who paid for this wing. The King may have turned down our expansion proposal, but that didn't stop him from donating another two million for your...ambition. Excuse me, I meant to say, research."

"He did what?"

"You heard me, don't act so shocked. You all want the fruits of my labor, but balk at me on how I get it. Your gifted hands—your skill,—can only do so much. You still need the funding and equipment to make the miracles happen. Move on with your life, man. Let her go. Do the surgery."

Absorbed in our conversation, we didn't hear his subtle cough to get our attention. We both looked up at the same time to see Walker Reed standing on the threshold of my office. I remained where I was, while McGovern practically leaped out of his chair to bow down to his feet.

"Come in, Mr. Reed. We didn't see you standing there," Christopher said.

"Clearly," Reed said. His tone was clipped and by the look on his face. He wasn't in the mood to have his ass kissed right now. For the first time, I actually could relate to him. I didn't want to have the conversation I just went through either, but Christopher insisted.

"Dr. McGovern, if you don't mind, I would like a word with Dr. Briggs," he said as he fully walked into my office and moved closer to my desk.

"Of course, Mr. Reed. I'll speak with you in the morning. You have my numbers if you need anything. Good night, Briggs."

Raising my hands up to Reed, I knew what he was thinking. "Yeah, he's pretty much a weasel, but the guy has his moments," I said. "What is it, Reed? To what do I owe the honor of a once again unannounced visit?"

"May I sit?"

"Is that a serious question? Are you actually asking my permission to sit in my office? Has hell frozen over?"

"Look, Briggs, stop being a dick. I'm trying here. Are we really going to keep doing this? Or can we have a real conversation?"

"Have a seat. Scotch or Bourbon? I have a feeling you might need a drink."

"Bourbon, please."

"What's on your mind?"

"What isn't on my mind? I know you hate me and blame me for everything that ever went wrong in your marriage to Reese, but why I'm here has nothing to do with that at all. This is about my son, and I'm asking you—no begging you—to save him."

"Reed, what Jackson has is not life threatening."

"Today it's not, but you know it can be, don't you? Briggs, what happened to his mother can happen to him."

"Yes. Yes it can."

"Please Samuel, help him. I won't stand in your way. You can have anything you want, just please save my son."

As I poured myself another shot of bourbon, I never expected to see this level of emotions coming from Walker Reed. *The man behind the mask has let his armor fall down around him. He's not the mogul who swims in his billions. He's just a worried father that will sell his soul to the devil if he had to. I almost feel sorry for him.*

I replied, "A few months ago, had you asked me this same question, we probably would be having a different conversation here today."

"No, Briggs, I don't think so. You are a doctor first. I know your patients matter, even the son of the bastard you hate matters to you. My boy is just eighteen years old and has a ticking bomb in his brain, not active now, but we have no guarantee when it will be set off. I can't just sit back and do nothing. I can't lose him like we lost his mother. I never knew back then, but I know now, and all my power and resources can't do what you can. Please, Samuel, save him and give my son a chance at the life and future that was robbed from his mother."

"Is she happy, Reed?"

Shaking his head at me, he questioned, "What?"

"Is Reese happy? Really happy?"

"Yes, she is. I can say that with my whole heart that we both are."

"When I first met her when she woke up in the hospital with me holding her hand, she was scared, but beyond beautiful even in her darkest time. Just looking at her, my breath hitched and made my heart skip a beat. I nearly stumbled over my words when I had to be the one to deliver the devastating news to her. We couldn't save her child. Believe me, Walker, I tried and I failed. He was just so small and not ready to be born. She suffered so much blood loss, I had thought for a second that I may have lost her as well. Your son was my first loss, and to this day, you never forget your first. Watching her sleep in a twilight bliss was calming to my unsteady nerves. I never felt that level of emotion with my patients before. She just captured me. I knew I had fallen in love with her. I helped her through her grief, pain, and loss. I convinced her to move on and take a chance with me. Reese was easy to love, and she healed me in some way that I never knew I needed. It's a wonder our marriage lasted as long as it did."

I continued, and Walker listened. "She wanted children right away. I wanted to wait. My career was my life, and Reese was my most prized possession. She was right to call me out on treating her like a trophy wife, because that's exactly what she was. I don't know how my beginning feelings for her shifted into something else. She needed another baby to truly be happy again. I don't think she got pregnant to replace or forget her loss, I think it was just a need to feel whole again. The day Riley was born, I thanked God for making me a father. I was holding a six pound miracle in my hands. I had never been happier in all of my life. Nothing in my life since that moment has even compared to witnessing her birth."

"Now here we are," I said to Walker. "You get your second chance at fatherhood. You get your miracle with Reese. I look to my daughter whose eyes once held so much adoration for me, and now all I see is contempt. She loves your son and hates me. I think I need another drink."

"Briggs, I get it. I can see the hurt you are carrying with you, but I swear to you that your daughter does not hate you. She's young and confused with her feelings, but hate is not one of them. The night I met Riley, she sang your praises. She put you on this pedestal of God-like status. She said you performed miracles, and that's what you do."

He took a sip of his Bourbon and continued, "Look, I'm not de-luded into thinking we will ever be friends, but sooner or later we will have to find the middle ground here. Riley and Jackson are as real as it gets. We will be connected through them."

"As for Reese," Walker went on, "I love her Samuel. I never stopped. Hate me for the rest of your life if that's what you need to do, but please don't take it out on Jackson. You may not have been able to save our child all those years ago, but you can save my son now."

"Stop talking, please. I can't hear this anymore. I'll do the surgery. I'll do it because it's the best course of treatment for my patient, and it will eradicate the AVM."

"Thank you, Samuel."

"It's for him, not you."

"I know that, but it doesn't mean I'm any less grateful."

There you have it, I thought as I watched Walker Reed walk out of my office. *Deep down I always knew I would say yes, and to hell with the drama that surrounded us. I am a doctor first. I always have been. I can think of no other thing in my life that drives me to the precipice of satisfaction. I knew I was taking a risk to agreeing to operate on Jackson. If anything were to go wrong with his surgery, how would I ever be able to look my daughter in the eyes again? I had to stow away those fears, and put the needs of my patient first. Keep the personal feelings out of it.*

I left everything where it was on my desk and called my driver to take me home. I needed a shower and some sleep to clear my head. This day was like nothing I expected it to be, but it has already changed my life.

Riley thinks I'm a rock star, but I'm not. I am a doctor. I have a gift, an extraordinary one. I went into medicine with the sole purpose to heal. My strong determination drives me in my commitment to take on the most impossible cases and give my patients possibility and hope. As I walked by Jackson's room, he was sleeping soundly. I smiled and shook my head. There she was…my daughter curled up beside him, as if my staff could keep her away.

The sight of Jackson and Riley wrapped around each other made my heart ache. They were so young, and their future was filled with promise. I never had what they have. Reese never looked at me the way Riley looks at Jackson. Love was shining in her eyes, and he was all she saw.

I silently promised her that I would do everything in my power to make this right, no matter how much it cost me personally.

Chapter Twenty-One

Needing you

Walker

STRUGGLING AGAINST MY want to stay close to Jackson and my need to be with Reese was consuming me.

This day had been a blinding blur. I had no concept of time. I felt numb from it all. After receiving the one call I always feared may happen, I felt at that moment that all I valued in my life could be lost. One call had the ability to bring me to my knees and make me succumb to my fear, a fear I showed no one, until today.

Jackson was in the hospital, every parent's worst nightmare come true. No matter what safeguards I had in place for my son, they could not protect him from the unknown: the silent killer that was now in his brain.

I could question "Why" all day long. It wouldn't change a damn thing. The answer would still be the same. I could lose my son the same way I lost his mother. I had never prayed so hard in all of my life than today. I threw myself at God's mercy.

Do I deserve my prayers answered?

My list of sins was long. I'd made my share of mistakes. I'd been uncompromising and unforgiving of others. My father was cold and remorseless. In our world, he knew no other way. His decisions later had cost him more than he ever realized.

Phillip outlined his sins in great detail in his last letters written to me, words from the grave he couldn't say to me in person. Maybe he could have if I had given him the chance. I wasn't fair to him. I should have listened but allowed my buried grief for Elizabeth and thoughts of Reese to consume me. Those feelings made me cold. I was catapulted back to a dark place where no light was in sight. I was drowning…again.

In hindsight, he was too. From the moment he decided to put his plan in motion to change the course of my life, his true hell began. To be under Townsend's control must have slowly destroyed my father.

A man like Phillip Reed did not *follow*…he *led* with no regrets. He taught me that, and he showed me that life lesson every single day while he was alive.

I can't be like him.

I have to be better than him.

I have to fight against my anger for him and truly forgive my father. But how?

I vowed never to forgive him for all the pain he caused me and Reese. He doesn't deserve it and neither does Henry.

Wise souls like Lila Mitchell, who believe in forgiveness would tell me this: "Forgive them for you and not for them. Free yourself of the ones that hurt you most. Break free of your past, a past you have no power to change. Free yourself of the binds that twist in your soul and break them once and for all. Be strong and have faith." *If only…*

As I stood in that darkened hallway with little light around me, I stared through the window, watching my son. I saw one thing perfectly clear. He slept soundly with Riley's arms wrapped tightly around him. They were each other's lifeline.

I know who I am. I am Walker Phillip Reed, a man who is un-forgiving of his enemies. But can I truly change? Will true for-giveness help me, help my son? Damn if I knew. I'm too tired to even try to figure it all out tonight.

"Sir, are you ready?"

I blinked and realized Richard was standing in front of me.

"Sir?" he asked again.

"I'm ready."

Two words that could change me completely, two words that I need to say to the one person who desperately needs to hear it. Look-ing back once more to my son, I have to try for Jackson. No matter what it costs me.

We made our way through the private parking garage of Samu-el's wing. I slid into the backseat of my waiting car. I probably could have crashed into a deep sleep if I allowed my brain to shut down. Emotionally exhausted and physically beaten down with all that happened here today, I needed the one person who could help me fight my demons. I needed my angel…Reese.

"Has Stephen arrived yet?" I asked Richard through the divider.

"Yes, sir. He's with Ms. Mitchell back at the hotel."

"Take me to Reese. I need her."

As I voiced out loud my vulnerabilities where Richard could hear them, I just didn't care. I needed my half—my better half—to heal me.

I phoned Stephen, and he had already been given a status update by Richard on today's events. I knew that once I cleared my head, I would have to phone my mother, check in with my office, and call the one person I never thought I would have to speak with again: Henry Townsend, Jackson's only living grandfather. My son would want him and his grandmothers to know. Maybe I can have Jenny place the calls. I can't think of that now. I'll decide tomorrow. Hell, it is tomorrow. It's way past two in the morning.

I made my way through our suite. Reese was sleeping and look-ing beautiful in her dream-like state. I stripped myself bare and let the hot water scold my skin, washing away the hurt I was feeling. I was lost in my thoughts when the shower door suddenly opened, letting the cool air in, along with a hot body. My eyes roamed over Reese's gloriously naked self. I was hungry for her and wanted nothing more than to lose myself in her, madly take her up against the shower walls and make her scream my name. I wasn't in the right frame of mind and wouldn't risk hurting her.

The way her eyes were piercing mine, I knew I could easily do anything I wanted at that moment, and Reese would easily submit and lose herself too. While the water showered down on her body, I also saw a few tears. *Please God, I could take no more tears today.*

I wiped them away and more fell. My mouth closed over Reese's very plump and inviting lips. She hesitated at first and then granted me access to her warm mouth. Sliding my tongue with hers, my dick stood at full mast. She turned away from me and placed her hands up against the wall with mine covering hers.

"Take me, Walker. Take what's yours. Heal yourself. Heal me. I love you, Walker. I need you inside of me...now. I just need... You."

One touch from Reese, and she has the power to completely bring me down to my knees. I wanted her in my bed and with me above her.

I was raging against the battles in my head. *Only Reese can calm me.* I was weary, but alive with carnal desire and pure want for her. She was waiting for me to touch her, as I continued to struggle against my control.

Closing my eyes and still holding her, I whispered, "Not here. I don't trust myself."

Kissing the top of her shoulder, as I glided my hands up her arms and turned her around to face me, I said, "You are the only one that I allow to see me. You have all the power here. You have it all, Reese. What do you want from me?"

She wrapped her arms around my neck, inching closer and closer to me. Placing gentle kisses along my neck and a soft bite to my earlobe, she whispered, "Do you really have to ask?"

"Yes," I replied.

"I need to hear it. More than you ever know."

She was driving me insane with her teasing. Biting her lower lip and tempting me with her gorgeous body, her curves were defined. Her swelled breasts were calling out to me like a siren's cry. Her nipples were hard. My desire for my woman was overflowing. The smell of her arousal was chipping away at what was left of my self-control.

She again whispered in her sexy silky voice.

"You. Walker. Just you. Now take me to bed and make love to me. I. Need. You."

Chapter Twenty-Two

Needing him

Reese

I COULD TELL by Walker's body language, he was struggling. I needed to lead him where his heart and mind wanted to go. He wouldn't say the words out loud, but I knew he was giving me the control to show him the way.

Our eyes were locked on with one another. He never looked away. Taking his hand in mine, I turned and exited the shower with Walker following. I reached for a towel to dry him, but he stopped me and took the towel from me. With no words spoken yet, he began gliding the towel up and down my body until I was dry, ignoring his own body to take care of me.

It was my turn to help him. I took my time with this simple act. Beads of water still remained on his skin, as I worked my way over and over his glorious body. He shuddered at my touch. I knew my teasing was affecting him. Stroke after stroke, I worked up and down his body until he was completely dried, but I purposely ignored his chest. This would send him over the edge. I lapped up the few droplets of water that remained around the flat disks of his nipples, biting down just a bit to awaken my man's desires. He let out a feral growl, and I knew what would come next.

I COULD TAKE no more.

"Enough," I shouted out.

Her eyes brightened. Reese knew exactly what she was doing to me, and now it was time to show her.

I carried her over to the bed and gently placed her down. She had been sick today. I knew I had to be careful with her, but Reese was beyond tempting. She began caressing her golden skin with her hands slowing reaching her entrance. I could take no more as I slowly entered her throbbing sex with my tongue.

She let me hear her, and with no restraint. Her cries of pleasure continued to ignite my desire for my woman. Reese was beyond excited. She was soaked with arousal. Her juices were intoxicating, and I wanted more. Two fingers separated her pink folds. I made my way deeper and deeper inside of her. Her sex tightened around my fingers, as her orgasm rocked her body. Her body was trembling, I wasn't done yet. I took a breath before entering her again with my tongue lapping up all of her juices. I flicked her clitoris one more time, causing Reese to completely shatter around me. Screams of satisfied pleasure resonated throughout our suite. We were slicked with sweat. I could taste her all night with no end in sight. God! She was beyond captivating. Reese was all I wanted.

I broke free of her embrace. My animalistic need for her was completely decimating me.

"Walker, Please. Why are you pulling away from me?" Her dejected eyes were piercing me like a knife.

"I don't want to lose control and hurt you. Baby, you were sick today and dehydrated. I was neglectful of your needs as well as the needs of our baby. You will never know how sorry I am for not being there for you both today."

"What? Oh Walker, you are breaking my heart," she whispered. Her words just broke me. I went to move, and she reached for me.

"You didn't neglect me or our child. Your child needed you today. Jackson needed you. Don't you ever apologize for you being a father. And as for hurting me? Look at me, dammit!"

She was now on her knees and holding my face in her hands.

"Look. At. Me. I. Love. You. I. Trust. You. You could never hurt me. Don't you know by now? You were the one that put me back together again. Now make love to me and make us both…whole again. I need you."

Reese was my Aphrodite, my beautiful goddess filled with beauty, raptures of sexual want, and love all for me. I took what was mine, over and over again. I entered her slowly until her fingernails clawed up my spine. She screamed out for me to go faster, harder, deeper. I could feel our bodies reaching the edge of our explosive orgasms. I loved coming with Reese. Our bodies were entwined, slicked in our juices and sweat. I stayed connected to Reese until I had nothing left to spill into her. I couldn't move. I swear I had to check to make sure she was still breathing. I knew I worked her over harder than I should have, but Reese took all of me with no hesitation.

Rolling over to my side with Reese in my arms, I whispered. "I love you." She smiled and returned the three simple words back to me. I watched her drift soundly into sleep. When I knew she was out, I detangled myself from her embrace and walked into the bathroom to get another towel. I gently and quietly cleaned her up and myself before getting back into bed. Her body shifted with her arm reaching out for me, feeling my absence.

I knew she was wrecked and needed sleep. I did too, but I wanted to watch her, to listen to her breathe, just be close to her. If I had to be addicted to anything, she was my drug. I craved her day and night. How did I ever survive all of those years without her in my life? It didn't matter. I couldn't revisit those thoughts. We promised each other we wouldn't do that anymore. I had her now where she belonged…in my arms…. forever.

What felt like feathers against my skin was Reese's long hair tickling and brushing up along my face. I opened my eyes to see her staring back at me. Tucking her long locks behind her ears, she kissed me and smiled. A perfect way to start what I knew would be a tough day.

"Good morning, beautiful," I greeted her.

I pulled Reese down to me, giving her a proper kiss.

Breathless, she whispered, "Good morning to you. Did you manage to get any sleep?"

"A couple of hours. Don't worry about me, baby. I can manage with less sleep than you can. You are the one that I'm worried about. All of this stress is not good for you or the baby."

"Walker, how many times do I have to tell you? Yesterday was just a small mishap. I am completely fine and so is your daughter."

"*Our* daughter. I wish you would stop trying to placate me and allow me to take care of you and our child. It's my job, Reese!"

"Hey, hey, now where did that come from?"

"I'm sorry. I'm sorry. I'm just completely beside myself here. I hate this feeling of helplessness. I can't help you, I can't help Jackson."

"Walker, I'm going to say this one more time, and you damn well better listen. Pissing off a hormonal pregnant woman is not in your best interest, so heed my warning. Stop with this self-deprecating attitude. You, Walker Reed—all of you—makes me whole. I love you with all of my heart and soul."

She grabbed my hands and perfectly placed them where our child was growing. It sent electric pulses throughout my body. Once again, Reese saved me.

"We love you, Walker. We need you. You. Are. Our. Everything. I love you. I love you. I love you," she recited over and over again, chipping away at my very existence. I lived and breathed for

Reese.

"I love you more, so much."

"Impossible, but I love hearing you say it."

I made love to Reese, as the early morning day light filled our room. She needed me as much as I needed her. I probably could have fallen asleep and remained in bed for the rest of the day with Reese, but I knew we needed to get to the hospital.

After our lovemaking, I checked my phone and read a text message from Liam, my friend and Jackson's doctor.

Liam: *Walker, I'm here at Johns Hopkins. It was a horrendous flight with all the delays due to the storm. I've only just arrived, so no need to rush. I am currently reviewing all of Jackson's labs and films. I haven't met with Dr. Briggs yet or Jackson. Talk with you soon.*

It was only six thirty. I truly was exhausted, but I wouldn't be telling Reese. She had her eyes closed, but I knew she wasn't sleeping. I held her as close as I could to me, breathing in her beautiful scent of jasmine flowers and our sex.

"Reese." I whispered close to her ear.

"Hmm?" She smiled, but kept her eyes closed.

"Can I ask you a question?"

Shifting in my arms, she answered, "Of course you can, and you know that."

"Even the hard questions?"

"Walker," she said with a warning, "ask me. Don't dance around it. Talk to me." Now she was fully awake and waiting on me to open up to her.

"I'm sorry I'm being so vague. I don't mean to be. With everything happening with Jackson, my mind is all over the place. Reese, something has been weighing on my mind, but I guess it really didn't hit me until now."

"Okay, what is it?" she asked.

Taking a deep breath and bracing myself for whatever reaction Reese would give me, I finally found the courage to ask her my question.

"Reese, if our son would have lived to be born, would you have told me?"

"Oh Walker, I think you know the answer to that."

"Please tell me, Reese. I know my father changed the course of your life, but I have to believe that you wouldn't have allowed him to stop you from me meeting our child."

"Walker, you're right about one thing. Yes, your father changed me and our life as we knew it. Losing our son was me hitting rock bottom. I had nothing left. Empty and broken, I didn't see any light in my future when I was told he was gone. Losing our baby meant you were really gone too. After my breakdown, I picked up the broken pieces of what was left of my life and started over. You know what happened next. I was determined to reveal the real truth to you. By the time I arrived in New York that was my goal. I had to find you and tell you everything. It didn't matter that you were with Elizabeth. That was never a factor in my mind. If I had the power to go back and relive that morning when I walked out of your home, believe me Walker, I would. Our life, our future, our baby meant everything to me, and yes I would have moved heaven and earth to reunite you with your son if he had lived. I swear on my life that is the truth."

"I'm so sorry, baby. I'm so sorry that motherfucker ever hurt you. God!!! I'm so fucking sorry."

Reese wrapped her arms around me and cried with me until we had no more tears to shed. If I was ever truly going to forgive my father, I had to allow myself to feel her pain, my pain, and his regret until it was completely gone.

"Reese, I'm sorry. I know I promised you, but I had to know."

"Stop apologizing. There is no time table on grief. If this is what you need to do to finally be free of these ghosts that you are still carrying with you, then please let me in and don't ever shut me out. I meant what I said to you, Walker. We can heal each other because our love is strong enough. We will get through this together. We will get Jackson through this. We will marry and welcome our daughter into the world. We will do all of those things…together. I love you, Walker Phillip Reed. Now kiss me."

"Yes ma'am. Never piss off a pregnant woman, right."

"Exactly right." I kissed Reese with all the love I had in my heart for her. Holding her for a few more precious moments, she whispered something I didn't expect to hear.

"About our son…I would have named him 'Thomas Mitchell Walker Reed.'"

A lone tear fell down my face as I took in her words. All I could do was hold her, love her, and simply whisper back…, "Thank you."

Chapter Twenty-Three

The day after

Jackson

A FEELING OF warmth surrounded my body as I slowly awakened. Riley was wrapped around me like a constricting snake. Through the night as I tried to move, her hands would instinctively tighten around my waist. She never opened her eyes, but I could almost read her mind: *Don't even think about moving, Jackson Reed.* The thought of her scolding me brought me to silent laughter. She was so protective of me, as I was of her.

My headache was completely gone, and I felt so much better. Yesterday's events were a blur, except my father's reaction to my deceit. He viewed my lies of omission as betrayal, as I viewed them as protection.

It was all out and in the open. I could do nothing to change it. I suspected something was wrong, but I never thought I would be told that I had an AVM in my brain. That was my father's fear, not mine.

I never allowed his fear of the unknown affect me. He had gone through hell losing my mother. I would never tell him how to feel.

I will admit that his overprotectiveness suffocated me at times, but it was something that I grew to accept. I knew it came from his need to always have control. This was my father. I knew how his mind worked. I was fooling myself in believing that I could truly keep anything from the long arm of Walker Reed.

He promised me that we were okay. We were always okay. I silently prayed that he meant the words he promised me. *I won't be able to fight this without him. I need my father. I need Riley. They are the most important people in my life. No more keeping secrets from them. They love me, and I love them back. They will get me through this and my angel above me. This I know to be true.*

Riley was beginning to wake, her body rubbing up against mine. Of course she picked the most awkward time to do so. I was sporting my morning wood. It was tenting under my hospital gown and at full salute. How freaking embarrassing. We've been sharing a bed since we began our summer adventure, but I've always respected and not pressured Riley into anything she wasn't ready for. It was usually Riley doing all the pushing.

Before we left California, my father had me join him in his study for "The Talk," like we didn't have that conversation a thousand times before. He knew I didn't cross that threshold with Riley yet, but he still gave me his fatherly advice. I sat there and endured a thirty minute torturous lecture. He wanted me to think with my head and not the one between my legs. Oh my goodness! I wanted it to be over, but I remained planted to the seat.

All I could do was promise my father that he could trust me with Riley. I would never disrespect her, this he knew, but I also knew the unspoken meaning of our talk. He wanted me to be safe and not only protect myself, but Riley. We had college to look forward to. The next four years would be challenging enough without any unexpected surprises we weren't ready for.

I don't know what made me think of that, but now I realize that advice may have been a bit hypocritical on my father's part. He did, after all, get Reese pregnant in their senior year of college. I couldn't imagine Grandfather Phillip treating my father with kid gloves the way my dad treated me. No matter, Riley and I have not reached that point yet in our relationship.

I wanted to make love with her so badly. I wanted to make it special for her, and this hospital bed was not the place I wanted to have our first time in.

"Riley, time to wake up."

I nudged her. She smiled, keeping her eyes closed. She must have felt my erection up against her. She was only wearing her shirt and panties under my blanket. I needed to get her up and dressed before our parents arrived. That would have been the last thing I needed to be explaining today!

"Good morning baby, and good morning to you too!"

Did she just say good morning to my dick? Yup, she did. Her hand was now wrapped around it and was giving me a hand job.

"Riley, please stop. We can't do this here."

"Shhh, this is a private room, and no one is going to come in without knocking. Let me take care of this for you."

She kissed my lips and made her way down toward my throbbing dick. Her one hand was cupped underneath my balls as she took me into her mouth. We've both pleasured each other orally, but have never completely gone all the way yet. *I can't believe I am allowing her to do this to me, and here, of all places.*

"Riley, please stop. I don't need your father or mine to catch us and in this compromising position. Oh god, that feels so fucking good!" I cried out as she worked me over and took all of me in her mouth.

Of course my natural instincts kicked in, and my hands went to the sides of her head. I tangled my fingers in her hair and just allowed myself to enjoy the pleasure Riley was giving me. I was so close to my release, but I never came in her mouth. That was something I didn't think she would be ready for yet, so I tried to pull away at my climactic moment but Riley clamped down and took in all of me. I couldn't hold back any longer.

Riley lapped up every last drop of me until I was clean. This intimate act we just shared was something I never expected her to do. Once again, she was the aggressor and full of surprises. Once I was tucked back into my briefs, she worked her way back up my body. Her lips found mine where I could taste myself on her.

"*Now* it's a good morning. I love you, Jackson."

"I love you too, so much baby."

Before I could say another word to her about what just happened here, she put her fingers to my lips to silence me.

"It's okay, Jackson, I promise," she said. "This was something I needed and wanted. Please don't give it another thought. Just wait until I fully take you. I'm going to rock your world, baby. I love you."

With those parting words and one last kiss, my very hot girlfriend bounced out of the bed and into the bathroom. My head was spinning in a thousand directions, but it was not due to any headache. Riley Taylor Briggs never ceased to throw a curve ball at me. *She just gave me a blow job and didn't even bat an eyelash. Not question her? How could I not? Oh my crazy girl. I love her so much, and the minute I am able to do so, I am definitely returning the favor.*

The knock on my door brought me out of my sex crazed thoughts.

"Come in," I called out.

"Good morning, Jackson. I'm Francesca. I work with Dr. Briggs."

"I remember who you are. Good morning."

I made sure to pull my blanket up to my chest. I suddenly felt exposed as if she knew what Riley and I were doing moments ago.

"Dr. Briggs will be in shortly to talk and to examine you. I'm just here to check your vitals. Is that okay?"

"Of course, it's your job, right?" I didn't mean to sound curt with her, but that's a stupid question.

"It's one of my jobs, but thank you for pointing that out to me."

Smart ass! I thought. Something about her just didn't sit well with me. I allowed her to take my temperature, blood pressure, and ask me question after question. I knew this would all be repeated once the doctor arrived. I knew my father would want everything repeated twice on me.

"Okay, Jackson, your blood pressure is excellent with a reading of 120/80. Any questions for me?" she asked.

"I'm good. Thank you."

Just as Francesca was gathering her things to exit, Riley bounced out of the bathroom. She was freshly showered and looked beautiful with her rose colored cheeks. Ignoring the nurse completely, Riley grabbed my face and crashed her lips onto mine, kissing me soundly.

"Good morning, baby!"

"I think we already established that it was a good morning, don't you agree?" I playfully asked her. She winked.

"Well, you never can have too many good mornings, right?"

"I guess not. Riley, we are not alone in here."

I flipped my chin upward at Francesca, who was patiently waiting for our little love fest to finish. I didn't care one way or another. After what I put Riley through yesterday, I allowed her to have fun. After another quick kiss to my lips, Riley remembered her manners and greeted the nurse.

Riley said to her, "Hello…and you are?"

"Francesca, my name is Francesca De Luca. I work with your father."

"Hi. Forgive me for how this sounds, but I don't remember ever meeting you. And I know the entire staff here, especially the ones that work closely with my father."

"No worries, I assure you. Other than last night, this is our official introduction. I worked with your father many years ago when I was just beginning my career as a nurse. I've only recently trans-

ferred here to Johns Hopkins. I wish we were meeting on better circumstances."

"Oh? And why is that?"

"Your father and I have been seeing each other. I was hoping we
would have a chance to get to know one another."

"Excuse me? You're seeing my father? As in dating him? This
is unbelievable!"

Francesca responded, "I'm sorry, Riley, but what's so hard to
believe? Your father is finally with someone that cares about him. I
would think you would be happy about that!"

"Oh my god! I can't believe what I'm hearing. Who the fuck do
you think you are? You bitch!"

"Riley! That's enough," I screamed. I had to break up this alter-
cation before my girl completely lost her shit with this nurse. Before
Francesca could respond, we all turned to see a very angry Dr.
Briggs standing in the doorway.

"Ahem," he loudly cleared his throat. "Good morning, Jackson.
Riley." That was all he said, as he turned to face Francesca.

"Will you two excuse me while I have a word with my nurse?"
he politely asked.

Riley was clearly angry and once again shot daggers at her father, no doubt to the revelation just delivered to her.

"Of course, Dr. Briggs, take your time," I said to break up the
obvious tension in my room. *As if I don't have enough to deal with
already. Now another fire I have to put out.* I silently laughed to myself. *My father hasn't even arrived yet, and the fireworks have already begun. I'm beginning to think this wasn't one of my smartest
decisions coming here.*

"Riley," I called out to her. She was completely ignoring me. I
called her name again and snapped my fingers to get her attention.

"What?" she shouted, and then immediately her beautiful face
showed regret. "I'm sorry, Jackson. I didn't mean to raise my voice.
Is your head okay?" she nervously asked.

"I'm fine, baby, and I'm not that fragile just because you raise your voice. Come up here and talk to me. What's going on in that head of yours?"

"I'm fine, Jackson. I don't want to talk about it."

"Come on, Riley. You think I don't know you by now? You are practically foaming at the mouth. Now one more time, talk to me."

"Who the hell is that whore who has sunken her claws into my father? After all the bullshit he put my mother through, he's been secretly dating? I had suspected something after he got back from London, but I wasn't sure. I want my father to find happiness again, but not with *her*. I can't believe the audacity of that woman, just waltzing in here and behaving as if she knew me and could talk to me about my father like that? I don't care what role she has here at this hospital. I don't like her. I don't want her near you, and certainly not with my father."

"Wow! That was a mouthful. Why don't you tell me how you really feel about Francesca?"

"Ugh...her name is *so* stupid." Riley couldn't resist and began laughing.

"Just think, my dad will be here soon," I said, sarcastically. "The day can only get better."

She looked back at me with wide eyes, a little nervousness to them.

I tried to reassure her, "Don't worry baby. We will be okay. We are always okay."

Chapter Twenty-Four

Blindsided

Samuel

LEADING FRANCESCA AWAY from the surgical suite to my private office was no easy task on my part. I was seething with anger and hanging on to the last thread of my self-control. This was not the place to have this conversation, but her actions left me no choice.

Ignoring my assistant Gretchen as she called out to me, I entered my office, slamming the door behind me. I took off my lab coat and almost threw the files I was carrying, choosing to place them on my desk instead. I buzzed Gretchen to tell her to hold my calls.

I took a seat behind my desk, leaving a now safe distance between Francesca and myself. I had never been so angry with a colleague before until right now.

"Samuel, before you say anything, please let me…"

"Be quiet! Take a seat. You said more than enough this morning. You will now listen to me. Am I making myself clear to you,

Nurse De Luca?"

"So, it's 'Nurse De Luca' now?" she said in her usual smartass tone.

"In here, yes it is."

"Too bad it wasn't when you were fucking me up against the wall. You remember that, don't you?"

"To answer your question, I wish I could forget that moment, because it was clearly a mistake and poor judgment on my part."

"The hell it was, Samuel. We shared more than just a quick fuck, and you know it. Why are you being like this toward me?"

"Francesca, your behavior this morning was completely out of line. You were in that room to be a nurse and a nurse only. Here at Johns Hopkins, what we do here we take very seriously, and you work for me. I will never have my reputation tarnished because of the rude and infantile behavior you clearly demonstrated today. I have never witnessed such a gross display of unprofessionalism until today with you. What the hell were you thinking, confronting my daughter! And to add insult to injury, you do it in front of Jackson Reed. As if I do not have enough to deal with knowing who his father is. Care to explain to me why you did this?"

"Oh, I can speak now? I thought I had to sit quietly and behave like a good subordinate with my mouth shut."

"Francesca, you really do not want to play this game with me. Do you? My patience is running out. Now, answer my question. Why did you do that?"

"If I displayed any unprofessionalism for my actions this morning, I will accept any corrective actions that you feel are appropriate. As for making it personal, this I will not apologize for. You, 'Dr. Briggs,' have been stringing me along since London, and I don't have a clue as to why? I thought after what we shared in London, we were going to move forward and publically announce our relationship. What happened to that?"

"Your definition and mine on this matter clearly mean two different things. Francesca, in London, we were two consenting adults that met at a conference, had a few drinks, and had sex. What did you think it was? True love? And now you are going around not only confronting my daughter, but also my ex-wife? You are out of control, and this behavior stops today."

"If I'm out of control, it's because of your actions, not mine. You have my head spinning out of control. I'm only acting like a crazy, jealous stalker girlfriend because you have shut me out. I have been there for you since we reconnected in London. I have supported you through your divorce. I've tried to help you with your therapy and with reconciling with your daughter. Now that the ex-wife and your daughter are now suddenly here, I'm nobody to you? How the hell do you expect me to feel?"

Francesca continued her rant, "I will not be used. And don't think I didn't hear your daughter's comment about me, as you dragged me from her boyfriend's room. I am no whore! And I will not be treated like one. If anything, your little princess deserved a slap across her face for that. I would have thought she was more graceful than that. The way you talk about her mother and her, all I imagined in my head was perfection. Now I see she's just another spoiled, selfish little daddy's girl not getting her own way."

"Enough!" I screamed, slamming my both hands down to my desk. "This conversation has gone way off course, and it stops now. Francesca De Luca, you are hereby off my surgical service. I expect all my patient files returned to this office within the hour. Am I clear?"

"Yes sir," she answered with no fight left in her voice, having been replaced with feeble cries.

I knew I had just shredded her. It didn't sit well with me to hurt her, but I wasn't a man to be challenged and pressured, especially when it came to my personal life. This was about work and work only. She was an amazing nurse when her head was in the game. I couldn't have her flying off the handle in a lover's quarrel because I couldn't measure up to her timetable.

I gathered my files and didn't look back at her as I exited my office. Passing Gretchen without a word spoken, I slammed out of my wing. *Dammit!! This can't be happening, not today. I have the biggest case of my life right now, and I need to focus all my attention on Jackson, nothing else.* I've yet to meet with Dr. O'Larien, and no doubt Walker will arrive soon with Reese in tow.

I climbed the stair access to the roof. By the time I reached the top, I was out of breath. I needed to clear my head and all I kept coming back to was Francesca. I hate myself for how I had spoken to her, but the tigress certainly gave it back to me. She could fight, that's for sure. She wasn't entirely wrong. We did share a connection in London, but I never promised her anything in return, I thought she understood that. Everyone in my life seemed to want me to just forget the life I was leading a few months ago and just magically move on without a care in the world. Christopher to Francesca, and even Reese all think that. But how can I? How can I just let it all go and take a chance on love again?

I pulled my buzzing cell phone from my pocket and saw it was Gretchen phoning me.

"Dr. Briggs here."

"Dr. Briggs, I'm sorry to disturb you, but I think we have a problem here."

"What is it, Gretchen?"

"Ms. De Luca, she's crying hysterically and hasn't left your office yet. How shall I proceed?"

"Leave her be. I'm on my way."

By the time I reached my office, Francesca was gone. I had her paged, and my calls went unanswered. *I could spend no more time on this matter right now. I had to concentrate on my patient. He was my priority at the moment. Even dealing with Riley and her anger toward me would have to wait. I guess I can add it to the long list of grievances she feels about me.*

As I tried to begin this day again, I left instructions with Gretchen. "Please try to locate Ms. De Luca for me. Once you do, send me a text, and I will take it from there."

She gave me a raised eyebrow look, but held her tongue. I left without another word spoken.

Chapter Twenty-Five

Breaking with the past

Walker

I LEFT REESE asleep in bed while I took in a quick workout with Stephen, not that the past few hours of making love to Reese wasn't a total body workout. I had to clear my head before seeing Jackson. After receiving updates from Liam, I called Jackson, and he assured me he was feeling better. He was with Riley and hadn't seen Samuel yet. The two doctors would be conferring this morning to go over Jackson's reports and come up with the best course of action for my son.

Asking Samuel Briggs for help was no easy task on my part. My pride meant everything to me. A man needs that, but I faced my struggles before, lord knows I had. I promised myself I would put aside my contemptuousness feelings for the doctor and put the needs of my son first.

I clocked four miles on the treadmill. It wasn't nearly enough, but it would have to do for now. Quickly showering and dressing, I looked for Reese, who was now missing from our bed. She wasn't in the sitting room either. *Where is she?* A panic suddenly washed over me. *I hadn't been gone that long.* I ripped the blankets off the bed and searched for a note. I found nothing, only accelerating my heart rate even more.

"Stephen!" I called out.

"Sir."

"Where the hell is Reese? I came back here to find the suite empty. Did she call you?"

"No sir, she didn't, but Richard is also not present. I can only assume she is with him."

"Never assume anything in my world, Stephen. Get him on the phone...now."

"Right away, sir."

Before Stephen could even dial, we heard the door to our suite open and close. My eyes dismissed Stephen and Richard. I only saw Reese. Rushing past Stephen like a linebacker, I made my way to Reese, who looked absolutely beautiful. Her cheeks were red and flushed. Carrying a bouquet of wild flowers, she sat them down on the table and began walking over to me. Unbeknownst to Reese that she nearly gave me a heart attack with her absence, I reined in my temper and took her in my opened arms. I didn't let her know how scared I was when I couldn't find her.

"Good morning, Walker...again. How was your workout?" she asked so innocently.

"It was fine. I'm more curious to know where you've been. Reese, where were you?" I tried to ask as calmly as I could manage.

"I went for a walk with Richard and then took a drive down to the outside market place where I picked up these flowers." She gestured over to where she placed them on the table. "Not as beautiful as the ones we have in Georgia, but they come pretty close. I thought they could brighten Jackson's room and his spirits."

"That was very thoughtful of you, but Reese, you can't just walk off without telling me. You left no note and never called me." I let out a breath; that was the best I could do without losing my shit right now.

"Walker, I did leave you a note. It's right on the nightstand table on your side of the bed. Even back home, that's where I always leave my notes for you. I would have called you, but my cell phone battery died. Why are you worrying so much? I was perfectly safe with Richard."

"Reese, your safety and well-being will always be a priority for me. Don't you know that by now? I hate not knowing where you are. It rips through me and wounds me deeply." *There I said it. I revealed what scares me the most, and now Reese knows too. I can't lose her again. I won't survive it.*

Reese looked at me with pure love in her eyes. No sadness, no pity, just love. Her arms tightened around me, and she kissed me on my neck.

"Come sit with me for a minute, please?" she asked.

I half-heartedly smiled as she led me to the couch, holding my hands in hers and bringing them up to her lips, where she placed soft kisses on them.

"Walker, talk to me," she said. "Other than the obvious with Jackson, what's going through your head right now?"

Her questions went unanswered until I had a chance to catch my breath. I got up and turned away from her. Grabbing onto the mantle of the fireplace, my knuckles were white from how tightly I was holding on.

I screamed, "I hate this! Why is this happening to us? We should all be in California right now, having the time of our lives, readying for our wedding. Instead, we are thousands of miles from home, and my son is in the hospital instead of preparing to leave for college."

Reese's arms wrapped around my waist. She pressed up against my back, waiting silently and patiently for me. I couldn't ignore Reese; that was impossible. I was instantly comforted and turned around to hold her as close as my arms were able to.

"I'm sorry, baby," I said. "It feels like that is all I've been saying to you lately."

"That's not true, and you know it. I'm here, Walker, and I'm yours always and forever. I promised you no more running. I will never leave you again."

Her words poured over me, wrapping me up in her love.

"I love you so much, Reese. It scared the hell out of me. I find myself lost in the moments where I don't know where you end, and I begin. You are my entire world. I can never be without you again. You have to promise me something."

"Anything my love. My answer is 'Yes' to anything you need."

Just a few simple words from Reese and my world felt right again.

"No matter what is happening right now, please don't let my pain over Jackson or my nightmares about my father push you away."

"Impossible. We are in this together."

"How come I feel so alone then?" I asked.

"Because you're in a place again that you have no control over. The past is colliding with the present, and your fears that you have for me and for Jackson are consuming you. Walker, what happened to Elizabeth will not repeat with your son. And I will not lose this baby I'm carrying. You will not come home one day to find me gone with no promise of return. All I have to make you believe that is my love for you and for us."

"You're breaking me down piece by piece."

"No, Walker, I'm not. I'm putting you back together, just like you did for me."

"The day you left me, was a day a part of my heart just died. I feared I would never feel love flow through my heart again. It's there, Reese, believe me it is. I'm deeply in love with you that I can only fear the unknown. And now with Jackson, it's almost hard to breathe. Do you understand that? I never want to hurt you. And I fear that the demons that I am struggling with will do just that."

"Don't worry, I won't let you," she said. "We will get through this and come out stronger in the end."

Her tears fell as she folded her arms around me. One lift and her legs were secured around my waist. No more words needed to be spoken between us. She took control as I easily allowed her to do so. My body totally submitted to her. We craved each other and shared the same addiction and carnal desires. I made sweet love to her, sealing my body with hers. Reese's love was my salvation and cure for my brokenness. The pieces were put back together again the day she walked back into my life.

The short car ride to the hospital was met with silence—not a bad kind, but peaceful. I held Reese's hand the entire time while she rested her head against my shoulders. We talked through so many issues that were weighing me down, and now that I shared my deepest fears with her, I felt lighter. I knew that sounded crazy with what we were all facing today, but I just did.

"Are you okay, Walker?" she asked me with hope in her eyes.

"Yeah, baby, surprisingly I am. I love you, Reese, and I'm never going to stop telling or showing you. There's something I need to tell you before we go see Jackson."

"Okay. Has something happened since you received your last update?"

"No, nothing like that. Jackson is fine and resting comfortably. Before I left the hospital last night, I went to talk with Samuel, and before you ask, we didn't argue. He was talking with Dr. McGovern when I got there."

"Oh, Christopher? Ha! I'm sure Samuel loved hearing him go on about you."

"Right about that. McGovern is pretty much a tool, but what he does for the hospital is for the greater good of the patients, so I won't judge him too harshly for his efforts."

"What happened with Samuel? What made you go talk with him?"

"It was Jackson, and what he said to me while we talked. Reese, you should have heard him go on about why he lied to me and then explaining to me his entire life plan. I am in awe of my son. He is an amazing individual, and although I want to believe I know him like no other, I saw him differently last night. He was determined to make me see what I never wanted to."

"Which was?"

"My fear. I never realized how much it truly affected him. Reese, I literally checked out of showing any kind of emotion after I lost Elizabeth. I put up walls that protected me from ever getting hurt, and it was those walls that I kept Jackson safely tucked behind. I think back now on how selfish I was to him. I never allowed him to play football or any contact sport. To hear him list why he kept his condition from me and the reasons behind it was a true epiphany for me. I love him, Reese, more than my own life, but he deserves to have his own too. I'm not saying I'm going to stop being overprotective tomorrow, but I have to give him some breathing room. After our talk, I almost forgot why I was angry in the first place."

"Where does Samuel fit in all of this?"

"Jackson opened my eyes, and he championed the good doctor and his abilities to help him. I had nothing left but to agree to Jackson's request. He wants Samuel to be the one to operate on him. With a heavy heart, I agreed to let him. That's why I found myself at Samuel's office last night. I was prepared to beg him if it came down to that, and I did Reese. I begged for my son's life."

I continued, "The conversation then shifted to you and the life you had with him. He touched on how he met you the night in the hospital and how sorry he was that he couldn't save our son. He was remorseful and repenting all at the same time. I almost felt bad for him, but I'm a selfish man and I was there and prepared for just about anything to have him agree to help Jackson."

"Did he agree? Will he do the surgery?"

"Yes, he agreed. He's a doctor first, and you know better than anyone that he just can't walk away when a patient needs him. Reese, I'm putting all my faith in the hands of your ex-husband, who probably deep down still hates me. Please help me with this? It wasn't easy for me to ask him for anything, let alone save my son. We could walk in there, and he could change his mind and be done with it."

"Walker, that's not Samuel. If he gave you his word to help Jackson, then he will keep it. Forget about what happened months ago, that is irrelevant. Samuel Briggs is one of the most honorable men I have ever known. He is a brilliant doctor."

"Careful, Reese, you know how jealous I can be."

"Oh, I know, but you never have to worry. I'm yours forever, and you're mine. I'm proud of you, Walker. Last night you took the first step on the path of forgiveness."

"Forgiveness? What do you mean?"

"You know what I mean. You took the first step in healing. You did something that your father could never do. And when he finally did have the balls to reach out to you, forgive my language, but he chickened the hell out. You could go round and round with your conscience about how you were the one that shut him out, but really, Walker? What did he expect from you? It was too late for Phillip to right his wrongs, but it is not too late for you."

"I'm trying, baby, but I would be a liar if I said I'm still so fucking angry."

"I get that, and you have a right to be, but staying angry at the people that hurt you the most just gives them more power in the end. You put up a strong front and it leaves your enemies in a state of fear, but I also know what it costs you. Maybe your father is trying to tell you what he couldn't say while he was alive. You're fighting a ghost, one that will keep coming back until you stop fighting. Listen to him, Walker, and just maybe you will finally be able to have the closure you need to move past all of this hurt. Whatever you choose, I will be here for you."

"That I know with my whole heart. It's your love that has made me whole again. I swore to all who hurt us that I would never forgive any of them for what they put us through. I got my revenge on

Ralston, and I cut Henry out of our lives, but he needs to know about Jackson. I have to tell my mother as well."

"Why don't you speak with Jackson first, and ask him how he feels about Henry. He is his only living grandfather. Please understand I am not saying this to you for his benefit. It's for Jackson, and if he wants his grandparents here, then you must respect his wishes. Let's go in and meet with Liam and Samuel, and then your son. The phone calls to the grandparents could wait for now."

We got out of the car and made our way through Samuel's hospital.

"Are you ready?" she asked me.

"Let's go. And Reese?"

"What is it?"

"I love you. Thank you for everything. You can't even begin to know how you help me. I don't think I would be able to get through this without you. You are so incredibly strong, and your faith is amazing. I hear Lila through your comforting words."

"That reminds me, she is another phone call we need to make today. I don't want to worry them."

"They're all fine. Stephen checked in with them this morning. They are still at the Grand Canyon and should be leaving sometime today to continue on to California. Let them have their fun, and we can call them later."

"Whatever you say, as long as I can have some fun with you later," she said with a wink.

"Well, we can have some fun right now. I do love a good elevator ride."

She flashed her beautiful smile at me and delivered a wink that could bring me down on my knees. This was Reese's way of helping me face what was beyond these doors. Just holding her hand set my mind at ease. *Breathe, Walker, breathe. Everything is going to be okay. It has to be.*

We reached Jackson's room and heard laughter coming from inside. I thought that was a good sign that my son was in good spirits.

Although we spoke already this morning, I was not reassured that he didn't just tell me what I wanted to hear.

"Good morning," I said as we made our way inside.

Jackson smiled and greeted us, but Riley's smile had fallen, no doubt because of how I spoke to her yesterday. Reese walked over to her and gave her daughter a hug. Riley took a step back and took a closer look at her mother.

"Oh my god! Mom, are you pregnant?" she asked, as Reese couldn't contain her smile any longer.

"Yes, sweetheart, I am."

What came next could seriously break the sound barrier. Riley screamed and then hugged Reese with such a force, she almost lost her balance. Thank goodness I was behind Reese to catch her.

"So sorry, mom, but wow, I can't believe you're pregnant. When? How?"

"Okay, Riley, take a breath. I would think you know the *how* part, but when? A few months ago. We wanted to wait until I was safely out of my first trimester to tell you the good news."

"Are you okay, mom? How's the baby?"

"I'm fine sweetheart, and your sister is perfect."

This time we were all prepared for the screams and covered our ears, even Jackson knew what was coming. We all laughed and my earlier anxiety was already forgotten. The next thing Riley did was touch her mother's stomach and asked if she could say hi to her little sister. Reese could barely answer through her tears, she was so happy. Riley whispered that she couldn't wait to meet her, as she promised to be the best sister ever.

"When is the baby due?" Riley asked.

"I'm due in January. Shortly after New Year's."

"That's amazing, mom. I can't wait to meet her. Any names yet?"

"We haven't gotten that far yet, but we'll let you know," Reese said, as she looked over my shoulder and winked.

The baby news helped with the obvious elephant in the room.

Riley still looked apprehensive around me. I needed to apologize and make her understand why I was upset. Knowing we had some time before the doctors would arrive, I asked Riley if she would take a walk with me.

"It's beautiful this time of year," I remarked as we took a quiet walk along the waterfront. I guided her to a bench, and we both took a seat. Riley sat, wringing her hands in her lap, while all of her confidence was replaced with worry.

"Riley, please accept my apologies on how I spoke to you yesterday. News of Jackson's collapse and all that was revealed was a shock to say the least. I never meant to lash out on you, but if you could just take a minute to see it from my point of view, I think you would understand how I was feeling."

"I was out of line, Mr. Reed. I should have never said what I said to you, but please understand I wasn't thinking clearly. I was deeply worried about Jackson, and all I wanted was for him to be okay."

"Oh sweetheart, you don't have to explain worry to me when it comes to my son. I think I own the patent on that one. I am very sorry for scaring you with my anger. It wasn't personally meant for you, but I was just surprised and of course, taken off guard. To find out that my son kept something so personal from me, and then add the marriage license on top of it? I just lost my head. The purpose of this trip was to surprise you and Jackson, to tell you both our good news and to catch up. Do you forgive me? I need us to be okay, Riley. You mean everything to your mom and Jackson, which means you are everything to me."

"Of course, Mr. Reed, and will you please forgive me?"

"I will, but on one condition."

"Anything."

"Call me 'Walker.'"

"Okay, Walker, it's going to take some getting used to. You are, well, you, and calling you by your first name feels weird."

"Okay. If it makes you uncomfortable, then by all means you

may still call me 'Mr. Reed.' Now before we go back, I do want to talk about something else. Riley, probably the biggest reason I reacted the way I did was out of fear, my fear for my son's health and well-being, and knowing the position you would have been in had you married my son?"

"I don't understand. What position?" she nervously questioned.

"If you two had been married, you would have been the legal advocate in regards to decision making for Jackson. Riley, you must understand the seriousness of this situation. According to the law, you would have been next of kin, and that means you make the decisions for your husband. I don't have a directive in place for my son. Why would I? He's eighteen years old and healthy. With facing a health crisis, anything could happen. You would be expected to make decisions, and that responsibility would fall on you."

"Mr. Reed, I highly doubt you would just sit back and let me take over."

"Now that is the girl that my son loves. Welcome back, Riley. You're right. I would have moved heaven and earth to take you out of the equation, but I'm happy it didn't come to that. To sit here and convince you that I'm not controlling or extremely protective of my son would be futile at this point. I'm all those things and so much more. Like I said, his well-being is everything to me, and that will never change. I know I can't protect him from everything in the world that can harm him, but this is different, sweetheart, and so very close to home. I know and understand why Jackson kept this from me, but now that it's out in the open, can you please do me a favor?"

"If I can, Mr. Reed."

"Fair enough. I understand your commitment to my son, but when it comes to his health, you must trust me to help him. We are a family now, Riley, and there is nothing you can't share with me or your mother, okay?"

"Okay, Mr. Reed. Again, I'm so very sorry."

"Let's not talk about this anymore. Let's concentrate on getting

Jackson well, okay?"

"Okay."

We walked through the lobby of her father's wing, and Riley stopped to admire Elizabeth's portrait, something she always did anytime she would visit her father here.

"She was very beautiful, Mr. Reed."

"Yes, she was."

"Don't worry Mr. Reed. My father has been blessed with gifted hands and a beautiful mind. He will save him."

I was taken aback with her admiration for her father. Jackson was right. She truly idolized him. She wiped a tear from her face and walked ahead to the bay of elevators, leaving me alone for a minute.

Looking to Elizabeth's portrait, I whispered my own silent vow, *our son will make it. I won't be hanging a portrait of him next to you anytime soon. Please forgive me, friend. I know how I sound right now, but it's who I am. You of all people know I make no apologies for who and what I am. Jackson is my whole world, and damn to destiny and my father's prophecies. I will not lose him. Please, God, save my son.*

Taking a deep breath, I made my way over to Riley, who was anxiously waiting for me. We took the elevator ride in silence as we made our way back to Jackson. We both needed this minute and respected the other's need for quietness. The doors opened and Riley speed walked back to Jackson, leaving me on my own. I followed a few steps behind and peered into the room. The doctors hadn't arrived yet. Reese spotted me by the door but stayed where she was. *Was I that obviously unapproachable? I'm scared out of my mind about what I'm going to hear from Samuel and Liam.*

I pulled out my phone. My fingers hovered over the keypad, and instead of calling my mother, I phoned my office instead.

"Jenny, I will not be returning to the office as planned. I need a status report e-mailed to me immediately, and then I will call you later with further instructions. Anything that requires my immediate attention can be filtered through Donovan. Are we clear?"

Never missing a beat, she agreed compliantly. "Yes sir. Is there anything else you need me to do?"

"No, not at this time. Have Donovan phone me when he gets in."

"Yes sir."

I ended my call and pocketed my phone. *That was a waste of time. Your office is fine, and you know it. My mother has a right to know, they all do, so why was I hesitating? I don't want to hurt my mother or Gail, but Henry, I owe him nothing. I don't want him here and especially not near Reese, but if Jackson wants him to know, then there really is nothing I can do about it.*

Just as I reached for my phone again, Liam, Samuel, and McGovern all arrived to Jackson's room. It was time to hear my son's fate.

Chapter Twenty-Six

The plan...

I ENTERED MY son's room and stood beside Reese. Jackson was now out of bed and sitting on the couch with Riley next to him. Considering the condition he was in the day prior, this was a miraculous sight to take in.

Their hands were entwined with each other as mine were with Reese's. I was trying with great effort to be calm and focused so I could concentrate on the matter at hand, not on one of the other million thoughts that were occupying my mind.

After the greetings were exchanged, we all took a seat and focused our attention on Samuel who began to explain his treatment plan for my son.

"Jackson, after reviewing your newest CT and MRI scans, Dr. O'Larien and I are both in agreement that surgery is your best course of action. As I explained, the AVM you have is small, almost too small to detect, but it's there. I've seen this before, but your case is different because of the symptoms that have been occurring. What concerns me is your blood pressure spikes and headaches. The AVM is located in your Occipital lobe which is the probable reason why these symptoms are evident at this time. I know this is a lot to take in with this medical jargon, but before I go on, do you have any questions, Jackson?"

I watched my son take a few deep breaths before answering. He looked at Riley, and then his eyes found mine. Without ever breaking contact with me, he asked his question.

"Dr. Briggs, am I at risk of going blind? You mentioned this as one of the side effects. Can this happen to me?"

"Jackson, temporary and permanent blindness are two very different things. Where this AVM is located does present a risk, but I am confident that you are not in danger of losing your eyesight. Let's go over the plan from the beginning, and then we will answer all your questions. Okay?"

"Okay, sir."

My son answered with his head down. He'd been incredibly strong up to now, but I could feel his fear of the unknown. This was a feeling that I knew all too well. I gave Jackson a reassuring smile as Samuel continued on.

"I will need to order some routine blood and urine tests again before surgery. It is also recommended to do a chest x-ray and an ECG. I have no doubt you are fit, but we exercise on every side of precaution. Dr. O'Larien will be observing, along with my highly skilled team of Anesthetists and nurses that will join me in my operating room."

"You will be taken in about 30 minutes before your operation. My nurses will prep the area on your head to be shaved and cleaned. The next step is my team of Anesthetists. They will prep and put you to sleep, but not before me answering any last questions you have. Once you are completely down, we begin.

"I will perform a craniotomy, which means an opening in the skull. I will carefully excise the AVM from the surrounding brain tissue. Without facing any obstructions or complications, this will take me several hours. Do you have any questions so far?"

"Where will you make the incision? Will you have to shave my entire head?"

"No, Jackson. Where the AVM is located, I will make the incision behind your ear. We will have to shave the surrounding area, but to answer your question, we do not have to shave the entire head. Don't worry, son, your hair is safe."

I watched my son's apprehension fall away, and he smiled a bit.

"As I was saying, once I close, a dressing will be applied to your head and you will be taken into recovery. You will not be here in this room. You will be moved to the Neurosurgical ICU to be observed closely by a team of nurses. They will be with you around the clock and giving me updates. You've never been under general anesthesia before, so you may feel nauseous when you wake, if not experience vomiting."

Jackson questioned, "How long will I have to be in the ICU?"

"Depending how you recover, most likely two days. If all goes well, I will have you discharged within a week. An angiogram will be performed once more to ensure the AVM has been completely eradicated."

"Dr. Briggs, what about the side effects? You make this sound so simple. Just cut into my brain and take out my big bad AVM, and slap a bandage on me like it was nothing at all. This is my brain!"

I watched Jackson stand and pace the room. He was at his breaking point. Hell, so was I, but this was happening to him, and he needed his space. He faced the window looking out and leaned his head on the glass while taking a deep breath. I eyed Riley to give him a minute, and she respectively did. Silence filled the room as we waited for Jackson to move or speak. He drank some water, rejoined his girl on the couch, and simply gestured to Samuel to continue, but it was Liam who spoke next.

"Jackson, I know you're scared and have many questions. We will answer them one by one until you understand them all. I don't think I could have explained what you're facing any different than

Dr. Briggs here. Believe me, son, this surgery is not simple by any means. Operating on a brain takes an insurmountable level of skill and precise timing. Both Dr. Briggs and I have performed this operation many times, and we are confident that we will not meet any complications while performing yours."

"But…with any surgery, side effects are always at risk of occurring. In your case, these are: Stroke-like symptoms such as weakness in your arms or legs. Numbness, tingling, speech, and visual problems can occur. If anything, I would wager on your vision being compromised, but not anything resulting in a permanent state. This is why you will be in the ICU for a couple of days if not more to watch for all of these signs. We have no way of knowing until post-op surgery. I have no doubt whatsoever that once the AVM is removed, you will make a full recovery without fear of this ever coming back."

We all let out a breath after Liam finished his explanation. Jackson appeared to be more at ease after switching over to Liam. He'd been his doctor for years, and they had a bond. But, personal feelings aside, Briggs was the best choice for my son. I saw and heard no doubt. This guy was the best for a reason, and I trusted him completely with my son.

"Dr. Briggs, when do you want to do this?" asked Jackson.

"I can have this scheduled as early as tomorrow, with all your pre-op testing done today."

"If you all don't mind, can I have some time with my father?"

"Of course. Why don't we all take a break and meet back here in an hour?"

McGovern seemed pleased and bid his goodbyes to us as he exited the suite. Riley hugged Jackson and followed Reese. For the first time since last night, I was alone again with my son. Not knowing what he would say, I prepared myself and waited for him to talk.

LOOKING AT MY father sitting there so composed was a bit un-nerving. I shouldn't be surprised by his demeanor. He wouldn't be the man he is if not for his level of discipline and control. My actions had disappointed him and our trust had been broken, but he made it clear to me that it's already forgotten. My actions were reckless, this I know, but at the time I felt like I was doing the right thing. *I'm scared, really scared and now is where I really need my father the most.*

"Are you okay, dad?"

"Me? I should be asking you, son. I can't imagine what's going through your mind right now."

"Well, probably the same thing going through yours. I'm scared."

"I know you are, son, but thank god you didn't let that fear hold you back and keep you from getting the help you need. I know I was angry yesterday, but this could have been a different outcome."

"Like what happened to mom?"

"Exactly. We always seem to come back to that, don't we? I'm sorry for that, son. I never really took in account how it affected you all of these years. I built this fortress around you and kept all that could harm you out, but never realized that I was the one that was hurting you most."

"That's not true. Please don't blame yourself. You did every-thing right by me, and I have had an amazing life. Not one day as your son have I felt unloved by you. I love you so much, dad, and it is an honor to be your son, to be a Reed."

"Jackson, it's not over. You have your entire life to look for-ward to. Talk to me son, and please don't hold back for me. If you have something to say to me, by all means, do it."

"Okay."

I WATCHED JACKSON walk over to the closet to retrieve his backpack. He pulled out a smaller bag from it. I didn't know what it contained, because all I found yesterday was the marriage license without searching it any further. He pulled out a small porcelain box in the shape of a heart. I recognized it belonging to Elizabeth, but I hadn't seen it in years.

"Where ever did you find that?" I asked my son with curiosity.

"Grandma Gail gave it to me when we visited Arizona months ago."

"I don't even remember you carrying anything when we left."

"That's probably because you were angry and that's all that you saw. I apologize, dad, but I can't really say it any other way."

"After our talk, I thought you understood why I was angry with your grandfather and the reasons behind it."

"I do understand, dad, and hold no fault toward you, but it is what it is. You clearly hate my grandfather, and probably your own father as well. I don't, dad. I could never hate them. I don't agree with their actions, and I am disappointed in them because they hurt you, but hate is not one of my feelings I feel when it comes to them. Grandfather Phillip is gone, and I miss him. If he were here today, I would be the first one to call him out on his actions, but all I could do now is just pray for him and hope he will find peace in the next life. As for Grandpa Henry, I have to imagine he is hurting and feeling lost. I've only spoken to him a handful of times, then a short visit with him when I graduated."

"What are you saying to me, son? Why are we even talking about him?"

"Because we need to, dad. I need to know that the people in my life who I love will be okay even if I'm not here."

"No!!! You stop this right now. I will not sit here and listen to this. You heard Samuel and Liam. You will be fine. What the hell? Why are you preparing yourself for the worst? You are so young to be this fucking cynical. What is it, Jackson? You want to die? Do you want to join your mother? Because if I lose you, I have no doubt I'll be right behind you. I will not lose my son. You will be fine. You need to believe that."

"And what if I don't believe it? What if I have a small part of me that is just blindly scared of the unknown? Just because I'm scared doesn't mean I'm giving up, but I also have to prepare myself for anything. Dad, this is not like getting your tonsils out; this is brain surgery. I don't care what they said and how minimal the risks are. Anything can happen while I'm on that table, and I'm preparing myself for every outcome."

"Even death, Jackson?"

"Yes, dad, even death. I'm sorry if this hurts you, but you have to know what I'm feeling. I love you. I want nothing more than to love Riley for the rest of my life. I want to see my little sister be born and hold her. I want to teach her everything, and scare the crap out of her future boyfriends. Believe me, dad, I don't want to go into that surgery thinking I'm not going to wake up. I know what I would be leaving behind, and that's not an option for me. I just wanted to say it out loud and really come to terms with all of this. If I hadn't hidden this from you, maybe this conversation would be taking a different direction. Maybe this is my guilt, but I can't keep it inside any longer. You always demand honesty, well this is me being honest. Which brings me back to this box."

Jackson continued, "I didn't have much time to tell Grandma Gail about Riley, but what I did say was that I found the person that I planned to spend my life with. She of course smiled, and at first I expected her to give me the speech on how young I was, but she didn't. Instead she walked over to her hope chest in the family room and handed me this box. She wiped her tears away and explained that it belonged to mother. She would want me to give it to the one that I love."

"Jackson, I haven't seen that box in years. I don't even know what it contains. When your mother died, I allowed your grandmother to go through your mother's personal things and keep what she wanted. I was so devastated after Elizabeth's death, I didn't care. I had the greatest piece of her, and that was you, anything else didn't matter. Will you show me what the box contains?"

I watched him lift the clasp, as the memories of my wedding to his mother came flooding back to me. Inside was a small piece of folded paper that had my vows written down on it. I was so nervous I would forget what to say that day, so I held the paper in my hand. Elizabeth's eyes were filled with tears as I made my promises to her and our child. Jackson handed me the heart-shaped box, and I looked at the rest of the contents: a small dried flower and her wedding rings. Back in my vault at home, I had Elizabeth's jewelry collection and pieces that I kept for my son, but I never knew Gail had taken the rings. I remember a staff member handing me her personal items and Gail taking the bag from me. It never occurred to me to even check.

"Are you upset, dad? I thought you knew what was inside."

"No, Jackson, I'm not upset. I'm just a bit overwhelmed by all of this. How could I not know where your mother's wedding rings were? I'm sorry."

"Dad, don't be sorry. They have been in safekeeping all of these years, and now they are mine. You remember telling me how you felt the first time you visited Pottersville? That meadow claimed a piece of me that day I spent with Riley. We talked about our love and the future we wanted. I sealed my heart with Riley Taylor Briggs that day, and I knew she was the one. The night before I left for my trip, I opened this box and read your vows. I knew at that moment what I wanted to say to Riley. I never imagined my crazy girl proposing to me, but I also had never been happier that I had this box with me. I feel close to mom every time I read this. I want Riley to have her ring, and believe in all the promises I will recite to her on our wedding day."

"Dad, I want her to have this ring today." Jackson declared. "She needs to have this on her finger to show her that I'll be coming back to her. I will keep my word and not leave her. This ring is one of many 'Forever Promises' that I intend to give my girl. Are you okay with this? Dad, I need your support and understanding."

"Of course I am. Nothing would please me more than knowing

your mother's ring will now belong to Riley."

"I was hoping you would say that. Now I need something else from you."

"Anything."

"You promise, dad?"

"Yes, I promise."

"Allow Grandpa Henry to be here. I want my grandparents around me. I can't move forward with this surgery without seeing them first. I know what I'm asking, but please make this happen. I'm not asking you to forget what he did. I know that's not who you are, but why hang on to something that you can never change? It's in the past, and it really shouldn't matter anymore dad."

"Jackson, it does matter. Your grandfathers changed my life without me ever knowing it. You can't imagine how I felt and still feel about all they did. I just can't magically wave my wand and forget it all. They don't deserve my forgiveness."

"I'm sorry to hear that dad, but I disagree. They made their fair share of mistakes, but it's nothing that can't be forgiven. You say you're not like your father? Prove it. Be better than him and move past your anger. I need you to do this for me, and for you. Please think about it."

"Jackson, you are asking the impossible. When have I ever second guessed any decision I made? Stressing over the problems I have with your grandfather should be the last thing on your mind. Please just let this go."

"I can't, and I won't."

"Why are you doing this? Haven't I already made enough concessions already? Now you expect me to just roll over and play nice with your grandfather? I can't do it, son. Not for your mother's memory, and not for you. It's not fair to ask this of me. I won't be emotionally blackmailed like this. You are using the feelings I have for you to get what you want, and that's not fair."

"Aren't you the one that says life's not fair? Nothing about this is fair. I shouldn't be here right now, but I am, and I don't think what

I'm asking is unattainable. I'm about to face the toughest challenge in my life, and all I want is my family around me. I could have called him already, but I wanted to talk to you first. You promised me that you would not make me choose between the two of you. You said he's still my grandfather, no matter what, and it would be up to me to decide what kind of relationship I wanted with him. Well I've decided that I can't have him on the outside anymore with you hating him."

"Jackson, I would never stand in your way of having a relationship with your grandfather, but to ask me to just move on from all he did is not fair to ask. Yes, I use the word 'fair' because this is exactly how I feel. I meant what I said to you back in Arizona. Henry Townsend is no longer a part of my life, but I will not stand in your way of having a relationship with him. You want him here? Fine! I will call him, but enough with trying to force my hand. I won't be topped by anyone, and that includes you. I need to check on Reese, and I'm sure Riley wants to see you. Please rest and concentrate on getting well. I'll be back later. I love you, son."

"Dad, please wa..."

I raised my hands to him and turned to leave. I was suffocating back there with him. *I can't be here for one more minute. I need Reese, and I need her now.* I almost crashed into Liam as I made my exit.

"Whoa! Where's the fire, Reed? Are you okay?"

"That seems to be the question of the day, but no, I'm far from being okay. I just need to get out of here for a little while."

"I was coming to find you. Samuel is back in his office. We agreed to take today to let Jackson process all that was said, and tomorrow we will begin all of his pre-op work with the operation taking place the following morning. If you're in agreement, then we can move forward."

"That's fine, Liam. Do what you have to do, and we can go over it when I get back."

"Do you want to talk about it? I can take my doctor hat off and just be a friend that listens."

"Don't worry about me, Liam. Just take care of my son."

Not giving my long-time friend another chance to speak, I left the surgery floor. *Fuck! How did my conversation with Jackson take such a drastic turn? I knew he had much on his mind, but to sit there and defend his grandfather to me? He is so like his mother. His heart is filled with love and compassion. It's abhorrent to him to hold grudges. He's kind and forgiving, but at the same time, he used that to get what he wants. I don't play that way, but Jackson does. He knows I will move heaven and earth for him. But this? ...I don't see how I can.*

Reese has encouraged me to move on. The ghosts of Elizabeth and Phillip have begged me as well, and now Jackson. Why can't I do it? It's not like I will burst into flames if I change my mind. I promised I wouldn't carry out my original plans for Henry if he had stayed away and out of my life. Now with Jackson facing this medical crisis, I'm being forced to pull Henry back in for the sake of my son. He loves him, he loves them all. I hate this, but I love Jackson more.

This is for Jackson. I took out my phone and dialed Henry's number. He answered before the second ring.

"Hello, Walker," he said with a guarded tone. I kept the pleasantries out of it and got right to the point of the call.

"I need you and Gail to fly out to Maryland, Johns Hopkins Hospital to be exact. Jackson is here and is requesting your presence."

"What's happened to my grandson? Please tell me, Walker."

My heart was in my throat. I could hardly speak through my unshed tears. I would not show my vulnerability to this man ever again. He was now screaming through the phone and demanding an explanation. I could hear Gail in the background questioning her husband. My answer silenced him.

"He has an AVM in his brain. He wants to see you before his surgery."

I heard the phone drop and Henry cry. He was screaming, "No! Please God, not again."

I couldn't take anymore and ended my call. I wasn't going to feel sorry for that bastard. I then dialed my mother and pretty much got the same reaction, but did my best to calm her. She would be on the next flight out.

I was spent, utterly exhausted and sitting on the cold hospital floor. I closed my eyes, wanting to shut the world out. I was bled out with no emotion left…until I heard her voice.

Chapter Twenty-Seven

Let me help you...

"WALKER, OPEN YOUR eyes." I slowly opened them to see her again before me, Elizabeth, with light shining all around her.

"So…is this going to be a regular thing? Or can I count on you haunting me just on Halloween?"

"Ha ha! You are just a barrel of laughs today. I'm not haunting you. I'm trying to help you, if you would take your head out of your stubborn ass."

"I wish that was my biggest problem, but we both know it is so much more than just me being stubborn. Our son is facing a medical crisis. All he cares about is me making up with your father. I can't do this, Elizabeth. I just can't."

"Oh, Walker! I can see I have my work cut out for me. No one is trying to—what was the word you used—oh yes, *top* you. Our son was just trying to help you. He is far from being cynical. He was just trying to make you see his point of view from all sides. He needs you, Walker, and is depending on you to get him through this. Open your heart, and see what you have been trying so hard to block out."

"What if I can't? What happens then?

"You try harder. You have to do this, Walker. Our son needs you."

AFTER CALLING HIS cell phone and repeatedly going straight to voicemail, I began searching the hospital for Walker. When I went back to Jackson's room, he had already left. Jackson explained to me what happened and the heated conversation that followed. I tried my best to calm him and reassured him that his father would be fine and just needed some time to think.

Walker was in the habit of shutting down when he faced a situation he could not control. What Jackson was going through would be the ultimate test to Walker's strength and resolve.

Stephen and Richard were both on alert after unsuccessfully tracking his phone. I don't know what made me search a particular stairwell, but my hunch was right because when I did, Walker was there. Maybe it was our connection that led me to the right passage. Whenever he was close by, I could feel his presence. My heart began to race as I felt him closer. I saw him from the top of the landing. He was sitting at the bottom of the stairwell with his head positioned between his legs, and one smashed iPhone next to him. I made my way down the stairs as he lifted his head to greet me. His eyes were red and puffy with no light behind them.

"Walker, I've been so worried. Please talk to me. Have you been here this entire time?"

No response.

"Walker, come on. You need to get up and go see Jackson."

"I can't, Reese. I don't know how to help him."

"Yes, you do. You're his father, and he loves you. Let love be your guide to help him."

"She came back you know."

"Who? Who came back?"

"Elizabeth. She's fucking haunting me, Reese. She and my father won't leave me alone. Why the fuck are they doing this to me? They're dead. Stay fucking dead, and leave me alone! I love you so much, baby, I need you. Let me love you," he cried out, as he reached for me.

"Walker, we need to get you up and out of this stairwell."

"No! I'm not going anywhere. Stay with me, Reese, please?"

"I'm here."

I'd never seen him like this before, so I wasn't really sure what to do next. The mere mention of Elizabeth had me a bit alarmed. I knew he'd been struggling with nightmares of his father, but I couldn't imagine him seeing Elizabeth haunt him everywhere too. He was exhausted and sleep deprived. I would do anything I could to help him, but I wasn't going to last too much longer in this stairwell. I was uncomfortable, and Walker had me in a tightly wrapped hug. *Did he just pass out?*

"Walker, I need to get up. Uncomfortable pregnant woman here. Please, can we move?"

"Reese?"

"Yes, baby, I'm here."

"Oh my god! Are you okay? Did I hurt you?" His voice sounding panicked.

"No, of course not. You've been drifting in and out. I just need to get off this floor. My legs are getting numb, and we need to get back to the kids."

He finally loosened his hold and helped me up.

"I'm so sorry, baby. I must have blacked out or something. What time is it?"

"It's almost noon," I replied.

"Noon! What the hell? I guess I hadn't realized how tired I was."

"Smashing your phone doesn't help either when you have people looking for you." I showed him his phone, and his eyes just widened.

"I was angry and so fucking lost. After my talk with Jackson, I just needed to breathe. I wanted to come find you, but somehow I ended up here. I did what my son asked me to do. I called his grandparents. Has my mother arrived yet?"

"No, not yet, but she called and will be here soon. I arranged to have a car pick her up at the airport and bring her directly here. Stephen and Richard were busy looking for you, and I didn't want to leave the kids."

"I'm such an ass to worry you like this. I am so out of my element right now. I don't know what I'm doing. Please help me, Reese?"

"You never have to ask, baby. I'm here for you always. Let's go check in with Jackson and Riley, and then we can get something to eat. You haven't eaten since breakfast, and that was very little."

"I'm so sorry I frightened you. I love you."

"I love you too, and I'm fine."

Not really, but I wouldn't let Walker know that. He had enough on his mind without worrying about me. I'm just as scared as he was, but even more so now that I know the Townsends will be here soon. The last time I saw Henry Townsend was the day Walker introduced me to his parents. Elizabeth and her family were there for brunch. Her mother was kind, but her father's coldness was hidden behind his impeccable manners. He and Phillip were definitely cut from the same cloth. This time around, I was not a scared, innocent girl. I could take anything Henry or anyone threw my way.

I texted Stephen our location, and he met us on the floor just below the surgical unit. None of the grandparents arrived yet. Even with their own jet, the Townsends couldn't rush time. They would probably still have a few hours of flying time. I wanted to get Walker out of here for a while to rest and prepare for their arrival.

"How's Jackson?" he asked Stephen.

"He's fine, sir. He's resting comfortably in his room. He was just examined by Dr's Briggs and O'Larien. Nothing to be alarmed about, they called it routine testing. They told me that they would confer with you this evening."

It was just like Stephen to get right to the point in his most professional tone. It didn't take much convincing to get Walker to leave for a little while. Richard called ahead and had lunch waiting for us. I was famished, but so thankful my morning sickness didn't rear its ugly head today.

The car ride back to the hotel was met with calming silence. Walker stared out the window the entire time. I checked my messages with my right hand, as he never let go of my left. My mercurial man was here with me, and he was safe. The door opened and I was pulled back into his chest of tight corded muscles.

"I love you, Reese, and when we get upstairs, I'm going to show you just how much."

All I could do was nod in my response. Walker was full of sexiness and charm. He led me through the lobby toward the bay of elevators that would take us to the penthouse floor. Once he entered our private suite, I would have thought Walker would have picked me up and carried me off to the bedroom, but he didn't. I was picked up, but taken to the dining area to eat the lunch that was waiting for us under the large silver dome covers.

He whispered in my ear. "As much as I want you, need you, hell…crave you, I also know you need to eat and so does our daughter. Forgive me once more for not taking care of you today. You are my world."

"Will you stop? There is nothing to forgive. We are both fine."

"Don't ever let me off the hook. I know you better than that, Reese, and you're just pacifying me because of Jackson."

"Please join me? You need to eat too, Walker. You passed out in the hospital stairway and were hallucinating before that."

"I will, baby. You start and I'll join you in a few. I have to make some calls to my office and check the flight statuses."

"Stephen could do all that. Now sit and eat with me, or I'm not going to."

"Reese," he enunciated my name in a "warning tone." "I mean it, Walker, either you join me at this table or no one eats."

Who was I kidding? I was starving and he knew it. My stomach had been growling, and the smell alone had my mouth salivating. The aroma of the delectable dishes must have wafted towards Walker too. He wasn't a man to be pushed, but I think I won this round. He smiled, kissed me barely on my lips and sat down next to me.

"I'll eat, but you, my love, are the dessert. And I will enjoy every last mouthful of your decadent flavor."

He's got me, and I have the soaked panties to prove it.

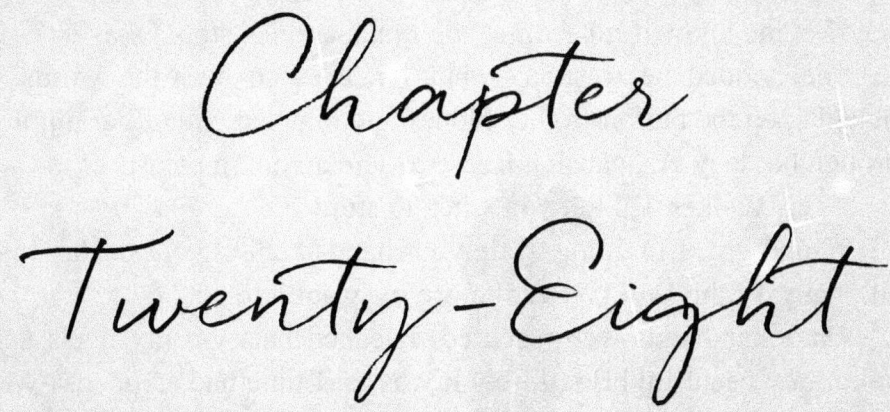

Chapter Twenty-Eight

Mine...

"**H**AVE YOU HAD enough to eat?" I asked Reese, as she wiped her lip with her linen napkin.

"Yes. Thank you. It was delicious."

She smiled sweetly as she uncrossed her legs. I could feel the tablecloth shift several times throughout our lunch, as I playfully teased her. I loved every minute of it, and now it was time to please her…with my mouth.

Kneeling before my woman, she began to loosen my tie.

"Do you want to play?" I asked her.

"Depends. What do you have in mind?"

"If I could, I would tie you to my bed and devour you for days, but we don't have that kind of time."

"You never have to ask, Walker. I'm yours and yours alone."

"Yes, I do baby. I don't want to lose control and hurt you. I just need to forget things for a little while. Can you help me to do that?"

"Yes," she coaxed.

I took my tie from her hands and glided it down her cheek. It was pure silk and velvety smooth like her skin.

"Let me know if it becomes too much and I'll stop. Okay?"

She nodded her response, but I needed to hear the words. I flicked open the buttons to her blouse and pinched one of her nipples through her lacy bra, causing Reese to scream out in pleasure.

"Yes, Walker, I'll tell you when to stop!"

"Good girl. I'm going to tie your hands behind your back. Hold still, baby, or this will be over before we want it to be."

Once her hands were secured, I leaned back on my heels and took in my beautiful bride-to-be. It was as if time had stopped. I was back there again to our first time making love. Reese was innocent, breathtakingly beautiful, and all mine for the taking. She completely opened up to me without any barriers between us. The same intensified feeling I had back then is flowing through me right here at this moment.

She knew what I was doing. I was so easily distracted when it came to Reese. I wouldn't let her wait another second for me to taste her. Her bra opened at the front, how lucky was I? Freeing her swelled breasts, I took in one of her nipples into my mouth as I pinched the other between my two fingers. She threw her head back as I bit down, not too hard, but just enough to elicit her rising pleasure.

"You are so wet and ready for me baby. I can smell your arousal."

I sucked and sucked her hardened nipples as I plunged two fingers deep inside her folds.

"Fuck! Walker! I need you…now. I'm going to come."

"Not yet baby. I still have plans for you."

"Ugh!! You are frustrating. I can't even touch you. Please, Walker, don't make me beg. Fuck me now, or I'm going to scream as loud as I can, and it won't be from your pleasure."

"There's my vixen. I love getting you worked up into a frenzy. Scream as loud as you need to baby."

This was it. She was spent after her first orgasm, but so needed to be fucked, and fucked hard. I was readying her, so I wouldn't hurt her. She would take all of me, no matter what, and never say no. My hands were on her thighs as I entered her wet, slick folds with my thrusting tongue. All she could do was thrash her head back, and let out her cries of unadulterated pleasure.

"That's two," I said, feeling accomplished.

"Fuck you, Walker, and fuck me...now."

"Your wish is my command, my naughty vixen."

"What are you doing?"

"I want you so much, Reese, but not here. I need you in my bed, opened and ready for me."

I untied her hands, and she was in my arms in seconds, as I carried her off to the bedroom. Kicking the door shut behind me, I placed Reese down in the middle of the bed. I removed my clothing and made my way up to my woman.

Her arousal was running down the inside of her thigh. Having shed her panties, she laid there completely bared to me. I loved tasting her. Her juices were intoxicating as they danced on my tongue. With our naked bodies skin to skin, I tried with my best effort not to be rough with her, but I still entered her with a penetrating force, causing Reese to cry out. I pulled back, and that's when her long slender legs wrapped themselves around my waist.

"Don't you dare stop!" she screamed. "I am not made of glass that will shatter at any moment. Fuck me, Walker. Don't be afraid give yourself over to me."

Her words were my undoing as I pushed deeper and deeper inside of her. I was hitting her deepest core over and over again until we both reached the edge of the precipice. I was so close, she was too. It took all my strength not to lay my body on top of hers. We were slick in sweat as my arms began to shake. I could hold on no longer as I spilled inside of her, filling her tight channel with all of my essence.

"Oh hell, baby! You take my breath away," she breathed out.

Still buried deep inside of her, I had no desire to break our connection. Her legs were gliding over my hips as I felt my dick begin to harden inside of her again. My sexual need for her was heightened already from our amazing fucking, and now just looking into her eyes, I was ready to go again.

"I love you, Reese, so much. You are mine…forever."

"Yes! Forever, Walker…forever."

I slowly made love to my beautiful angel. We entwined our hands together as we came together once more, not just committing our bodies, but our souls forever. Holding her in my arms, this was where I needed to be.

Unfortunately, thoughts continued to rush into my head. *Richard was with Jackson, and would phone me immediately if something happened. My son was in capable hands with Liam overseeing his case.*

"What are you thinking about?" Reese asked. She always sensed when I was distracted. I pulled her even closer to my body if that was even possible.

"Your body is changing," I said to her.

"Come again?" she retorted.

"Oh baby, I will, just give me a few minutes."

"Stop it, Walker, you know what I mean."

"You are so adorable baby, I love teasing you. It's a good thing, I promise. Holding you like this in my arms, I can take a moment to really appreciate your body changing with our child growing inside of you. Your breasts are fuller. Your hourglass shape is even curvier, if that's even possible, and where our child grows is perfectly round. I couldn't be happier knowing that she's safe inside of you, and it was our love that made her."

"And to think she wouldn't be here had you used a condom."

"Yeah, I guess that never occurred to me. I never wanted any barriers between us, I still don't. After our first time, I just didn't care what happened. I knew I loved you and would love you forever no matter what. Having a child would only have made me love you more. Now we have our second chance at that amazing gift."

"I feel the same way, baby. I don't mean to bring up the past, but he's still a part of me, even now after all of these years."

"Don't ever apologize for missing our son, especially to me. Even for the short time you carried him, I know he was loved."

I wiped away her tears before they even had a chance to fall. I knew she carried the memory of our son and what she lost with her every day. I would never allow anyone to ever hurt my angel again. I moved the sheet away from her protruding belly and placed my cheek on her bump. I couldn't wait to feel my child kick from inside of Reese. I loved her so much. She would be a daddy's girl, without question.

"Hey you, come back to me," Reese called out. "Where did you go?"

"I was just thinking how much I plan to spoil our daughter."

"You say that now, but just wait. Girls are so different than boys."

"I don't care. I'll take it all and love it… every bit of it. She's going to look just like you, only a smaller version."

"You sound better. Do you want to get ready to go back to the hospital?"

"Not yet. Jackson is with Riley, and the way we left things, I'm just not emotionally ready to put myself through anything else right now. As is, I will have my mother to deal with and then of course, Henry and Gail. After I told him about Jackson, Henry wailed out loud. I almost could hear him falling to the floor before hanging up. His cries were reminiscent to the ones he shed when we lost Elizabeth, but this time, I simply didn't care."

"We don't have to talk about this if you don't want to."

"It's okay. It doesn't bother me like it once did. After I left Jackson's room, I just wanted to hit something. I wished I was in front of my punching bag or going three rounds with Tyler. After I made my phone calls, throwing my phone was the best thing I could do to let go of some of my rage. I just fell down on my ass after that and remained on the floor until you found me."

"Do you remember your vision of Elizabeth?"

"What do you mean? Elizabeth? At the hospital? No, that's not possible. Maybe I was dreaming of her, but nothing like I experienced before."

"Walker, you told me that she was haunting you. And you wanted her to leave you alone."

"I'm sorry baby, but I just don't remember that. Maybe I was confusing her with my father. Reese, I don't want you to worry yourself over this. Yes I'm having nightmares, but it's nothing I can't handle."

"I don't doubt you ever, but that doesn't mean I can't be worried about you. I know what I heard. You clearly said 'Elizabeth,' and now with her parents arriving soon, I just want to make sure you are okay."

"I'm fine, baby. I made the call for my son. When I'm ready—if I'm ready—to forgive and lay the ghosts of my past to rest, then you will be the first person I tell. Now let's shower."

Cutting Reese off was the only way to stop her from questioning me. I couldn't even begin to understand why I was having all these crazy dreams, but with Henry arriving soon, this was all I was capable of right now.

He was the last person I want to see. I knew he would hover over my son, and if Jackson wished him to be here, then I really didn't have much say in the matter. For Henry's sake, he'd better remember my warning and keep his distance from me and from Reese. If he even attempted to come near her, all bets were off.

While Reese was getting dressed, I checked in with Stephen. He looked just as tired as I was. Jackson's condition was on all of our minds.

"Has my mother arrived yet?"

"Yes sir, her flight just reached the gate. All arrangements have been made here at the hotel, and the driver will call me once they arrive at the hospital."

"Excellent. Any word on Townsend?"

"They are still in the air. They flew commercial. His plane is out of service, and he just booked the next available flight. They are not expected until later on this evening."

"That's fine by me. The less I see of Henry, the better. We'll be heading out in a few minutes. Anything else we need to discuss before we leave?"

"I spoke to Jenny. Everything is steady at the office. Donovan and Tom are sharing the responsibilities in the day-to-day operations along with sending me daily reports. Ms. Mitchell's grandparents should arrive in California by tomorrow."

"Sounds good. Keep me informed. Once I know they are all settled in, I will have Reese phone them. We didn't want to worry them until we knew for sure what Jackson's condition was. I sure could use a dose of Lila right about now. She has the patience of a saint and the wisdom of a thousand philosophers."

"I look forward to meeting her."

"That's right, you haven't had the pleasure of meeting Lila or Thomas Mitchell yet. Stephen, they are amazing people. I am very fortunate to call them family. I only wish Reese would have trusted them enough to help her when I couldn't. Thomas likes to remind me that no matter his age, Mitchell's come from strong Irish stock. You don't mess with an Irishman, especially a Mitchell."

"Shall I arrange to have them fly out here?"

"No, Stephen, that won't be necessary. He doesn't fly anymore on account of his heart. He's in good health, thank god, but the cabin pressure can affect him, and Reese didn't want to take any chances. This is why we arranged the alternative form of transportation. The last time I spoke to them, they were having a great time, and it helps they are not alone. Their friends are just as fiery as they are. You may want to get some ear plugs when you meet those southern ladies."

It was nice to laugh a bit and that's when I heard my angel interrupt us.

Reese said, "Well, Stephen, I'm also a southern gal, I sure hope you don't need ear plugs around me."

If only Stephen could see himself right now. His cheeks were actually changing color before me.

"Um…Stephen. Please bring the car around," I said.

"Ha ha ha! That was too funny. Who would have thought I could make him blush? Stephen of all people," Reese laughed.

"Now, my naughty vixen, that obvious flirting with my staff has definitely earned you a spanking or two. I will certainly take pleasure in the task later on this evening."

"Oh my love, I look forward to it. I love you."

"I love you more. Let's go before I take you again."

"Promises, promises."

"Oh, Reese, I am a man of my word."

Chapter Twenty-Nine

This I promise you

Jackson

AFTER I KNEW my father had been located and was now with Reese, I could concentrate on Riley and the surprise I had waiting for her. In two days, I was going to undergo brain surgery. I was scared out of my mind and was trying so hard to hide my fear from her.

She knew me better, sometimes better than I knew myself. *How does that even happen? Do you just one day completely hand over your heart and trust to the person you believe will love you forever? And never hurt you? And be by your side always? For me, Riley is that person. Meeting her felt like the stars were aligning with each other. Probably sounds lame like something from a Hallmark card, but I can't help myself.*

Most guys my age were chasing tail whenever they could. My friends Brandon and Clay were whores, but at least they're honest.

They voiced their strong opinions against being tied down to one girl. They said this was the time to party their asses off in college, be stupid, and just enjoy their youth. No judgment on my best friends, but I just wanted something more, and my more was Riley. That girl owned me body and soul. I wanted nothing more than to completely give myself over to her, and I couldn't think of a better day than today. I opened up my mother's jewelry box and took in the sparkling ring shining back at me. The sun was hitting it at the right spot, making the room flicker with an array of colors. I didn't share my plans with my father yet, but I did with Dr. O'Larien, who cleared me medically. Other than the AVM occupying space in my brain, I was in perfect health.

My father and I were at a crossroads, so to speak. I forced him to call my grandfather. My father was 100% correct in calling me out for my actions. I absolutely manipulated him to get what I wanted, and the part that I'm sorry for is how I hurt my dad.

I didn't want to be in the middle of this war between the two men I loved most in this world. Cross my father once, and you're dead to him. I couldn't do that when it came to my grandfather. I was angry with him for hurting my father, but I was able to reconcile the feelings I had. But as for my father...Hell would have to freeze over before he backed down and chose to forgive.

I closed the box and stowed it safely back inside my bag. I showered again after my testing. I smelled like antiseptic. They took more blood than a hungry vampire. More scans were performed, and my chest was still sticky from the probes. I guess I should have been happy I possessed no chest hair.

By the time Grandpa Henry arrived, I'd be long gone with Riley. With me not here, maybe he would try to talk with my father and mend fences. *I know it's a long shot, but I still hope.* Riley is going to go crazy when I bring her to the surprise I have planned, and then we will be off to our own private bubble, where I intend to make love to Riley, giving myself only to her.

"Penny for your thoughts?" she asked as she wrapped her arms around my waist.

My back was turned to her as I stared out the window. *I swear the perfume she wore had mind altering powers.* I pulled her hands to my lips and kissed them gently. She giggled and planted her face on my back, leaving shivers down my spine.

"Hey, Riley, how was your walk? Sorry I couldn't join you."

"It was good. I cleared my head. I love the waterfront. I used to go down and watch the boats all the time. Inner Harbor is one of my favorite places, but my list is short. I've only recently begun to travel outside of Maryland, thanks to my incredible tour guide. What's his name?"

"Oh you know his name, and one day you will share that name as your own."

"Promise?"

"I promise. You have my forever promise. I love you so much, and I will show you every day for as long as you will have me."

"Good. Let's start today."

"You read my mind, sweetheart. I spoke with Liam, and I've been cleared to leave the hospital today. You and I are going to go somewhere to be alone and talk. I need that baby, and I think you do too."

"What about my father?"

"Sorry, sweets, he's not invited, but maybe next time."

"Stop it, Jackson. Don't tease me when you know what I'm saying. He's your primary doctor. Don't you think he should have a say if you just get up and leave? What if you have another seizure? I'm not trained to help you. No!! We are not going anywhere."

Now how come I thought this would be easier? She broke away from me and sat on my bed with her legs dangling over the sides. Her eyes said it all, she's worried for me. I hate that I've put that fear there when her eyes should be showing happiness. Deciding not to give her another minute to bite her nails, I quickly walked over to her and held her in my arms.

"Riley, I give you my word that I'm fine and you have no cause for worry. I will not have another seizure, and if I do, I'm already prepared for that. I promised my father and you that I would never be reckless again, so measures are in place."

"Where are we going?" she asked, all upset. *Oh she breaks my heart with her tears.*

"Trust me?"

"With all that I have," she replied.

"That's all I need to hear and all you need to know…for now. Let's go."

"One more question, and then we can leave?"

"Go! You have 30 seconds," I said.

"Your father? I've already gone a few rounds with him already. He's going to lose his shit when he comes back to find you gone."

"No, he won't, and please don't worry about my father. Your mother will take care of him. Liam has cleared me, and Richard will be with us."

"He will?"

"Yes. A safe distance, but he won't be far behind. I left a note here for my father and grandparents. Don't worry, baby. It's going to be okay."

I wiped the last of her tears and held her beautiful face in my hands.

"I need this night with you, Riley, please?"

"Okay, anything for you, Jackson."

"Thank you. You won't regret it."

I heard her whisper "I hope not," but I wasn't going to say anymore. Her nerves were rattled enough and arguing with Riley was not an option.

Richard already had our bag packed in the car. He was positive my father was going to fire him for sure, but I squashed that quickly and told him I would never allow that to happen. Richard was more than a driver and bodyguard to me, he was family. We made our way down to the underground garage and didn't turn back as the hospital became a distant sight.

"Okay, Mr. Reed, now that you have me here, what do you intend to do with me?" Riley asked innocently, but with a hint of playfulness.

"Do you know why we are in a car with blackened windows?" I asked.

"To torture me?"

"Hey! You got it right! Obviously no, not to torture you, but rather to keep you guessing until we reach the first destination."

"And where might that be? You know I love and hate surprises."

"I do know. Can you close your eyes for a minute?"

"Jackson..."

"Close them, Riley. Do not open them until I say so, okay?"

"I get it. You can be so frustrating at times, boyfriend."

I took in a deep breath and smiled as I looked at her. I could feel my pants tighten, especially in my lower region. I loved this girl, and someday she will no longer be my girlfriend, but my wife.

"Hold out your hands," I asked.

She bounced in her seat with excitement. Who was she kidding? She loved every bit of this little game. I placed her gift in her hands, as her fingers ran over the soft surface.

"Open your eyes, baby."

Her eyes brightened at the sight of her new furry friends. She eyed the bears and smiled.

"Really? Mr. & Mrs. Yankee bears? Oh you play dirty. You know I am an Oriole's fan for life by the way."

"That's only because you've been misguided all of these years, but now you have me to set you straight. Be nice sweetheart, or I will take back my bears and give you a stuffed bird instead."

"I love them and you, Jackson."

"I love you too, and I'm happy you like your first gift. Are you ready for your next one? Because we're at the first destination."

Before she could ask, I crushed my mouth down onto hers and kissed her until she was silenced. She ran her fingers though my hair and pulled me closer. I wanted her so badly, but not like this. Riley had been more than patient with me, but tonight she would wait no longer.

"Behave, Riley. Let's go in before I change my mind."

Richard waited a minute before opening our door, just enough time for me to push down my growing erection. She knew what she just did and wasn't sorry at all for it.

"Keep your eyes closed until I say open, okay?"

"Yes, dear."

Her long hair was cascading down her shoulders. Riley's hair was thick and gorgeous, and I wasn't sure the hat would even fit on her thick mane of hair. I tucked her waves of caramel brown behind her ears and put her baseball hat on. I wore mine and had our shirts in my hand. *She is going to flip out when she sees what I'm wearing.*

I wanted to give her one more tease before I let her open her eyes. I kissed her behind her ear, placing five kisses down her cheek.

"Open your eyes, babe"

"What the...? How?"

"I have my ways. Are you surprised? Do you like it?"

"Oh, you amazing boyfriend! I freaking love it. This game has been sold out for months with pretty much season ticket holders. Camden Yards, Jackson!! I love this ballpark. Oh. My. Goodness! We are at our first baseball game with our teams playing against each other. How are you not freaking out right now?"

I couldn't help but laugh. Riley was just too adorable. I scooped her up in my arms and twirled her around. She needed this laugh, and so did I.

"Jackson, can I ask you a question?"

"Go for it."

"Why are you wearing an Orioles shirt, and I have a Yankees shirt in my hand?"

"Do you remember what I wrote in my card when I gave you Mr. Yankee Bear?"

"Of course, I memorized your lovely note."

"Good. Now, I've had time to think about it and realize that I can't force you to love the Yankees like I do, as you can't make me like your team. So I decided to have a little wager with you. I love you, Riley, and that means all parts of you, even as far as supporting your team, so here's the deal. If the Yankees win tonight against your birds, then you cross the arbitrary line you have drawn in the sand and cross over to the New York side. If your team wins, then I will do the same for you. How does that sound?"

"I agree to your terms, but I'll add a clause to our new deal."

"And what might that be?"

"No matter whose team wins tonight, the only team I truly care about is 'our team,' you and me."

"I agree to your terms," I said.

And that was just one of the reasons why I loved my girl so much. My legs felt like jelly as I took in her innocence and beauty. Her eyes were shining like diamonds. All I see was my reflection when I leaned in to kiss her. It could only get better from here.

"Um…one more thing?" she asked.

"Yes, my love?"

"I want a crab mac-n-cheese dog. Stuggy's makes them, and they are the best."

"Only in Maryland," I chuckled. "I'll take your word for it and just have a good old fashioned dog with kraut and mustard."

"Oh baby, you don't know what you're missing."

"I'll survive. Let's go watch The Captain. I'm feeling a home run and a three run lead in the first inning alone."

"Confident much?"

"Oh, yes. A Reed never loses."

The banter between us was just what we needed after the last few stressful days we endured. I wanted Riley to remember every last detail of our time together. She would need the comfort of the good memories to help her when I'm in surgery. Seeing her cry broke me down and hurt my heart. I needed her to be strong not just for me, but for us. It was her love that was getting me through this.

Driving to our next destination, my head was spinning with shock. My girl was grinning and laughed so hard, I thought she was going to wet herself. My Yankees got beat tonight, and not by just a run or two, but creamed. They only scored three runs against Baltimore's eleven. Eleven? Seriously? She's still smiling at me. I guess I would be doing the same thing if my team had won, but my girl can really gloat.

"Are you finished?" I asked her. I was trying to be a good sport about it, but this was a tough pill to swallow.

"Not by a long shot, but I will take mercy on you. Oh, Jackson, come on. Let me have my fun. I know in your Yankee loving heart you must see how happy I am? What were the chances?"

Honestly at this point, I didn't even care about who won. I already felt I had won by just admiring the smile on Riley's beautiful face. She was glowing, and I was happy. My girl wanted ice cream to complete her happy dance, but little did she know I had so much more planned. I stayed back in the car while she and Richard ordered our sundaes.

My vibrating phone was going off nonstop for the past couple of hours. I knew it was my father, and that's exactly why I was ignoring it. I had Richard take the tracers off our phones, another act that would make my father lose his mind, but as I explained in my note, I needed this night with Riley.

Curiosity won out and I scrolled through my 43 text messages, all from my father. It was the usual, "Where are you" to "Come back to the hospital right now." And then the last message read:

Walker: *I love you, son. Be safe.*

I figured that by the time he texted me the last message, all the fight had gone out of him, or Reese talked him down. No matter what, I wasn't going back until tomorrow morning. I promised Liam we would be back by nine. I had no regrets of the plan I set in motion, but I still didn't want to hurt my father, so I sent him a short reply:

Me: *I love you too, dad. I'm safe. Please do not worry. And dad? Don't blame Richard. He's got my back and will make sure I safely return in the morning.*

I waited a few minutes and received no response. Hopefully this was a good sign that he trusted me, and we were okay. His one promise to me was that we were always okay. He didn't even know how much I needed that to be true. I wiped away a few tears before the back door swung open. Riley's hands were filled with delicious ice cream.

"Take your pick. We have vanilla with hot fudge or chocolate swirl with hot fudge."

"You kept it pretty simple. I would have thought you would have went toppings crazy and layered them up," I said as I reached for the vanilla cup.

"You know me too well, but we did indulge a bit much at the ballpark, so dessert is light tonight. You like it, right?"

"I love it."

We sat and enjoyed our sundaes. Riley couldn't stop smiling. The divider was lowered and I couldn't help but notice Richard texting away. No doubt he was going round and round with my father. Richard was ex-military. I have no doubt he couldn't handle my dad. To have Riley here and snuggled up in my arms was so worth my father's potential eventual wrath.

The drive to the next destination wasn't too long. My girl had fallen asleep and was looking so peaceful. I almost hated to wake her, but we were at our final stop of the evening.

"Baby, open your eyes," I requested.

I brushed her hair away from her face and eyes, and her nose twitched when I did it. She let out a light giggle and then snuggled closer to my chest. If I could, I would put her in my back pocket and keep her there forever.

"Come on, sleepyhead, I want to show you something." I stepped out first and reached for her hand. She slipped hers in mine, a perfect fit. The sun had set hours ago, leaving us with a clear night filled with stars dancing over the water below.

"Inner Harbor! I love it here."

"I know you do, and this is why I brought you here tonight. Walk with me?"

Hand in hand we walked around the harbor. It was still summer here in Maryland. The harbor was filled with tourists, the restaurants were packed, and the street musicians were out and about. Two guitar players were singing one of our favorite songs by The Goo Goo Dolls, "Let love in." Riley squealed, she was so happy. I twirled around as we passed them. We walked for a little while taking in the beautiful scenery and the boats that lined the marina.

Throughout our talk, Riley talked about all of her long-gone, happy memories spent here with her father. They used to go sailing on the weekends when he could get away from his hospital. They would come down here every Fourth of July to watch the fireworks display. She tried to hide her sadness, but I knew better. I gestured over to a bench to sit for a minute. Riley didn't know, but we had reached the end of our walk. I turned to my girl and took her in my arms.

"It's okay to miss your father. Don't you think it's time for you to forgive him?"

"I wish I would have listened to you when you asked me to. I still feel you're in this position because of me. I behaved so foolishly and adolescent with my father."

"Hey, we've been over this already, and it is not your fault. You wouldn't be you if you tried to hide your feelings. Life is too short, baby, let the hurt fall away and move on from it. He is the only father you will ever have, and I know he loves you. Find your way back to him and make things right between you two."

"What's wrong, Jackson? Are you okay?"

"I'm fine, and I was fine when I asked you this a few days ago.

You need to make up with your father and put the past where it belongs. Being angry will not change anything that has already happened. Your dad is going to be okay. I'm sure it would help him, knowing that you forgive him and love him like you always have."

"I do, Jackson. I love my father very much. I'm not even angry anymore. The moment I realized what happened to you back at the restaurant, I only wanted my hero, my father, the great doctor who could come flying in to help you. How could I be angry with him anymore? He's operating on your brain in two days."

"That he is, but that's not why I want you to forgive him. I want you to reconcile with your father for *you* and to make things right between the two of you again."

"I promise I will talk to him tomorrow, okay?"

"Okay," I agreed. "Now… are you ready for your last surprise?"

"Another one? My goodness, Jackson. You've given me so much already. You should be resting right now, not taking me all over the place."

"For the last time, I'm fine and will be better very soon. Do you see what we are sitting in front of?"

Her eyes smiled at me, and she really took in the beauty of the boat that was in the harbor. It belonged to Brandon's uncle Vincent. He was an investment banker in New York. This was his summer toy, and until tomorrow, I got to enjoy some private time with my girl. It wasn't like I could immediately use my father's yacht that was docked in California, so when Brandon told me about his uncle's boat, all these ideas went off in my head.

Riley got up and examined our floating hotel. She studied it very closely and then turned back to me.

"Um…Jackson, this is not just an everyday boat. This is a yacht, and quite an expensive one at that. This is a Sunreef 80 Carbon Line Superyacht. By looking at this beauty, this has got to be about a year old. It's breathtaking. Who does it belong to?" She asked so innocently.

I was just shaking my head at her obvious knowledge of boats. I thought I was being slick by bringing her here, but she showed me. *Another amazing thing I love about her. She can bamboozle me and make my head spin in a thousand directions.*

"Riley, once again you beguile me. How do you know so much about boats?"

"Yachts, Jackson. This bad boy is a yacht, not a boat. I spent my childhood down at this harbor, and I love to sail. My father took me to a Charter Club yacht show once a few years back, so this at the time was just a model in progress. Anything else you want to know?"

"No, I'm good. To answer your question, this belongs to Brandon's uncle, and it's on loan to us for the night."

I reached for her hand and led her to the ramp that would bring us onboard.

"Wow! This is just out of this world amazing. Are you sure it's okay for us to be here?" she asked.

"It's more than okay, baby. We have it all to ourselves, and no one will bother us. Come, let me show you around."

After giving her the grand tour of this magnificent yacht, I led her downstairs to the cabins, bypassing the guest quarters, straight to the master bedroom. This Catamaran slept ten people. It had four large cabins with private baths/en-suites. There was a large size dining room, sun-bathing area. It was absolutely grandiose for the rich. My father raised me in this lavish lifestyle, but everything I had, he made me earn. He used to tell me that he hated the labels that followed him growing up in New York and the Hamptons. I was born into wealth, but that didn't mean I was allowed to behave like a spoiled brat.

Leading her into the master cabin, Riley gasped at the sight of it. I had candles lit around the entire room. Rose petals covered the white bed linens. John Legend was crooning in the background on my iPod. Sparkling cider was chilling in the ice bucket, right beside a platter of fruits and cheeses. My girl wasn't saying too much, which was beginning to make me nervous. Had I misjudged her?

Only one way to find out.

"Riley, talk to me."

I turned her around to face me as I could feel her skin tremble under my touch. Her beautiful skin was now lined with goosebumps. Her smile would be an image I would never forget. Her silhouette was glowing off the back wall from the candle flickering all around her.

"Make love to me," was all she said, four words that she asked of me before, and now I would give her all of me.

"I love you, Riley Taylor Briggs, so very much. Yes, we will make love tonight. I can't wait to show you how much you mean to me, but first I would like to give you something. Come here, baby, and sit with me."

I led her to the couch. I couldn't choose the bed, not now with how much I wanted her. This day and night was everything I wanted it to be, and now it was time to present my mother's ring to her.

Chapter Thirty

Our forever promise

Riley AND Jackson...

"WHEN YOU FIRST asked me to marry you back in New York, I thought you were completely nuts. I knew I wanted to marry you and after we left Georgia. I knew for sure you were the one."

I continued, "I had everything planned out on how I would ask you and the exact location where I would propose. Somehow that doesn't really matter to me anymore, because I know in my heart that right here, right now is our time. I truly believe I was meant to find you on the day of my mother's dedication ceremony. I even told my father that I believed my mother sent you to me. After listening to our parents' love story and seeing how love stands the test of time for Lila and Thomas, I know that can be our story too."

"Many years ago," I said to Riley, "the fates were aligned, and the love story for Walker and Reese began. Through the years of separation, their love remained true and found its way back to each other through us. If you think about it, it's pretty incredible. You, Riley, are incredible. I am so thankful for you and what you bring to my life. You are out of this world, spontaneous, crazy emotions all over the place, and beauty that stops me where I stand. I can't breathe without you, and I don't want to spend one day not loving you."

"Riley, I want you to have something. This belonged to my mother. What's in this box was given to her by my father. Now although they didn't have much time together, they did have a special love that began in friendship and became something more. How lucky for me that I was the product from that love. Although I never got to meet my mom, she's very much part of my life and our life together. I look to her for guidance and strength, and I feel her protection over me. After my talk with my father, all the fear that I had just faded away into thin air. This incredible heavy burden just disappeared. I'm not afraid anymore. I have to believe and trust that I will be fine after my surgery. And when I wake up, I expect to be able to lose myself in your beautiful eyes."

"Riley, you're the one that I want to spend every day with for the rest of my life. I want to fight with you and know we will be making up at night. I want to share everything with you and experience all our firsts together. Tonight I will be making love for the first time with the love of my life, but first, please open this box."

I rendered her completely speechless. Thank god she wasn't a mascara wearing girl, or her face would be lined up by now. She's cried quite a bit today, and once again I was brushing away her happy tears. Her hands were shaking as she opened the heart-shaped jewelry box. My heart was in my chest. *I hope the ring will fit. I didn't even think of that when I put my plan in motion.*

"Oh, Jackson! It's the most beautiful ring I have ever seen. I can't believe this is happening. This is real, right?"

"Yes, baby it is," I took the ring and slowly slid it on her finger. "Riley Taylor Briggs, will you make me the happiest ex-Yankee-now Oriole-loving fan and be my wife? I've accepted my fate and will forever love your birds. I see no one else beside me in this life. Allow me to be your husband, the father of your children, and the reason your eyes brighten. You have my promise—our forever promise—of an amazing life to look forward to. Please say yes?"

Waiting for her response added years to my life. She was crying, moving her mouth, but no sound was coming out. I knew her answer was coming, as this was my girl in all of her wonderment. She was either going to scream at the top of her lungs and break the sound barrier, or kiss me senseless. I was hoping for option two.

She wiped her face and looked at her ring. Taking my face in her delicate hands, she kissed me so softly on my lips, I could hardly feel her. Then she gave me the words I'd been waiting to here.

"Yes. I will marry you, Jackson Walker Reed. I will love you forever, be all types of crazy, and not hold you to loving the birds. I will go to your Yankee games and cheer your team on, because I know it makes you happy. I can't wait to tell you when I'm pregnant with our child. You will be an amazing father. I don't know what I did to deserve you, but I will not argue with the universe, the heavens, and every spiritual being out there. I'm yours, and I can't wait to say…I do."

"I'm going to make you so happy."

"You already have. Make love to me, Jackson."

As I took in Riley's beautiful face, once again the candles glowed around her, I almost had to pinch myself. I said my silent prayer to my angel above and thanked her for my angel here on earth. *Riley is here and with me in my arms. I'm a dreamer. I believe in the sun, moon, and the stars. Riley is my other half of my heart and she's said yes to becoming my wife. I wish I could stay here forever with her, but the night will slowly become the dawn, and we have to cherish what we have right now.*

"I'll be right back," she whispered to me, but not before leaving a trail of kisses along my face. *God! I wanted her so much. I feel like doing push-ups. I'm praying I last more than two minutes. Take a breath Jackson. You made it this far, and your girl is on the other side of that door about to come out and make all your dreams come true.* I gently knocked on the door to make sure she was okay. She said she would be out in a minute. We've done other things with each other that have been leading up to this point, but this was our big moment. I couldn't really blame her for being nervous. I knew I was.

I turned down the bed and got undressed. I stripped down to my boxers. My heart was beating way too fast. I took in a few calming breaths to steady myself, which was beginning to work until Riley walked out from the bathroom, looking breathtaking. I actually put my hand across my heart. My world completely stopped. She brushed her hair out, and it was full and wild running down her back. She was dressed only in her baby blue lacy bra with matching thong panties. They looked like dental floss with a triangle patch that barely covered her most intimate spot. They left little to the imagination. I bit back my lip imagining my mouth on her. *Yeah, I was going to rip that tiny scrap of material with my teeth.*

She slowly walked over to me, and began running her fingers through my hair, pulling me closer to meet her lips. Our mouths met as our tongues tangled with each other. She tasted delicious. I wanted more and couldn't wait one more second. I loved pleasuring Riley with my tongue, but we always stopped ourselves. Oral sex was amazing, but I wanted all of her now. I easily picked her up and carried her to the rose covered bed. She was sprawled out in the middle and began to open for me. I was on my knees and over her, taking in every inch of her natural beauty.

"I love you so much, Riley. I can't wait to be inside of you."

"Don't make me wait any longer. Please love me, and love me now."

Her pleas were making me lose my mind. She took her bra off and led me to her perfectly round breasts. Her nipples were pebbled and so inviting for me to suck. I took them in my mouth one by one as she cried out from the tantalizing sensation coursing through her body. I couldn't help my desire for her as I marked her breasts. She went wild at the sight of my love bites. Trailing my tongue down her sternum and to her swollen clit, she was tight, so tight, and I knew I had to take it slow. She lifted her pelvis, meeting my mouth at her entrance. I entered her with my tongue and began to fuck her with my mouth. All thoughts of erotic fantasies were filling my mind. How many times did the guys come over and play porn in my media room. I wanted more with Riley, but she was so fucking hot, I couldn't help it.

"Oh my god! Jackson, suck me please. I'm going to come so freaking hard."

And she did, all over my face. She was soaking with arousal and waiting for me to push deep inside of her. Sitting up to kiss me, she showed no resistance. Kissing me and tasting the remnants of her orgasm on my lips and tongue, she took it all. I fucking loved it. We were marking each other.

"I'm on the pill, you know this, but I would still be happy if you used a condom for our first time. Do you have one?" she asked so innocently.

"Of course."

I kissed her again and rolled off the bed to retrieve it from my pocket. I pulled down my boxers as my hard throbbing erection sprang free. Her eyes widened at the sight of it. We've seen each other naked before, but the expression on her face was priceless. Compared to other guys, I was rather fortunate. I crawled back up the bed to my girl and reassured her that it would indeed fit inside of her. That was it, I knew it. Her cheeks reddened, and she ducked her chin to her chest.

"Hey, look at me. Please don't ever turn away from me. You have nothing to be embarrassed about. I'm nervous too. Let's take this slow, and if you want me to stop, I'll stop."

"Okay. I trust you Jackson. Please don't make me wait any longer."

"I love you so much."

With my five words, I easily slipped inside of her. I watched every emotion play out on her beautiful face. She pinched her eyes shut a couple of times. When I tried to pull away, she pulled me back down.

"It's okay, baby," she said, holding her breath. "Just go slow and let me get used to it." She let out her breath.

Inch by inch I went deeper inside of her. "I'm almost all the way in baby, just a bit more."

Once I was completely inside her body, I began to go faster, but not too much that she couldn't handle. Our bodies began a steady rhythm of perfect unison. Sweat trickled down in between her breasts as I lapped it up with my tongue.

"You taste amazing, Riley, and feel so good. Wrapping her legs around my waist, I couldn't hold back anymore as I listened to her commands to go faster. I pumped and pumped every last drop into her, filling the condom. I collapsed on top of Riley. Our bodies were entwined with each other. I wanted to stay with her forever.

"I love you so fucking much. You are my life," I said to her.

I crushed my lips onto hers, making them swell before me. I licked, bit, and kissed her madly until I had to come up for air. How I waited this long was a miracle.

I slowly pulled out of her, causing her to wince a little. I was already feeling the loss of our connection. I disposed of the condom and climbed back in bed with her.

"Are you okay baby?"

"Fantastic. Can we take a bath?" she asked.

"We can do anything you want. I'll go start it. Be right back."

I kissed her again and made my way to the bathroom. This bathroom wasn't small by any means. It had a huge oval tub that we would easily fit in and still have room. I filled it with jasmine flower bath oils, one of Riley's favorites. I turned to see her standing in the doorway, and she looked scared.

"Baby? What's wrong?" I kissed and held her face.

"There's blood on the sheets." I looked over her shoulder and saw the evidence of her lost virginity.

"It's okay, baby. They're just sheets. It's supposed to be normal for your first time."

"I know, but when I saw the blood, I just got scared."

"Come on, let's take a bath, and you'll feel better."

I picked her up once more and placed her in the warm bath. She winced again, but then fell backward to my chest. I wrapped my long legs around her and kept her snuggled close to me.

"Are you okay, Riley, I mean really okay? This was a big step for us. Please tell me that I didn't hurt you?"

"Jackson, are you crazy or something? You did not hurt me. I loved what we just did and can't wait to do it again. I guess the reality of it all just slammed in to me. We're not virgins anymore, and we're engaged."

"Is that a bad thing?" I asked.

"No!!! It's an amazing thing, and I will always remember this night with you for the rest of my life. I love you with all my heart. Thank you for making it so special. I knew so many girls in school that did it in the back of some boy's car, or a quick fuck at a party. What we shared, you and me, was something from a movie, like a fairy tale love story. You are amazing, Jackson. I will spend every day proving that I'm deserving of your love."

"You are, baby. I'm the lucky one. It was the same for me. I had plenty of opportunities to be with girls, but none of them held my heart. I was just waiting for you. You have my heart, body, and soul for you, and only you."

After declaring our love for one another once more, nothing at all needed to be said. We belonged to each other. The fear and tension blissfully faded away as Riley straddled my hips and lowered herself on to my dick.

"Are you sure? I can get a condom."

"No barriers between us. I trust you Jackson. Now let me show you how much I love you."

Her inhibitions gone, Riley took me over and over again. My

eyeballs were rolling to the back of my head as she took control. Water was splashing over the sides of the tub. She gripped my shoulders as I held on to her hips and guided her up and down. I was so deep inside her.

"I'm going to come..," I breathed.

She bent backwards with her hair falling into the water. I held her hips so tightly, I was sure I bruised her. We came together in a catapulting thunder of pure pleasure.

"I can't move, Jackson. Oh my god, what the hell was that?"

"If you have to ask, maybe I didn't do it right."

"Shut up, you jerk. Oh, you did it right. Not sure if I'll be able to walk in the morning, but you're good babe."

We kissed and held the other in our arms as the bath water turned cold. I wrapped her up in a warm bath sheet the size of a blanket and carried her back to the bed. Riley was all I needed. Her body fit mine perfectly. She ran her fingers across my chest, stopping over my heart.

"I love you so much. Always believe that, Jackson, okay?"

"I do, baby, I do."

"Your father is going to be so mad that you left. Probably will blame me."

"Stop it. He's not going to be mad at you. Everything is fine with my father. Let's not talk about him right now. The only people that matter are in this room. Me and you. Got it?"

"Got it."

The drums of her heart were slowly lulling me to sleep. No matter what happened after tomorrow, Riley and I would always have this night.

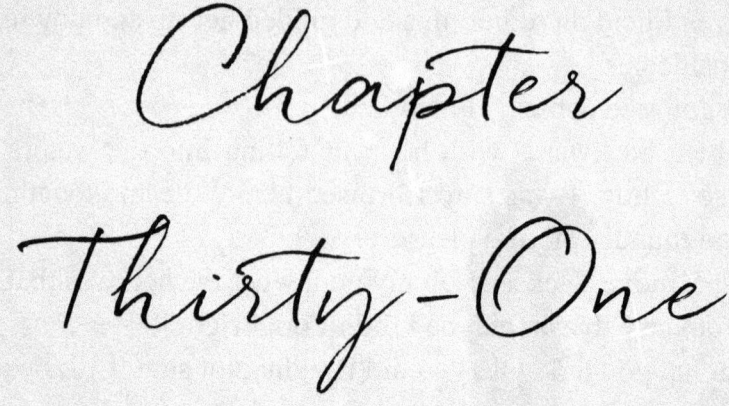

Chapter Thirty-One

Fool me once

Walker

"*GOOD MORNING, BALTIMORE! It's going to be a beautiful day here in the city.*" I heard this all too cheery greeting blasting from the television. *A beautiful day? Um...I don't think so. My son will be getting brain surgery in twenty-four hours and there's Henry Townsend to deal with.*

As I sipped my morning coffee and stared out to the rising dawn, I replayed the previous night's events that led to the confrontation with the man I despised most in the world. I had just been finishing up a meeting with Liam, when unexpectedly coming face to face with my former father-in-law.

"Liam, are you absolutely positive it was okay for Jackson to leave the hospital?"

"I do. I medically cleared him myself. Don't forget, Walker, he's not alone, he's with your guy, Richard, who I'm sure is trained and more than capable of assisting if anything happens."

"That's just it, Liam, what if he has another seizure? I can't even begin to have my mind go there."

"Then don't, Walker, you need to relax and get some sleep. Tomorrow is a big day for your son and he is going to need not only you, but his entire family for support."

I couldn't help notice Samuel's grim expression. He had to be thinking what every father did not want to believe, his little girl was all grown up. He, along with Liam, reassured me that Jackson would be fine. It had been a rough few days, and Jackson needed to relax before his operation. I trusted them both and tried to relax, but finding my son's note sent me spiraling.

Dear Dad,

I've left the hospital with Riley for some time alone with my girl. Please don't worry about me. The docs say I'm good to go. As an added precaution, I have Richard accompanying us. See you tomorrow morning at nine am.

I love you, dad.

Yours,

Jackson

Does he not know me at all? Me not worry? Yeah that's like asking the sun not to rise in the morning. Reese calmed me as best as she could, but I was still livid. My calls and text messages went unanswered, which proved to be more frustrating.

As angry as I was with Jackson for sneaking off with Riley, I was thankful he wasn't present to witness my confrontation with his grandfather. They had just arrived as I was leaving my meeting with Samuel and Liam. He didn't see me at first, but I certainly heard him demand information on his grandson. He certainly had balls, I'll give him that: to walk in and begin shouting out his demands, as if he was entitled to them. In my eyes, he lost that right after he screwed with my life. Jackson was my son, and he would not lay claim to him.

After discovering Jackson's leaving, I phoned my mother and explained to her that she would be driven to the hospital in the morning. She insisted on meeting me tonight, but without Jackson here, tomorrow was a new day. Olivia wasn't happy about it, but she did as I asked.

Now if it was only that simple with Townsend. Going unnoticed, I continued to listen to his rants. Stephen asked me if I wanted him to handle the situation Henry was causing at the nurse's station, but I refused. Gail saw me first and rushed over to me for an embrace. I accepted her affection as she immediately began crying over Jackson.

"Oh, Walker, where is he? They're telling us he's been discharged. How can that be if he's about to have surgery?"

Before I could answer her questions, Henry lunged forward at me only to have Stephen jump in and block him.

"You asshole, Reed! Where the hell is my grandson? You can't keep him from us. I know he's here."

A small gathering quickly surrounded us. Samuel immediately walked toward me, and I assured him I would silence the irate man in front of me. He didn't want his other patients disturbed, and rightfully so.

I excused myself from Henry's derogatory rant, and he had no choice but to follow. I led him into an empty conference room and out of sight from the rest of the floor. I was thankful that I sent Reese back to the hotel while I finished up my meeting with the doctors. Once we were all inside, I closed the door and turned around to face my former father-in-law.

"You will lower your voice and show respect for the patients who are residing on this floor," I sternly said to him.

He wasted no time and began spewing his ugliness once again.

"*Respect?* You want to know about respect, son. Well, what about my respect? How dare you! My grandson needs me. I will not be pushed aside because the great Walker Reed says so. I will fight you with everything I have."

"Henry! What has gotten into you? Why are you so angry with Walker?" Gail cried out.

"Quiet, woman! Let me talk to my son-in-law."

"Excuse me?" she replied.

"You heard me."

That's all he said as Gail appeared to be shocked by her husband's tone he had taken with her. Now, where is he, Walker?" he spat at me.

Stephen wanted to throw Henry out on his ass. I could see him balling his fists at his side, but I gestured that I had the situation under control. I first turned to Gail who was now wringing her hands in a crumpled tissue. She didn't deserve this treatment, and I would make it clear that I wasn't angry with her. I comfortingly put my hand on her shoulder as I yelled at her husband.

"Henry, let me be clear once and for all, I am not your son, and do not ever reference me by that term again. Secondly, you are here on the request of your grandson and grandson only. I don't give a rat's ass about your feelings and what you think you are entitled to. You make me sick, and if I had my wish, I would never lay eyes on you again. As for hiding my son somewhere in this hospital, that is absurd. He's not here, but will return tomorrow morning. He's not in immediate danger, and is under supervision while he's away tonight. He even left a note for you. Care to hear what it says?"

I mockingly waved it out in front of him. After his behavior, I was not going to give him Jackson's note. I opened it right in front of him, making him angrier than before.

Dear Grandpa

Thank you for coming out to see me.
Please don't worry about me. I will see
you tomorrow morning. And Grandpa...
please don't argue with my father.
Try to reconcile your differences, if
not for yourselves, then for me. Hug
Grandma and tell her that I love her.
Love you,
Jackson

I crumpled up the note and threw it at his feet, causing Gail to gasp at my actions. I immediately turned to her and explained.

"I'm sorry, Gail. Clearly your husband here has some explaining to do and hasn't already told you the truth to why we are at odds."

"Shut your mouth, Reed!" Henry screamed.

"No! You shut yours, and hear me, old man, because this is your only warning. You stay the fuck out of my way. You are only here because of Jackson. You try one thing, or say another word out of line, and I will have you removed from this hospital. And don't think for one second that you can play my son against me. You. Will. Fail. You've been warned."

"Gail, again my apologies. My mother will be here in the morning. I'm sure she will be happy to see you. Good night."

Without another word, I left the room with Stephen following my lead. All I wanted to do was forget these last few days, but that wasn't my reality. My boy would be back here tomorrow, and knowing what he would be facing was crushing my heart.

I was again seeking out divine intervention to help me, help my son. I sat in the dark chapel only lit with candles. I could take no more appearances from Elizabeth or my father, but that still didn't stop me from throwing myself at her mercy.

"Please, Elizabeth, watch over our son. He's got to be alright."

I then lit candles, hoping for my prayers to be answered: One for Elizabeth, one for Jackson, and one for my baby boy in heaven.

As Stephen and I made our way back to the hotel, my phone buzzed with an incoming message. I expected it to be Reese asking where I was, but it was from Jackson. He was telling me that he was safe and for me not to worry. He was with Riley, and she was all he needed at the moment.

I didn't bother responding, because I knew deep in my heart he was okay. *I'm not angry anymore, but that doesn't mean that I'm not worried. I will always be this way when it comes to him. I know where his heart was leading him tonight. The apple doesn't fall from the tree when it comes to how we love our women. He is knee deep, head over heels in love with Riley. They are each other's match. It's no wonder at all, she's Reese's daughter. She's beautiful, smart, and incredibly kind. I have no doubt in my mind that she will make my son very happy.*

We sure did have quite the growing family. As I thought about all I had, the anger I felt a short time ago with Henry was just gone. *They can't hurt us, ever again. Reese tells me this every single day, it's about time I start believing it.* I tiptoed back into the bedroom where Reese was still soundly sleeping. She was up so late with me and battled another round of morning sickness.

Sitting in a hospital was the last place she should be, but try making her leave. She could be just as obstinate as me, sometimes even more so when she was determined. I could try to convince myself that I would be okay if she went home to California, but that would be a lie. I needed her with me at all times, and she was the only one that was keeping me sane.

"Good morning," her silky voice greeted me.

I let out my breath and walked over to take my angel in my arms. She looked beautiful with her hair in a tangled sexy mess, her cheeks flushed with crimson all for me. She dropped her sheet and was naked in my arms. I was only wearing sleep pants and my obvious arousal was pushing against her stomach.

"Good morning, baby. You should still be sleeping."

"Only if you join me," she said, a proposal I could never deny, but I would have to say no for her own good.

"You are tempting, my love, but I will exhibit self-control this morning and just hold you instead.

"Come again?"

"You heard me, love, and no sex for you this morning. Do you remember how sick you were last night? And earlier in the day? Reese, I've been neglectful with you, and I have to be more careful. It's not just about you anymore. You're carrying our child, and I can't just take your body whenever I need release.

"Wow, what was in your morning coffee? Are you not you anymore? Because the man that I love—the father of this baby—would never hurt me, use me, and certainly not just fuck me because he needed to come. No matter what manner we make love in, it's always making love. Don't you know that by now? And if I couldn't handle it, I would say no and trust you to stop. Why, Walker? This deprecating attitude is grating on my last nerve. Stop it already!"

"Reese, you misunderstand, I…"

"The hell I do. Don't pacify me. I'm taking a shower…Alone!"

I watched her stomp off and into the bathroom, slamming the door behind her.

What the hell just happened here? And that will be the day when she takes a shower alone, I thought to myself. I stalked into the bathroom, pulling off my pants and joining her. Her back was to me. She stepped forward under the multiple sprays of water beading down her skin. I gently grabbed her arms as I felt her shiver beneath my touch.

"Please don't be angry with me," I said. "I can't take it."

"I'm not angry. I need time to think."

"The hell you do. Don't hide from me…ever!"

I turned her around to face me. Taking her face in my hands, I crushed my mouth down onto hers. She resisted at first and then opened up for me.

"We will never hide from each other again. I fucking love you, Reese, and I need you with every fiber of my being. Fight with me until your voice is hoarse, but please don't take time to think. That scares the hell out of me, and I can't lose you."

"Oh, Walker, is that what you believe? That if I take a few moments to myself, I'm drumming up ways to leave you? This is what I'm talking about. This is why I referred to you as deprecating. This is your pain talking for you. I understand your concerns for my health and the well-being for our daughter, but I'm the one that is carrying her, and I know my body. I know my limits, and you truly have nothing to worry about. To say 'I love you' pales in comparison to how I feel right now. We need a new dictionary written just for us that will *try* to explain my deepest love for you. I'm all in, forever with you, Walker. Please love me."

I tightly closed my eyes as if I were in pain. Her words were a blanket covering up all my open wounds. I easily wore my feelings on my sleeve when it came to Reese. She saw me and accepted me anyway. Her aptitude to read my thoughts was even scary at times.

"All parts of you, remember?" she said.

"All parts of us," I answered.

I was drained. She was drained. All her fight was gone, and I was there to heal us both. I didn't want to take her here, though. Reese needed to be in my bed. Turning the water off, not even remembering if we were finished, I led her out to dry her body off. I took my time with the process. This simple act gave Reese so much pleasure, as I began at her feet and worked my way up one leg at a time, giving each equal attention. I gently kissed my way up to her sensitive bud as it was calling out to me to enter her with my tongue. I so did. Her immediate response to my touch was to grab my hair. Reese pulled me toward her as I delved deeper inside her, making her cry out her pleasures with my name on her tongue. Taking her in my arms and carrying her to the bed, she opened up for me. I was so crazy with intense desire for Reese, I wanted to fuck her and fuck her hard, but held back no matter how much she demanded. This would be slow and she would feel every part of me, piece by piece.

"I know what you're doing. Stop it and go faster. I won't shatter like a porcelain doll."

"Shhh, let me love you baby. And remember who submits to whom."

That was it. Just a few last flicks of my tongue and Reese was spiraling down from her orgasm. I fucking loved to hear her and watch her body move as she took all of me and reveled in the pleasure only I could give to her. Without hesitation, I plunged deep inside of her, pulling back ever so slightly and then pushed deep again. Her back was arched and matching me thrust for thrust. I gripped her hair as I exploded inside of her. It was at such a force, it immediately began to spill out of her. I wanted to go again, I was so turned on.

"Holy shit! Walker, I can't move. You fucked me into the mattress."

I couldn't help but laugh out loud. We went from zero to a hundred in seconds.

"You can't move? I want to stay buried inside you forever."

Now she was smiling as she leaned up to kiss me. I lifted myself off of her and padded off to the bathroom for a warm washcloth. She was raw after our past few days of hard lovemaking. She would never say it, but I wasn't blind to it. I cleaned her up and kissed where I left my marks, while she let out her sighs and easily drifted off into a restful slumber. I climbed in and joined her.

It was barely seven. We had more than enough time to get some extra sleep. I was almost contemplating leave Reese here, while I went on ahead to the hospital, but she would want to be with me. I held my sleeping angel in my arms and thanked the universe for her. The bastard in me didn't deserve her, but she was here and that could never be challenged to as to why. We were meant for each other, we always were.

"I love you, Reese, always and forever." I whispered in her ear.

"I love you more." she answered back.

Oh, my impossible girl! I thought to myself as I continued to hold her, touching every inch of her body. Every touch calmed me, the goosebumps that lined her skin were a hairline trigger for me to take her again, but I let out my breaths and appreciated the moment with her.

Today would be hard, this I knew, but Reese would get me through it. Always...

Chapter Thirty-Two

Samuel Briggs

I SAT AT my desk, reveling in the quiet. The past few days had been the nosiest of my life. I still hadn't heard from Francesca. All my calls and texts to her had gone unanswered. She said we shared a connection, so if that's true, then she should have had the decency to call me back. I felt shameful how I had to speak with her. I was correct on calling her out on her unprofessionalism and would not waver on my decision to remove her from my service. The fact is, she's a damn good surgical nurse, and we crossed a personal line that should have never happened.

Today would be about Jackson Reed and preparing him for his operation that would take place tomorrow morning. Last night's commotion did not help at all with his grandfather causing a scene on my floor. This family had more drama than a Lifetime movie. *Not my concern, only the welfare of my patient, and securing the future happiness for my daughter. If his surgery is a success, I'm a hero once again in her eyes.* She'd been softening to me since this entire ordeal unfolded. With all that I had going on, I hoped I could at least speak with her and mend some of the broken fences that separated us.

I was going over some of my notes when a timid knock at my door interrupted me. To my surprise, it was Francesca. She looked exhausted with nearly swollen red eyes. No doubt I was to blame for her condition. I sat behind my desk not really sure what to do, but simply gestured to her to have a seat. She closed the door behind her and just stared at me.

"I've been calling you," was all I could say to break the obvious tension between us.

"I know, Samuel. I listened to all your voicemails and read your text messages over and over again until I had no more tears to release. Why Samuel? How did we get here?"

She sat looking defeated and broken. As much as I felt bad for my harshness with her yesterday, I couldn't sit here and give her false hope just because I called her out of concern. She ran from my office and hospital without even signing out. I couldn't lead her to believe that my natural concern for her well-being was nothing more than friendship. I knew how that sounded coming from someone who slept with her, but to me it was just sex. I never knew it was more for her.

"Francesca, I'm relieved to see that you are okay, but you and I are not a 'we.' I am sorry that you believed otherwise."

"That's just it, Samuel, I did believe it, because I allowed myself to. I thought you wanted me as much as I wanted you, and I was wrong. I have loved you from a distance for years now, and with your wife leaving you, I thought it was finally my turn. I must have been crazy to believe that you would want to start something with me after all those years married to her. I messed up, what do you want me to say?"

"Nothing. You don't have to say anything. You were not alone in this, I was right there with you. It was not my intention to lead you on and give you hope for something more between us."

"I guess it's really over?"

"I'm sorry, Fran, but we never really began."

"Okay then, thanks for that. Um…here's your case files and my resignation. I've already turned in my formal letter to HR."

"What? You're leaving? Just because I took you off my service doesn't mean you have to leave Johns Hopkins. Why are you doing this?"

"You know why? Because I love you, and I know you don't love me. How the hell can I remain working here and come to terms with that? You made it perfectly clear to me yesterday how you felt. If I even had the slightest doubt, well you certainly summed it up for me today. Don't worry about me, Dr. Briggs, I know I am a kick-ass nurse and will do fine anywhere I get a job. I trust you will give me a recommendation for my future employer."

"I will."

"Good. That will help. And Samuel…I truly hope one day you will be able to open your heart again to someone who is deserving of you. My girlfriends would probably smack me upside my head right now if they heard me being compassionate toward you, but they don't know you like I do. You're not ready, I get it, but I can't wait around forever until you are. I deserve more too. Hopefully letting you go won't be as hard as it was for you with your ex-wife. She clearly is happy and moved on. Good luck doing the same."

And with that, she turned and left my office. I whispered… "Goodbye Francesca."

You ever have one of those moments that completely blindsides you? Francesca just accomplished that.

"Wow! That woman has some fierce fire coursing through her veins. Your loss, Briggs."

"Ah, Satan incarnate, good morning to you. Now my full circle of hell has been complete, and it's not even eight o'clock," I said to Dr. McGovern as he made his intrusive way into my office. Of course, my friend and colleague always had a unique way of putting his perspective on my problems.

"What is it?" I asked him. "And why are you making yourself comfortable in my chair? I don't need this right now, especially from you."

"Relax, Briggs, I just came to check-in with you before my day got started with my meetings. All jokes aside, I'm sorry about your girl."

"She wasn't my girl. She was nothing more than a distraction and now, my *former* lead surgical nurse. I fucked up and hurt her. She just quit."

"This is not going to be a sexual harassment suit, is it? Let me know, so I can get the lawyers on it."

"Gee thanks for your concern, but no worries there. She quit on her own. As for a personal relationship? It never existed."

"Good. Keep it that way. That girl is a pot stirrer, and one you do not need right now, or ever for that matter. Keep your head in the game and concentrate on tomorrow."

"That's all I think about, Christopher"

"Good. Keep it that way. I'll see you later."

I didn't have time to respond back to him. He exited my office as quickly as he entered. After Francesca's outburst yesterday, I would have thought she would have put up a bigger fight with me today. I'm not sure what it was, but something was off with her. *Did I dodge a bullet? Or did I let my second chance at happiness slip through my fingers? What the hell am I doing? I can't sit here and ponder what might have been with her. I have my work and that's what I need to focus on.*

She was right about one thing. Yes, my ex-wife is happy and clearly moved on with Reed, but that doesn't mean I am. I've accepted the fact that my marriage is over and I will never get my old life back, but to try to have that all over again with someone new is just unrealistic for me. Who knows when I will find "the one" to share my life with? I thought I already had with Reese.

I need a serious do-over already!

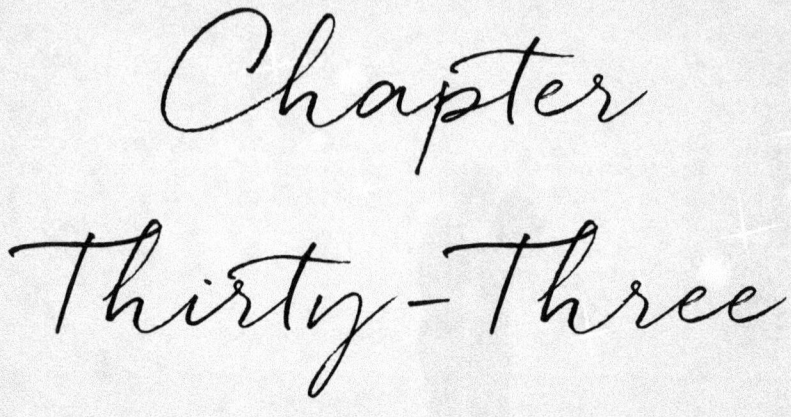

Chapter Thirty-Three

Trust your heart

Riley AND Jackson...

"**A**RE YOU READY?**"** I asked my beautiful girl as she continued to stare down at her ring. She was completely blissed out after the incredible night we shared. *Here we are, engaged and ready to begin the next chapter in our story. She said yes to become my wife. A promise between the two of us to become a reality someday in the future.*

We agreed to take it one day at a time and not worry about things that were not changeable. I had no doubt about my surgery tomorrow. My trust was with my doctors, God, and my angel above, who will protect me. I believed that undeniable fact with my whole heart. I just wanted to put this behind me and move forward with Riley.

"Earth to Riley, hello?"

She was still in a daze and completely ignored me. I knew she was in there somewhere under her glowing smile. I walked up behind her and hugged her. She let out the sweetest laugh and turned to kiss me.

"Good morning Jackson. I love you so much."

"I love you too, beautiful girl. Breakfast is ready. You need to eat before we head out."

"What about you? Aren't you hungry?"

"I am, but not for food." I arched my eyebrows and she laughed again.

"I'm going to hold off eating until we get back to the hospital. I'm not sure what kind of tests they need to do on me, and I may need an empty stomach. They took so much blood from me yesterday, and I can't imagine how much more they might need."

"I guess they are just exercising on the side of caution, especially with your father now involved. Jackson, how are we going to tell him our news? I can't imagine he will be exactly thrilled with his only son proposing to his flaky girlfriend."

"Stop it right now. What did I tell you about talking down about yourself? You are incredible babe, no bullshit talk about yourself. I love your personality. I love all parts of you. So, squash it, now. Babe, he already knows. Once I showed him my mother's ring that is now yours, he gave me his blessing."

She lunged herself in my arms, almost knocking over the breakfast table. I think she needed that reassurance.

"Hey, it's okay. No tears today. Is this why you were tossing and turning last night? Are you that worried about my father's reaction to our news?"

"Yes and no. Jackson, you weren't there when he overheard my conversation with my mom. He was so angry with me, and I was scared."

"He apologized to you once he calmed down, right?"

"He did, but I'm still a little nervous about it all."

"You have nothing to worry about when it comes to my father. His reaction was solely based on his anger toward me. It was completely my fault for lying to him and you were the first person he took it out on. He told me how much he regrets speaking to you like that. Of course, your mother set him straight after that. No worries, babe, please? I want you to forget all about it and concentrate on other things today, beginning with your father."

"What about him?"

"I want you to take some time today and talk with him. It's time, babe. Forgive him and move on from all the hurt that has separated you. Life is too short to be angry, especially with the people that love you the most. He's your father. He made a mistake, but you haven't been exactly a saint either. Forgive each other and move on. Plus, he doesn't need this added stress when he should be focusing on your fiancé's surgery."

"You're right Jackson, you always are. I so regret everything that came out of my mouth when I was with my father. After what happened to you, and seeing him just leap into action without hesitation, I already forgot why I was angry in the first place. I also have to apologize to him for speaking like that to…what's her name? Francesca? I was out of line."

"You were, but I love you for acknowledging and owning your faults."

"I don't know what's going on between them, and not sure if I really care, but that embarrassed him, and it was petty on my part. It's time to be a grown up and accept the things I cannot change, right?"

"Exactly. Eat your breakfast."

"I am, Mr. Bossy. Don't get any crazy ideas that you can just order me around now that I'm wearing your ring. I will always be fiercely independent."

"Oh baby, I have no doubt when it comes to your spirit. As long as you love me at the end of the day, all is forever right in my world."

Richard drove us back to the hospital and personally escorted us back to my private suite. More flowers had been delivered along with balloons, cards, and big "Get Well Soon" signs. I started to read them and laughed out loud when I read Brandon's card. He was the biggest male slut of our group. His card had a picture of three sexy nurses on it, and when you opened the flap, they flashed you with their big breasts. *I'm sure Riley would love seeing this above my bed...not!* I just moved it to the side.

Riley looked over my shoulder and laughed. "Is that from Brandon?"

"Yes, the one and only."

"Are you sure you don't want your friends here with you?"

"Yes, positive. I have all that I can handle right now. We will see them soon once we get back in New York and begin school."

At the mention of school, she detached herself from me and began to pace the floor. A sure sign she was worried about something.

"What is it, babe? Come here."

She let out a deep winded sigh and turned to look at me.

"Jackson, do you really believe that you will be able to begin school next month? I can't even think about that right now."

"Hey, where is this coming from? I'm going to be fine, and my recovery will be supervised by Dr. O'Larien. Nothing is going to change babe, trust me."

"I do. I'm really trying to be positive here, but we have no absolutes in life. And I don't want to keep bringing him up, but what about your father? Do you honestly believe he will allow you stay in New York after this?"

"Yes, I do. I'm an adult, and he will not force me into anything I don't want to do. We are moving forward with our plans to remain in New York and attend school at NYU. That's the plan babe... our plan."

"Okay," she whispered and wrapped her arms around my waist with her face burrowing into my chest.

I didn't say anything else on the subject. She was hanging on by a thread right now. I knew she was scared and was struggling to hide it from me. Holding her like this made me want to run back to the marina and make love to her for the rest of the day, but that wasn't my reality. My reality just walked through the door. Her father was looking way too serious with Dr. O'Larien. I'm sure my father was not far behind him.

"Good morning, Jackson, Riley," Dr. Briggs greeted us both with a curt formality. Riley turned in my arms and waited for her father to soften his features before greeting him. Once they looked at each other, she left my arms for his. He lovingly embraced her, and I saw a tear fall down her face. More fell as her father held her. She needed him as much as he needed her. *They would be okay, I just know it.*

"I'm sorry, daddy. Hormones," she said, and they both laughed. "Daddy, can we spend some time together today to talk?"

He let out a sigh and smiled warmly back at his daughter. "Nothing would please me more. How about we grab lunch down at Inner Harbor?"

"Sounds great," she answered back, but winked over to me.

Of course she was remembering our night spent together. Of course, I kept my thoughts to myself. We took a seat at the round table in my room. He had my chart with him, along with my scans. We covered everything we needed to discuss about my surgery tomorrow. All my tests came back in normal range, and my blood pressure was excellent.

"Jackson, I expect to be in the O.R. for about four hours, pending no complications. We will monitor you closely and hopefully you have no issues with anesthesia. Dr. O'Larien will of course assist me, but I'm confident we will get this AVM, and you will make a complete recovery. Any questions for me?"

"You keep mentioning complications. Do you think I will experience any?"

"I have to completely be prepared for anything that will arise tomorrow, including any unforeseen complications which I've already explained to you. Worrying about what might happen is superfluous at this time. You're in good hands, son, trust me."

"I do, sir. I do."

"Good man. Take today to relax, and if you need me for anything, I will be here."

Riley hugged her father again, only to be interrupted by our arriving parents. It didn't go unnoticed by my father how Dr. Briggs looked at Reese. They both greeted me with hugs, and my father raised an eyebrow at me. He was looking for confirmation if I went through with my proposal. I gestured to Riley's hand, and he grinned.

I wasn't ready to have another heavy conversation with my father, but with Walker Reed, anything was possible.

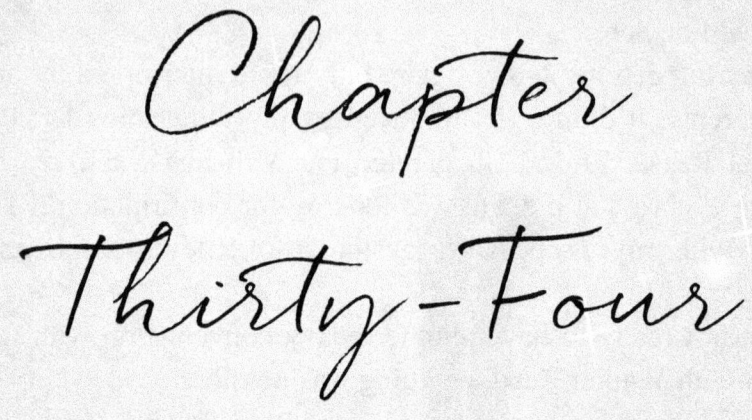

Chapter Thirty-Four

Coming together

Walker

AFTER A QUICK status with Briggs about Jackson, he left us to our privacy. I had so much I wanted to say to my son, "Where to begin?" was the question.

Reese and I both glanced down at Riley's hand, and she made no effort to hide it from us. This was the first thing that needed to be addressed. No reason to wait any longer.

"Congratulations on your engagement." Those four words spilled out of my mouth, surprising Reese, and even the kids. I took Riley in my arms and hugged her with all that I had.

"I love you, Riley, and you make my son very happy. I know this in my heart, and that's where it matters. We are a family, and our family is growing," I said.

"I still can't believe you kept it a secret from us." Said Riley, as she pretended to pout.

"It wasn't our intention to keep you out of the loop, but finally being all together again, we are so happy you both know."

"I'm going to be a big sister! I love how that sounds. I always wanted mom to have another baby, and now she is. Oh I can't wait to take my little sister shopping."

We knew what was coming next. She got up and threw her hands in the air and did a happy dance. She shrieked so loudly in excitement that a nurse came to check on the commotion. I assured her that we were fine, and she made her exit.

"Oh mom, I still can't believe it. I am so happy. You look a little green. Are you sure it's a girl? It could be a little linebacker in there. Boys are tough. What if you're having twins? Maybe that's why you're so sick."

"Take a breath darling," Reese calmed her. "We are positive it's a girl. She's perfectly healthy, and so am I. I've been dealing with morning sickness, hoping I am nearing the end. Oh, my sweet girl, we wanted to tell you, but please don't feel left out that we didn't do it sooner."

"I'm not mad. Okay, maybe a little. Jackson, you knew?"

"Yes. I did, but I think my father slipped."

"Men!" Riley humphed.

We all laughed. She hugged her mother, me, and finally Jackson. They linked their hands together. I saw so much of us in our children. Knowing they were so in love warmed my heart. A parent only wants the very best for their children. I have no doubt in my mind that Jackson had found his match, as I had with Reese.

We talked, and the kids told us all about their day and night, leaving out the parts we didn't want to know. Jackson looked really good. His attitude from our conversation yesterday to today was a complete turnaround. My mood was too. I had never experienced so much struggling with my thoughts, and I'd come to terms that I was ready to move on from my anger regarding my father. As for Henry Townsend, that was an entirely different problem. He was here, alive and well, and ready to take me on. His actions spoke volumes yesterday with me. I wasn't sure how he would react toward me today, but I had to try for my son.

Riley and Reese excused themselves while I stayed with Jackson to talk. My mother would be arriving shortly and no doubt, Henry and Gail would be here too.

"Are you okay, dad?" my son asked me in the most earnest tone I had ever heard from him. We didn't leave things on a positive note yesterday, and today I walked in like everything's fine. When it came to my son, we were fine. I couldn't be angry with him, not even for an hour.

"I'm fine, son. I'm sorry for storming out like I did yesterday. It was irrational on my part and wrong to leave the way I did. I don't want to defend my feelings to you and keep this disagreement on repeat. You must understand and respect my feelings, son, as I respect yours. You choosing to present Riley with your mother's ring was a huge decision and commitment. I've given you my blessing and will not stand in your way. Having said that, you need to show and give me the same in return. Your relationships are your own, and so are mine. Please do not worry about your grandfather and me. It's my problem, not yours. Understand?"

"I'm trying dad, and I give you my word to stay out of it."

"Jackson, that's not what I want at all. Don't ever feel that you can't express what you are feeling to me, but when I tell you an answer that you may not agree with, you can't use that against me. I totally felt blindsided by you yesterday, and that was not fair to me. I was angry with you, but I've also had time to think and take to heart what you said. I can only give you my word that I will try my best to see reason with your grandfather. He showed up here last night and we didn't have the most positive encounter. He was completely enraged and out of control, mostly out of concern for you. I can't promise how today will turn out once he arrives, but he's here for you. Let's keep that in mind."

"Thank you, dad, I love you so much. Thank you for supporting my relationship with Riley. I needed to hear that more than you know. And I'm sorry for pushing you yesterday. I was wrong, and you're absolutely right. It's between you and grandpa, and I have to keep our relationships separate. It was my fear that did most of the talking for me, but after sharing last night with Riley, I see things clearer today. Does that sound crazy?"

"Of course not. For a young man, you have the wisdom of ten men. I'm so proud of you and honored to be your father."

"I'm honored to be your son. You are everything to me, dad."

"Now that's what I needed to hear. I love you, son, so much."

No matter how old he was, I never missed an opportunity to take him in my arms. I hugged him tightly until we were interrupted by a staff member.

"Excuse me, Mr. Reed?"

Jackson and I both turned and answered, "Yes."

She laughed and told us that Jackson had a visitor waiting to be escorted in. My stomach dropped at that moment, but then my spirit lifted when I saw it was my mother. She looked beautiful with the epitome of grace and beauty, dressed in her classic Chanel suit and pearls gracing her neck. If she was worried, her appearance certainly didn't show it.

"Oh, my Jackson, come here and give me a hug." He quickly greeted his grandmother with a warm embrace, lifting her effortlessly off the floor, making my mother cry out in laughter. "Put me down! Oh, you Reed men and your love for picking up women. No pun intended."

"That's a good one, grandma."

"I try my best. How are you? Are you okay? What can I do to help?"

"Just you being here is enough for me." Jackson answered and hugged her back.

"I'll leave you two alone to catch up," I said.

They both went on about their conversation as I exited my son's room. Richard was standing guard in the hallway, no doubt wondering about my reaction to him leaving with my son last night.

"Sir," he greeted me.

"Hello, Richard, thank you for taking care of my son. You are not fired. I want you to remain here while I go take care of some business that needs my attention. Townsend is here along with his wife. I don't want any disturbances today that will upset Jackson. Please notify me immediately if anything arises. Are we clear?"

"Yes sir. I will take care of everything. Thank you, sir."

"I have no doubt, Richard."

My actions surprised even me, but like I promised, this was me trying.

I found Reese in the atrium with Riley, laughing over milkshakes and greasy French fries. You could hear Riley's excitement all the way down the hallway. She was so happy about our news.

"Hey you two," I said to them, curiously.

My girl gave me a "Don't worry" look when I saw what her second breakfast was. She knew I would have preferred fresh vegetables, but I was soon learning not to anger a pregnant woman. She needed to eat, and I was just happy she was keeping something down.

"Will you excuse us for a moment?" I asked Riley. She nodded and began playing on her phone.

"What is it, Walker?" Reese asked. "Are you okay?"

"Never better, love. I talked to Jackson, and now my mother is with him. I have to leave for a while. Will you be alright without me for a few hours?"

"Yes, of course I will be, but where are you going?"

"I need to go out to the Hamptons and see my father."

She let out a gasp, but it was a relieving one. Once and for all, I was putting the past where it belonged, and beginning with my father was the first step.

"If you tire for any reason, please go back to the hotel and rest," I pleaded with her.

"I will. I promise."

"Stay close to Richard today. If anything or anyone upsets you,

you are to call me immediately."

"Please don't worry. I'll be fine."

"All the reassurance in the world will never stop me from worrying, but I'm trying, and I try for you."

"I know you are, and I love you for it. Are you sure you don't want me to come with you? I can be with you if you need a shoulder to lean on."

"That warms my heart more than you will ever know, but this is something I need to do alone. I have many conflicted memories when it comes to that house. My mother likes to remind me that I remember the bad before the good."

"Don't you have any happy memories of time spent there?" Reese asked. "I can't believe you don't. What about summers in the Hamptons? Your early days of friendship with Elizabeth?"

"That was another life, and I don't wish to revisit it. This trip is about closing the door to my past with my father, and that is what I plan to do."

"Walker, please remember it's about your father. He doesn't get the power to darken every memory. Open your heart, the good feelings will come back, and there will be more good than bad. Don't worry, I won't tell your mother that she was right."

"How do you do it?"

"What?"

"You give me hope, Reese. I see things differently with new perspective and understanding. I can be so closed off, and then the good you have in your heart shifts me off course, and I'm steady."

"You are all those things and more, Walker. This is what healing does. Today when you walk through and crossover the threshold, know I am with you. Let our love be your guide to finally wash away the pain, loss, anger, and your father's sins. Remember our promise? We walk hand in hand on our new path to Forever. It's time, my love… our time."

"I love you, Reese, more than my own life. Thank you for coming back to me and putting me back together."

Tears began to fall as I took her in my arms and crushed my lips onto to her delicious sweet mouth. I didn't want to be away from her for a second, but I knew what I had to do. Holding her in my arms, this was my home. I knelt down before her, worshipping the very ground she stood on. I placed a kiss to her stomach and whispered "I love you" to our baby.

"I love you, Walker. Be safe and hurry back to me," Reese whispered.

Kissing her once more, I led her back to Riley.

"Take care of each other. I'll see you later."

Riley smiled. I turned and made my way to the airport with Stephen.

Chapter Thirty-Five

Forgiveness

Walker

WE TOUCHED DOWN on my family's Hampton compound. The flowers were in bloom with bursting colors. The surf was rising. Today would be a perfect summer day. I would have loved to share it with Reese, but I was here for something else.

I took a breath and walked through my former home. Every antique was in perfect arrangement, not a dust particle to be found on anything. My mother kept her home in a meticulous manner. It's been photographed for magazines more times than I care to remember. She would never leave this house. She shared this home with my father for over thirty years. This was where she was most comfortable.

After learning of my father's duplicity, I threatened to burn this house to the ground, but that would destroy my mother. Learning of her husband's betrayals was enough pain she would ever endure by me. My issues with Phillip were my own.

My relationship with my mother had been better, especially with Reese now back in my life. She'd only been out to California twice to visit with us. Mostly she spent her time with Jackson before he left for his trip, but we also had our time to reconnect. Reese had a way of bringing me out of my dark and into the light. I didn't think I would be baking cookies with Olivia Walker Reed and singing songs by a fire, but we were definitely trying to mend our hurt and begin a new relationship as mother and son.

Pausing at the entrance to his office, I let out a breath and walked through the one room I vowed not long ago to ever return to. It was just as I remembered it, but one thing clearly stuck out. My father's defaced portrait had been removed and replaced with one of my mother's precious Picasso paintings. I looked around and didn't see it anywhere. I would have to make a note to ask her about it. I destroyed it by throwing the decanter of scotch at it. I was blinded by rage and lost all control on that day. Miles Jacobson took the brunt of my anger and was so deserving of it.

My feet felt like lead as I tried to move about the room. After months of him being gone, I still strongly felt my father's presence. I planned on saying my peace at his gravesite, but I thought this is the better choice, right here where he spent his final days and penned all of his sins in letters to me.

Sitting behind his desk felt almost forbidden. As a child, I was never allowed to play in here. My father's office was his and his alone. When I was summoned to this room, it was usually to listen to a lecture on responsibility, my future role in the company, my choice for a wife. He certainly did have my life planned out for me before I knew myself, and then meeting Reese changed his plans for me. It's amazing how following my heart changed my father and forced him to commit unthinkable acts, a fact I was still trying to wrap my head around and come to terms with. This was why I was here. I was moving forward and finally laying old ghosts to rest.

As I looked around the room, my eyes found a framed picture

on his mantle above the fireplace. I don't ever remember it being displayed in here of all places, but there it was. I got up and studied it closer. It was a collage of me. It contained my high school graduation picture, my college graduation picture, and a picture of the two of us when we christened the new Reed Global building in California. I guess it would be considered milestones of my life. He was actually smiling in this one. It was one of the few times he said he was proud of me. I took the framed photo with me and sat again behind his desk, staring at the man that led me back here.

"I'm here, father. I'm here to give you what you want ... forgiveness. Where do I begin? Since reuniting with Reese and discovering piece by piece of your deceptions, I've been a man filled with rage, hungry for revenge. All I wanted was to make the people that hurt Reese to suffer. I followed through with some of it, and left the rest to suffer in their own pool of guilt and regret."

"I won't deny how much your betrayal has hurt me. You took my choices away and made them your own. For years, I suffered with pain and loss and never truly understood why I was going through it at all. I was so in love with Reese and planned my entire future around her. To lose her without ever knowing why gutted me through like a piercing blade. Why, father? What was it all for? For the sake of your ambition? Our company? Why didn't you trust me to help you? We could have faced the problems you were having together, but you allowed Henry Townsend to manipulate you, ultimately changing my life. You made it your life's mission to groom me to be the perfect mogul. I was a boy that had to grow up way before I was ready to, because this is what you wanted for me."

"Was I ready, father? You seemed to believe I was. So why didn't you trust me to help you? This is the one question that has been weighing heavily on my mind. If you were in front of me right now, this is the question I would ask you. I believed you got off easy by dying, but not anymore. If I hadn't been so blind and arrogant the day you came to me, maybe I would have seen beyond my own sins, and acknowledged yours."

"Then there's your good friend, Henry Townsend. He said the reason behind his motives was securing his daughter's happiness? Was that fair to her in the end? I can't change what happened and what led you to do what you did, but I can change my destiny. It begins here."

I ran my fingers over the framed photo and voiced the words out loud.

"I forgive you, father. I forgive you for me. I forgive you for Reese. I forgive you for Elizabeth. I forgive you for my mother. I forgive you for Jackson, and I forgive you for the life that you took…my son, Thomas Mitchell Walker Reed."

"Yes, father, my son…my first son. You tormented, hunted, and never gave Reese a moment of peace. She wasn't strong enough in the end to carry our baby to term. On your road to absolution, did you ever think of him? Reese is pregnant again, this time with a girl. She is just at the same mark in her pregnancy that she was with our son when she miscarried. You can't even imagine how fucking scared I am at this moment. I watch her sleep. I watch her eat. I just watch her and look for any sign of distress. She is my life. Do you hear me, father? She was everything I ever wanted back then, and she still is today. You did not break her! You did not break us! I can't spend the rest of my life hating you. Life is too short, and I lost so much time already. My future is with Reese and our daughter. My son—your grandson—will survive. Life is not that merciless to take away one more person I love."

My breath was ragged, and my chest felt heavy. I screamed out to thin air in hopes he was listening. Yes, I vowed to forgive him, but it still hurts like hell to say the words out loud. I returned the photo to its rightful place and walked out of my father's office, already feeling lighter.

Walking through my mother's prized rose garden, I picked a few white roses. I felt they would deem best on how I was feeling about today. My mother loved to show them off. She always explained what each color meant and the right times to give them. I had chosen white, because they can mean a new beginning or a farewell. For me, it was both. I was saying farewell to the past, and my new beginning was with my family and all the good that was yet to come.

The sun was warm on my face and a light breeze wafted at my back. I placed the flowers down on my father's grave and knelt before it. I shrugged at what was in front of me, almost in bewilderment that this was his last mark on the world. For a man that lived larger than life, his stone was simple. His name was carved into the solid granite stone. No personal touch to tell you who the man was who laid beneath the earth. I traced out his name with my finger. "Phillip Alexander Reed."

I wanted to feel something for this man who was my father. No tears fell, I was numb. I said a prayer for my father in hopes that he would hear it. It was a simple prayer for his peace. And then I said my final words to him.

"You never apologized for who you were. I guess that is one thing we have in common, but I declare, we have many things we share. I don't hate you, father. I just hate what you did. I may have thought that I hated you at one time, but now I know that's not true. You were my father. I believe you did love me the best way you knew how. I always knew who you were. You never justified that fact and still stood behind every decision you ever made."

"The good you had in you was a legacy you left for your grandson. Jackson loves you, father, and misses you. Jackson has your watch with him, and it's giving him the strength he needs to get through tomorrow and on the road to recovery. You don't have to be in the dark anymore. I'm not a man that throws out false words and not stand behind them, another trait from you. Reese told me that when I was truly ready, I would know the right time to say the words. Did it take nearly losing my son to make me realize it? I'm not sure. I'm tired. I'm tired of analyzing every emotion that I'm feeling."

"I'm sorry that my walls were up on the day you chose to break down yours. I wasn't ready to listen. But all roads lead back to our past, whether we like them to or not. Sometimes we don't have the power to stop it. I will no longer be guided by your sins.

"I. Forgive. You. Father."

"You. Are. Free."

"I hope what I've said here today is enough. I hope it brings you peace and the closure you need for the next life."

"Goodbye, Father."

Chapter Thirty-Six

You've got a friend

Reese

REMEMBERING THE LOOK on Samuel's face as we arrived this morning saddened me more than I realized. I knew he had many things weighing heavily on his mind, and I felt his loneliness radiate off of him. We were friends first, and he needed one right about now. If the tables were turned and I was in his shoes, I wouldn't be feeling too hot either. It wasn't as if we were parading our relationship in front of him, but Walker never eased back on his public displays of affection. I noticed that when Samuel was around, Walker became even more aggressive.

Walker would always be a possessive man. He valued what's his and let no man stand in his way. Samuel was no exception.

Riley had lunch with her father today, a "do-over," if that's what you want to call it. It was her second chance at making things right between them again. They met down by the waterfront and dined at his favorite restaurant, Henningers. This time, father and daughter enjoyed a delicious lunch and had the talk that needed to happen months ago. I was so proud of her for finally letting go of her anger and animosity toward Samuel. They were always so very close. It hurt me that they were so at odds with each other. She had to come to terms with the fact that he wasn't the only one in the wrong, as I also played a role in the separation.

When Riley returned from lunch with her father, she looked happy and carefree. The worry I saw this morning was gone. She hugged me, and we chatted about her lunch with Samuel. I asked her where he was, and her simple reply was enough to tell me that my instincts were correct. He was on the roof. This was his one private place that he could go and clear his mind. With Walker still not back yet, this was my chance to speak with Samuel without being interrupted or my mercurial man losing his mind.

"Ms. Mitchell, are you sure? The roof?" Richard had nervously questioned me.

"I'll be okay. Please wait here for me. If Mr. Reed calls you, please tell him that I'm perfectly fine. Understand?"

"Yes, ma'am, as you wish."

Poor Richard. He constantly plays the buffer for Jackson, Riley, and now me.

I found Samuel where I knew he would be. Samuel was a creature of habit and rarely changed up his way of doing things, at least personally. He was in a corner with his head in his hands. I slowly made my way over to him without startling him of my presence.

"Samuel" I whispered to him, as I sat down beside him.

"Reese, what are doing up here? And in your condition? It's dangerous and you can fall and get hurt. What is it?"

"I was looking for you."

"You found me. If you don't mind, I would rather be alone. Call your security dogs to come and retrieve you."

"Are you finished being mean? I didn't come up here to argue with you. And being alone is the last thing you need right now. And one more thing, stop being an ass."

"I wasn't trying to be, I'm sorry. I just can't be here with you, especially right now."

"Why not?" I asked.

"Because..."

"Oh Samuel, you can do better than that. 'Because...' is a child's answer. I came up here to speak with you, and Dr. Briggs, you will listen."

He went to respond, and I raised my hands to stop him. Placing my hands on top of his, his eyes widened as if he was surprised with my intimate gesture. For me to touch another man would not go over well with Walker, but this wasn't just any man. He was a huge part of my entire adult life, and he was Riley's father. We would always be connected. Nana always encouraged forgiveness, compassion, and understanding. Right here on this roof, Samuel needed all three.

"Thank you, Samuel," I said to him.

"For what?" He looked incredulously at me.

"For being the man I always knew you to be. The man that held my hand in the hospital all those years ago when he thought I would be scared when I woke up. You showed kindness to a complete stranger when you could have just treated me like any other patient under your care."

"You were so much more to me than a patient, Reese. You were the sun that lit up my life. I was blind and foolish to not value what I had. I should be thanking you for staying with me as long as you did."

"Oh, Samuel, stop it. Please do not devalue what our marriage was or wasn't. We had more good than bad, and I will never regret the time we had together. And please, you shouldn't either."

He broke away from me, as if my touch was hurting him. His back was to me. I asked him to sit back down, but he refused. I stepped behind him and placed my hand on his right shoulder. He jerked away.

"Please don't. Please don't build me up to something I used to be. I'm not that guy anymore. That man died the day he hurt you. I do not deserve your compassion," he sulked.

"You are wrong, so wrong. Forget about being the great brain surgeon. Forget about the awards that line your office wall. Forget it all, and just remember who you are. You deserve compassion, friendship, and most of all…love. You are an amazing man, and I will not listen to you break yourself down as if you don't matter. Your daughter is the same way, I might add. If at any given moment you don't rise to meet someone's expectation of you, then you feel less of a person and undeserving, which in my opinion is a bunch of bullshit."

"Careful, Reese. Where's your southern manners?" he joked and smiled.

"They're right where your self-esteem is, in the shitter."

That broke the tension. He was laughing so hard, he was holding his stomach. I wasn't one to use these words, but when I did, he always laughed. It was one of Nana's words that I used from time to time. I didn't want him to retreat back to his dark mood, so I continued to talk.

"Samuel, do you want to know why I came up here to find you?"

He quietly nodded.

I continued, "Because I know you're still struggling with what happened between us back on that island, and what followed afterwards. Do yourself a favor, and let it go. Forgive yourself, because I have, and move on from it, never to talk about it again."

"So what you're saying is move on from you? And behave as if the past eighteen years didn't happen? You sound like Christopher and Francesca. Believe me, Reese, I'm trying to move on, but it's a daily effort to do so. For months our daughter refused my calls and any contact with me. I was so disheartened by her."

"I'm sorry for that, and I know she is too. You talked it all out and are fine now, right?"

"She forgives me, and I her, but it's still hard to come to terms on how we got there. After months of rejection and then to hear from her, it made me so unbelievably happy. She accepted my invitation of reconciliation, and to find out that it was laced with lies and deception hurt like hell. A few days ago, she was the same angry girl that shut me out of her life. She used me, Reese, to help her boyfriend. Now that young man has put all of his trust in my hands to help him. Of all the surgeons in the world, he wants me. How am I supposed to feel about this? He's our daughter's boyfriend—no, scratch that—her fiancé. I'm too close to this, but I can't not do it."

He continued, "I sat in my office on the night Jackson was brought in and listened to Walker Reed beg me to save his son. Again, I ask you: 'How the hell am I supposed to wrap my mind around this conundrum that has brought us all together?'"

"Why question it at all?" I asked Samuel. "He chose you because you are the best at what you do. He trusts you to help him, and so do I."

"Our daughter will never forgive me if something goes wrong. How will I ever be able to look into Riley's beautiful eyes if I can't save the love of her life?"

"I'm not worried." I reached for his hands and held them in my own. "I know these hands heal and will be the same ones that save Jackson. You are a brilliant surgeon. You have been blessed with an extraordinary gift, one that gives your patients their lives back and hope for their future. Jackson's life is just beginning, and it will be shared with our daughter. Please, Samuel, this will be the last time I ever ask you this again. Forgive yourself. Please stop blaming yourself for failing me. You were not the only one in this marriage. I'm so sorry for hurting you. You were my friend first, and I want us to be friends again. Please, Samuel, can you try?"

Tears began to fall down his hardened features. He ran his hands through his hair and tried to hide once again from me, but I was crying too.

"Reese," he sighed, "for you...I will try."

"Thank you," I whispered to him.

As I remained in his arms, I felt the weight of his stress leave him. Putting the past behind you and leaving it there was harder than it looked, but we were all trying. Today, Walker, Riley, and Samuel all took the first step forward.

I WAS PRETTY much gone the entire day. All I wanted was to be with Reese. She was my home, and I needed to be comforted by her. I phoned her immediately, and my calls went straight to voicemail. She knew how I detested when she ignored her phone. My second option was to call Richard. If he valued his job, he'd better be with her. He answered on the third ring, raising my alarms even more.

"Hello, Mr. Reed."

"Where the hell are you? And where is Reese? She is not answering her phone." I was trying to keep myself in check, but how I just spent my day, my patience level ceased to exist.

"Mr. Reed, I assure you Ms. Mitchell is fine. She is speaking with Dr. Briggs at the moment and didn't want to be disturbed."

"And you're not with her? I'm coming to you. Where are you? Hello? Richard? Answer me. Where are you?"

His silence was peeling away the last layer of my patience and then he answered my question.

"The roof sir. I'm up here with Ms. Mitchell and Dr. Briggs. They are speaking to one another, and I have a clear sight of them."

"I'm on my way. Words cannot begin to describe how angry I am with you."

I hung up before he could respond. Stephen was following behind and tried to keep up. I had never moved so fast in my life. I was nearly out of breath by the time I reached the entrance to the roof access.

"Sir, I…"

"Not a fucking word from you, Richard. I will deal with you later. Where is Reese?"

He directed me and Stephen to where she and Briggs were. I

witnessed an intimate moment they seemed to be having. She was in his arms, and he was lovingly stroking her hair.

What the fuck! I wanted to throw him off the roof, but hell had frozen over because I remained in control and dauntingly calm.

"Reese," I called out to her. She immediately smiled and walked toward me. It was my arms that were now wrapped around her, as I glowered toward him. He remained where he was standing.

"What are you doing up here?" I asked. "This is not a safe place for you. What were you thinking?"

My hands were now cupping her face and waiting for an answer. She didn't respond and turned back to Samuel. She asked if he was okay, and he simply told her, "Yes." Entwining her hand with mine, she led me away, but not before I shot him one last look.

My hand was at the nape of her neck, as I guided her down from the roof. She remained silent as we were now heading to my car in the private underground garage.

HE TOLD STEPHEN and Richard to leave us, and to wait for him back inside. No doubt they were on their way back up to watch over Jackson and Riley. His hand hold did not lessen on me until I was in the backseat of the car. His eyes were flaming pools of fire. He began to loosen his tie, and before I could register what was happening, he had my hands bound.

"Walker!" I shouted. "What are you doing?"

It's not as if we didn't have this type of play in our life, but here in this car? He was treading on thin ice. This right here was not him having fun, but punishing me for being with Samuel. It was finding me in Samuel's arms. I might as well have thrown gasoline on Walker and lit the match.

"Walker, please talk to me?"

"I think you did enough talking already today, Reese. Now I get my turn, but on your body instead."

I'm sure he wanted to shred my clothes, but he had impeccable control and deftly unbuttoned my blouse. He lifted my skirt and made his way to my panties, which he tore.

"Why, Reese?" he asked has he plunged two fingers inside of me, making me cry out.

"Answer me. You were alone with your ex-husband in an area you knew would make me lose my mind? And in his arms? I can't bear to see another man touch you, least of all, him."

Before I could answer, Walker was fucking me with his fingers. I came soon, as he entered me with his tongue, bringing me to the edge of my second orgasm.

"I'm going to fuck you now, and hard," he slowly spoke while clenching his jaw.

I was defenseless against his sensual assault. He placed my tied hands around his neck and entered me not as hard as he warned me he would. I loved every piece of this man inside me. With every thrust, I wanted more, but he glanced down at my growing belly and held back. He wouldn't risk hurting me, not that he could. This was who we were. When he was inside of me, he was all I saw and wanted. The way we made love was a force to be reckoned with. We had no boundaries, we never did. I was about to come so hard, and he was close too. Grabbing my hair, he filled me with his release and called out my name. My body was shaking with him still buried deep inside of me.

"I love you so much," he said as he kissed me all over and swiftly untied my hands, rubbing them over and making sure I was fine. We cleaned ourselves up, and then I was pulled onto his lap with his arms securing me in a tight hold.

"I'm sorry, baby. Trying doesn't mean I will completely change everything about me. I am a man who protects what's his. And never forget who you belong to. You. Are. Mine. No matter what the reason to why you were up there, you had to know it would never sit well with me. To see you in his arms, I just about lost my fucking mind. I will make concessions, Reese, but not on this. He is never to touch you like what I walked in on. I'm not a fool to believe that you will never embrace. You do share a daughter, but the way he was touching you was not exactly friendly. I know the difference, and I'm quite sure, he does too."

"I love you too."

"That's it? You're not going to fight with me? You're not going to tell me that I'm a crazy, possessive caveman?"

I was laughing now with my mercurial man. *Oh, I love him so much.*

"Walker, you are all those things and so much more. I love all parts of you, you know this. Walker, Samuel is part of my life, and he always will be, but not for the reason you believe. Please try for both our sakes to come to terms with this. Sooner rather than later would be best. You weren't the only one breaking with the past and starting over. He needed a friend today. I was happy to be there for him. He was hugging me because of what he will be facing tomorrow when he operates on Jackson. I have no doubt he can do this surgery and come out successful. It's too close to home and emotions are high. It's perfectly natural to be apprehensive."

"He's not having doubts, is he?"

"No. Nothing like that. He and Riley reconciled their differences today, and I felt it was my turn to do the same. Before you protest, hear me out. I forgave him a long time ago, but he didn't forgive himself. He needed to let this go before tomorrow. We talked everything out and when you saw us hugging, that was Samuel promising me that he would try his best to move on. Are we okay? Do you now understand?"

"I do. More than you know. I'm sorry. We are always…okay. I know he's a good man, and I understand how he feels. It's an emotion I felt for years when we were apart. The rational side of me gets it, but tell that to my caveman side. Reese, it's just impossible for me to know any other way."

"I understand, baby. More than you know. Do you want to tell me about your trip to the Hamptons?"

"Someday."

"Walker? What is it?"

"I'm fine. Can you do something for me?" he asked as his shoulders fell and he visibly relaxed.

"Anything."

"No more talking. Just let me hold you."

Chapter Thirty-Seven

I never really knew you

Jackson

IF I DIDN'T know I was getting brain surgery tomorrow, you would think my stay here was a vacation. I had staff doting on me. My suite was filled with fresh flowers, and I had all the amenities a five star hotel would offer. This had my father written all over it. After all, he did design this building.

My mind kept going back to my night spent with Riley. She was the best thing that ever happened to me. Her body beckoned my desire to take her all night long. We fit perfectly together as two lovers could. I FaceTimed with Brandon earlier, and he told me that monogamy was too cruel a rule. I couldn't help but laugh. They could have their fill of nameless faces and the quick flings. What I had with Riley was real, and it was for a lifetime.

Losing myself deeper in my thoughts, I didn't hear the knock at my door. I looked up to see my grandpa Henry standing there. He was wearing a pained expression on his face, kind of like when I saw him last at my graduation. I wasn't sure why he hadn't entered yet, but I decided to make it easier for him and walked toward him.

"Hi, grandpa. I'm happy you were able to make it."

Before I could say anything else, he stepped forward and grabbed me by my shoulders. His fingers dug into my shoulders to the point of pain, but I stayed still and waited for him to say something. He looked me up and down then pulled me forward to hug me. His grip was tight, and then he broke down into tears.

"Oh, my boy, my precious boy, are you okay?"

"I'm fine. I promise you. Please, grandpa, don't cry."

"I can't lose you, Jackson. I won't survive it."

"Grandpa, please don't talk that way. I'm going to be fine."

"And how in the hell do you know that?" His tone made me step back.

"I'm sorry, son. This news has certainly rocked me to my core, and I admit I'm not handling it very well."

I guess there was no better time than to address his issue with my father. I asked him to have a seat, so we could talk. He wiped his eyes and joined me at the table.

"Am I the reason you argued with my father last night?" I think my question surprised him.

"Jackson, it's more complicated than you realize," he answered back.

"Enlighten me. And before you sugarcoat your answer for my benefit, I know why my father is angry with you. The one thing I don't know is why you did what you did?"

"I'm not having this conversation with you, Jackson, and not before you are about to undergo brain surgery tomorrow. You should be resting and not worrying about the adults in your life."

"Grandpa, if you haven't noticed, I'm an adult too."

"I know, my boy. I was there when you were born. I just don't want to burden you with my problems that concern your father. He's been standoffish and obstinate when it comes to you. He barred us from even sitting in the family section at your graduation. You can't even begin to know how much that hurt your grandmother. I respected his wishes then, but all cards are off the table now. I will not be dismissed and kept away from you."

"Grandpa, no one is keeping you from me. You are here because I want you here, but if you argue with my father and make an intense situation even worse, I will be forced to choose sides. I mean, he's my *father*."

"And I'm your grandfather who has rights. We deserve to be with our daughter's child, and not even your bastard of a father will keep me from you, son."

Who was this man before me? It's as if he has lost his humanity. He has never raised his voice to me, let alone speak in a derogatory manner toward anyone. After he slammed his fists onto the table, I literally jumped. His expression instantly softened and filled with regret, but it was too late. My eyes found his, and they were filled with rage. I wasn't sure how long my father had been standing there, but judging by the glacial daggers he was now directing at my grandfather, I knew he heard enough.

"HE'S NOT *YOUR* son. He's *my* son," I proclaimed as I walked in Jackson's room. Jackson was frozen where he sat, but Henry quickly turned to face me, not caring about what I just interrupted.

"You!" he shouted.

"Because of you, my Gail is sick with worry and is in bed back at the hotel. You and your 'truth' caused more harm than you can imagine."

"Are you for fucking real?"

"Dad…"

"Not now, Jackson," I said. "This is between me and your grandfather. He obviously has something he needs to get off his chest. If he wants to do it here, then we do it here. So it's my fault Gail is sick? I love how you can stand here and feign innocence when you are the one that caused years of heartache for me. Your presence was requested here because of Jackson, and him alone. I don't owe you anything but a punch to the mouth. I don't know what it is with you, Townsend? I warned you months ago to stay the hell away from me and out of my life. We are finished. I really don't give a fuck what happens to you, but my *son* does. You have a choice to make right here, right now. Shut the hell up, and be the grandfather that Jackson needs, or go back to Arizona. I can't have you flying off the handle like this. My son should be resting and not having to witness your temper tantrums."

"You are such a smug bastard. You think you can twist the truth and use it to your advantage. This is your fault, Reed. Everything is your fault. If you would have just stepped up and chosen Elizabeth from the beginning, I wouldn't have had to do what I did."

"I already know what you did, Henry. Please spare your grandson any pain, and not repeat it."

"I have nothing to lose, Reed, not a thing. I already see Jackson looking at me differently, and that's because of you."

"Grandpa, that's not true," Jackson pleaded. "Please let's just talk it out?"

Henry interrupted, "It's too late for talking, son. Your father is not the man you believe him to be. He used my Elizabeth, then threw her away like garbage because of some whore from Georgia."

The moment I heard him spit out his malevolence toward Reese, I completely stepped outside of my body and became unhinged. *Never will another person ever hurt her again. Even with words, I would make them suffer.* I punched Henry so hard that he flew back into the wall, denting the sheetrock. He lunged at me as if he could take me. By this time, Stephen had come rushing in to the room and restrained him.

"Fuck you, Reed. Fuck you and your Reese Mitchell. You didn't deserve my precious daughter, and you don't deserve her son. Your father wasn't man enough to keep you away from her, so I took over."

"What the hell are you talking about?" I said.

"I fucked with and sabotaged your company. I arranged for that accident to happen on that job site so I could have your father right where I wanted. He was under *my* control. And you, Walker, were under *his*. Did you honestly think that Phillip Reed gave that much interest to who you were fucking? He lived for his company. Sure he wanted you matched with the perfect woman, but he knew you loved her. When I saw him slowly changing his mind, I had no choice but to change the game. Thank god, she lost the only leverage leading her back to you. It paved the way for you to be with Elizabeth. When I found out she was pregnant with Jackson, I knew I had you. I knew you would never walk away from your responsibility. After you brought her home, my good friend Phillip easily cowered down to my demands."

Was this really happening? This couldn't be my life right now. Just when I thought I had put the past pain behind me, Henry Townsend upped the ante and changed everything. I knew he was the puppet master pulling the strings, but not to this extent. *He was the one?* It didn't dismiss my father's role in this fucked up story, but it showed me that I truly never knew my former father-in-law.

I JUST STOOD there in shock and disbelief. *Who was this man?* Five months ago, he was my grandpa, a man I respected and loved with all of my heart. The man standing here now was not that guy. He was unhinged. His words were filled with poisonous venom, all aimed at my father, ready to strike. What am I saying? He already did. My father was silent. My grandpa had now been released from Stephen's hold, but all eyes were on him. They were all ready to pounce if he made any sudden moves.

Richard now joined them, along with two more men I had never met before. I was thanking God that Riley wasn't here to witness this. My head was beginning to slowly pound. I took a few deep breaths and looked at my grandfather. He tried to come closer, but my father blocked him. After what happened here, I knew there was no recovering from this. Grandpa Henry, and his hatred for my father and Reese, did this. I didn't know if I could even speak, but slowly tried.

"Is it true, Grandpa? Don't worry, I don't need to hear you confirm it. Your actions here speak volumes of a man I truly never knew. Please leave, and don't come back here again."

"No! Jackson, it was your father. He's trying to keep us apart. You must believe me, son. I did it for your mother. You are what binds us together. Don't let your father take that away from you. I am your grandfather, and I love you. Please, Jackson, don't let him do this."

"I'm sorry, grandpa, but you did this all on your own. The only person that's wrong here is you. How could you disgrace my mother's memory like this? She loved my father, and my father loved her. For you to say otherwise makes me sick. I feel sorry for you. You've spent years hating on a woman that did nothing to you, and all she did was love my father. You destroyed lives. I'm looking at you, but all I see is an angry shell of a man I used to know. You're not even sorry for it. You say you loved my mother? How could you when you are filled with so much hate? You vilify what my father shared with my mother. It may have not been what you created in your head, but it was real, and their story belonged to them. You don't get to stand here and rewrite history to ease your conscience. Get out! And don't come back."

I went to move and nearly fell over. My head was spinning, and I felt sick, causing my father to react immediately. I could feel my heart beating faster, faster than ever before. My eyes began to blur. *No, please!!!* I silently prayed.

"Jackson! Are you alright?" My father asked me in a panicked voice. "Get a doctor!"

My father lifted me up into his arms and carried me back over to my bed. As soon as he laid me down, I reached for the basin and emptied the contents of my lunch. My grandfather was shouting for help at this point and wanting to come over to me, but the security team held him in place. Dr. O'Larien rushed in with hospital security following him. He cleared the room and began flashing a bright light into my eyes. But not before I witnessed my grandfather dragged out of my room.

"Jackson. Eyes on me. Tell me the pain level. 1-10?" Dr. O'Larien asked me.

I was shaking my head back and forth. I was talking, but heard no words. My father was screaming at me. His strangled cries were resonating throughout the entire vast room. Speckles of light was all I could see. I heard Dr. O'Larien call out commands to nurses who were surrounding me. I could feel a hand wrapped around mine like a vice. It was my father's hand, I think. He was crying, screaming, begging.

"You stay with me, Jackson!" His cries became faint, as I struggled to keep them focused on the light. *This can't be happening.* I felt my body rising as I was looking down at the scene below me.

I was dying. And in front of my father, just like my mother. *No! I have to hang on.* Dr. O'Larien was working over me. A tube was being inserted in my throat, and I was being wheeled out.

"Page Dr. Briggs…Stat to O.R. One." Dr. O'Larien screamed.

I heard one medical term being called out after another, as I tried to hang on and not go to sleep.

"Come on people…move!" he shouted as we crashed through another room. My father was held back by security as he tried to claw his way in to follow me. I will never forget his cries, as my world went dark.

"Jackson!!!"

"You fight, son."

"Don't let go."

"Stay with me."

This is not my destiny. My future is with Riley. How can history repeat itself in two lifetimes? I wouldn't believe that fate could deliver that type of pain to my father again. I woke to Riley in my arms this morning, my beautiful girl, happy and so in love with me. I would lay my life down for her, but not like this. She's not here to hold my hand. I need her. I need my crazy girl to tell me that she loves me. I need to feel her breath on me with her hot kisses. I need to see her walk down the aisle toward me.

I promised her forever. My forever promise to Riley was to love her all the days of my life. I would have never asked her to marry me if I didn't believe I could keep that promise to her. No! I can't leave her. I can't leave any of them, especially my father.

This cannot be how my story ends...

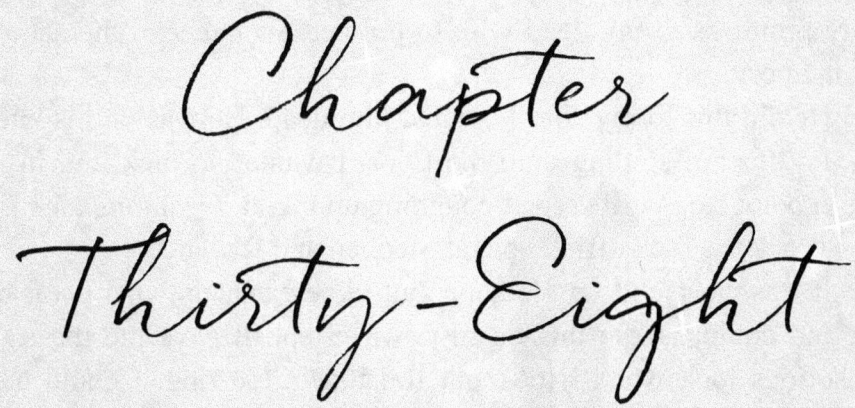

Chapter Thirty-Eight

Lost

Walker

"**J**ACKSON!!!

"You fight son."

"Don't let go."

"Stay with me."

I continued to shout as my voice became hoarse. *This is not happening, not again.* I was rooted to the floor, as Stephen and Richard helped me up. They led me to a chair where I nearly collapsed in. I thought I had no strength left until I saw Henry cowering in a corner, crying for my son.

"You son of a bitch!" I screamed, as I lunged for Henry Townsend with intent of killing him with my bare hands. My hands wrapped tightly around his neck, constricting his airway. I allowed this monster to come in reach of my son. I went against all my internal instincts and let Jackson change my mind. I knew he was a bastard after I discovered his duplicitous side, but never in a million lifetimes did I ever believe he could be this hateful. His legs were buckling, as my guys pulled me off of him. All bets were off. No more promises to my dead wife to protect her father in the sake of her memory.

He did this to my son. I wanted him dead. He was on his knees gasping for air, spitting onto the floor. I wanted to kick him in his ribs and not stop until he was coughing up blood. *I want him dead.*

"Back the fuck off!" I spat at Stephen and Richard.

It was their job to protect me, but I knew exactly what I was doing and could handle this on my own. Stephen gave me the same censorious look when I took out Ralston in the ring. I could have easily ended Jake's life, but taking his life would not give me back the years that were taken from me. Ending him and Henry would only take away my future. *Fuck that! I have too much to live for.*

I knelt down in front of the man I thought I knew. The man I once loved and respected. *Oh, how I was fooled by him.*

My jaw ticked as I gritted my teeth. My anger completely consumed me. What I did say would be the final words I ever would say to this man.

"I want nothing more than to see you suffer for the pain you caused here today. My son could be dying because of you. If I could, you would die by these two hands. I would relish in the fact that I was the one that ended you. I hate you, but even in hate, a man can find redemption for his enemies. My father did. And so could I. Hear this old man, because I will only say it once. If you ever come near any member of my family again…I. Will. Kill. You. There is a special place in Hell, reserved and waiting for you. You deserve nothing less."

With what I had left of my control, I summoned over Stephen and Richard.

"Get this piece of shit out of my sight," I told them.

They didn't hesitate to pick him up and carry him away to the nearest exit. I was questioned by security, no doubt the cameras had caught everything. I didn't care. My son was fighting for his life because of his grandfather's hate for me. McGovern was filled in on the events that took place and hurried over to my side. He informed me that Briggs was with Jackson. He was in his office going over my son's records once more. He answered his page immediately, and I thanked God that Samuel was nearby.

I slid my body down the wall with no strength left to hold me up. *Please God...don't take my son. Please...*

I silently prayed for my pleas to be answered. Arms were enveloping me with love and warmth. My blurry eyes found hers.

"Reese," I whispered.

"I'm here, baby. I'm here."

I cried in her arms. Riley was crying and being held by Richard.

"I can't lose him, Reese. Not like this...not ever."

"You won't, Walker. He will make it. I promise you. He will make it."

"How do you know?" I questioned my love.

"Because I believe. Fate is not that cruel. Jackson will come back to us. This...I know."

I didn't say anything else. My throat was burning, and it hurt to even talk. All I could do was silently pray that Reese was right .

Chapter Thirty-Nine

Moment of clarity

Jackson

CROSSING OVER FROM the life you had on earth to the next is nothing like you see in the movies. No one really knows what Heaven is like. Who knows if this is where I am right now. I feel free and light as a feather. *How is this happening? I feel like I'm flying, a weightless gravity that has me suspended with no ability to feel the surface below.*

I'm in an operating room where Dr. Briggs and Dr. O'Larien are working side by side to save my life. The nurses are working furiously around them and acting on every command they direct at them. With precision and calmness, Dr. Briggs begins to work on my brain. *I think I feel sick and shouldn't be watching this.* I'm starring in my own horror flick, but it's not the mad scientist working on my brain, it's Riley's father. This was not the way this was supposed to happen. I should be surrounded by my family with Riley at my side.

I didn't have the chance to say goodbye. What will happen to her if I don't make it? What about my father? The look in his eyes will forever be burned into my memory. He was devastated.

I can't look anymore. *I need to get out of here, but where do I go? I don't even understand why I'm here or what's happening right now.* At my moment of confusion, all became clear and was standing in front of me to show me the way. At first, all I could see was a shimmering light, almost how Riley's ring sparkled and it shot off a rainbow of colors. This light was different though. It was calming and protecting. I wasn't scared anymore. I felt the presence come closer to me as I tried to bring the image into focus.

I looked all around me, but was only surrounded by light. I could no longer see my body in the O.R. It was gone. Once again my fear of the unknown crept in and took hold of me. *Was I dead? And this was the afterlife?* Panic was setting in. *What is this place? I want to go home!* I shouted. And then I saw a hand reach for mine.

"Hello Jackson. Take my hand. And don't be afraid."

If this were a movie, I would probably be on the edge of my seat waiting to see what comes next. This was no movie. This was real, and it was standing right in front of me. The image was clear and there was no mistaking who it was. I was staring at my mother. *My mother has come for me.*

"Mom?" I barely got out above a whisper. "You look exactly like your portrait in the hospital. But if you're here and I'm here, then it can only mean one thing…I'm dead."

"No, son, you're not dead, just sleeping. You called for me, so I'm here…for you."

She was beautiful as I imagined her to be. Her hair was dark like mine, almost black. It was wavy with curls that went past her shoulders and down her back. I saw myself through her eyes. I was looking at a mirror, and my image was staring back at me. *A life cut short by something that wasn't controllable, and yet it's happening again with me.* Somehow looking at her took away all my fear and anxiety.

We walked in silence until we reached a tall tree, probably the tallest tree I have ever seen. We were in Big Sur. I was standing in front of the same tree where I had carved our names in. This was the place I had intended to propose to my girl. This was the same spot I professed my love and commitment to Riley. Pottersville was the turning point for us, but it was here where we made Our Forever Promise to one another. This was our place. And ours alone. I vowed to love Riley for the rest of my life and knew I would marry her one day.

I turned to look at my mother, who was smiling at me.

"Why have you brought me here?" I demanded to know. "I will never have this again. I can't bear it. Please take me anywhere but here."

I could feel my eyes moisten with tears until my mother leaned in and wiped them away.

"Don't be afraid son. You will see this place again, I promise. I brought you here to remember why you need to fight. I know you believe that what ended my life is now ending yours, but that's not true. It's scary, but it will all be over soon. I'm so sorry for my father. The answers to your long list of questions as to why do not matter anymore. He chose his path a long time ago. He alone has to be responsible for the choices he made. It will be him that has to live with them, not you."

She took my hand and guided my fingers over our carved names. I felt the bark rub against my skin and the memory of that day crashed through me. I felt Riley. I felt her love for me in that moment of clarity. *I had to get back to her, to all of them. I would fight forever to spend one more moment with Riley.*

"Mom, I can't be here. I want to go home. Please help me?"

"Like I said, Jackson, your life does not end here. It's just beginning, I promise. I love you so much. I will always be here in your heart where it matters most. I'm never too far away, and I will always look over you."

I felt her arms around me. I have never been so comforted in all of my life. Knowing her through other people's memories would never even come close to what I'm feeling at this moment. I can touch her. I can see her beautiful emerald eyes shining back at me. Now I can understand why I've been told all of my life how we have this one trait in common. I'm lost in them.

Our hands were entwined as we began walking again, this time towards a doorway. I once again was surrounded by light, the brightest I have ever seen. She held my hands and looked into my eyes.

"I love you, Jackson. I will always be with you, but here is where I say goodbye...for now. One day we will be together again. You must go now. You have people who love you and are waiting."

"How can I say goodbye to you, mother when I just found you?"

"It's never goodbye, my son. It's just a pause until we meet again. Take care of your father. I will always be with you both. I love you, son. Forever and ever."

She led me through the door, and I was back in the O.R. I didn't want to be here, not after where I've just been. I had to trust my mother and what she said.

Warmth radiated through me, and I heard her once more. "Don't be afraid, son. And Jackson? It's time to wake up!"

"WE GOT HIM back. His heartbeat and pulse are back in normal range. This fucker was a bitch to get, but we got it," I said to Liam and the rest of my team who accomplished a near impossible feat today. It was touch and go for a while there, but my daughter's fiancé survived. Before I arrived, Liam had almost panicked with the thought of losing Jackson. He thought for sure that Jackson's pupils were about to blow and that would sever all hope of saving this boy's life.

With only minutes to spare, I located the AVM. Unbeknownst to me, there was a second one located directly behind the first. We took countless images, but this shadow never came into focus until we saw it with our own eyes. It was the second that nearly ruptured. Something bigger played a role here today that helped me save him.

It wasn't just these hands, it was something so much more. Jackson should have died here on this table, but he made it. We eradicated both AVM's and have ruled out a stroke. It was the blood pressure spike that he experienced beforehand that set all of this in motion. A rupture was always to be considered and taken into account. The level of stress he experienced led to what could have culminated his life. Thank God it didn't.

There was no way of knowing how long it would take for Jackson to wake. The stress of the seizure and hours under sedation, it would be a waiting game now. He would be taken to the I.C.U. of my Neurosurgery Center to be monitored closely throughout the night. I knew it would break my daughter's heart to not be with him, but he needed to rest, and his brain needed to begin the healing process.

The route to the recovery units were off from the O.R. He would bypass his waiting family and be taken directly to his room. They were anxiously awaiting news, but I needed to catch my breath first. Liam did too!

"I was scared in there," Liam admitted.

"I was too. I've done this operation more times than I can count. This was like something I never experienced before. Maybe it was because this case hit too close to home. We had no time to second guess our steps. We came so close to losing him, and then his heart rate steadied and there was a chance. How do we begin to even understand that?"

"I don't know, Samuel, but what you did in there was miraculous. We were thrown together by the force of nature called Walker Reed. I'm damn proud to know you, friend. It was an honor sharing the O.R. with you. You are a truly gifted surgeon."

"Thank you, Liam, but I did my job. I couldn't have done it without you. Your initial reaction was probably what saved him in the end. One minute wasted could have changed this outcome. Do you want to tell the family? Or shall I?"

"I'll walk out with you, but you're the one they want to hear from."

"Okay," I replied.

My scrubs were soaked through. I quickly changed into fresh ones and cleaned up my appearance. Liam and I both checked on Jackson before making our way to speak with the family. He was stable and holding his own. My natural expression always came across as serious. I knew I couldn't walk out there and show anything else but hopeful. Liam stopped me as we came to the door.

"Ready?" he asked.

"Yes. I'm ready," I confidently replied. Jackson made it. That's all that mattered.

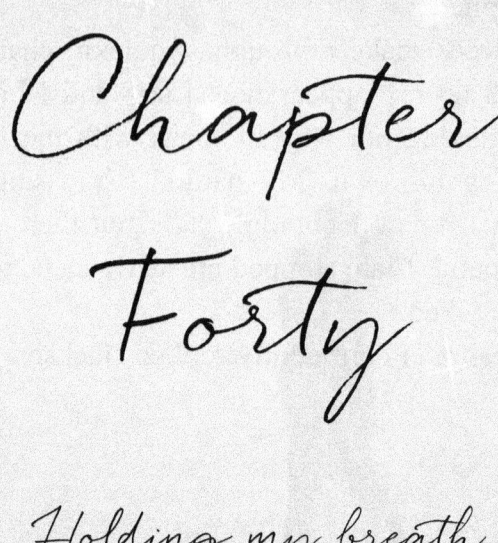

Chapter Forty

Holding my breath

Walker

DAYS LIKE THIS are days when you look at your life, and hope you still have more moments to come with the people you love most in the world.

I just want to believe that everything is going to be okay. I want my life back to last week when I was making love to Reese and dreaming of our wedding day, laughing and imagining our future together with the new life our love created.

How do I get back there? To the best moments of my life? I'm a selfish man and I usually get what I want, but this? I have no control over, and that is the hardest part of it. I'm standing on the outside looking in. I'm suspended and held back by my fear, my fear of losing everything that matters to me, beginning with Jackson.

Reese made me believe in second chances, fate, the universe, and all it represents. Our future has been written. Some say our destinies are planned out for us before birth, but not our story. We changed it and took back what was always ours to have. Now I sit here and hope for the same conclusion for my son and Riley. They are so young, carefree, with light all around them. This is not their story.

I've been here before. I'm here again in this darkened room with candles and nothing else but my silent pleas screaming from inside of my head. I once again looked up to the man on the cross. Millions of faithful believers prayed to him every single day. Now I'm no different than the countless others, praying and hoping for good news.

I'm here again! Praying for divine intervention to save my son. I'll never forget his first cry. The shrill of his newborn cry resonated throughout the entire operating room. I was holding Elizabeth's hand and just praying for confirmation that our son made it.

My eyes never left His, as I heard my thoughts become words.

"I know it doesn't seem fair that people from all walks of life sit here and ask for their wishes to be granted, prayers to be answered, and wrongs to be righted. We ask so much of you and hardly ever give back. I'll do anything to save my son. When I lost Reese, and then lost Elizabeth, my son was all I had left. Jackson saved me a long time ago. He deserves this miracle. Please allow him to have it."

I was going out of my mind with worry and was not sure if I could take much more of this waiting. It had been hours and no word yet. Not even a nurse had updated us. I had to get back to Reese and Riley. Riley broke down upon hearing what happened to Jackson. For a time, she was inconsolable. She looked broken and was rocking in Reese's arms. When she glanced over to me, I wasn't sure if I was reading her eyes right. They were filled with tears, but hardened at the same time. Did she blame me for what took place here? Her expression almost mimicked my own when I initially found out about Jackson and the secrets they both kept from me.

I was angry then, kind of the same way Riley was looking at me now. I couldn't blame her. As much as I tried to justify my actions here today, I didn't have to go off on Henry. I could have had him simply removed from the hospital, but his vile words enraged a fire within me and all I wanted was my pound of flesh. He deserved it and so much more. He was filled with hate and no remorse. Gail had to witness firsthand who her husband really was. He, like my father, always protected the women in their lives by not revealing his duplicitous side. He kept them at bay and protected the women from the ugly side of business. It's how they increased their wealth and became the men they were. They were feared by many, but loved unconditionally by the women who held their hearts.

That is probably the hardest to come to terms with. I'm still struggling with how my father could lead two very different lives. Henry was no different in the end. He was disheveled as my men dragged him out. Gail didn't appear to be fragile like Henry said, and, if anything, she wore an expression of strength. He was begging her to come with him, but she gave him her answer in the way of a stinging slap across his shocked face. She made her choice, and it wasn't him. Gail turned away from her husband and took me in my arms. She whispered "I'm sorry" for only me to hear. She joined my mother, and they both prayed for their grandson's survival.

"You know my story by now. You know their story. I've spent months holding onto my deep rooted anger toward my father and the ones who hurt me. I understand that sometimes to move forward, we have to go back. I did that today by forgiving the one man that hurt me the most. Please give me more moments with my son. Please give him back the life and future he deserves."

I said all I could say. Now, I wait for His answer. Tick tock...tick tock

"Walker! Can you hear me? Please, baby. Open your eyes."

I could hear her soft voice as I slowly opened my eyes. It was a few hours later. I was still here in the chapel, but I was on the floor and before the man on the cross.

"Reese?" I answered her. Once my eyes were fully awake, Stephen was also by my side, helping me up.

"Are you okay?" she asked me. "You must have blacked out

again from exhaustion. I had a hard time waking you. I thought something was terribly wrong when you didn't come back to the waiting room."

"Can you stand sir?" Stephen questioned me as he got me to my feet.

"Yes. I'm fine. I don't remember too much. Is there any news yet about Jackson?" All my senses became vividly clear, and I remembered exactly why I was here.

"A nurse just came out to tell us that the surgery is over. Samuel would be out shortly."

"And Jackson? Did he make it, Reese? Please tell me he's okay." My voice was shaky as my eyes focused in on Reese.

"He made it, Walker. He's in recovery. That's all I know."

He made it Walker, and is in recovery kept playing over and over in my head. My son was alive, and that's all that mattered. I took Reese in my arms and held her as tightly as I could. I whispered my love for her and looked up to whisper "Thank you" to Him. My prayers had been answered for my son. I would spend the rest of my days being thankful for this blessing we'd been given here today. I ushered Reese out of the chapel, and we made our way back to meet with Samuel.

Riley joined us, nearly knocking me over with her hug. We all huddled together, cried with one another, and waited for Samuel and Liam. At that moment, the doors swung opened and in walked through the two men that saved my son's life...a debt I would never be able to repay.

We waited in silence as the two men approached us, assessing their facial expressions down to their walk.

Reserved and to the point, Samuel simply said, "We got it. Both of them. We have no doubt that Jackson will make a full recovery."

"What? I thought you said he only had the one AVM? There were two?" I questioned.

"Yes. Where the AVM was intricately located made the other be concealed. We never saw it on the scans until we were inside."

"The stress of the seizure and blood pressure spike nearly caused the second to rupture. Upon thorough examination and quick thinking on Dr. O'Larien's part, I was able to excise it before it ever reached that point. During the surgery, Jackson flat lined, but only for a mere second or two. We stabilized him and shortly after, his blood pressure and pulse returned to normal range."

His heart stopped? I could have lost him today. The man that I hated just on sight for loving the same woman I loved was responsible for saving my son's life today. I was at a loss for words and the only two words I can manage to say were "Thank you." He nodded and said nothing else. I was just numb and reeling from all that had happened here today.

I watched Riley hug her father, cry onto his shoulder, and lovingly thank him. Reese was next to embrace him. She was also crying happy tears and thanking him for all that he had done. I gauged Samuel's expression as he took her in his arms. He looked exhausted, but at peace. The malice he once wore in his eyes were gone and replaced with closure.

"When can we see him?" Riley was first to ask.

Liam answered her question and addressed anything else we wanted to know. "He's being monitored and will continue to be watched closely for the next twenty-four hours. He's going through some post-op checks right now. Let's give him some time to sleep. You all will all be able to visit with him soon."

I shook Liam's hand and then pulled him into a brother hug. He was as close as they come to the real thing. I was eternally grateful for not only his friendship, but for what he did today for Jackson.

"Thank you, my friend...thank you."

"No thanks needed. I'm a doctor. This is what I do." He turned to Samuel, and then back to me. "Correction, this is what *we* do. It's going to be a long night here, Walker. You look like shit. Take a breath before you collapse. He made it. Go grab a shower and then see your son. He'll be waiting for you...I promise."

I hugged my friend again and then walked over to Samuel. I

don't believe I could give him the same thank you I gave to Liam, but I wanted to let him know how grateful I was. He stood tall, taller than I had ever seen him, and he did the one thing that surprised me. He extended his hand. No hesitation, I shook his hand and once again gave him thanks. His response didn't surprise me, nor Reese for that matter.

"I'm a doctor first. It's the only way I know how to be."

And with that, Dr. Samuel Briggs walked away and didn't look back.

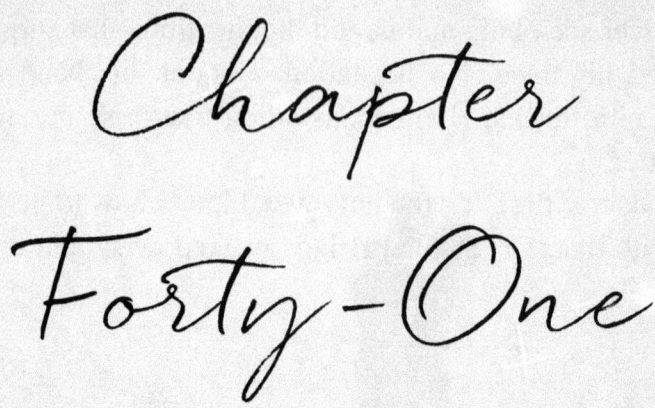

Chapter Forty-One

Time to wake up

Jackson

DID I DREAM it? Or was it a hallucination I experienced while under sedation? No, it was real. I met my mother for the first time. She told me she loved me and held me in her arms. I heard her voice, felt her skin on mine, and she was incredibly beautiful. Photographs could never capture who my mother was. You could only truly know by seeing her in person and hearing her voice. My out-of-body experience, or whatever they call it, achieved that long awaited dream. My mother, my guardian angel, never stopped protecting and watching over me when I needed her most.

"Wake up, baby, it's time to wake up."

I heard whispered voices all around me, but I was still deeply under that I couldn't make out who was talking to me.

I could feel my hands wrapped up in another. Was it my father? Riley? They had to be with me. Then I heard her voice again, and it was as clear as the first time I heard it. My mother was with me, willing me to wake up.

"Don't be afraid, son. Your father is waiting for you to come back to him, and so is your beautiful girl. I love you, son, but it's time to wake up."

I blinked my eyes open to find Riley staring back at me. She was smiling through her falling tears. She nearly broke me every time she cried. Before I could even say hi, her lips found mine. She gently held my face in her hands and whispered "I love you" over and over again. My voice was dry to the point of hurting. I knew a tube had been inserted in my throat while I was in surgery, I could feel the remnants of that now. She kissed me again and began pressing the call button next to my bed. Not a minute later, my father rushed in with relief showing all over his face. With red rimmed eyes, more tears fell as he leaned over to kiss my forehead, and thanked God for saving me.

Reese was next. Then my grandmother Olivia, Stephen, and Richard. The one that stayed back was my grandma Gail. My vision was blurred a bit, but I could still make out how tired she looked. My limbs were heavy and not easy to lift. I was praying my eyes showed her what she needed to see. She wiped away more tears and came over to me. She almost touched my head, but recoiled back because of my bandage. I always had shaggy hair. My grandmothers were constantly brushing it away from my face.

"Hi," I croaked out. My throat hurt.

Grandma Gail leaned in and kissed my cheek.

"Oh my precious boy! Thank God you are alright. How do you feel?"

"Like I just had brain surgery."

She smiled, but my father gave me an admonishing look. Yeah this wasn't the time for jokes, but come on! I'm alive and I've seen enough tears to last me a lifetime.

I asked for a few minutes alone with grandma Gail, only requesting my father to stay. Riley promised to be right outside. I knew she would be, but I encouraged her to sit and relax. "Not a chance," she said.

They each held my hand with my grandmother speaking first. "Jackson darling, I am so very sorry for what happened here with your grandfather."

My father interrupted her immediately with the mention of Henry.

"Gail, this is not the time," he said, giving her a cautionary look, a look I knew well. This was my father in protection mode once again, but he didn't have to be when it came to her.

"Walker, this may not be the time, but it wasn't right earlier with Henry, but did you stop? As far as I am concerned, you both played a part in why my only grandson is lying here in this bed. And before you say anything else, I know what led up to you attacking him. I know, because I heard it all with my own ears, down the hall from the both of you. I was sickened by the one man who I vowed to love forever. He was my entire world up until that moment I heard his enraged hatred for you and Ms. Mitchell. I am deeply sorry that you ever had to suffer one day at his hand. My Elizabeth would be so disappointed in him, as I am."

She continued, "Jackson, you are truly the only thing I have left of my daughter. I love you with all of my heart and can only hope your grandfather's sins don't separate us. I so very much want to be part of your life today, and your future tomorrow. Your fiancé is simply wonderful. It took my breath away when I saw your mother's ring on her hand. She would be so proud of you."

"I love you, grandma. No one could ever come between us. Please believe that," I struggled to say.

"I do now, my boy. I love you. Get some rest, and I'll see you soon. Walker, can I have a word before I head back over to my hotel?"

He nodded and led her out of my room.

"GAIL, WHATEVER IT is should wait. I need to return to my son."

"What I have to say won't take long. Please hear me out?" Her eyes pleaded with me to say yes.

It was night with a warm summer breeze that touched our skin as we walked outside. The fresh air would do me some good. I didn't want anyone else to be privy to our conversation, no matter what would be said here.

"Please say what you have to say, so I can get back to Jackson."

"After all we've been through, are you really going to stand there with this cold manner? We could have lost him today, and here you stand as if that reality didn't almost happen."

"You're wrong, Gail. I do know how close I came to losing my son. You do not need to remind me of that fact. What I will not do is stand here and listen to you defend *him* to me. I never wish to speak of that man again."

"That's too damn bad, because you are. Why, Walker? Why couldn't you have told me when you discovered what Henry did? I had a right to know. Elizabeth was my daughter too, and Jackson is my grandson. After your visit to Arizona all those months ago, you completely shut me out. You refused my calls. You didn't allow me to sit with you at the graduation. Why, I'll ask you again? You should have told me what was going on instead of punishing me for being married to the man that hurt you. It wasn't fair, Walker, and that is why we are having this conversation now, because I am damn mad at you! And him for causing all of this pain."

For some strange reason, I was preparing to be slapped. After witnessing Gail hit Henry, I thought she would deliver the same to me, but she didn't. She threw her hands in the air and shouted a few obscenities, surprising us both. I never saw Gail behave this way, let alone raise her voice and curse. I barely was able to contain my smile, and it didn't go unnoticed by her, because she laughed as well, breaking the obvious tension between us.

"I'm sorry, Gail. I'm sorry for hurting you, but I was reeling from all that I discovered and I was fighting to get back what I lost."

"Reese Mitchell?" she raised her eyebrows up at me.

"Yes, it began with her."

"I'm happy you found your way back to each other. I guess true love never fails when it's meant to be."

I couldn't argue with her statement. It was true, and I believed it with my whole heart.

"I did love and care about your daughter. It was just a different kind of love."

"I know." She softly said.

"You will always have a place in your grandson's life, but it's over for Henry. There's no coming back after what happened here today."

"I know that too."

"What will you do now, Gail?" I asked her.

"I'm going to stay up here for a few more days and make sure Jackson is okay, and then I'm going back home to Arizona to begin divorce proceedings." You're right about one thing, Walker. There is no coming back after today. I can only move forward with the rest of my life, and hope he can too. You may think your mother and I are foolish women who were blinded by the men in their lives, but really Walker? Do you truly believe that? Take it from someone who has been married for a very long time. When you truly love someone, you want to see and believe in them, believe wholeheartedly that they will never cause you one minute of hurt. You believe they will unconditionally love you for the rest of their life. Isn't that what you believe you have with your Reese? I'm not a fool son, neither is Olivia. We just loved. But sometimes… it was love that was the only thing we could see."

I had Richard drive Gail back to her hotel, while Stephen gave me a quick report on Henry. After he was removed from the hospital property, they lost track of his whereabouts. Not that I gave any direct orders to monitor his movement. He was the last thing on my mind at that time, but to discover that he wasn't where he was supposed to be was alarming. Stephen received confirmation that Henry checked out of their hotel suite, leaving Gail there on her own. I asked Stephen to check the outgoing flights and gather Intel on him immediately. At this point, he was a loose cannon with a thirst for revenge. I couldn't take any chances with my family.

While I was with Gail, Reese never left Jackson's side, nor did Riley. We didn't even bother asking Riley to return to the hotel with us. She would remain with Jackson tonight, and probably until he would be discharged. I returned to see Reese asleep in the chair and Riley nestled carefully next to Jackson.

"Reese, baby," I said, as I woke her with my feather light kisses to her forehead and temple. She shivered awake and smiled up at me.

"Hey," she whispered back.

"Hey, back at you. I'm going to send you home with Richard. Stephen and I will be back shortly."

"No. I'm staying with you."

"You know I love you for that, but you're exhausted and you need your rest. Sleeping in this chair is not going to work for me. So please be compliant and wait for me back at the hotel. This is not a request."

"And if I say no? What then?"

"Do you really want to play with me?"

"Maybe I do," she said with a wink.

"Reese. Please don't push me. I have zero control left, and who knows what I'm capable of at this point. I want to fuck you so hard into the mattress, you won't be able to stand for a week, but I know I can't do that."

"Why ever not? You won't hurt me. After today, I think we both need it rough and hard. We need to feel alive, and fucking each other into the mattress will accomplish that. I need you, Walker, and I know you need me, so don't send me away."

"You stubborn girl. Never will I ever send you away. How about going with Stephen for a snack and some orange juice? Take Riley with you. I'll be along after I visit with Jackson. Deal?"

"Deal. And then we'll play."

343

I kissed her with a bruising kiss and whispered my answer, "Absolutely." She smiled and waited.

Riley was reluctant to leave Jackson, but she didn't put up too much of a fight when asked to get up for a snack. I gave her a quick hug, and she walked hand in hand with Reese.

Pulling up a chair, I sat next to Jackson and held his hand in my own. "How are you feeling, son?"

"Not too sure with all the great drugs they're pumping into me. I'll get back to you on that one." We both lightly smiled. "Dr. Briggs saved my life dad."

"I know, son. I am eternally grateful to him, and to Liam."

"I was scared, dad. I didn't know if I was going to come through it."

"Shhh, you don't have to worry about that anymore. You are going to be fine, and soon this will all be put behind you."

"I saw mom."

And those three words nearly broke me. I never told Jackson about my visions of her, and the nightmares I experienced with my father.

"What did you say?" I asked him, already believing what I heard.

"I saw mom…in Heaven. At least I thought it was Heaven. I thought I was dead and mom was coming for me, but that's not what happened."

"What do you remember?"

"The sound of your voice, begging me to hold on. I'm so sorry, dad, that you ever had to go through that. As I closed my eyes, all I could hear was your voice. Then I was surrounded by light and felt a strong familiar presence. It was mom asking me to take her hand and not be afraid. I could see my body below me, but I also could see her standing in front of me. I asked her if I was dead, and she said I was just sleeping. She showed me my future with Riley, and what I would be losing if I stopped fighting. Do you believe me, dad?"

"No question, son. I believe you, because she has also come to me in recent days."

"She has? And you never told me?"

"No time. Everything happened so fast. This was one of the reasons why I wanted to come to New York and see you. Something had felt off from our last phone conversation and then I experienced a terrible nightmare. I bolted from home and ran for miles until my legs gave out. I found myself at your mother's grave, where she appeared before me like an angel. I didn't welcome her at first. She wanted to help me get over my anger with your grandfathers, and when I refused her request, she slapped me. I know it sounds crazy, but I actually felt the sting of it on my cheek. Then she left me with something so disturbing that I had no choice, but to come here for you."

"What did mother say?"

"She told me that you would need me more than you have ever before. Of course, I screamed at her, but she just kept fading away until her image was gone."

"Do you think mom knew what was going to happen to me?"

"I don't know for sure, Jackson, but I'm not going to argue with the angels or God...ever again. You're alive and here with me. I will always believe. I always knew she was with me, but to see her again after all of these years, it was just something I will truly never be able to make anyone understand."

"I understand, dad."

"I imagine you are the only one. I love you, Jackson."

"I love you too!"

"You need to rest. Please get some sleep, and I'll be back in the morning."

"Dad, before you go, can I ask you something?"

"Make it a quick one?"

"What are you going to do to Grandpa Henry?"

"Jackson. Please don't worry about him."

"I need to know, dad."

"He's still alive, if that's what you're asking me. As long as he stays away, he will remain alive. I'm done talking about him. You are too! Now get some rest. I love you, son."

My heart hurt to leave him, but I needed to get back to Reese. I checked in with Liam before leaving for the night. Jackson was stable. He was up for several hours, which was a great sign. My son would be fine, and we could put this nightmare behind us.

Reese and I took a cab back to the hotel, leaving Stephen to remain with Jackson. My last status report on Henry came up empty. He disappeared without a trace, and knowing that worried me. The minute Jackson would be cleared to be discharged, I would take him back home to California. The thought of Jackson remaining in New York, and on his own, didn't sit well with me after what we just went through. I would discuss his recovery and rehabilitation with Liam in the morning. Certainly Jackson couldn't argue with me about the betterment of his health?

I was probably reaching for the impossible. He was a Reed, and would not be challenged.

It was time to return to our lives. We had a wedding in our future and a baby to prepare for. I needed to get out of this city and back home to my life with Reese.

Chapter Forty-Two

Reese

"HOW ABOUT A hot bath? I sure could use one after today."

"Before or after we *play*?" Walker said wickedly with a gleam in his eye.

"Before. My muscles are tight and I need to be warmed up first."

"Oh baby! I can do that with my hands tied behind my back, or even better, yours."

"As tempting as that sounds, my body needs a soak."

I gave him a sly smile and wink. My body was calling out for his pleasure, and being tied to a bed with Walker in Dom mode was exactly what my brain was telling me I needed. I removed my blouse and stepped out of my skirt, leaving me with only my bra and panties on. I looked over my shoulder to catch him staring at me. He looked lost, but in a good way. His eyes were roving up and down my body, sending shivers through me. For the first time in days, I saw the man I loved, and not the tortured lost soul who's been worrying over his son, Samuel, Henry, and his father.

"Coming, my love?" I teasingly asked him.

"Yes, my love. I will make it my mission to hear you scream my name all night long."

Without another word, Walker freed himself from his clothing and pounced on me before I could even blink. He carried me into the bathroom and gently placed me in the coconut scented bath. Walker climbed in behind me and wrapped his long muscular legs over mine.

"I love you so much, Reese. Thank you for never leaving my side throughout this ordeal. My biggest fear was that I was going to push you away."

I turned in his arms and tried not look at him with sadness in my eyes. He was deeply hurting, and that needed to stop.

"Don't you know how much I love you?" I said. "Where am I going to go? No place exists without you. Look at me. Be here…with me. I love you."

Once again, our universal body language spoke for us with Walker taking control and leading me where he wanted us both to go.

"You on top," he commanded.

Lifting me effortlessly over his thick crown, my heated core milked his cock into a steady rhythm between us. Walker continued to grind into me, gripping my hips as I arched back into sheer ecstasy and pleasure. With my eyes rolling to the back of my head, I thought I was going to pass out with how hard I came. Walker screamed out inaudible words until one was perfectly clear, my name. He had my body spinning out of control. As easy as it was to straddle him, now I was turned around with Walker entering me from behind. His front was pressed into my back with one hand tangled through my long hair, pulling me back to kiss him. It wasn't painful as it was completely erotic and intoxicating. Our tongues danced in unison as he continued to take me higher and higher.

"Oh, baby, you feel so fucking good. This is where I want to be, buried balls deep inside of you. Come for me baby. Tell me you love me. Scream it like you mean it," he said.

He tugged tighter on my hair as my orgasm continued to build. I was on the precipice of heightened arousal.

"Oh, Walker. I'm close, so close."

With his two fingers pinching my over sensitive nipples, I came again with such a climactic force that I nearly collapsed forward. I didn't get too far with Walker's strong arms around me and capturing my mouth once again.

"Rough enough for you?" he asked with a twinge of naughtiness in his voice.

I was beyond sated and completely exhausted. Still enfolded in his arms, he kissed, licked, bit, and left love bites all over me.

"I love you, Reese, so fucking much. You. Are. Mine. Forever. And. I'm. Yours."

As if I could forget? This is what he needed tonight, and so did I. Walker climbed out of the tub first and lifted me into his arms. He took his time drying me from head to toe, of course kissing me everywhere and sending me into another erotic tailspin.

"You are so wet for me, baby" he whispered against my thighs, plunging his tongue between my folds, lapping up my juices as he continued to bury himself into my heat.

"No more baby!" I cried. "I'm going to pass out!"

"Control, baby. Hold on for me," he whispered.

My hands found his hair with my nails clawing into his scalp. Wincing from the grip I had on him, he didn't relent on me and sucked harder until I exploded my essence all over him.

"My perfect girl, now you can sleep."

And with that, I was once again carried by him and placed in bed, with Walker laying right behind and pulling me tightly to his chest.

"Sleep baby. I love you," he said, placing light kisses on the back of my neck.

I lost track after the three mind blowing orgasms Walker gave me. His steady breathing lulled me into a contented sound sleep.

I awoke sometime in the night and realized he was not in bed.

"Walker!" I called out to him, my hand reaching out for him and only feeling the now cold side of the bed. *Where is he?* I turned on the side light, making my eyes adjust and reading the time on the clock. It was just a little past three. I stretched out my sore muscles, giving me some relief. I felt like I just did twelve rounds of sexual twister. Grabbing my robe, I searched for my missing man.

When I found him, he was outside on the balcony with an amber filled drink in hand. Lost in his thoughts, he didn't hear me come up from behind him. He didn't flinch when I encircled him with my arms and hands folding over each other. He let out a sigh and turned around to kiss me.

"You should be in bed," he quietly reprimanded me.

"I could say the same about you. Come back to bed." When he didn't easily follow, I looked at him questioningly until he crushed his lips onto mine. Dropping to his knees, he hugged me to him with his cheek to my stomach. This was not about sex; this was about Walker needing assurance that we were okay. *My mercurial man!* I vowed to love him, all parts of him. My husband-to-be was hurting beyond anything he had ever experienced before. I stood there in silence until I knew he was okay, or at least on his way.

"Come back to bed, baby, and let me hold you." I asked again, and Walker, this time, followed me. He stripped out of his sleep bottoms and removed me from my robe. Skin on skin, we couldn't be any closer. Walker gently kissed me and fell asleep with me by his side.

We slept soundly for the next five hours with me waking first. It was very rare this happens with Walker only requiring a few hours of sleep each night. I carefully lifted myself on one elbow and took in the beautiful man sleeping beside me. He looked at peace. His long eyelashes looked like sweeping feathers. He was dreaming, and I knew it was a good one because I saw a hint of a smile. Leaving the bed would waken him, but I needed to capture this stolen moment between us. Very carefully, I reached for my cellphone and snapped his picture. I then leaned in and took a selfie of the two of us. I was silently laughing. I never did this before. What would he think if he caught me? I didn't have to ponder long, because he was the one now staring at me. I was so lost in my thoughts of him, I didn't even notice.

"Good morning, baby," he crooned with his sexy, raspy morning voice.

"Good morning. How did you sleep?" I asked as I placed soft kisses on his chest and made circles along his tight corded stomach muscles.

I was starving for food, but hungered for him more. He was naked already, making my task that much easier to do. Without another thought, I gripped the base of his hardness and took him deep into my mouth, causing Walker to buck his hips forward. I loved taking him by surprise. His hands were already tangled through my hair as he pushed me further to take him deeper.

"That's it baby, fuck me with your mouth. Feels so fucking good."

He was close as I felt his balls tighten in my hand. I silently counted to five, and by three, Walker exploded into my mouth and down my throat. I swallowed quickly as he pumped the very last drop.

"Holy hell! Reese, I wasn't expecting that, but thank you, baby, for the wake-up call."

He pulled me up on top of him and plunged into me. I held his hands for support as I rode him to my next round of mind blowing orgasms. This is not what I had in mind when I decided to give him a morning blow job, but Walker always reciprocated with an even exchange. Collapsing on top of his slicked chest, his heartbeat was racing and matching my own.

"I love you, Reese."

He kissed me and made his tongue dance with mine.

"You taste like me. I love that. Are you okay? Was I too rough?"

He anxiously awaited my answer. I slid off of him and snuggled beside him.

"I'm fine, baby. You did not hurt me, but there is one thing you can do for me," I asked him, now gaining his full attention.

"Anything, baby." he answered with more kisses and a love bite on my pebbled nipple.

"I'm hungry. Feed me now," I said, grabbing his face and kissing him back.

Walker ordered everything on the breakfast menu and fed me course after course. His only request was for me to stay in bed and to remain naked. *Oh, what a hardship! I think I could easily manage to do this every day and twice on Sunday.*

"I'm stuffed. No more please."

I patted my round belly, as I took in his widening eyes. He loved to kiss my stomach and talk to our daughter. I was beginning to be more pronounced and you could easily tell I was pregnant. I was like this with Riley too. My stomach was flat for months, and then overnight I was sporting a small basketball under my shirt. I loved being pregnant again and with his child, a miracle I never thought I would ever experience again.

"What are you thinking?" I asked and watched him for his reaction.

"I'm thinking how much I love you. How happy you make me. You are my entire world. I need you like my next breath. There is no life without you in it."

"So you've said. Hey, where is this coming from? All the ghosts of our past have now been laid to rest. We are together, and nothing will ever change that."

He smiled and said, "I know that, baby, and I love you. Last night was the first time in nearly two months that I have been able to get a decent night's sleep. By truly giving forgiveness to my father, my nightmares are no more. Reese, I love you more than I can ever possibly explain. I feel our life together has been a constant test and every time we are close to finally having it all, we are yet again faced with another obstacle."

I take her hand and place it over my heart. "Do you feel that?" I asked her.

"Yes," she replied softly.

"This is how much I love you. You mean everything to me. My desire for you makes me absolutely crazy to prove not only to you, but to the rest of the world how much you mean to me. I intend to keep you for the rest of my life."

Chapter Forty-Three

Walker

MAKING LOVE TO Reese again solidified my earlier fears of losing her. She was my life, it was that simple. I would fight to keep her with me always and forever. Too many years spent without her had left me vulnerable and gutted wide open. These were feelings I once knew and now had rediscovered again.

Jackson's health crisis, Henry's confrontation, and facing my demons with my father had tested the bounds of my control. I insisted on Reese taking a nap before leaving for the hospital. She wanted me to join her, but I had too much work to catch up on. Staying days away from my office was not the norm for me.

Stephen called me first thing and gave me a status on my son. All was well at the hospital with Jackson resting comfortably with no complications through the night. Confirmed by Liam, I was assured that my son was on the road to recovery. He would be undergoing some tests today for his post-op checks. I wanted him home and safely protected in our compound in California.

Henry's whereabouts were still unknown. Gail and mother visited Jackson this morning together with no new information on her husband. Stephen had the hotel checked again, and had a man on Gail. On all accounts, she was telling the truth and did not know where Townsend was.

He needed to be located immediately. Surely he wouldn't be that foolish to come at me again after the warning I delivered to him, right? But he's not thinking clearly, and when a man like Townsend goes rogue, he could be dangerous.

I called Jenny with a task list that I expected to be completed by end of business hours today. I also checked in with Tom and Donovan. We were on schedule with all of our high end projects, especially the Reinhart Building in Germany. When asked about a dedication for the front name plate, I hadn't decided what I wanted, but now I have. I will reveal my plans to Donovan upon my return.

One last call needed to be made before waking my sleeping princess. I called Priscilla to check in and make sure all was right back at the house. She answered quickly, and I got right to the point.

"How are our house guests? Are all their needs being met?'

"Yes sir. The Mitchells and their friends arrived a couple of days ago and are settling in just fine. Mr. Mac and his husband are also here, but not staying at night," she said in her most efficient tone. "How is young Mr. Reed? We've been praying for him."

Cursing myself for not keeping her better informed, I answered her questions quickly. "Thank you for asking. His surgery was successful with no complications. I hope to return home soon with Jackson. Please make sure his room is ready and accommodations are in place for Ms. Riley Briggs as well."

"Yes sir. Will there be anything else?"

"Just one question."

"Yes sir, "she responded.

"Do I have anymore wine and champagne left in my cellar?"

This made my house manager lose her professional manner and laugh out loud.

"Yes, sir, you do, but I needed to place another order for your favorite 2002 Cristal to be restocked."

I shook my head because I already knew that Freddy had his own personal party at my expense. I would immediately be changing the alarm code upon my return. In hindsight, I didn't really care. His friendship meant everything to me because of the happiness it brought to Reese's life. She had spent the past years alone and isolated from her friendships. I would do anything to change that, but it's just another part of our past that we now found closure with. We lived in the now and concentrated on the future we would spend as husband and wife.

With all my pressing matters now taken care of, I made the mistake of opening up my personal e-mail to find seventeen frantic ones from Rosalyn Baker Davenport, our wedding planner. I quickly skimmed through them, and mainly they contained pleasantries and gibberish. Clearly she didn't understand my one and only e-mail instructing her to put all on hold until we return home. Rubbing my temples, I didn't have time for this, but made the call anyway.

After she answered her private line, I skipped the formalities and got right to the point of my call. "Rosalyn, why is my e-mail flooded with correspondence from you?" I curtly questioned her.

"Mr. Reed, I was simply following up with you. It's my job to stay on top of events, especially when they are for my best clients."

"I understand that, Ms. Baker, but seventeen e-mails are not warranted. I specifically directed you to put all plans on hold and wait for my call. What part of that did you not understand?"

"My apologies, Mr. Reed. I understand and will wait for further instruction from you."

"Very good. Our family is facing a personal matter and as much as I want to move forward with my wedding, I have no direction for you at this time. If this becomes a future complication for you, I will have no problem taking my business elsewhere. I expected more from you, Ms. Baker, considering your fee I have already paid in full."

"Again, sir, my apologies. I will certainly speak with my assistant as well to not send you anything else."

"You do that, Ms. Baker, good day."

She could pass the buck and blame her assistant all she wanted, but I knew better. Ms. Baker was a social climber, and having me on as a client would give her the brass ring. I would give her some leeway here and let this infraction go. Her work spoke for itself, and I'd been very pleased with all she managed to complete to date. I sure did have fun riling her feathers in the meantime.

"It's nice to see you smile again," Catching me off guard, there was my beauty admiring me from the doorframe.

"Come here, Reese." My arms opened and waited for her. She climbed on my lap, and I hugged her closely to me. "Good morning again. How's my daughter?"

"We are both fine, and ready when you are."

"Lead the way, my love."

"Stephen was back and driving us to the hospital. He switched posts with Richard to catch up on his own work. Still no leads on Townsend, but I wasn't going to worry Reese with that. Her hands were locked together as we drove on. She touched on a subject earlier about my visit to my family's home, but with all that happened yesterday, we never had an opportunity to discuss it again. *Should I tell her? Of course I should, but I'm so over it.*

"Reese, baby?"

"What's up?" she turned to me.

"My visit yesterday to the Hamptons. You never asked me again about it."

"You're right, I didn't. You needed time to process it. When you were ready to talk about it, all hell broke loose with Elizabeth's father. I figured when you were ready, you would tell me."

"Reese, I endeavor to always be honest with you and never hide or keep anything from you."

"I know you try, but some subject matters can't be helped."

"What does that mean? Subject matters?"

"Walker, come on, my love? You can't be that obtuse."

"Reese, obtuse is not a word in my vocabulary. Explain yourself…now."

"I'm sorry. I didn't mean to offend you, love. What I meant was that I understand you can't share everything with me. You close parts of you off to protect me, and I love you for that."

"I'm sorry too, baby. I didn't mean to snap at you. You are the most important person in my life. I promise to share everything with you. I just need time to come to terms with it all."

"I know. Another reason why I didn't bring it up again. Now kiss me, you big bear." She laughed.

"Big bear, huh? I would show you something big, but we're here. Maybe we can sneak off later for a little fun."

"A girl can dream."

"Not dream, baby. I mean what I say. You know that. Come! Before I change my mind and take you in the backseat."

"Now you're talking. I love backseat car sex!"

"Reese! As much as I love to hear you scream out your desires for me, this is certainly not the place, but as always you have delighted me. I love you."

"I love you too!"

We walked through the private entrance to Samuel's wing. I was informed by my security team that some members of the press have camped outside the main entrance. I had issued a press release through my office, but now the vultures have circled. With the wedding suddenly put on hold, that led to rumors of our possible break-up and reasons leading up to calling off the wedding. I had shielded Reese from most of the media garbage that was being played out, but some of it she already had seen. My girl took it all in stride, and if it bothered her, she didn't show it.

Dr. McGovern greeted us when we stepped off the elevator. I swear this guy had me on his own personal radar whenever I was close by. We exchanged pleasantries, and I continued on to my son.

Jackson was just getting settled back into bed when we arrived at his room. Two nurses were checking his vitals and making notes on their tablets.

"I'm fine, really. You can go now," I heard him say to one as she continued to tuck him in.

"Thank you, ladies." I said as they took their leave.

"A Reed man never objects to a woman's comfort. You'd do well to remember that, son."

I couldn't help but tease Jackson. His cheeks reddened, especially when he saw Reese behind me.

"Very funny, dad."

"How are you feeling, son?"

"As if you don't know already? How many reports have you received since this morning?"

Kidding aside, his tone worried me.

"What's wrong, Jackson?"

"I don't want to talk about it."

"Well, I do, so spill it," I said. "What's wrong with you?"

He looked nervously over at Reese, and then back to me.

"Jackson," I encouraged him to go on.

"Dad, I can't talk about it right now. Please just let it go."

"Like hell, I will. Talk to me, son. If there is something I need to know, please say it."

"Walker, maybe I can clear some things up for you, with Jackson's consent of course."

I turned around to see Liam and Samuel standing in the doorway, with Samuel waiting for my son's answer. Jackson gave his consent, and we all took a seat at the table in his room. Jackson looked suddenly tired. Reese stayed with him, while I talked to his doctors.

"What don't I know?" I kept my voice lowered.

"We are hopeful and confident that Jackson is on his way of making a full recovery, but we do have some concerns. We have already spoken with him and needless to say, he didn't take the news well." Samuel said.

"Which is what?" I demanded to know.

"Jackson seems to have some numbness on his right side, causing difficulty when walking. His vision is still impaired, but improving. Post-op scans and the ones performed this morning all indicate our initial findings. The AVM's are gone."

"I understand the vision impairment, but the numbness? How is that? You said he didn't have a stroke, so what is causing this?"

Samuel clarified, "He did not have a stroke, but we discussed the possibility of stroke-like symptoms that could occur post-op surgery. If this is all that Jackson will experience, I consider this a win-win outcome. He is very lucky considering how close we came to losing him. Walker, if you don't mind, I would like to continue this conversation in my office."

After hearing Samuel say "almost losing him" I readily followed him back to his office. Reese stayed with Jackson, while I continued being brought up to speed with the doctors. What I did notably notice was Riley's absence. Where was she? I told them to continue on without me, and I would catch up in a few minutes. I couldn't go back in and ask Jackson. He was in a foul mood, and I didn't want to upset him further or cause concern for Reese. Richard told me that Riley had left after Jackson's discussion with Briggs. He asked her to go and get some fresh air, but he didn't think there was cause for concern.

"I want you to find her. I'm sure she's fine, but I still want her located. Am I clear?"

"Yes sir. I believe I know where Ms. Briggs could be."

"Then go get her and bring her back here." I snapped at Richard.

And the hits just keep on coming. On top of everything else, this was all I needed now. A lover's quarrel between Riley and Jackson. He needs his rest above anything else. I rejoined the doctors back in Samuel's private office. I was almost tempted to see if he had anymore Bourbon tucked away in his hidden bar. I could use one to take the edge off.

"As I was saying earlier," Samuel continued, "we got very lucky yesterday. With the stress his brain was under and the manner how we had to proceed, these bare minimum setbacks are trivial to what could have happened. I tried to explain all of this to Jackson, but he became agitated and increasingly hostile as I continued on with my findings."

I turned to Liam for clarity at this point. "What do you make of this?"

"He's scared. Knowing Jackson as well as I do, leads me to believe his problems lie with you, Walker."

"Me? When I left here last night, he was fine. What the hell changed since then?"

"Walker, what's happening or what should be happening in a matter of a few weeks?" Liam questioned me, and all I did was draw a blank for a few seconds. Then it came to me, but as far as I was concerned this was not up for debate.

"You mean going to school, don't you? He still wants to go to NYU, doesn't he?"

He nodded.

Briggs jumped in and continued explaining Jackson's rehabilitation plans. "His vision alone can be impaired for a couple of weeks to several months. His brain needs to heal. This is not a process that can be rushed. With a direction in place for him, he can begin to do out-patient therapy to regain his strength. Once he improves over time, he can continue with home therapy in your gym with the assistance of a personal physical therapist, or a trainer of your choice that is skilled in this field."

"This is all positive news, Walker, but once I said it, the look on your son's face changed to complete fear and anxiety. Riley tried to help him, but he just shut down. From what Riley has filled me in on, his dream is to attend NYU Film School, of course with Riley with him. At this time, I believe those plans should be put on hold until he is completely cleared."

"You've told him all this? And your personal opinions as well?" I questioned him.

The look on his face told me all that I needed to know.

"Fuck!" I screamed. "You could have at least warned me before I saw my son today. It's no wonder why he is upset, but he needs to get over it and move on. I had already intended on bringing my son home to California the minute you discharged him. I can't in good conscience leave him on his own after everything he has just gone through."

"And I think right there is the root of the problem." Liam stood up and walked toward me. "Walker, you never wanted him in New York in the first place, but conceded anyway. Now do you understand why he hid his medical condition from you in the first place? Because he knew exactly what would happen once you found out. I'm speaking to you as your friend now, and not his doctor. You need to give him some breathing room and let him be the man you raised him to be."

"And If I don't?"

"If you don't, then you risk losing him all together. That boy loves you with all he's got in him, but he's a man now and wants to begin living his life separately from yours. His life begins in New York with Riley. I can say this freely to you because it's nothing you don't already know, and I have discussed this with Jackson, countless times."

"He needs to recover. That alone is not up for debate. I suggest he takes the fall semester off, and we will revisit after the first of the year. He can begin in the spring. If not, just take a deferment for the first year and plan on next September."

"And you, Briggs, do you agree with this plan?"

"Are you asking me as a father or a doctor?"

"Both, if you don't mind."

"Yes, of course I agree. If this was Riley, I would put her health first. School is not going anywhere. Not that my opinion holds water here, but if Jackson knows he has your support and promise of allowing him to return to New York, I believe he will be more agreea-ble. He's very emotional right now. I think the enormity of the situa-tion has begun to set in, and he needs to process it. He's only twenty-four hours post-surgery. Right now, all of this should be the last thing on his mind. I've ordered a mild sedative in his IV line to keep him calm."

"And what about Riley? Will she defer for a year as well?"

"I'm not sure. She didn't say."

"Do you know where she is? I have my team looking for her."

"She's at the marina. She likes to go there to think."

"Thank you, Samuel. I…"

"You're welcome, Reed. I'll check in with your son later. He should be out for the next few hours."

"Are you okay?" Liam asked me.

"No, but I have to make this right with my son, and I will."

"You always have his back. I don't doubt that, just tread lightly, okay?"

Reluctantly, I agreed and knew my friend was right. I texted Richard, who had Riley in his sight. I told him to stay back and wait for me to arrive. I texted Reese with a quick update. She told me that Jackson was sleeping, and she was fine with Stephen.

I texted Reese:

Walker: *I love you baby. I'll be back soon.*

Reese texted back:

Reese: *Take your time. No scratch that. Hurry back…xo!*

Her response warmed my heart. I arrived at the marina and met up with Richard. Riley was down a ways near the larger yachts that were being housed for the summer. I found her sitting on a bench, staring out to the water. She reminded me so much of Reese, but she also carried so much of her father. She could be funny and outgoing like Reese, but then so serious like Samuel.

"Mind if I join you?" I asked, breaking her out of her thoughts.

"Mr. Reed, what are you doing here?"

"Looking for you. Can I sit?"

"Of course, please."

She looked on the verge of tears, a sight I probably couldn't endure now. I invited her in for a hug and she took it.

"I've been in to see Jackson and have spoken with your father. I know, Riley."

She let out a sigh and wiped her tears.

"I love him Mr. Reed, but he can be so stubborn."

Welcome to loving a Reed man! I silently thought, barely containing my laughter. If Reese were here, she would know exactly what I was thinking.

"In his defense, he's just reeling from yesterday, and I'm sure it's all hitting him at once. Give him some time, Riley. I'm sure things will look brighter once he's had some time to rest and think about things."

"Mr. Reed, as far as I'm concerned, there is nothing to think about. I will follow him anywhere, he knows that. I can easily go to UCLA for the first year and then transfer back to New York next fall. We already discussed the possibility of this happening. I thought he was okay with it, but then he just shut down on me. I think it's because of you."

"I've been hearing that a lot this morning."

"I'm sorry. I didn't mean to offend you, but it's what Jackson believes."

"I promise you Riley, I will not stand in my son's way in pursuing his dream of attending film school in New York with you, but I also can't ignore that I need to be a father and choose what's best for my child's health. Two doctors, one being your father, just told me that Jackson's health has to come first above anything else. Once he has been cleared medically, then New York will be back on the table, but for now, he is to return home with me as soon as he is able to travel. Our home is your home Riley, and you are welcomed to stay with us."

"Thank you, Mr. Reed. I needed to hear that. I'm going to make plans to attend school in California until we can both be in New York."

"Are you ready to go back and tell your fiancé the good news?"

"I'm not sure he will see it that way, but yes, I'm ready to go back. I need to talk to my mom too."

Chapter Forty-Four

Jackson

WAS I HEARING a lullaby, or was I dreaming it? I slowly opened my eyes to see Reese curled up in the recliner next to my bed and singing softly to her stomach. Her head was turned, so I didn't want to startle her. I closed my eyes again, but moved my left leg to show her that I was waking up. I opened my eyes again to see her smiling.

"Hey, you, how are you feeling?" she asked and leaned over to kiss my cheek.

"I'm better. Thank you. Where's my dad?"

"He's with Riley down at the harbor."

"No thanks to me, I'm sure."

"Why do you say it that way?"

"Because I'm an ass, and I hurt her this morning by behaving like one."

"A wise man owns up to his errors in judgment, and you are one of those men. Are you sure you're only eighteen?" she giggled.

"I hate this, Reese. I just want this to be over, and I can return back to my life. I just feel helpless and so unsure now."

"Jackson, you have just been through a life changing surgery, one that saved your life. Do you even get that? How close we all came to losing you? You are going to be fine, and why do I know that? Because you had the best surgeon in the world operate on you. In order for you to get better and make that full recovery he promised you, you need to follow his orders and be patient. Now I get that the Reed men don't roll that way, but you be the one Reed man to change that. I promise you, sweetie, this is nothing compared to what could have been. Please try to see all points of view?"

"I promise, Reese, and I'm sorry."

"Oh, Jackson, stop apologizing and just get well. I love you."

"I love you too."

"I'm going to step out for a bit. I'll be back soon."

OH THAT BOY! He is so much like his father, I thought to myself as I exited his room, only to be swept up into Walker's strong arms.

"Hey! That is quite the welcome."

"Thank you, baby."

"For what?"

"For being you, that's all."

He kissed me passionately on my lips and in front of Riley, who was just smiling from cheek to cheek. I pinched him to put me down, but it had the opposite effect. Walker continued to kiss me until I was breathless.

"Stop it," I whispered in his ear. His erection was evidently clear, I slid down his body and concealed it with my tall frame.

"Hello, my darling Riley girl. How was your walk? Feel better about things?" I questioned my daughter, but by the look of her face, I knew she already felt good.

"I'm great, mom. How's Jackson? Is he still sleeping?"

"He just woke up, and I'm sure he is waiting for you. By the way, he says he's sorry."

"I know, I heard when he was telling you. I'm going to talk to him. Love you, mom. And thank you, Mr. Reed."

"You're most welcomed, Riley."

MY FIANCÉ LOOKED so cute and sad just sitting in that hospital bed, looking all apologetic and contrite. I wanted to cheer him up.

"Special delivery. Hi! My name is Candy, and my job here at this hospital is to give our gold star patients very special treatment. I come with gifts. I have here two very delicious, mouthwatering hot fudge sundaes with all the trimmings here in this bag. I can feed it to you myself, if you need assistance," I said.

"Come here, Candy!" he motioned with his finger, keeping his eyes focused on me.

"I'm here. Now what, sir? Perhaps a sponge bath? Or something else that might interest you?" I pointed to the bag.

"You want this, don't you? Hmm, it sure is good. I may have to sample some of the delicious whipped cream."

I removed the lid from the now melting sundae. I lapped up the ice cream that had dripped down the side.

"Hmm, this is so good."

I continued to tease him with my mouth and then went in for the kill. I took the cherry and dipped it into the cream, rubbing it over my lips.

"Delicious," I said as I bit into the cherry.

Jackson growled and pulled me practically on top of him. Crashing his lips onto my own, I loved to get him all worked up. If he was going to have another blood pressure spike, this was one I would happily be responsible for. We tangled our tongues until he broke the connection. He was breathing heavily, but still held on to me.

"I love you baby, so much. Forgive me for being an ass again!"

"I love you too, and you are forgiven. Jackson, we are going to get through this. Months from now, this is going to be just another memory that we will add to our story."

"Absolutely. Can I have my ice cream now, Candy?"

"You may."

We talked for as long as Jackson had the strength to do so. A nurse came in and checked his vitals, all was good. After we finished our desserts, I snuggled very carefully next to him.

"I spoke to your father."

"And?"

"And he's fine, Jackson. He loves you so much. My father and Dr. O'Larien told him exactly what they told you. They are all in agreement with you taking some time off from school to get better and make a full recovery."

"That's not what I want though! And what about you? I can't expect you to just give up your plans for me."

"You see this ring? The same ring that you put on my finger with the promise of forever? The same ring that holds all of our promises we made to each other? Yeah, Jackson, you can expect me to just change my plans for you, because this ring makes it okay. I love you. And because I love you, I will follow you anywhere. I would expect the same promise in return from you. So we wait a year for NYU. Big deal! Don't ever put me in the position of choosing anything above us and what we have. I will always choose you. I would have never accepted this ring if I didn't feel that way. Now, you have used up your "being an ass" card enough for one day. Kiss me before I find myself an Italian prince and run off with him."

"I'd like to see you try. I will find you and beat his ass down, and then show you who you belong to. Now kiss me before I forget why I'm in this bed and tie you to it."

"I love you Jackson...so much."

"I love you too Riley. Thank you for loving me."

WE STAYED IN each other's arms until the next shift change of nurses. My father and Reese hadn't returned yet, but my father did text me to tell me he would be arriving soon. I couldn't thank him enough for giving me this time with Riley. I didn't deserve his patience, but was thankful for it just the same. I owed him an explanation and probably an apology for the way I behaved this morning. They all kept saying it was because of all I'd been through, but I'd like to know that even with valid reasons, I should be able to keep my manners in check.

She looked beautiful in my arms. This is where I wanted her to be for the rest of my life. She was the one. I always knew from the first moment our eyes connected. She was now wearing my ring. I meant every promise I made to her. I gently nudged her to wake. She must have been exhausted.

"Hey, baby." I kissed her on the top of her head, as she slowly stirred.

"Hi. Are you okay?"

"I'm perfect, and you?"

"Perfect. I want to make love with you. It's all I dream about, especially when I'm in your arms."

"You're killing me, baby. I thought the 'Candy' bit pushed me to the edge of my insanity, but hearing you talk this way sends me into a downward spiral. I want you…badly. Every time you're near me, my body wakes to your voice, and then I have a bone crushing hard-on for the rest of the day."

"I can help you out with that part, if you want."

"Not a chance. I love you for offering, but until I can love you the same way, I will just walk around with a case of blue balls."

"Oh my goodness! Jackson, you are too much."

We kissed each other madly until we heard a very distinctive clearing of someone's throat. *Oh god, was he listening to me talk about my erections?*

"Daddy!" she screamed and jumped off the bed.

"Feeling better, Jackson?" Dr. Briggs had asked me, clearly not happy finding his daughter all over me.

"I'm fine, sir. Thank you."

Riley hugged her father, and he welcomed the hug in return, but glaring over her shoulder at me in a disapproving look. *Way to go Jackson. Piss off your future father-in-law.*

"Riley, I'm going to examine Jackson. Can you give us some privacy?" Her father asked her.

"Sure daddy, I'll go grab a coffee. I love you, Jackson. I'll be back soon."

"I love you too, beautiful girl."

Riley practically bounced out of my room, causing her father to shake his head, but with a smile to go along with it.

"Okay Jackson, let's have a chat. Clearly you seem to be in a better mood since the last time we spoke, but I'm more concerned with how you're feeling post-surgery."

"Look, Dr. Briggs, I'm sorry for my earlier reaction when you explained everything to me, I was just taken off guard. I'm also sorry for what you walked in on just now."

"Jackson, I'm not that naïve, so relax, son. I know your relationship with Riley is not just for fun. I see how much she loves you. I know my daughter. She would have never agreed to marry you if it wasn't for real."

"Thank you, sir, for saying that. I promise to love your daughter forever. She's all I want. I know I can make her happy."

"You already do, son, this I know without any uncertainty. This entire experience with you has been a revelation for me. You are a good man, Jackson. Thank you for giving me back my daughter. I never wanted to hurt her or cause her one day of pain. I was dealing with my own loss, and I'm so very sorry for my actions. I see Reese, and how happy she is with your father. I never had that with her. Anyway, I'm getting off track here. We're good, son. Now, let me be the doctor again and get back to examining you."

When Dr. Briggs finished his examinations, he said to me, "Okay son, your scans are clean and AVM free. As for the numbness and tingling, we just have to take that day by day. You can wake to-morrow and it could be completely gone, or it can take weeks to go away. Once you are released, I would like you to begin out-patient physical therapy. Once you have the exercises down, you can continue on at home. I will always be available for any questions you may have, but your primary care will move forward with Dr. O'Larien. Once you are discharged from Johns Hopkins, your file will be sent over to Dr. O'Larien, okay?"

"I understand, sir. How will I ever be able to thank you for all you have done for me?"

"Jackson, I did my job as your doctor, now do your job as my patient, and follow my orders. And please, if you ever experience anything like you went through, you must promise to be proactive and tell someone. I don't ever foresee another AVM reoccurring. Having said that, you still will have to be monitored, and if meds are needed for any reason, you must follow your plan."

"I promise, sir. I have too much to live for to take stupid risks again."

"Good man. Now get some rest. You will need your strength for tomorrow."

"What's tomorrow?"

"We begin your Physical Therapy. Time to get you up and walking. I can see the apprehension written all over your face, but try not to worry. You came through with flying colors with all of your follow-up tests. I wouldn't be recommending this if I wasn't confident in my assessment. Get some rest."

"Thank you, sir. I will."

Just as Dr. Briggs walked out, my Riley walked back in.

"Hey, I just saw my father leave. Are you okay? He didn't give you too much of a hard time?"

"No, he didn't. We're cool. He just told me that tomorrow I begin my physical therapy."

"That's great news. The sooner you're up and around, the sooner we can get out of here."

"Yeah, back home to Fort Reed. It will probably be under armed supervision."

"Stop it. Remember how you reminded me to keep an open mind when it came to my father, well the same advice applies to you. He loves you so much. There is nothing he wouldn't do for you. Meet him halfway, Jackson, please?"

"I know what you're saying, babe. Your mother gave me the same speech. I know I must sound like a selfish brat, but giving up NYU is a hard pill to swallow. I kind of feel like he's getting his way. He never wanted me in New York. I argued every possible point with him until I was blue in the face. You can't imagine how I felt when he finally agreed. Once I'm enrolled in UCLA, I feel like I'll be stuck there. Bye-bye, New York."

"UCLA is not a bad back-up plan. You don't have to decide any of this right now. All you need to worry about now is concentrating on getting well. Please, Jackson, promise me that you will do that."

"I promise, beautiful girl. How can I ever say no to you?"

"You can't, so don't even try. Now kiss me!"

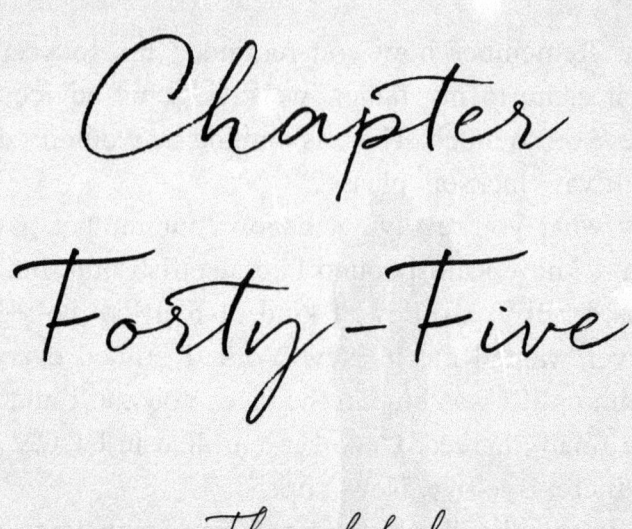

Chapter Forty-Five

Thankful

Walker

AFTER THE STORM cleared and we came to a mutual understanding, Jackson was on his way to recovery. Although he was disappointed about not attending school in New York, he finally made peace with it and focused all his attention on his physical therapy.

To argue with me was a miracle in its own right. I read countless medical journal entries that my son could have had any number of setbacks: Behavioral changes, Loss of Speech, Memory Loss. The list went on. Once he awakened and was alert, he still should have been tired and weak, but not my son. He was fired up and determined to put this entire ordeal behind him. I promised not to interfere with Samuel and Liam's plan for him, but as a father, I felt making him walk so soon after his surgery was out of the question. I wanted him to rest several more days before beginning anything.

I also made Riley spend her nights back in the hotel with her

mother and me. Jackson wasn't happy about it, but enough concessions were already given, and I had to draw a line somewhere. A
physiotherapist was brought in from London. Dr. Gillian Taylor met
Samuel during the medical conference he had attended during the
spring. She was more than qualified. Her credentials spoke volumes
of her success rate in helping post-surgical patients regain full mobil-
ity, especially patients like my son. She devised an aggressive plan
that consisted of daily workouts in the gym combined with weight
training, swimming, and yoga.

Samuel argued that it wasn't necessary to bring someone in
from the UK, but I spared no expense when it came to my son's
health, and I wanted the best...Dr. Gillian Taylor was the best. Before beginning his PT, Jackson went through another intensive round
of testing to show Dr. Taylor where he was post-surgery. He did re-
markably well. I never had a doubt, but he tired easily. He only had
mild tingling down his right side. Jackson described it as pins and
needles. He had weakness, but slowly he was able to move with the
assistance of a walker.

Not to risk injury, the first week he was harnessed in between
the bars to avoid falling. He did several reps until he could take no
more. Gillian pushed him to his limits, but without being overbear-
ing. She was compassionate to his feelings, having a daughter who
experienced something similar to Jackson. Her own daughter served
as a reminder to why she worked as hard as she did.

We talked over coffee one day, and she shared her personal story with me. Her then twenty one year old daughter had suffered a
stroke while away at university. She wasn't found right away and by
the time she was taken to the hospital, it was nearly touch and go.
Her chance at survival was reduced to the lowest numbers. She was
in the hospital for over eight months and suffered many complications that changed her life.

She would never be able to walk on her own without the assistance of equipment to help her. She only regained partial speech. Her
mental state had been reduced to a child of under seven years old.

My heart broke to hear this. I was thanking the heavens for sparing my own child. After I shared this story with Jackson, he never complained again and was the perfect patient. Of course we were all understanding to him, but putting things in perspective made life easier for all of us.

Although his complications were not as severe as they could have been, nothing was to be taken lightly. His recovery could not be rushed. The doctors were confident that by this time next year, this would all be a memory.

Three weeks later, Jackson was cleared to go home. I was ready to go home. This was the longest month of my life. I pushed for more time to make sure he was ready. Dr. Taylor could not accompany us back home to California, but she recommended several colleagues to assist us once we were home and settled. I already had everything in place for him.

Liam had flown back to Maryland to see us off on the day my son was discharged from Johns Hopkins. Nurses lined the hallway saying goodbye to my son. He was their star patient. He couldn't help flashing his perfect smile at them, especially at the younger ones. His flirtatious smiles had Riley turning into the green-eyed monster. He only had eyes for her, but I could definitely relate.

We all said our goodbyes, as Samuel handed off a file to me filled with more post-op instructions, as if I didn't have it all memorized by now. McGovern of course made his presence known. I in turn thanked him for all of his assistance, by way of a very generous donation to the hospital. Money well spent. I would do it a thousand times over if it meant securing the well-being for my son.

Riley stepped out to say a private goodbye with her father, promising she would see him soon. Reese also had said her goodbyes and gave him a friendly hug. Her pregnancy progressed over this past month and was clearly showing beautifully with our daughter growing every day.

I stayed behind to speak with Samuel privately. I watched my son be escorted down the hall to the private elevators. Everyone was smiling and relieved that this ending was a happy one. It had been weeks since the day I rushed through these doors to hear the fate of my son. I had never been so scared in all of my life, every fiber of my being was tested. Once they were out of sight, I turned to the man that saved my life by saving my son.

"Thank you, Samuel. I owe you a debt that I will probably never be able to pay back. You did the impossible and gave my son his future. You put your personal feelings aside when you didn't have to. I was wrong, so very wrong to judge you all those months ago. And for that reason alone, I am truly sorry. Thank you for not making Jackson pay for my mistakes."

He stood there calm and composed. I could say nothing more that he didn't already hear a thousand times already, so I simply extended my hand out for him to take.

"You're welcome, Reed. And, not that it matters, but I truly wish Reese to be happy. If you're the one to do that, then all has been righted."

"Thank you, Samuel, and it does matter…everything in my life matters."

I nodded at him and made my way to the one place I needed to be. It was as if it was calling out to me. The last piece of the puzzle I needed to put in place before leaving for home. I entered the quiet candle lit room and sat down before him. I once again prayed to the man before me. The same man that I begged to save my son. I screamed my demands at him and took no mercy on myself. I fought my own personal demons in this room. I had come full circle, and I truly believed that closure had been found.

I felt a presence beside me. It wasn't dark as the times before. It was lighter and freer. I turned, and it was my father.

"Hello, son."

"Father." I barely could get out above a whisper. He looked like the man I remembered him to be when I was in my younger years. He was still him, but no hardness in his features. He looked at me filled with love and pride. I blinked a few times to make sure this was real and not a hallucination.

"Thank you, Walker. Thank you for forgiving me. I thought I would be bound to my sins forever with no light ever to be seen again. You are my son. And I know I failed as a father, and I have failed you. You are a good man. A better man than I ever was."

I took a breath and opened my eyes. He was gone. It was over, truly over. I could walk out of here and finally leave the past behind, and begin the first day toward the rest of my life with Reese…

Chapter Forty-Six

Home is where you are...

AS OUR CAR made its long trek up our driveway, the path was lined with "Welcome Home" signs and balloons, and of course, Lila and Thomas Mitchell. Reese's grandparents decided to stay for an extended length of time with no date to return home to Georgia. I had their home in Pottersville closed up, and their shop in town was still going with their trusted staff. Their manager sent me weekly reports. Lila asked her dear friend Mabel to help with some of the more personalized baking in her absence.

Her friends had flown home only a week after their arrival in California. With the wedding still on hold, they wanted to return to their homes. They would fly back to California when we were back on track with our plans.

Riley was first to jump out of the limo and leaped right into the waiting arms of her great grandfather. He swiftly picked her up and swung her around. Where did he get his strength? He looked young-er than his given age and was in great health. He took his heart med-icine daily, exercised, and ate well. During our phone conversations, he expressed how much he was looking forward to helping Jackson. Reese cried while listening on the extension. She loved Thomas as if he was her own father.

Next was Reese to get a lift, but Thomas was very careful with her. This was the first time they were seeing her since we announced our good news to them over the video chat. Lila wiped away her tears as she took in Reese and all of her beauty. They were both cry-ing, hugging and simply glowing. The Mitchell women were amaz-ing, and I was damn lucky to soon be marrying my Georgia Peach.

The last of the welcoming party made their way over to us. Freddy and Fabrizio walked hand in hand over to us. They both took a turn hugging Riley, and then hugging Reese with Fabrizio kissing her on her cheeks.

He preferred to speak to Reese in Italian. He animatedly spoke to her in Italian with my girl responding perfectly back to him. I un-derstood the language, but sometimes I felt they had their own pri-vate way of speaking to one another that made me feel left out. Freddy had spent most of his career in Italy, so he spoke it fluently as if he was born there. Their friendship was solid and now with Fabrizio in the mix, it was a beautiful sight to take in. Anyone that can make my angel smile like that is alright in my book.

FABRIZIO WAS SO adorable with his hello kisses to me. "Ciao bella ragazza. Sembri positivamente raggiante. Ci sei mancata."

The worldliness of my modeling days long ago meant I had to learn a few words in other languages, Italian included. I responded, "Grazie Fabrizio. Siamo tutti contenti di essere a casa.È rimasto del Cristal in cantina?"

Fabrizio of course flashed me his sexy smile and kissed me again on my cheeks, gaining a smirk from Walker. He knew and understood how much I loved Freddy and Fabrizio, so his jealousy was mildly contained.

Fabrizio whispered in Italian that they had been discovered, and the cellar was re-stocked, but the code had been changed. That new piece of information made me look over to my man, who was now laughing. *What a devil, squashing his and Freddy's fun.*

Other than Walker and Freddy, who understood what Fabrizio and I exchanged, the rest of our party were standing and looking confused. I simply announced that Fabrizio had told me that I looked glowing due to the pregnancy and how happy they were to have us home.

My grandfather huffed, but Nana smiled. *This was quite the eclectic bunch*, I thought to myself. As we made our way into our home, Freddy whispered into my ear for only me to hear. He said that he had Priscilla, our house manager, wrapped around his finger. He gestured his hand, and then said he already knew the new number sequence to the wine cellar. I laughed so hard, I nearly wet myself. Oh it was good to be home and with everyone that I loved.

"Oh my sweet girl! Let me take a look at you." Nana happily took my hands and looked me over from top to bottom. "I have never seen you look more beautiful in all of my life."

"You do realize you say that all the time, Nana. You would think I was the Mona Lisa with the way you describe me. I'm just simply happy and so in love with him." I turned to see Walker watching me. He touched his heart and blew me a kiss. Oh I can't wait to revisit our gazebo. My mind was already spinning out of control, as well as my desire for him.

I never wanted to leave our home again. The minute I walked through the door, I felt the warmth and love greet me. This was our new beginning right here. We would fill this home with many new memories to share as husband and wife, and parents to our little girl who will soon arrive. I couldn't contain the smile that I was showing. I blew back a kiss to Walker, and gave him the silent promise of a wonderful night to come for us.

I spent some time with the guys, having promised to catch up with them. With my growing belly, Freddy would have to work on my dress and fit it to my body. We knew we wanted to get the wedding plans up and going again with marrying the soonest we could, but we needed to make sure Jackson was settled in first. He argued with Walker that we shouldn't put off one more day because of him, but we wouldn't hear of that. We didn't want him blaming himself for our postponed wedding. All would work out. We would soon have our day.

Freddy and Fabrizio were leaving for New York in the morning. They had to tie up some loose ends before returning back to California for our wedding. They promised to only be gone for a few days and would return by the weekend. I was beyond excited and was ready to see the masterpiece Freddy designed for me. He was so secretive about it. Freddy did some new measurements once he took in the size of my belly. He said to Fabrizio that a trip back home was necessary. That didn't help my self-esteem, but Fabrizio assured me that this was his beautiful creative mind at work, and to trust him. I did. Not only with a dress, but with my life.

After a delicious dinner prepared by Nana, we spent the next hour catching up, trying to keep the conversation on a positive note. Walker was worried that Jackson would be depressed. He was quiet all throughout dinner, but kept close to Riley, which was a good sign. They kept to themselves in their quiet conversation. I wasn't too worried. They would both be taking off the fall semester, with Riley beginning the new term in January. We would have to wait and see for Jackson. Walker had taken a video conference call with the dean over at UCLA to begin the enrollment process for Jackson and Riley.

This didn't sit well with Samuel at first, on account that Riley was our daughter, but I quickly helped him work through it and move on from it. No reason to argue over who was helping with the arrangements. Samuel was her father, and only father. He was a proud man and disliked the fact that Walker had a strong active role in his daughter's day-to-day life. This was the area we all needed help with. We would forever be in each other's lives because of our children. The fathers would eventually find their way of understanding the other's role. We had already come so far while we were in Maryland. I wasn't going to go backwards now. It was a new beginning for all of us.

"You look tired sweetheart. Let's get you upstairs and settled into your room." I said to Riley. I made it very clear that she and Jackson would have their own quarters. No arguments from my daughter, and none from Jackson. We had the long put off conversation with both our children. We knew the dynamics of their relationship had changed in more ways than one, but we still wanted the boundaries and rules of our home followed. Once those words left my mouth, I knew what Walker had been thinking. I kind of thought it also, that these two were in love and would probably move heaven to be with each other, even under our roof. I believe Jackson understood the meaning of discretion, so it would be Riley that would need more guidance on this subject matter.

"This room is huge, mom. It's bigger than the one I had at our house back home."

"I'm happy you like it, honey. As you can see, all your personal things have arrived. Your closet is fully stocked with some new Freddy Mac Originals, and of course, Mr. Yankee Bear."

"Oh mom! Thank you so much for being amazing. I love you so much."

"I love you too Riley. You have grown so much since the last time you left this house. It feels like forever already. I'm so proud of the way you handled all of this with Jackson. You are strong and fierce down to your core."

"Don't give me too much credit. If I'm anything it's because of Jackson. He makes me better, and his love gives me the strength that I need to take on anything we are challenged with."

"You sound like someone I know."

"Who?" Riley asked.

"Me. It's exactly how I feel when it comes to Walker. We are part of one another, two halves that make one. That's what real love is, baby. I don't know how I lived all of these years without him, but so very thankful that I will never have to know that feeling of loss again."

"Mom, does that mean you regret your past with daddy?"

"No, honey, not at all. In life, we all have our share of regrets and what might have been, but I would never trade up one day as your mom. I couldn't say that if I regretted my time spent with your father. The love we did have for each other made you, and that will always be cherished between us. Do you understand that?"

"I do. I guess I needed to hear it again."

"I will explain it to you as much as you need me to. Don't worry about your dad. He's going to be okay. We all are. Now, get some much needed sleep. Tomorrow is going to be a big day for Jackson. His new physical therapy team arrives. With the improvements made to the gym, he is all set to continue with his therapy."

"Mom, I was kind of hoping to take a few days to relax with him, and just spend some time alone."

"You will have that Riley, but his therapy has to come first. This is not up for discussion, especially with Walker. Am I clear?"

"Yes, mom, you are."

"I love you. Go to sleep and dream about Nana's homemade cinnamon rolls. I had mentioned to her that the baby had yet to taste the decadent flavors of her gooey breakfast treat. Well, that did it, and I saw Nana go into the kitchen, no doubt already preparing the batter."

"Mom, do I have to remind you that you have a wedding dress to fit into? Nana's cinnamon rolls are the size of a softball."

"Thank you for the reminder, but I will be careful. Go to sleep, my darling daughter. And worry about your own figure."

"Punk," I called out to Riley, as I closed her bedroom door, earning a breakout of laughter from my daughter.

"Gotcha!" Walker screamed at me as he grabbed me from behind and lifted me effortlessly in his strong arms.

"Oh my goodness, Walker! Thank you for the heart attack. You scared me." I pouted. He crushed his lips down onto mine and began walking toward our bedroom. Once inside, he kicked the door closed behind us and locked the rest of the world out.

"I'm so happy that your daughter cares about your body, but no need to worry, baby, that's my job. A job that I take very seriously. And I am about to inspect every delicious part of you."

"Oh yeah? Where will you begin your exploration?"

He bit my lip and then winked. I was already craving him to be inside of me. It was days since we last made love, and I wanted him now!

He placed me down on our bed, but on the edge where my legs could dangle over. Kneeling in front of me, Walker began to lift my leg and remove my shoe, giving the now freed foot a massage. I let out a pleasured moan, and then he proceeded to give the other foot the same attention. He knew what he was doing, and it was driving me insane. Next came my stockings, unfastening them by their garters, one by one. I was leaning back onto my elbows with my back already in an arched position. He was leaving a wet trail of kisses up and down my thighs until he reached my swollen clit and inhaled my arousal for him…only for him.

I was beyond mad with want. My skin was heated and my body was screaming for a release, but it wasn't to be found anytime soon. Walker was slowly torturing me with his skillful tongue and stimulating every nerve ending in my body. He would pull me to the edge of ecstasy where my voice would go hoarse from screaming his name, and then begin all over again. I wasn't sure how much more I could take, and just when I was about to claw my fingers down his sculpted back, Walker plunged his pulsing dick into my slick hot heat.

"Yes!" I screamed out.

He silenced my screams with his mouth. Our tongues were twisting together inside of my mouth. This was what I wanted. This was what I needed…we needed. No matter what happened, we would always have this moment where we could lose ourselves to the other without any barriers between us.

"I love you, Reese. You own every part of me. I am yours …forever. You feel so good baby. You're my home. You're my life."

He screamed as he let go of his release and climaxed so hard deep inside of me. My hands were clenching the sheets as I rode out my own orgasm. Walker's body was shaking as he stayed in me and poured every last drop of his essence into my body. He was right. I did own every part of him, as he owned every last part of me. As the man that I've loved for twenty years was still on top me, in me, my mind drifted back to the day his simple three words changed my life.

It was one of those moments in life you never forget. Every last detail was etched in my memory. It was the memory of that day I always carried with me:

"I love you, Reese, so much that I'm afraid to blink and you're going to disappear. You are my air, I need you to breathe. You are my first thought when I wake in the morning, and my last thought when I go to sleep. When I hold you in my arms, my world feels right. For the first time in my life, I'm home."

"I love you, Reese." His words broke me out of my blissful memories of our past. His words were true then, as they are right now. Another beautiful moment forever sealed in my memories shared with this incredible man.

He carefully broke our connection, and I was already feeling the loss. I was exhausted, but my mind was wide awake, and all thoughts were of Walker. In his darkest hours, he submitted all control over to me, as if I was his lifeline for survival. Didn't he know that he did the same for me? I am a woman deeply in love.

He was back with a warm Jasmine scented washcloth. With gentle strokes he cleaned down and in between my legs, and then onto my stomach. Lifting and placing me down under the soft duvet where he climbed in behind me and pulled me as close as two lovers can be.

"Don't over think it, babe. I love you. Now sleep, baby."

"How does he do it?"

"Do what?"

"Oh my goodness! I actually said that out loud."

Now he was laughing.

"Stop it, Walker. I'm serious. How do you do it?"

"And my love, I've already answered you. How do I do what?"

"Know my thoughts before I say them? You always did that with me. It drove me crazy."

"What can I say? I'm a man in love. I never really stopped from the first day I said those words to you. I love you, Reese Mitchell. You are my life, and please spend the rest of yours by my side as my wife. Will you marry me?"

"Yes. I will marry you Walker Reed, but I believe you already asked me. Come to think of it, you asked me several times. Do I have to worry about early memory problems?"

"Nah, no worries babe, I just like asking you. The way you breathlessly answer makes my heart beat just about out of my chest."

And with that loving sentiment, I took him by surprise and straddled his hips. The feeling of Walker filling me with his powerful erection was addicting. This was home. Here with Walker, inside of each other, making love and falling in love with him. Over and over, again and again. My love for him is on forever repeat.

"Marry me tomorrow. Seriously, babe, I can't wait one more day."

"It is tomorrow."

"Perfect, then I'm ready when you are. Are you ready to become Mrs. Walker Reed?"

"Absolutely, my love."

Chapter Forty-Seven

Finding our way back

Walker

ALTHOUGH I KNEW he was in good hands, I still had taken a few more days off to be at home with my son. I wanted him to settle in and return to a familiar routine. When he left this home three months ago, it was with Riley to begin their summer long vacation, and then off to New York to begin college. He's less mopey, but not the same as I knew him to be. He seems to get along with his new physical therapist, but to air on an extra side of precaution, I called my good friend, Tyler McVee, to lend a helping hand.

He was my personal trainer and was happy to step in to assist Jackson with his rehabilitation. Tyler, a former UFC Champion, was now retired. He'd worked with Jackson before and developed a friendship with my son. A personal touch was just the very thing I was hoping would get him out of his foul mood. Liam checked in daily and we'd discussed this matter. It was part of the healing process, and I was encouraged to be patient with him. I needed to be in the office today. I had a mountain sized pile of work waiting for me, and Jenny has already texted me twice this morning. I didn't want to leave Reese or Jackson.

Lila wanted to shop the Farmer's Market with Reese and Thomas. I immediately said no, but as always, Reese manipulated the hell out of me with her sexy smile and promises to rock my world tonight. I easily caved under her sexual hypnosis. I still didn't have a location on Townsend. That fucker disappeared off the map with no clues left behind. He was a man of great wealth and could easily disappear if he wanted to. I had Gail and all of their properties under surveillance. I told him to never come near my family again, but when I said it, it fell onto dead, soulless eyes. The man had lost everything. When you had nothing else to lose, you become dangerous.

"Jackson, may I have a word please?" I tapped on his door before entering his room. He was focused on his laptop, squinting furiously at the screen.

"What are you working on?" I cautiously asked him. He completely ignored me, which frustrated the hell out of me.

"Jackson," I called out once more and loud enough for him to hear me.

"What?" he answered, shoving away from his desk. He placed his head down in his hands. I knew what he was doing. He was frustrated and hurting. As his father, it hurt like to hell to see him in pain.

"Talk to me son, please. Don't shut me out again."

His voice quivered as he tried to hold back his tears. "I can't see the screen. The images are blurry and when I try to focus, my head begins to throb."

"Jackson, you have to give yourself time to heal. It is a miracle you've progressed this far already. Now in order to see more improvement, you have to be patient. Your sight is getting better, but there is no way of knowing when you will regain it to full capacity."

"What if I never get it back? What then, dad? I'm fucked, and my future is fucked! I can't be a blind film maker."

"Jackson, I don't know what I can say to help you right now, but maybe we need to have you talk to someone that can."

"Like a shrink? No thanks. I'll be fine."

"Why don't you get out of the house today? Maybe take a walk along the grounds? The exercise will do you some good, and it's a beautiful day."

"I'm fine here, dad. I just want to be alone."

"Okay. Get some rest, and I'll call you in a couple of hours. I love you."

He said nothing back, as I closed the door to his room, shutting him in with his thoughts. I hated to leave him, but I really needed to get to the office. I instructed Richard to stay close to Jackson today, and keep me updated throughout the day.

"Priscilla."

"Yes sir."

"I'm leaving for the office and I won't be home until later this evening. Please keep an eye on Jackson, and call me immediately with any changes I need to know. Also keep in mind of the extra security here at the house and on the grounds. No one is to enter the property without being cleared by security first, understand?"

"Yes sir."

"Thank you Priscilla. I'll see you later." I grabbed my briefcase and handed it off to Stephen, who was waiting for me by my car.

"Good morning, sir." He greeted me with his usual professional manner.

"Is it?" I answered morosely, and then slid into the back.

"Good morning sir. Welcome back!" Jenny greeted me as I stepped off the elevator to the executive floor of Reed Global.

"That seems to be the consensus this morning, but less of the cheeriness. Hello, Jenny, and thank you. Can you please bring me in some coffee and a muffin? Get me Donovan and Tom, and I need all my correspondence."

"Coffee and muffin are waiting for you on your desk. Donovan and Tom will be here in ten minutes, and all your pressing matters are on your left side of your desk. Will there be anything else sir?" She dutifully waited for my response.

I sighed and thanked the assistant gods for giving me Jenny. "Thank you Jenny, and e-mail me a reminder to give you a raise. Send them in when they arrive, and of course put through any calls from my home."

"Yes sir. Happy you're back."

"Me too."

Before diving into the long day that was a head of me, I enjoyed the quiet and sanctuary of my office. The last time I was here, I had made love to Reese in my private hidden bedroom. She came to me here wrapped up in nothing but a sheet hiding her gorgeous body under it. This was the last place I wanted to be today, but I have a company to run, and Jackson wasn't the only one that needed to get back into a routine. Before Reese came back into my life, this was my life. This company and this office. I spent fourteen hour work days here, six days a week. Now it's the last place I want to be.

As I finished my coffee and muffin, Donovan and Tom entered my office.

"Good morning, Walker. Happy to have you back." Donovan greeted me first.

"Hello, sir." Simple greeting by the more reserved Tom.

"Gentlemen, I take it no major crises occurred while I was away? I've already gone through this stack of reports, and we seem to be on schedule with Germany."

"On schedule and moving ahead as planned. The Reinhart's are thrilled with the progression of the building. After the completion, we will have to set the date on the official dedication ceremony and opening of the complex."

"That all sounds great, but when is our end date? We are all in-vested two plus years already. We need an end date. So when is it?"

"I see the completion by spring 2015," Donovan replied.

"Fair enough. I will hold you to that time frame. I want this building ready by April, and not one month later. Now moving on…"

I spent hours going over each project that was on my desk with the Reinhart building at the top of the list. I had spoken to Sebastian Reinhart, and as Donovan earlier stated, he was more than happy.

Jenny buzzed in, "Excuse me sir, you have a visitor."

"Who is it, Jenny? I'm very busy and see no appointments." Before she could answer, my door swung open and in walked Thomas, Lila, Reese, and Riley. Jenny was covering her mouth from her laughter spilling out. I could imagine my expression that I was wearing when they barged in, but now it was a welcomed surprise…the best.

Reese greeted me first with a kiss and hug. How did she know this is exactly what I needed? I would have loved to take her to the back, but we had company. "Nana wanted to see where you worked. Is it okay that we stopped by?"

"Of course it is. You never need a reason." I shook Thomas's hand, and hugged Lila and Riley. Thomas walked around the room and took in the antiques that were prominently displayed throughout my office.

"This is quite the office you have here, son. You've done good, kid, real good."

"Why thank you, sir, and coming from you that is quite the compliment."

"Just telling you how it is. Now son if you don't mind, I would like to speak with you about a few things."

"Of course, Thomas. Do we need privacy or can you tell me in front of the others?" I asked him.

"Here's just fine."

"Very well. Have a seat. What's on your mind?"

"Wedding" he stated.

"When are you going to marry my granddaughter here? She's carrying your child and we need to get you two married."

"Granddaddy. I've already explained that we will be planning it soon."

"And I told you, my sweet girl, that there is no time like the present."

I sat there for a minute in silence, deciding on how to answer his request. Lila was uncharacteristically quiet, and Riley was just smiling. I think it was at my expense.

"I couldn't agree with you more, Thomas. I plan on speaking with our wedding planner today. Once I do that, all will be back on track. I promise to give Reese an amazing day."

Thinking that answer would appease him, my response did not make Thomas happy.

"Walker, you don't need any fancy planner. Lila is here and has been waiting to throw you one hell of a party. My heart hurt for you, and for your son, but you all are home now, so I see no reason to wait. Don't you agree, Reese?"

"Granddaddy, can you give me some time with Walker? I'll join you in a few minutes, and then we can go to lunch, okay?"

"Okay, sweet girl. Walker." I nodded at her grandfather and watched them exit my office. Jenny would chat with Lila. She was looking forward to meeting her.

"I'm sorry. I'm sorry. I'm sorry," Reese said to me. "I can't believe how standoffish granddaddy was behaving."

"Come here, baby. Talk to me. What has gotten him all riled up? Do I need to worry? Did he bring his shotgun with him?"

"Stop it. That's not funny."

"Okay, I'm sorry. What's up?"

"He's not mad at you, he's just mad in general. I've never seen him so upset."

"I can't help unless I know the whole story."

"After we arrived home from the market, Nana and I were talking in the kitchen and didn't realize granddaddy was around the corner. He heard most of the conversation about Henry, and what happened at the hospital. Nana began asking questions, and I had to tell her who he was and how I fit into the story. Well granddaddy finally lost it and demanded to know everything. We never really explained our entire history to him, and Nana and I felt that he didn't need to know. The short version always worked for him, and this time, it didn't. I tried to explain it the best way I could, but I think after he heard it all, he just wanted to hit something. The gardener gave him an ax to break up some firewood. That helped his tension a little bit. He's also upset for Jackson. He hasn't come out of his room all day, and has refused lunch."

"Reese, why didn't you call me immediately? Or better yet, Priscilla or Richard? This is what I pay them for and quite fucking well I might add."

"Walker, it is not Priscilla's fault. This is a family matter, and we discussed it as a family. I'm fine. He's just upset for me and felt he let me down by not being there to help me all those years ago. The fault lies on me. We all know it. No point to deny it."

"No, it doesn't! I refuse to listen to this garbage. I agree, Thomas does have a right to be upset, but it's not right to make you feel bad about it. Secondly, my son nearly died weeks ago. We are all trying to get our feet back onto the ground. Baby, our wedding will happen. I promise you."

"I know that, Walker. I don't want you to feel pressured by my grandparents or by me."

"Impossible. Are you forgetting our conversation last night in bed?"

"No! Never. It was one of the best nights of my life."

"Good. Mine too." I pulled Reese to me and kissed her passionately.

"Not one more day, baby." She looked at me with widened eyes, as I pulled out my phone and dialed her number.

"Rosalyn. Walker Reed here. I need you to drop everything and proceed with our wedding plans. Oh and one more thing…you have ten days to pull it off." Without waiting for an answer, I disconnected the call and kissed my beautiful bride to be. "Baby, I'm going to make all of your dreams come true. Marry me next Saturday in our meadow and under our gazebo. I'll be the handsome prince waiting for you."

"You already made all my dreams come true. I love you so much."

"You render me speechless, baby. Do you think we can send them home, and I can have my way with you?"

"As much as I would love that, I have to say no. And Walker?"

"Yes my love."

"Granddaddy does have his shot gun with him."

"Oh fuck!"

"Exactly. I love you, and I'll see you at home."

I said my goodbyes to Lila, Thomas, and Riley. Thomas's mood changed with the news of our wedding next week. Lila was smiling and Riley was happy too. Lila couldn't wait to begin cooking and getting everything on her end done. Their smiles were worth the office invasion I endured earlier.

"Jenny!" I didn't bother buzzing her.

"Yes sir."

"Time to turn the office back into wedding central. If I turn into groomzilla, reel me in quickly."

"Will do, sir."

"Follow up with Rosalyn, and put out a press release for tomorrow morning. I need Stephen here immediately, and another coffee would be great."

"Yes sir. Did I tell you how happy I am to have you back?"

"You may have mentioned it. Now go! We have a lot of work to do and not a lot of time to do it in."

The rest of my day flew by with making call after call. Reese would have her wedding. I left no detail to chance. Freddy would arrive by the weekend with the finished dress in hand. Before he left, he took new measurements of Reese, and began working on her dress. She looked gorgeous, and now being pregnant, she was just off the charts beautiful. In the beginning, my planning went to the extreme. I didn't even know how I let things get out of hand, but all was on track now. Reese didn't care about much. She just wanted her family and closest friends with us on our day. With her life in front of the cameras, she left that behind a long time ago. I was sorry that I had forgotten that for a while, but I truly believed Reese and her grandparents would be very happy with what I'd come up with.

After my very long day, I arrived home to a very quiet house. I called out and no one answered me back. Not even Priscilla greeted me by the door. I searched the house and still found no one.

"Calm yourself Reed, and get yourself in check," I said out loud as I continued to search the house. I pulled out my cell to dial Reese, when I heard noise coming from the media room. Not knowing what was on the other side, I slowly opened the door to find everyone, including Priscilla and Richard watching home movies of Reese.

"You're home!" Reese called out to me.

"So it appears. I was worried when I couldn't find anyone."

"Oh I'm sorry baby. We've been in here for a couple of hours now. I didn't even know that Nana had brought all of my childhood home movies with her. Come here, let me show you my mama and daddy."

I sat beside Reese, as she explained in great detail the memories that were being played out in front of me. She looked just like her mother. Her father resembled a younger looking Thomas. I caught a few of her falling tears as the camera zoomed in on her parents at times. I got to see the famous Bubba, her grandfather's golden retriever. He was in all the footage, and at times dressed up. I laughed out loud with my girl. Her tears ceased, and she smiled as she snuggled up to me.

"Your parents are always with you, baby. They'll be with you on our wedding day too," I said.

"I know. Seeing them again brought it all back for me. I haven't watched these movies in years. I didn't know that Nana had them restored. It's a wedding present for me. They're all mine now. She even made copies for Riley to have."

"That's beautiful, baby. I can't wait to watch them all with you.

Speaking of family, I can't help but notice, where's Jackson?"

"He's upstairs. He didn't want to come down."

"Okay. Will you excuse me for a few minutes?"

"Walker, don't be upset with him."

"I'm just going to talk with him. I'll be back soon."

Reese and Riley both looked up at me with apprehension in their faces. Clearly what we were doing wasn't working, so it was time for a talk with my son.

Without knocking this time, I walked in to his room. He was sleeping with his headphones on and a movie now on its credits. I carefully removed his headphones and gently shook him awake.

"Dad," he groggily responded.

"Hey, how are you feeling? Any more headaches?"

"I'm good. It was just eye strain earlier this morning. Tyler came by and we worked out for a while, but just strength training. I was tired after that and just relaxed here."

"Why didn't you join the others down in the media room?"

"I wasn't up for it."

"But spending time alone in this room, is that what you're up for?"

"Dad, I don't want to get into this right now."

"That's too bad because we're already knee deep into it, and we're going to talk this through, right now."

"What do you want from me, dad? So I stayed in my room today. It's not a crime to want to be alone."

"You're right. Shutting your family out, and the girl you're supposed to love, is not right either. How do you think she feels knowing you won't talk to her and have completely shut her out?"

"Did Riley say something to you?"

"She didn't have to, son. It's written all over her face. Now for the last time, talk to me."

"I'm sorry. I don't know what else you want me to say?"

"Jackson, I want you to rejoin the living. Hiding up here in the solace of your room is not going to make you feel better, in the long run. Shutting everyone out who loves you is not going to help you feel better, if anything, it's going to make you feel worse. I'm not going to sit here and try to minimize what you've been through. I know because I was right there with you, son. It nearly destroyed me to discover your secret. I don't ever want to think about what could have happened if I lost you. How many times do I have to tell you this? I love you, Jackson, with every fiber in my soul, but as much as I love you, I will not sit back and lose you to this depression that has taken hold of you."

"You are getting stronger every day. And your vision is improving. Please son, give yourself time to heal and be thankful that you're still here."

I gave him a minute to process all that I said. Times like this I wish he had his mother to comfort him. I tried my best to keep myself in check and not get angry. I watched Jackson pull himself up with now his back to his headboard. I extended my hand, but he refused it. He wanted to get up on his own. He reached for his cane before placing his feet to the floor. With the assistance of his cane, he stood up tall and gave me a hug. It was a hug I welcomed and needed.

"I'm sorry, dad. I'll try harder and do better. I should have never lied to you from the beginning. I'm so sorry for putting you through this."

"Jackson, none of this is your fault. We have already made peace with this a long time ago. I just want you to live in the now with me, and not let the past keep interfering with your present. Don't make the same mistakes I made. You are so young and have so much to look forward to. None of it has to be spent alone. You have an amazing girl who loves you and is waiting for you downstairs. Go to her and make things right. By the way, I have a question to ask you. It's more like a favor."

"Anything, dad, name it."

"Good. I was hoping you would say that. Next Saturday, I'm going to marry Reese. I would love nothing more than to have the best man I know, well…stand up for me."

"Me? You want me to be your best man?"

"I don't see anyone else around. Yes, Jackson, I want you to stand up for me. Will you?"

"Yes! Of course I'll do it. It would be my honor, dad."

"Excellent. I was hoping you would say yes. Thank you, son. You don't know how happy you just made me."

"No, dad. Thank you."

Chapter Forty-Eight

I'm still me

Jackson

AFTER MY TALK with my father, I took a few minutes to myself to gather what I wanted to say to Riley. My girl had been more than patient with me while I'd been an ass. My father was right on all counts. I was shutting out my family and my girl. I'd been so selfish and consumed with focusing on school and my wants, that I never even considered how it was affecting Riley.

She had been nothing but supportive and loving toward me, even when I didn't deserve it. I just wanted "me" back, and I had to find some way to make her understand how I felt, and without pushing her away. I loved this house. The grounds were beautifully lined with blossoming trees and flowers. I knew I couldn't walk too far without getting tired. My sight was improving as well as my balance. I couldn't wait to throw this cane away, but for now it was my saving grace. I lowered myself to the ground and leaned back to stare up at the night sky. Stars were blanketing the sky tonight and left me wishing that Riley was here with me. As if she had a secret portal to my thoughts, I didn't have to wish for long. I looked up to see her standing before me. She looked at me lovingly and waited patiently to be invited back in.

She looked absolutely beautiful with the moonlight shining all around her. We had our own connection and could almost hear the other's heartbeat. I opened my arms, and with no hesitation she dropped to her knees and fell forward into me. I folded her in, safe and protected. I loved her so much. It was time to show her how much.

"Hey, beautiful girl. What's with the tears? We've had enough of them lately, and they stop tonight."

"I can't help it, I'm sorry. When your father walked back into the media room without you, my heart just sank deeper and I felt...lost. Lost without you. Jackson, please don't give up. I am begging you to fight, and fight for us. I don't care about school, I don't care about New York. All I want is you, and for you to love me. Has that changed for you?"

Gutted. Totally sliced wide open with her words. I already knew how she could sit here and question me. This was my fault because I was the one that left her so unsure. Her confidence had now been shattered, and she was left with the uncertainty of facing a future without me. *Never! I could never be so lost for that to happen.*

"Riley, if I could, I would just hit rewind on the past month and take back every last tear you ever had to cry because of me. I am so sorry that I've hurt you. I never knew that I had a selfish side in my body until I was faced with losing something that I wanted so badly. I put my own wants before you, and for that alone, I am so very shameful. I know what I went through with having the AVM and the surgery that followed. I do know how fucking lucky I am to be alive, but even that didn't stop me. All I cared about was that I wasn't going to my dream school or city. My friends were moving on without me, and here I was, not getting to do what I had planned."

"Riley, I will never be that careless again with your feelings. Here you were putting everything on hold for me, and I just let you do it. I promise to work hard at getting 'me' back. I promise to listen to my doctors and follow my physical therapy. I survived baby, and that alone is a miracle. I'm done being an ass and taking for granted everything I still have. Specifically, you, my beautiful girl, are my life. If I'm ever selfish again it's going to be for us and for us alone. We matter most, and I promise to always put you first. I love you."

"I love you, too. You didn't have to say all of that, but I'm still happy you did. I've missed you so much. I can't help but feel insecure. It's a bad habit. I allow my overactive mind to analyze the shit out of everything."

"Don't apologize, baby. You were just taking cues from me. I want you, but this is not the place to show you how much."

"I know. This place is on lockdown and I'm not sure if we could go anywhere that's not being watched."

"My father is on high alert because of the press. And there's my missing grandfather to worry about."

"We never really talked about it, Jackson. How do you really feel about your grandfather and all that happened? I know you loved him very much."

"I still love him, but he's not the same person I knew as my grandpa. He's changed into someone I don't recognize. He hurt my father so much. Clearly after all of these years, he's still hating on your mother for simply loving my father. I don't get it, babe? But I'm done trying to understand it. My grandma is a mess. She's divorcing him. Can you believe that? After forty plus years of marriage?"

"It doesn't matter how old you are. Hurt is hurt, and your grandfather caused a lot of it for many people. Your grandmother has a right to her feelings. She probably has many of them right now to work through, but I'm sure she will be okay."

"I hope so. Anyway, enough of that. Did you know my father asked me to be his best man?"

"I did. I'll be standing up for my mom as her maid of honor. I can't believe they are finally getting married. We will both be witnessing a testament to their love story."

"It's been quite the journey for them. All has finally been righted in their world."

"Jackson."

"Hmm."

"Is everything right in *our* world?"

I pulled my girl on top of me and held her face in my hands. She was trying not to cry and be brave, but I knew any tears that would fall would be because she loved me so much. I saw myself in her reflection and let a tear or two fall down from my own eyes. I never felt more in love with Riley than at this moment with her under the night sky. I didn't answer her, I showed her. And I really didn't care about being seen. All I wanted at this moment was Riley seeing me, and feeling my love for her.

She hesitated at first, and then opened up for me, as my tongue met hers. I never loosened my grip on her, as my tongue twisted in unison with hers. She let out a soft moan, sounds that flowed straight down to my hard erection. My eager body wanted hers. Riley sat up and now was straddling my hips. She lifted her shirt from the hem and slowly removed it from her body, leaving her with her pink lace bra on. I sat up and wrapped my arms around her, and kissed her between her breasts, biting through the barely there material. I took her pebbled nipple into my mouth, as she screamed out her pleasure. I quickly silenced her with my mouth. We were away from the house, but we didn't need an audience.

"Please, Jackson, make love to me. I need you so much."

"I am making love to you, baby."

"I want you inside me. Stop teasing me, please."

"We have time, Riley, so let me love you and show you how much you mean to me."

My leg was tingling again. I'd been on the ground way longer than I should have. I could feel it begin to spasm, but I bit back the sensation and continued loving my girl. I placed my shirt on the ground and laid Riley on top of it. I kept her skirt on, but pulled off her panties. She was wet and ready for me. I inhaled her intoxicating scent as I drove my tongue into her inviting aroused bud. She cried out again and lifted her pelvis further to get my attention. *Oh I was there, and I wasn't going anywhere.* She withered beneath me, as she bit her lip to the point of ripping it open.

"Now, Jackson, right now!"

"You are a demanding little thing, aren't you?"

"Only for you. I need to feel you fill me, please, Jackson."

"Her words were my undoing as she handed me a condom, taking me by surprise again. I didn't question it. I slid the condom down my length and entered Riley slowly at first, and then picked up the pace. The pain in my leg was keeping me from going faster, but my girl wasn't complaining. She felt so good wrapped around me.

"Look at me, Riley. And don't close your eyes."

"You said that the first time we made love."

"I'll say it every time. I need to see you…always, and I want you to always see me. You make me come undone, baby. I am so head over heels in love with you."

"I love you, Jackson."

We were close as two people could be. Our bodies were tightening around the other, as we both came at the same synchronized moment. I felt alive, and so very strong. This was how Riley made me feel. We were one. I knew that we would be okay from this minute moving forward. My father was right. My future wasn't gone. It was just beginning, and with Riley. No more doubts. No more sad tears. I had it all. And had the girl of my dreams here in my arms.

"We better get back before they send a search party out to look for us." My girl giggled and quickly dressed. I tied off the condom and pocketed it until I could throw it out. I struggled to get up, but nothing got past Riley, as she noticed me wince in pain. Holding out her hand, I took it with no hesitation and got myself up.

"Team Reed, right?"

"Forever beautiful girl. I can't wait to make you mine forever."

"I'm already yours, Jackson. A piece of paper won't change that."

"Yes, it will. We will be married, Riley, and that will be the happiest day of my life."

"Our life," she said as she smiled at me.

"Absolutely."

"Our life."

Taking her hand in mine, as we walked back to the house, I whispered to myself, "Our life."

Chapter Forty-Nine

Countdown to the big day...

THE WEDDING PLANS were back on. Not a minute was wasted on finalizing every last detail for our big day. I felt like I could finally come up for air and just take a breath. With all that my family has been through, no family deserved a win more than we did.

My son was getting stronger every day. Reese's pregnancy was right on track. She wasn't getting sick anymore, and her little baby bump wasn't so little. She was nervous about fitting into her wedding dress, but Freddy assured her that she would look stunning in his one of a kind design. I downsized the wedding guest list to family and close friends only. I gave Reese what she wanted, an intimate wedding in our meadow. After we met with Rosalyn, and she revealed her revised plans, Reese was thrilled. And Lila? She was over the moon. Rosalyn had won them both over with all she had done.

My mother had arrived, along with Marsha Malin. Reese had insisted that Marsha stay with us. This was my first time having the opportunity to spend some time with Reese and Freddy's longtime friend. She was like no one I had ever met. She was loud, opinionated, and had no filter when it came to what was on her mind. Having Freddy, Marsha, and Lila all at the same table made the dinner conversation very animated, but we all had a great time as new friendships were born.

As much as my mother tried to be part of this fun group, I also saw some sadness on her face. I hadn't really had the opportunity to spend any real time with her. When I suggested a walk through the grounds, her eyes lit up and happily accepted my invitation.

We walked arm and arm through the garden that led to the meadow where Reese and I would marry.

"Are you okay Mother?" I asked her, as we sat in the gazebo.

"Of course. Why do you ask?"

"You say that you're okay, but your body language tells me differently. What is it? Haven't we made you feel welcomed in our home?"

"Oh, Walker, please don't be defensive. You know I am so happy for you and your lovely Reese. She's making me a grandmother again. That alone is the best news I could ever receive. You wouldn't understand if I told you."

"Try me. I may just surprise you."

"Please don't be angry with me, but I've been thinking about your father lately. I know you were at the house and you made your peace, Reese told me. But the bigger question is, why didn't *you* tell me? I could have been there for you, son, and helped you through it. I know your father hurt you very much, but I'm still here, Walker, and I feel disconnected from you."

"Mother, I'm sorry you feel this way, but it was not my intention to hurt or shut you out. I needed to be alone at the house, and with father. His presence is still so strong in that house, and I needed him to hear me. I no longer am carrying the anger I once had. I lost too much already to waste one more day being angry over something I cannot control."

"What does that mean exactly? Have you forgiven your father?"

"I have. I gave him his absolution. I truly hope he is at peace."

"And Henry? What will you do about him?"

"Nothing. Absolutely nothing. He's dead to me. He's alienated his grandson and his wife. The man has lost everything. He only has himself to blame. He's another subject I no longer wish to discuss. For what's it worth, I am very happy you are here with us. Reese couldn't be happier that her family and ours have finally come together. This is what we have always wanted, and now we have it."

"I'm happy too, son. You deserve all the happiness your heart can hold. You found your soul mate again. To have that happen once in a lifetime is miraculous, but twice? I would say you, Walker Phillip Reed, are the luckiest man in the world, and I'm damn proud to be your mother."

"Thank you, because I'm damn proud to be your son. I don't say it often enough, but I do love you very much."

"I love you, too. Come on, and let's go share a piece of pecan pie."

"*You* want pecan pie?" I laughed out loud with my mother's request.

"Yes, and what's so funny about that? That Lila Mitchell is one hell of a baker. One bite of that pie, and I was hooked. Now let's go back inside before that grandson of mine finishes it off."

"As you wish mother. You never cease to surprise me."

"Touché son, touché."

It was amazing how far we've come in our relationship. We went from not having one to laughing and enjoying each other's company. All was fitting into place.

IS THIS REALLY happening? How did I get here? I'm here with Walker. The man whom I have loved all my adult life. The man that has made all my dreams come true. My fantasies have now become realities.

I smiled and took it all in. The sun was warming my skin on this beautiful September morning in California. Our gardens were exploding with color from the hundreds of flowers blooming throughout the grounds. Our gazebo was ready. The dance floor had been installed, and the tents were presently being put up. It was like watching a movie play out in front of my eyes, and I had the front row seat in my balcony above.

"Ouch, little one. That was a hard kick."

I rubbed my growing belly as I talked to our daughter who was being very active this morning. I was just far enough along where I could feel her, but it was a little harder for Walker to. I told him that his time was coming soon, and he would love it. He talked to her every night and played his favorite melodies for her. Times like this, I often think of our son who we lost. He probably would have looked just like Walker. Jackson mirrored his father almost completely, except for his eyes which belonged to his mother.

I could sit here and daydream all day, but I had vows to write. *What could I say that I haven't said to Walker a thousand times before?* I thought about just waiting to the moment where his eyes would meet mine and the words would easily come, but decided it was best to write them down.

Freddy had given me some of his best one liners to use, but I would save them for when we didn't have an audience listening. I didn't think it was appropriate to call Walker "Mr. Wall Sex" in front of Nana. *Oh my goodness! I love my best friend.*

"Knock, knock. Come on, Peaches. It's time to meet my god daughter." Speak of the Devil, it was Freddy at my door.

"Hey, what time is it?" I nervously asked Freddy.

"It's time for your appointment. Hurry up and get dressed, or we are going to be late. I promised your very hot man that I would drive you to your appointment where he will meet us."

"I'm sorry, BFF. I just got lost in my thoughts."

"I hope it was all thoughts of Mr. Sex on a stick!"

"Of course, are there any other kinds?"

"Ha ha, very funny. Let's go, Peaches."

Freddy had driven me to my appointment at Dr. Lemay's office. Walker had early morning meetings, so they worked it out that he would meet us there. Freddy was so excited to see the baby. He never experienced something like this before, so I was happy to share it with him. He was also over the moon that we asked him to be god father to our daughter. Who else would love her more?

Arriving before Walker, I was taken into my exam room where we waited for the man of the hour to arrive. After consuming a gallon of water, I was going to burst any minute if he didn't get here soon. Freddy kept making faces at me and trying to make me laugh. I shooed him away after the last joke, when Dr. Lemay and Walker entered the room together. He looked incredibly handsome in his three piece grey pinstripe suit. I loved watching him dress, but this morning I missed my own private viewing because he left so early.

"Hello, baby. You look amazing," he said as he leaned down to kiss me.

"Why thank you, stud, but not in front of Reese. Our girl gets jealous." Freddy winked at my man.

"Freddy! You are terrible," I playfully slapped him.

"What? That compliment wasn't for me? Oh Walker! You hurt my feelings." Freddy feigned his hurt.

"Sorry, Mac, not this time," Walker said.

He winked and then kissed me without any care in the world that we weren't alone. Dr. Lemay cleared her throat. And Freddy? Well he's Freddy, and he mini-applauded our display of affection.

I bit on his lip in the kiss and Walker leaned in. He said, "Save that for later, baby. You can bite me anywhere you wish."

Freddy gasped and screamed, "Swoon!" as Dr. Lemay ignored everyone and focused on her job.

Walker held my hand with Freddy on the other side doing the same. Dr. Lemay lifted the sheet and exposed my belly, where she put the jelly on it.

"Oh that's cold." I shivered.

"Sorry, but it's necessary." Dr. Lemay replied. She stroked the scanner over my stomach and within seconds our little girl appeared on the screen. She was sucking her thumb and nestled all cozy inside of me. Dr. Lemay clicked and clicked until we had an album of images. She was absolutely beautiful. I looked up at Walker, who had tears in his eyes. Underneath the powerful mogul that the world sees, right here with me, is simply the man that I love and the father of our child.

"That's our baby," he whispered. "I have never loved you more, Reese. Thank you for making me a father again. I can't wait to hold our daughter."

"I love you too. Thank you for making me a mother again. We are blessed. To have this with you is simply a miracle, a dream I gave up having many years ago."

"Okay, you two, cut it out. I can actually feel a cavity beginning to form with all of this sweetness. Come on, Reed! Where's the hard core dirty talking 'Mr. Wall Sex' I love so much?"

We both just shook our heads at my best friend and laughed. Poor Dr. Lemay. She was as red as a rose, but she took all the fun in stride.

She went over all the details of my exam. Our baby's heartbeat was perfect. I could listen to that amazing sound all day long. I was at my halfway point of my pregnancy.

She told us that our little angel was just about the size of a banana. I looked over at Freddy, giving him a warning not to joke about this. He pretended to zip his mouth.

"All is progressing nicely, Reese. You are measuring perfectly. Although you think you are huge, you've only gained about twelve pounds. You are a star patient. Other than the early sickness you experienced, all looks great. I see no reason why you won't continue to have a healthy pregnancy. I do encourage a reasonable amount of exercise, but also rest too. Anything else you would like to go over?"

she asked.

Walker seemed to be satisfied with all that he heard, and with that, I got dressed. Arriving back home, Nana was cooking up a storm. The house smelled amazing. You would think scented candles were burning, but it was the aroma from the oven that had our tastes buds bursting. She was excited to see the baby pictures I brought home.

"That's not ready yet!" she screamed as scolded Freddy who took a taste from one of the pastry bowls.

He gave her a lifting hug and she laughed, while telling him he was forgiven. Jackson was resting in his room. Riley was in the media room making some videos that she called "book trailers," as she was an avid reader of many books on her Kindle. She said she was just messing around, but some of them were really good, and I encouraged her to pursue it further. She had been amazingly supportive of Jackson and waited along with him to begin school, but I knew my daughter. She was itching to get her creative juices flowing, so this was a good distraction for her. Who knew where it could lead to? Before she left for her vacation, she took Jackson to an author signing where she "fan-girled" over her favorite authors.

Riley described the leading men as her book boyfriends, and she adored the women responsible for bringing those men to life. She took a photo with authors Wendy Ferraro and Alice-Montalvo Tribue. Their men were Dylan and Victor. Riley talked my ear off for hours explaining every last detail of their books. I finally put my hands up in the air and conceded to read them. After all, I was living my real life story with Walker. What harm can it do to—what was her word she used—"fan girl" over a few book boyfriends.

"Wow! Oh my talented daughter. You did a great job with this one."

"Thanks mom, but I'm just messing around."

"Riley, this is more than messing around. You took their story and made it into a mini movie. Why don't you reach out to Wendy and show her what you've done? I bet as an author, she would be thrilled that one of her fans took this much time and effort to show-case her book."

"Thanks, mom. I'll think about it."

"Do more than think about it...do it. This may lead to other things. You never know."

My girl definitely was overflowing with her sparkle. We both were. If someone were to ask me six months ago if this is how I saw my life playing out, I would have not believed it. It happened...it really did happen. The dream of marrying Walker and sharing my life with him was something tucked away in my memories. Now all I wanted to do was scream it from the highest mountain how much I loved him. I was ready...we were ready. In just under forty eight hours, I would be...Reese Mitchell Reed.

"Mom, earth to mom."

"Oh, I'm sorry, honey. What did you say?"

"Nothing important. You must have been having some day-dream, huh?"

If she only knew.

STEPPING OUT OF the shadows, I observed without being seen or heard. I would wait for the perfect time to strike and make my presence known.

Fools, all of you. You conniving bitch. You smug bastard. The prince will fall...mark my words. Enjoy your happiness now, while it lasts.

You soon will discover what it means to lose everything. You took away what was most important in my life. So now, I will take away what you value most.

And the best part? You won't see me coming.

Chapter Fifty

Past...Present...Future

Walker

IT WAS FINALLY here, my wedding day, a day I dreamed about for more years than my son had been alive. Some cynical men have called marriage the death of romance, love, and bachelorhood, but I never saw it like that. ...Which made it slightly ironic that I found myself at the cemetery on my wedding day. In actuality, I was here with my son to pay respects to Elizabeth before the ceremony.

Last night, after I made love to her for the last time as Reese Mitchell, I talked to Reese about coming here. She always supported my decisions, and this time was no different. Reese encouraged me to come here today, which made me love her even more, if that was possible.

She said, "I will never stand in the way of the memories that you shared with Elizabeth. She will forever be a part of your life because of the son you share. Your life with her and your life with me is not the same, and both should be respected. If this is what you need to do, then you have my blessing to do so. Your son needs to know that his mother is not forgotten. Go together and share your loss with each other."

I hugged her and said, "I don't know what I ever did to deserve you, but I will never question fate. I love you Reese with all that I have, and tomorrow I am going to make you mine forever. All that I have is now yours, and I will love you all the days of my life until God calls me home, and even then, our love will live on."

When I asked Jackson to join me, he seemed relieved because he was intending to ask me to come with him. I always told Jackson he could talk to her anywhere, anytime, but today he felt he needed to be here. It was a need I understood all too well.

I watched him from afar as he waited his turn for me to finish paying my respects to my oldest friend, his mother. I placed her favorite flowers in the vase in front of her stone. I broke off some rose petals and scattered them on top of her angel.

"Hi, friend. I bet you're wondering what I'm doing here today of all days. I guess you can call it a rite of passage with one door closing and another opening, but that's only partly true. Elizabeth, our door will never be closed. I share a son with you, and your spirit lives on through him. I came so close to losing him, and then he was saved. Thank you for saving our son. Thank you for showing me the way on my darkest days when there was no light. I did it, Elizabeth. I opened my heart up to forgiving my father. I don't know if he will ever have peace, but it is something I wish for him. I'm sorry I wasn't able to do all that you asked of me, but I'm sure you know why. I'm still me, and there are some things that can never be undone. I have to protect my family the only way I know how. Our son is here. He's waiting patiently to talk to you, so I'm going go and give him the time he needs with you. I love you, friend."

As I walked away, I watched my son take a seat on the bench in front of his mother's grave. He needed this time with her.

"Are you okay son?" I asked him. He was silent as we left the cemetery.

"I'm fine."

"You don't seem fine. Do you want to talk about it?"

"Dad, I just need to work through a few things on my own. Is that okay if we don't talk about it right now?"

"Of course. I just want you to know that I'm here for you."

"That's one thing I'm sure of and never doubt. I love you very much, dad."

"I love you too, son. Thank you for standing up for me today. It means everything to me that you will be by my side."

"You deserve this day with Reese, and every bit of happiness she brings to your life. I'm telling you, dad. One day Riley and I are going to make your story into a movie."

"Whatever you say son, just pick an awesome actor to play my part. He's going to have lots of nude scenes."

"You sure are confident."

"Hell yeah! I'm a Reed."

We both laughed as we arrived back at the house. The heavy heartbreak that we were both feeling after leaving the cemetery had been lifted and replaced with laughter.

Today was a happy day…a new start for all of us. I kept patting down my pocket to feel the rings and my vows. Jackson told me to relax, but I was too excited to take a breath. I had worked on my vows for the past few days, making sure it was perfect like the angel I was marrying.

We walked into the house, where the staff was buzzing around, and Priscilla with her clipboard was managing it all. Rosalyn was here wearing her headset and shooting off commands to her assistants. Flower arrangements and candles beautifully decorated the tables. Everything was in place. Nana's dessert display was something out of *Bon Appetit Magazine*. She baked all of Reese's favorites, and surprised even me with creating some French pastries. Was there ever any doubt that Lila couldn't have pulled this off? Shame on me for entertaining that thought. I glanced over to her and she gave me the biggest "I told you so" smile. Yes, I deserved it, and smiled back.

Reese

AS I SAT at my dressing table to take my first look at my hair and make-up, all created by Freddy, I heard *oohs* and *aahs* coming from behind me. I wore my hair down layered with curls as it cascaded down my back. Freddy braided both sides and wrapped them around as if they were a crown. He threaded flowers through the braids, and placed my great-grandmother's Irish Claddagh pin in the middle, another heirloom I get to pass down to Riley someday.

"The pin is perfect. I knew it would look beautiful on you." Nana said as she wiped away a tear. I turned to reach for her hands and folded them with mine.

"Thank you, Nana. How can I ever say it enough for you and granddaddy loving and caring for me all of these years?"

"Oh, my sweet girl. Your smile is thanks enough. We only want you to be happy and live the life you were destined for. You have that with Walker, and soon you will be holding another precious life. A miracle from God, wrapped up in the love you have for each other. I could ask for nothing more for you."

"Do you think mama and daddy are watching from heaven?"

"Always my sweet girl…always."

"Stop!" Freddy called out.

With his hands flailing in the air he rushed over to me. "Don't cry Reese, breathe beautiful girl, and do not wreck my masterpiece. Your make-up is flawless."

"Will you stop it? I'm fine and I'm wearing waterproof mascara."

We all laughed as Freddy took a big gulp of his champagne and poured another. It was time to begin to get dressed, but I wanted a few minutes with Riley first. I gave hugs to Nana and Freddy, and then to Riley, who patiently waited to talk to me.

"You do look beautiful, mom."

"Thank you, my daughter. Come and sit with me. Speaking of beautiful, you look amazing, Riley. Jackson is going to lose it when he sees you walking down the aisle."

"I sure hope so, mom, but it's what I'm wearing underneath that I can't wait to show him."

"Oh my goodness! I'm covering my ears. TMI, daughter, way too much."

"Sorry mom. No filter, remember?"

"How could I forget? Oh, Riley! Not a day spent as your mother, have I not laughed or smiled at least five times a day when I look into your eyes. You have been my greatest joy in this life. I love you so much."

"I love you too, mom. I am so happy you are finally getting your happily ever after with Mr. Reed."

"Thank you for saying that. Somehow, I still wasn't sure how you felt about it."

"Mom, I'm sorry you ever had to doubt me. You have my unconditional support. You made me a believer. What you and Mr. Reed share is truly magical. It's something dreams are made of. It's beyond any fairytale I ever read. I don't have to wish anything for you, because you already have it."

"You're pretty amazing yourself. It's no wonder why Jackson loves you so much. Your story is just beginning, and I'm so happy you found your own prince to love. Having said that, please never forget who you are. When you're in love, it's like no other feeling you will ever get to experience, especially when it's with the right person, someone who can see you all the way through to the deepest depths of your soul. Take it one day at a time. Live and have fun in all the moments between you, okay?"

"Okay, mom. I promise. Now can we get you married already?"

"Absolutely. I just need a few minutes to compose myself, and then we can call the team back in."

"You got it. I'm going to check on Jackson. I'll be back soon. Love you."

"Love you more."

Wiping my tears that managed to fall, I thanked the make-up gods for waterproof mascara. My make-up was still flawless and Freddy's blood pressure intact and steady. My dressing room was filled with flowers, but one rose was placed here on my table. Of course, it was from Walker. He left me a note with a few simple words:

My Dearest Reese,
Our day is finally here, where I make you mine ... forever.
See you at the altar.
Love,
Walker

Lost in my thoughts, I didn't hear the door open and close. I looked up to the horror standing behind me.

"Hello, Ms. Mitchell."

"Henry," I whispered.

Elizabeth's father, Henry Townsend, is standing with a gun directed right at me. I instinctively cover my stomach to protect my baby.

"I said hello, Ms. Mitchell. Where are your manners? Don't you remember me? Of course you do. I can see it in your eyes. I'm the man that changed your life. And today, I will do it all over again."

I'm silent. I'm stunned. I'm shaking. I'm crying.

"Nothing to say? You seemed pretty talkative a few minutes ago. Spouting tales of unrequited love and dreams coming true. Isn't that what you said to your daughter? She's quite beautiful and very reminiscent of you at that age. I can see why my grandson is infatuated with her, the same way his father was with you. I wouldn't count on this day ending the way you have pictured it. You don't have your 'happily ever after' just yet. Today, I change your story by taking away what matters most to Walker Reed."

"Please don't hurt me. I'll give you anything, but please don't hurt me. I'm pregnant." I sat frozen to the chair as my frightened eyes stared back at his manic ones.

"Yes, I see that. Another bastard child of Reed's."

"Shut up! How dare you say such vile things? You don't know anything about Walker and me, and our children as you say, are not bastards. This baby, as well as the son I lost, was conceived in love, a forever love that is unending."

"Bravo, Ms. Mitchell, you certainly do have a feisty side, don't you? I remember Phillip telling me all about it when you were down on your knees begging not to be thrown out of his son's life, and yet here you are, begging again."

He continued, "You protected your family from the wrath of Phillip all those years ago. So I ask you: *Will you do the same today? Will you sacrifice yourself for the safety and well-being of your family?* Because we know family means everything to you, and I also know what it means to Walker. This is the one thing we do have in common. My Elizabeth was my world. Her happiness meant everything to me, and when it was threatened, that's when I decided to remove the problem. You, Ms. Mitchell are still the problem. You need to be gone, but this time, you won't be coming back. Now, get up!"

"You are out of your mind if you think I'm going anywhere with you. Walker has this house surrounded by security. We will never make it out of the front door."

"Wrong again, Ms. Mitchell. Your entire staff, down to your lovely grey haired grandmother, is busy with today's event, and clearly not paying attention. How else do you think I got in here? I've been watching you for days. I could have taken you several times, but I think today is fitting, don't you think? Here you sit and wait to meet your groom, to take your vows to become husband and wife. A dream, as you say, you've been waiting to come true. I can just picture the devastation on his face when he discovers that you have left him…yet again."

"You are delusional. Somewhere deep inside of you, you have lost your humanity. Grieving for your daughter has left you lost and empty. You feel alone right now because you are on the outside looking in, but it doesn't have to be that way. You can right this wrong before it's too late. Your grandson loves and misses you. It is never too late for forgiveness, and it is not too late for you. Please don't do this, Henry. Please don't hurt me or my baby. You still have a chance."

"Wrong, yet again. My grandson hates me now because of his father. Gail, my wife. She hates me too. Walker has turned them against me. When you have nothing left, you have nothing to lose. I won't ask again, Ms. Mitchell. Get. Up!"

My entire body was shaking and silently begging for Walker to save me. But Riley was now back and knocking on the bedroom door. I had to think quickly to send her a message without Henry knowing what I was doing.

"Mom! Why is the door locked? Are you in there with Mr. Reed? Oh I love it mom, but you are going to be late for your own wedding. Mom?"

Before I could see him coming, I was roughly pulled up from where I sat with his gun pressing into my side. He hauled me against the door, nearly avoiding my cheek crashing into it.

"Answer your daughter now, or I will put a bullet in her head."

"I'm here, honey. Sorry."

"Um…okay. Can I come in?"

"Not right now. Can you do me a favor, sweetie?"

"Anything."

"Do you remember what I told you about believing in forever love and dreams coming true?"

"Come on, mom. This is crazy. Open the door."

"Just answer the question. Do you remember?"

"Yes, mom, of course I do. Your dream is finally coming true today."

"Yes. That's right. Dreams do come true. This is what I'm praying for today. I love you, Taylor."

"Mom?"

"Always and Forever. I love you, Taylor. I love you so much. Now let me finish getting ready on my own. I'll see you soon."

"Mom?" She began to bang on the door while Henry's gun was still pressed into my side. I was praying Riley would have understood, but she was now pleading with me to open the door. I had to do something before he really became unhinged.

"Taylor! Leave me be for five fucking minutes. I swear you are a brat sometimes. Take the hint. I want to be alone. Now get the hell out of here!"

"Shhh, do not make a sound," he warned as he listened to her footsteps fading away. "Very good Ms. Mitchell, very good. Now, where does this door lead to?"

"It's a connecting door to my sitting room, and then another hallway and stairs."

"Perfect. Let's go."

"Please, Henry. Don't do this."

He ignored my pleas and dragged me along with him, never removing his gun. I began praying as my tears began to fall. *Please Walker. Save us.*

Riley

MY MOTHER HAS never called me by my middle name alone. Something was wrong, and she was trying to message me somehow. I took my shoes off and ran in a fast pace for help. I ran as fast as my legs could take me until I found Mr. Reed surrounded by Jackson and my great grandparents. They looked so happy, toasting with champagne.

"Mr. Reed! Mr. Reed!" I screamed out as if I was in pain. My mother was in danger.

"Riley, what's wrong? Is it your mother, or the baby?"

"Both Mr. Reed. She needs help, something's wrong. I think she's in danger."

"Danger? Where is she? You must calm down, and tell me everything."

"We were talking and laughing, and I left her for only a few minutes, and when I came back to help her dress, the door was locked. I asked mom to let me in, but she refused. She kept calling me Taylor. She has never addressed me by middle name in all of my life, and then she asked me to remember."

"Remember what?" he shouted.

"She told me to remember my dreams of coming true, and how she was hoping hers would come true too."

"Motherfucker! Stephen, check the feed surrounding the hallway and the back stairs coming off our bedroom. That's the only way out from that part of the house. She couldn't have gone far. Find

Reese, Now!"

I never felt so helpless in all of my life. Where was my mother? Jackson took me in his arms as I wept onto his chest. He quietly soothed me, until Stephen called out from the office.

"Sir, we have them in site. They are on the north side of the property. Stephen shouted out, as he secured the security teams in place.

"Who's with her? Mr. Reed asked as he focused in on the picture before him. Before he could answer, Jackson whispered... "It's my grandfather. He's kidnapped your mother."

"That fucker is dead!" shouted Mr. Reed.

"Not if I don't get to him first," Thomas joined in.

"Thomas, I will get Reese back. I swear to you on my life, I will get her back."

"I'm coming with you."

"No! Thomas. Please stay here with Lila, Riley, and my son. They need you. And Reese needs me."

Mr. Reed and his team fled the house. The guards were armed, and I was afraid for my mother.

"COME HERE RILEY, follow me."

"What's wrong?"

"I have to go. I need you to stay here."

"Jackson, it's too dangerous. Please stay here with me. You saw the video. Your grandfather has a gun, and it was aimed right at my mother. How could he do this?"

"Riley, I wish I knew, but I have to try to talk with him. He will listen to me."

"And how do you know that? The last time you saw him was right before you collapsed, and you were so angry with him."

"It doesn't matter. He will listen to me. I have to try and help both our parents. Stay here, please? I love you, beautiful girl."

"I love you too. Please be careful."

I knew I couldn't make it there on foot. The sound of the motorcycle would alert them of my presence. Not that I could drive it anyway with my sight still a little blurry at times. Then I remembered I could take one of the golf carts. They practically steer themselves. I had to get to my grandfather before he did something he couldn't take back.

HANG ON BABY, I'm on my way. That fucker better have not harmed one hair on your head.

"He's mine when we get to Reese," I said to Stephen, as we approached the barn and stables that were still under construction. They could be anywhere in there. We had nothing up and running yet, so every inch of ground would have to be searched, and quietly without alerting them of our presence. Stephen began to scan the area with his binoculars. We didn't have them in sight yet.

The building that would be the barn consisted of three levels, with only the first floor completed. They wouldn't be able to get to the top, which worked in our benefit. Stephen secured all points of entry with his men. They were told to stand down until he gave them the signal to take Henry out, if it came to that. I demanded a gun from Stephen, but he refused to give me one, assuring me that he would take the shot. My focus was to get to Reese, and get her out before she or our baby were harmed.

"Sir, we have movement. It's an assailant coming down the road on a golf cart. How do you want me to proceed?" his man asked over the walkie.

"Who is it?" I questioned. Using the binoculars to get a better look, I was horrified to see who it was.

"Stand down. It's my son! Stand down!" I commanded through the walkie. "What the hell is he doing? Stephen, we have to get to Jackson before he reaches the barn."

"It's too late, sir. He's already there."

"This can't be fucking happening. That mad man has Reese, and now he will have my son too? Do we have a clear shot? Can we take him out?"

"We need to get closer, sir. We don't even have him on sight yet." Stephen said.

"Stephen, I have to do something. I need to get in there."

"Sir, you can't go in there unprotected. I'll have no visual on you once you're inside."

"Then I'll take my chances. I have no life without Reese and Jackson."

I LEFT WITHOUT my cane, causing me to stumble a few times before reaching the entrance to the barn. My leg was tingling with painful pins and needles. I needed to get to my grandfather before he hurt Reese. I knew I wasn't alone. I saw my father and his team trying to get closer, and I didn't miss the terrifying look my father wore on his face when he realized it was me coming down the path. I had to do something and not let my grandfather cause any more pain to the people I loved.

"Grandpa, it's me, Jackson. I'm alone and unarmed. Please come out." I called out with no response back. I searched several stalls before finding Reese tied, bound, and unconscious. She was bleeding from her head.

"Reese! Oh my God!" I reached for her, and that's when I heard him behind me.

"That's far enough, Jackson. Do not touch her." I slowly turned around to see my grandfather aiming a gun right at me. Here was a man that I loved my entire life. He was my hero. A man I respected and looked up to. The same man who cheered me on at my baseball games, took me fishing, and taught me how to ride a horse. The man standing before me is no one I recognize.

"What are you doing grandpa? Are you going to shoot me?"

The minute I said the words to him, the realization of the grave situation we were in registered on his face. He immediately put the gun away and began walking toward me. I put my hands up to him and stopped him where he stood.

"Don't come any closer, grandpa. You stay back and let me help Reese. What did you do to her?"

"Nothing she didn't deserve," he coldly replied.

I tried to kneel down beside her, but my leg stopped me.

"Stand back, Jackson. Do not touch her. I will not say it again."

"I'm getting her out of here if I have to drag her myself. I can't let her die." I tried again to get to Reese, this time making it to the ground.

That's when the first shot was fired.

"I said…Do. Not. Touch. Her. Get up, Jackson, and move away, now!"

"No! You're going to have to shoot me, grandpa. There is no way in hell that I'm leaving her."

"This is your father's fault!" he shouted.

"It's all his doing. Don't you see, Jackson? He's turned you against me. Your grandmother tried to leave me, and now you hate me too. Here you protect this woman who destroyed your mother. How could you, son? How could you do this to me?"

"Grandpa, stop this now. You don't know what you're saying. Mother died because she was sick, not because of my father or Reese. No one could have predicted what was going to happen to my mother. Please, grandpa, let me help you. I don't hate you. I could never hate you. I love you."

"Liar! You don't love me, not anymore, not after what I've done here today. All I wanted was to scare her, and then she fought me. What was I to do?"

He rambled on as he became more and more lost in his warped

427

mind. He was pacing back and forth, twiddling the gun in his hand. I checked Reese, and she was still breathing. She had an open wound on her head. I untied her hands and tried to get her to wake before he stopped me again with his gun.

"I told you not to touch her."

"And I told you that I couldn't do that. I have to get her help. Grandpa, you are surrounded. There is no way out of here. Please give me the gun, and this will end now. Please grandpa, you need help. Let me get you help, and I promise I will not leave you. You have to trust me, please?"

"I'm sorry son. I love you, Jackson. I always will, but we know what will happen the minute I step outside. Your father promised death would come for me if I ever hurt him again. It's too late for me, Jackson. My Elizabeth is dead. My Gail is dead. And now my precious grandson? You and I will join them. I love you, Jackson."

I love you Riley. I said silently, as I threw myself over Reese's still body. And that's when the loud shots rang out.

WE CHARGED THROUGH the barn and came upon the bloody scene. Henry was dead with a bullet wound to the head. My son was on top of Reese. I didn't know if he was hit until I reached him.

"Jackson, are you hurt?" I ran my hands all over his body, but he was okay.

"I'm fine, dad. It's Reese, she's hurt." My son was crying over her limp body he was still protecting.

"Stephen, get an ambulance right away!" I screamed out.

"Reese, baby. Please wake up." I begged her to open her eyes. I threw my jacket off and used my shirt to wrap her head. She wasn't shot, but she had a nasty cut and bump on the side of her head. She wasn't bleeding anywhere else from her body. Her wrists were cut and bruised. I was praying for her and our child's survival.

I held her in my arms until the paramedics arrived on the scene. Stephen had to pull me off of Reese. I didn't want to let her go, but I had to let the paramedics help her. My son and I just took it all in. We held onto the other for support, as Henry's body was now being placed in a bag. Stephen joined us along with my security team.

"Who took the shot?" I questioned.

Stephen gestured over to the railing where Thomas, Reese's grandfather was being questioned by the police.

"It was Thomas?" I asked Stephen.

"Yes, sir, so it seems. Reese's grandfather is an excellent marksman."

I looked over to Jackson, who I knew heard what Stephen said. He would forever have to live with the fact that Reese's grandfather killed his own. The rational side would help him realize it was self-defense, but what to tell his breaking heart? My son loved his grandfather and would mourn his loss. Not the grandfather he was today, but the man he once was.

"Sir, she's ready to be transported," said the paramedic. I quickly stepped inside the ambulance, leaving Jackson with Stephen. They would follow us out along with Lila and Riley, and the rest of our family.

Reese was taken immediately upon arriving at the hospital. Dr. Lemay, her ob/gyn was waiting for us in the Emergency Room. Commands were being called out, as I stayed back and watched for the second time, another person I loved being taken away from me. *Not this time would I find myself in a chapel, and praying for their survival? I think I used up all my requests when Jackson was fighting for his life. Reese and our child were in God's hands, and all I could do is silently pray once more for fate not to be so cruel again.*

One by one, I was joined by our friends and family who loved Reese. Freddy was being comforted by Fabrizio and Marsha. He was crying out loud for Reese. Lila and Thomas were in the chapel, and Riley was with Jackson. He sat quietly with Riley in his arms. He wasn't crying, or showing any emotion, we were just numb. After Thomas was questioned by the police, he was free to come to the hospital. No charges would be filed, clearing him of any wrongdoing. He did what he had to do to protect Reese. It was also confirmed that Gail was dead. She had been shot and left for dead for several days before her body was recovered today. A note was left by the bedside table, and it simply read:

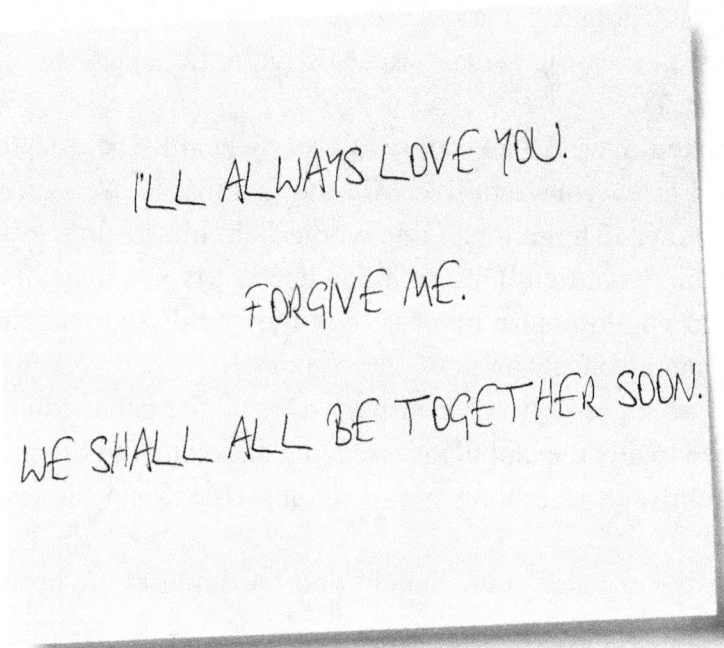

I'LL ALWAYS LOVE YOU.

FORGIVE ME.

WE SHALL ALL BE TOGETHER SOON.

Gail was an extraordinary woman who survived breast cancer and the loss of her only child. She didn't deserve one day of pain. In the end, the man she loved and stood by every day through her marriage took her life. He was a gutless coward in the end. She was with Elizabeth now in heaven. I recited a silent prayer for Gail, and continued to wait for news on Reese.

Thomas and Lila rejoined me in the waiting room.

"She's going to make it Walker. Do not give up on your faith now." Lila said as she hugged me. I prayed she was right.

"She's a Mitchell. Mitchell's come from a strong Irish line. The sun will shine on my granddaughter. Lila is right. Do not give up on your faith, and do not give up on Reese." He slapped my back and then pulled me into a strong hug. I promised I would never give up on her, and again waited for news.

Dr. Lemay, along with another doctor, updated us on Reese's condition.

"Mr. Reed, this is Dr. Sloan, a neurologist here on staff." I said hello and hoped they would both be telling me good news.

"Mr. Reed, your wife has a contusion to the left side of her brain, along with a cut that required five stitches. She has a concussion, but thankfully no fractures or bleeds. We have performed both a CT scan and MRI, confirming my diagnosis. She hasn't regained consciousness yet, but we are hopeful she will wake soon. I know it doesn't look like it now, but she was very lucky. The outcome could have been much worse."

"And the baby?" I barely got out the words. Dr. Lemay quickly answered my question.

"She's stable with a steady heartbeat. We will wait for Reese to wake, and then I will perform more tests. She will need to stay for a few days so both she and the baby can be monitored. Just to err on the side of caution."

"That's fine with me. Can I see her?"

"Yes you may. Give us a few minutes to get her settled in her room, and then my nurse will come out and get you."

"Thank you, Dr. Lemay, for saving both of them."

I hugged Reese's doctor taking her by surprise, but I didn't care. Reese and our daughter would be okay.

I knew once I was in there, I would never leave, not without Reese walking out with me. I let Lila, Thomas, Riley, and the rest of our friends and family visit with Reese, before I camped out by her bedside. My mother stayed behind and held my hand while I waited. She mourned and cried for Gail.

"Why, Walker? How did it ever come to this?"

My mother wanted answers, and hell, so did I. I never imagined someone having that much hatred for me that they would succumb to doing something so horrifying.

"I wish I knew, mother. I was supposed to be married by now, but the love of my life is recovering from a vicious attack."

"She's strong, and so is your daughter. They will both be fine."

"Thank you."

I gave her a hug and a chaste kiss to her cheek. Jackson and Riley approached me.

"Dad, I'm going to take Riley home. We're exhausted. I just can't be here knowing my grandfather is dead in the morgue."

"For you son, I am so very sorry."

"I know, dad. This wasn't your fault. Somewhere along the way, grandpa lost himself. The man that hurt Reese and my grandma is not the same man I shall remember. I can't hate him, dad. Please understand."

"I do, son. More than you know. Take Riley home and please, get some rest. How's your head? Any headaches? How's your leg?"

"I'm fine, dad. I'm just tired."

"I'm proud of you, son. You were so brave back there. You were ready to sacrifice yourself for Reese, and your sister. I love you so much. She's not even born yet, and you're already her hero."

"I wouldn't go that far, dad, but thank you for saying it. I love you too!"

I hugged Riley goodbye. Her tears were still falling. I promised her I would not leave her mother's side. The grandparents also followed the kids. Freddy wouldn't leave until I gave him the same promise.

Tick tock...tick tock. Tick tock...tick tock. This sound was making me crazy. Hours later, and after lots of praying, crying, and hoping, Reese still hasn't woken up yet. I've been talking to her and our daughter. I leaned over her and kissed her soft cheek. Her delicate wrists were bandaged. My heart hurt as I took in her bruised skin.

"Time to wake up, baby" I said to Reese, as I held her hands in mine. She looked peaceful as she slept. You wouldn't know she just survived what she went through if not for the physical signs. I tried once again to avoid looking at her bandages that covered up what Henry did to her. A monitoring belt was wrapped around her belly. The sweetest sounds of our daughter's heartbeat filled the room. Tears filled my eyes as I once again talked to my daughter.

"Hey Princess, it's daddy. I'm here with you. Your mommy was so brave today. She fought against the bad wolf in our story. She protected you with all the love she has for me and you baby girl. Every fairytale needs a prince. Well you already know who he is, but now we have a hero too. Your big brother, Jackson. He loves you so much and can't wait to meet you. So princess, you listen to your daddy now. You stay put until you're ready to be born and meet us. Promise me, princess? Stay with mommy, and soon I'll be holding you."

"She promises." I heard her say. I lifted my head and looked to Reese, who was slowly opening her eyes.

"Reese, squeeze my hand." I urged her. She tightened her hold with mine, and it was the best feeling in the world next to hearing her voice. "Oh, thank god! You're alright. I love you baby...so much."

"I love you too, Walker. I'm so sorry I scared you."

"You didn't." *I lied.*

"Whatever you say." She quietly laughed, knowing me all too well.

"Henry," she whispered.

I shuttered just at the sound of his name. I leaned in to kiss my angel and wipe away her tears. "You never have to worry about him again. He will never be able to hurt us, not ever. I will never let any-one hurt you or us, again."

"What happened? Please tell me." She implored me to do so.

"Okay, the short version. Jackson got to you first and protected you against Henry. You were unconscious. It appears Henry was go-ing to shoot Jackson before taking his own life, but someone stopped him first."

"Who was it?"

"Your grandfather. Thomas and his rifle stopped Henry from hurting you, and my son. One bullet straight to the back of his head. I wouldn't have believed it, if I didn't see it with my own eyes."

"How's Jackson?"

"He's numb. Reese, there's something you don't know."

"The baby? Is she okay?" Reese was now struggling to sit-up.

"Shhh, calm down. Our daughter is fine. Riley's okay too. I'm sorry to have frightened you, but you weren't the only one that Henry had hurt. He murdered Gail. They found her body in their Arizona home."

"Oh my god! That poor woman. Walker, you need to go to Jackson, and make sure he's alright."

"He's with Riley, and the rest of the family. My son is not alone, believe me."

"I still would feel better if you were with him."

"Reese, give me a minute to just look at you. I need to feel your heartbeat against my own. I need to hear you speak, and get lost in your touch. I'm done with people trying to take you away from me. I love you so much. There is no way I'm leaving you."

"You stole my line."

"I think it was mine first, but who cares? I love you, Reese…Always."

"I love you, Walker…Forever"

Chapter Fifty-One

Reese

Two months later

WE CHOSE TO be married around Thanksgiving. It was a time to be thankful for all of life's blessings. After surviving my attack, and then supporting Jackson through his grandparents' funerals, it was time for our family to come together to come to terms with what happened and finding the closure we needed to move forward.

Jackson never looked back after that day. He didn't hold any ill will toward my grandfather, Thomas. He understood his need to protect his family. After the funerals, he refocused on his recovery. Samuel even took a flight out to spend some time with Riley, and oversee Jackson's therapy. Always obsessing over his son's health, Walker insisted he go through tests to make sure all was okay after what he endured. Samuel didn't disagree and ran the necessary tests to put Walker's mind at ease. Jackson was in perfect health. His sight now returned to perfect 20/20 vision, and his post-op complication with his leg was now healed as well. His therapy was intense, but all paid off in the end.

I was able to spend some time with Samuel before he left for London. He would be attending another medical conference on the study of strokes and AVM's. It was championed by Dr. Gillian Taylor, whom I suspected Samuel was getting closer too. He denied it, but of course, that was Samuel. He was discreet when it came to his personal life. I was no longer a part of that, but still wished him well. He was happy. We all were. I was ready to become Mrs. Walker Reed.

With waiting the extra months, the wedding dress I was to wear back in September no longer fit. My baby girl had grown and so did my expanding belly. Walker didn't care what I wore, as long as he was able to remove it with his teeth on our wedding night. This time around, we had no wedding planners, no press releases. It was just us, marrying under our gazebo, and surrounded by our family and friends.

On the eve before I said I do, Freddy and Nana presented me with a huge ribbon tied box. My eyes lit up, because I loved surprises. I tried not to tear the beautiful paper, but was excited to see what the box contained. Riley was jumping up and down, of course she knew. I lifted the paper, and my eyes immediately filled with tears.

"This belonged to your mother, Susan. She wore this dress on the day she married my Daniel. I think your mother would love to see her beautiful daughter wear the same dress she married her prince in." Nana had said.

"Oh Nana! It's gorgeous, and so well preserved."

"Well it had help from your Freddy Macaroons over here." I looked to Freddy, and we both laughed with Nana's nickname for my best friend.

"I had to rip out some *hideous* shoulder pads, but I added all new sequins with an overlay of new lace from your original dress.

And don't worry, Peaches, it will fit."

"I don't know what to say?"

Nana leaned in to hug me. "Just say yes to the dress, and let's get you married."

"Yes! A thousand times yes!" We all did a group hug. With twenty two hours to go, I would be wearing this amazing dress, walking toward the man of my dreams.

The day of the wedding, once again, a single red rose was delivered to me with a note from Walker. I held the thorn free flower to my chest and inhaled the beautiful smell.

My Dearest Reese,

Here we go again! Third time's a charm, right?

As much as I missed waking with you this morning, I know how our night will end, with you sleeping soundly next to me as my wife. This has been a dream of mine since the first moment my eyes connected with yours. You are my forever love, and I am yours. I love you, Reese Mitchell, for today is the last time I will ever use that name. You were destined to be a Reed.

Hurry, my love, we've waited long enough.

Walker

"Oh mom! You look beautiful." Riley said as she made me turn around and model for her. My mother's dress fit my tall frame perfectly. Freddy had turned it into my own, and I truly loved it. I was scared and reluctant at first to wear it because I feared it would bring me bad luck. My parent's story didn't end magically, and their time together was cut short. Nana quickly stomped all over my silly worrying like she was turning grapes to wine. She reminded me that although their time wasn't long enough, what they did have was timeless. They were in love with each other since their younger years in school. Inseparable to the very end, and not a day went by that they didn't show their love for the other. Walker and I had our share of bad luck, missed encounters, and too many years apart. This was our time. No one would ever stand in our way again.

"Ready?" Granddaddy asked, as he tucked my arm in his.

"Ready as I'll ever be." I smiled and fought back the tears. With the help from Riley and Jackson, we had chosen the perfect song to get married to. The melody played as I walked down the rose line walkway leading to Walker. We would dance to the words later as husband and wife. "Two is better than one" by the band, Boys like Girls. After listening to the lyrics, Walker and I agreed this was the perfect song for us.

Riley took her place, and Jackson stood by Walker. Freddy was already crying, along with Nana. Walker's eyes never left mine. He stepped down the three steps, and reached for my hand, but not before granddaddy placed a kiss and handed me over to my prince. "I love you," I mouthed to him. He replied, "Impossible, I love you more."

We reached the top and faced the minister who began speaking over us to our family and friends. We kept our ceremony simple, with both of us reciting our vows. I handed over my bouquet to Riley and took out my folded paper with my words to Walker.

Taking a breath and looking over to Freddy, who gave me the "you've got this" look, I turned to the beautiful man standing in front of me.

"Once upon a time, a shy girl from Georgia made her way to the big city, to live in the real-life world, where a simple prediction from her Nana came true. It was where love found a home in the hearts of two believers, who believed in…Forever."

"Two strangers who came from different worlds defied the odds. They became two hearts, one love. This is the only way I can truly describe "us" to the rest of the world who are listening. You are the other half of my heart and soul. There is no greater measure of time than time spent with you. To share every tender moment between us reminds me how beautiful our love story is. There will never be anyone ever that will love you as much as I do. I am so proud to have found the love of my life in you. Happy Wedding Day, Walker. For today is the beginning of the rest of our life. I love you today, tomorrow, and forever."

NOT A DRY eye in the house, including myself, who struggled to stand in front of Reese as she recited her vows to me. She never looked more beautiful. It was now my turn to pledge my forever love to her.

"I love you angel, let's start with that. You came into my life like a speeding train. I never saw you coming. Once I did, I knew I would never be the same. You sat in that library hiding behind your glasses and trying to go unnoticed, but how could that be? When you were the most beautiful sight these eyes have ever seen. Love at first sight took on a whole new meaning when it came to you. Sometimes you just know, and to hell with the people who don't believe. Our story is like no other ever told. I promised you forever a long time ago, and today I make that same promise. On this day, you truly become mine. I love you, Reese. I always have. Even when our love was tested and I had to face life without you, you never left the one piece of me that mattered the most." I took her hand and placed it over my heart. "Right here, is where you stayed, as I waited for you to come back to me."

"Do you feel that? That's my heart and it's beating for you. It became whole again on the day you walked back in to my life and sealed your fate with mine. I love you with crazy, head over heels to the edge of obsessive love. I want to scream it as loud as my voice will allow me to. I know no other way to love you. Our love is based on second chances, forever promises, and falling stars. Meadows filled with wild flowers, and the night sky to make love under. Our love is lyrics to a song I will forever play on repeat. That's our story, and it's timeless. I've carried it with me while we were apart, and it's as real now as it was back then."

"By the way, if you didn't know it then, that whole knocking into you at the coffee station, yeah, all planned by me."

She smiled, and said…"Yeah, of course I knew. Are you done yet? Because I really want to kiss you." I couldn't help but smile, as our family and friends laughed.

"Almost, I still have some ground to cover."

"Show off." she said.

"With all my lines I used on you that day, you still managed to laugh at me. By doing that, you pulled me in like a magnet. Once you agreed to going out on a date with me, I watched you leave with your books in hand. I let out my breath. You literally stopped me in my tracks and completely captivated me. Thank you for loving me Reese. Thank you for giving me a second chance at forever. I promise to love, honor, protect, and never forget to kiss you good night."

"Have I said how beautiful you look today? How's our daughter?" I asked her as I placed my hand over her swelled belly where our princess kicked for me. Thank you, Reese, for making all of my dreams come true. Thank you for giving me the greatest gift a man could ever receive, and thank you God. Not a day will go by that I don't thank him for allowing me to keep my vow to make good on my forever promise to you."

I took my thumb and wiped away her falling tears, as she did the same for me. We joined our hands and looked back to the minister. He said…

"Walker Phillip Reed, do you take Reese Mitchell to be your lawful wife?"

"I do."

"And do you, Reese Mitchell, take Walker Phillip Reed, to be your lawful husband?"

"I do." She replied.

"With the vows you have pledged here today to one another, and the power by the State of California, I hereby pronounce you, husband and wife. Let no one ever come between the love you have for each other, and the love you have pledged in front of God, and his witnesses. You may kiss your bride."

Never again, will I ever let anyone come between us. I placed my hands to her beautiful face and kissed her softly on her lips. Our tears fell as our kissed intensified.

"I love you, Reese. You. Are. Mine."

"I love you too, Walker. I was always yours, and forever will be."

With Freddy leading, applause and whistles could be heard for miles as we again were officially announced as husband and wife.

I took her hand and led her out onto the dance floor. Our song played, as I twirled her around the dance floor. She never looked more beautiful. The band played for hours, and toasts were made in our honor. From Jackson to Riley, to Nana to Thomas. We were loved by many, and it was the perfect ending to our blessed day... that is, until Freddy had one more announcement to make. Reese giggled because she knew her best friend like no other.

"TODAY, YOU'VE ALL stood witness to a love story that has spanned nearly twenty years in the making. A love that beat the odds and came back stronger than ever. I knew it from the moment our boy here met my girl, they would forever be destined to live as one. You are my best friend, Peaches. Some people are meant to come in your life, and easily walk right back out. You stayed, and became a permanent fixture in my heart. The years when I didn't know where you were, I still prayed for you every day and waited for my best friend. Don't ever leave me again, because you are the wind beneath my wings."

"Really, Freddy? Bette Midler?" I heard her call out.

She smiled while laughing and holding back her tears. I blew my best friend a kiss, as she playfully caught it. I winked over at Fabrizio who was grinning like the sexy beast he is. It was hard to stay focused with all of the love in this room, but another smile from Reese, and I continued.

"Yes, my Georgia Peach, we will always have *Beaches* in our life. But do you want to know what's really perfect just about now?"

"Yes! Tell me." She giggled and clapped her hands in excitement.

"Okay, if you insist. I was thinking of getting some help from another amazing guy named Freddy."

I turned to the DJ who was waiting on my signal. I walked over to where Reese was sitting and reached for her hand to take mine. I pulled her to me and lifted my beautiful best friend in my arms. She begged me to put her down, but I wasn't losing this moment with her. I placed a kiss on her cheek, and grabbed the microphone. "Happy Wedding Day Best Friend. I love you with all my heart."

As the music began to play, I sang, "You're My Best Friend" by Queen. It was my favorite song and it said it all for me and Reese. I brought it home with the last verse, as she wrapped her arms around my neck, and we sang it together. She was my sunshine, my forever best friend, and I will love her always.

AFTER FREDDY'S LOVING tribute to Reese, my girl was spent. We shared one last dance before we said our goodbyes to all who loved us. It was truly a magical day. Another chapter has now been written in our story. We would have many more to write and share with each other. All the days of our life…

Chapter Fifty-Two

Happy New Year...
And baby makes three

FOLLOWING OUR WEDDING, it was a nonstop celebration. Reese had asked to post-pone our honeymoon until after the baby was born. She wanted to be back into shape. I almost laughed, but not wanting to hurt her feelings, I agreed. My girl was absolutely without fail the most beautiful woman in the world, but she felt huge with her nine month pregnant belly. I never stopped touching her. I would never tire of feeling for kicks and talking to my little girl. We couldn't wait for our daughter to arrive.

We were weeks away to her due date, as we made all the final preparations for her birth. I surprised Reese with the nursery of her dreams. I had made changes to the adjoining room, now a playroom for our daughter. Maybe my best design ever. Our daughter's view would be overlooking our meadow. Just below her balcony, I had a tree planted for her, a Peach tree. As our daughter would grow, so would her tree. Reese loved it. All was perfect in my world with the smile she gave me.

Lila and Thomas stayed on with us, as we waited for our daughter to be born. They were getting accustomed to living out on the West Coast, but their home was in Georgia, and we knew how much they missed it. Jackson was doing amazingly well, and Riley too. With much insistence, we encouraged them to continue with their deferment from school, and wait until the summer to begin their long awaited adventure. I knew Jackson would never be happy attending UCLA, so we went back to his original plan and NYU was back on the table, as if it never was off. After much negotiation, we agreed to their housing plans. Jackson didn't want to live in my penthouse, and wanted to have as close as the normal college experience he could manage.

We found an apartment close to the campus, where Jackson and Riley would live with two other roommates. Jackson's best friends, Brandon and Clay, would be sharing the place with them. I no longer laid the law down with Jackson. I trusted him emphatically, and Riley too. They were ready, beyond ready to begin their life together, and away from our watchful eyes. Just thinking about that makes me laugh because I didn't think I would ever stop being overprotective when it came to my son, and now I'd get to do it all over again with my daughter. When you are a father, you are a father forever. The worry never stops, but knowing the man he had become had made me so proud. He was still hurting over the loss of his grandparents, but Riley was forever his support system. I would never truly understand what drove Henry to the brink of madness, but that door to that story was closed a long time ago, and I would never re-open it again.

Lila explained it best. You never know what drives a person to commit any act of selfishness. He acted cowardly and hurt many people. She said it was no longer my responsibility to seek out the answers to why? That was reserved for God himself. My job was to be happy and make Reese happy. I can do that. It would be my life's mission for the rest of my life.

"Do you realize this is our first New Year's Eve we've spent together in nineteen years?" I asked Reese, as we clinked our glasses filled with sparkling apple cider.

"You're right, it is. At least this time around, we will ring in the New Year together." She giggled and then winced in pain.

"Reese, are you okay?" I took her glass, as she held her back.

"Wow! That was a powerful kick your daughter just delivered to me. Ow, there she goes again."

"I guess ballerina lessons are out of the question, and onto soccer." I said, as I rubbed her belly. She'll be here soon, baby."

"You got that right, babe, because soon is right now."

"What?"

"My water just broke. Looks like our daughter is trying to be a New Year's Baby."

"Oh my god! You're in labor? We have to get to the hospital."

"Sounds good to me."

I crushed my lips down onto hers, and held her to my chest, kissing her once more before releasing her.

"We're going to meet our daughter tonight. I love you baby. Stay right here. I'll be right back."

"Love you too! I'm not going anywhere."

I called for Stephen, who had our car packed and ready to go. Lila and Thomas were waiting and so ready to meet their newest great-grandchild. I helped Reese change her clothes, and got her into the car. Her contractions were coming quickly, too quickly for me to handle. She said her labor with Riley only took a few hours. Dr. Lemay told us every baby and birth was different. Reese had been uncomfortable the past few days, but who knew she would go into labor on New Year's Eve of all days. She wasn't due until the 26th, but the women in my life made their own rules, and I was only to follow.

Dr. Lemay met us on the Labor & Delivery floor with our room already ready. Jackson and Riley were up in Big Sur ringing in the New Year with friends. I would wait to call and share our news. What a New Year's Day gift. The newest member of our family crashed our party, and came early.

It was nearing midnight, and Reese had been in labor for several hours already. Lila was holding her hand, as Thomas paced outside of her room. Even with the epidural, Reese was in pain and discomfort. She was doing great and concentrating on her breathing. Talks of a C-Section were discussed early on, but Reese wouldn't hear it. She was in good health, and strong enough to deliver our daughter naturally, but I also said I would make the decision for her, if it came down to it. Luckily I never had to, because Reese was ready to push. She gripped my hand tighter with every push, as the contractions became stronger. Falling back onto the pillow, she was exhausted.

Dr. Lemay kept encouraging her on. "Come on Reese, I know you're tired, but we are almost there. Work for your baby and push as hard as you can. Her head is crowning, I think one big one should do it."

I couldn't help, but look. Her head was full with dark hair that matched mine.

"Oh babe, you are doing so well. I love you so much. Hold my hand, break it if you have to, and let's meet our daughter." I kissed her and prayed that Reese had the strength for one last push.

"I'm tired Walker, so tired," she cried.

"I know baby, but she's almost here. You can do this. You are the strongest person I know. I love you so fucking much."

"Language!" Lila scolded me.

"I'm sorry, Lila, slipped out."

"Come on, sweet girl, you can do this. I ain't getting any younger."

"Gee thanks Nana for the support." Reese had let out a deep breath, and then sucked one in deeply preparing to push once again.

Dr. Lemay commanded Reese to push. "1, 2, 3, 4, 5, and hold it, Reese. Come on princess, mommy and daddy want to meet you. Her shoulders are stuck. I need to turn her. Bear down and when I say to push, you push with all your might."

"Walker! Oh my god, I can't do it," she cried.

"Yes you can, Reese. Yes you can."

I wrapped my arms across her back and helped her as she waited for Dr. Lemay to call out her commands.

"Okay, Reese, here we go. 1, 2, and 3!"

Reese gripped the side bars of the bed and with all of her strength, she pushed and pushed hard, as our daughter screamed her way out. Dr. Lemay quickly suctioned her airway, and tied off the umbilical cord. She was holding a little piece of heaven in her arms, our daughter.

"Do you want to do the honors, daddy?" Dr. Lemay asked me. Without hesitation, I cut the cord and our daughter was freed from Reese. She was handed off to me, and I kissed her little forehead. The nurse covered her with a pink hat that had a princess crown on it. *Perfect for our daughter.* Lila was crying, as was Thomas who was hugging Reese. I handed our daughter to Reese, and folded them both in my protective arms. I wasn't going to let them out of my sight.

"Thank you, Reese. I love you."

"I love you more."

"Impossible." I replied back, as I continued to hug and love them both.

"Have you decided a name for this little one?" Thomas asked with curiosity.

Reese and I both looked at our daughter, and then to Lila. Lila never gave up faith on us being together. She always believed that true love would find its way back and bring two souls together. Reese was wearing her great-grandmother's ring, the same that had been passed down to her father for her mother. We had several names in mind, all with strong Irish meanings, which made Thomas very happy. I kissed my daughter and proudly announced her name. "Lila, Thomas, we would like you to wish a very Happy Birthday to our daughter, Fallon Ryann Reed."

Lila and Thomas were beyond happy. Fallon was Lila's mother's name, which means, "grand-child of the ruler" it was so fitting because Lila was the strength behind the Mitchell Family. And which was even more perfect was the meaning of our daughter's middle name, it meant "little ruler," so perfect for a Reed. She would be the ruler of my heart, along with her amazing mother who stole my heart many years ago.

Our miracle…our daughter.

Epilogue

My legacy

Walker

Three months later

THIS WASN'T JUST another ribbon cutting ceremony to commemorate the completion of just some building I had designed. It was a project that took nearly three years to complete, The Reinhart Building in Frankfurt, Germany. It towered to fifty eight floors, bypassing Main Tower, which was currently the fourth tallest building in Germany.

The Reinhart's, never to be outdone, wanted their new building to outshine the rest in Frankfurt. They had not two, but three public viewing platforms, and an observatory that overlooked the river. I was the only architect that was commissioned to bring their dream to reality. It was shining in all of its glory as the sun's reflection bounced off the glass panels.

The foyer of the building housed several living art installations that were open to the public. Every building I designed, including Samuel's wing at Johns Hopkins, carried a special piece of my mark, my personal legacy that would carry on for years to come. Donovan and Tom relentlessly asked me how I would mark this building. The Reinhart's left it to me. With their blessing, I included a children's park, which I fully funded on my own. Being a new father, I wanted to give back something for the community to know children were rejoicing and playing happily. The park included state of the art equipment. For the summer months, a splash play area would be utilized for the smaller children, and a rock climbing wall was available for ages ten and up.

We couldn't have asked for a better day. It was sunny with a temperature of sixty six degrees. I was introduced by Sebastian and Viktor Reinhart. They aptly named their building "Hart."

As I made my way up to the podium to say a few words, I looked out to the crowd below. My family was here. Reese was holding Fallon securely in her arms. She was cocooned in pink blankets. Jackson and Riley, along with my mother were proudly smiling at me. And for a brief moment, I almost felt as if my father was here too. I vowed never to question the universe again and prayed he would find peace…Today is that day where I feel his presence most. He took pride in our work and our company. It was just beginning to go global at the time I had joined my father. It was my vision to take our company to reach new innovative heights. Now a year after his death, here I am celebrating yet another accomplishment in my career. Surrounded by all the reasons I do what I do. My heart warmed as they cheered me on, as I took my place.

"Hello. I'm Walker Phillip Reed, CEO of Reed Global. I am profoundly honored to be standing here today, as we officially cut the ribbon to this extraordinary building, a vision by my friends here, Sebastian and Viktor Reinhart. Collectors of art, who commission artists from all over the world to bring their fruits of their labors to the public. As you have already seen, Hart currently houses three remarkable living art installations. It is a sight to see, and I truly hope you take in of all its wonderment and beauty."

"And now to another work of art I would like you all to visit and be familiar with. A gift for the children. I know many of you are working parents who put in many long hours to provide for your families. Time is so precious when your children are young. You want to spend every minute you can with them and hold close to your heart every memory you create. Let this playground be a new memory for you and your children of all ages to enjoy."

"I've recently become a new father again. After nineteen years raising my son, I begin this amazing journey all over again. I look forward to the day where I am able to push my little girl in a swing and hear her squeals of laughter, as she urges me to push her higher. I will promise to bring my 'Fallon' back here one day and play with her until she tires me out. Thank you again for sharing this wonderful day with us. Now if you're ready, please follow me as we open and celebrate 'The Thomas Mitchell Walker Reed Playground' for the young at heart."

As soon as I said his name, Reese hugged our daughter closer, and let go of the balloon she was holding. We watched it soar through the bright sky and through the clouds. We would never forget the son we lost. Now, in his honor, children would always have a place to play, laugh, and dream.

OUR STORY BEGAN on a college campus, where two strangers met and fell in love. While their love was tested beyond measure, it was the kind of love that was precious and rare to find. Two souls patiently waited until they were reunited by fate. New promises of forever were made, even when they were constantly being tested and pushed beyond any reasonable limits. Their love never wavered, and hope was never lost. It was celebrated and cherished through the eyes of their daughter. They would count their blessings and create new memories to share.

Our story already had the greatest ending.

Three hearts...One love

Our love...Forever.

...And they lived happily ever after

The End.

Acknowledgments

For my amazing husband, Henry:

You know I can write all the book boyfriends I want, but you, my love, were my first. Life truly does imitate art. With every book I write, there's a piece of you and me in it. You are my Forever love.

For my sisters:

"Family isn't always blood. It's the people in your life who want you in theirs; the ones who accept you for who you are. The ones who would do anything to see you smile, and who love you, no matter what." I chose this quote for you. I love each and every one of you. Thank you for your friendships and filling my heart with your love.

For Mindy Guerreiros:

If I had to sum up one word that defines you, I would have to go with "Everything." That's what you are to me. Your friendship has taken up a space in my heart, and I am forever thankful for you. You are incredibly talented with amazing mad skills. You bring my characters to life with your unique way of making the perfect teaser. Thank you for your love and support. I value you as a critique partner. Your creative feedback is welcomed and appreciated.

For Wendy Ferraro:

We're not sisters by blood, but the universe brought us together to be connected as sisters, forever in each other's hearts. Always remember, my friend, if you fall, I will pick you up. We not only share the laughter, but the tears too. The best friendships happen when you don't see them coming. Thank you for steamrolling right into my heart. That's where you will forever remain.

Special Thanks to...

Julie Titus of JT Formatting: Words are one thing, but your creative style makes them sparkle on every page. Thank you so much for all you do to bring my book to life.

Sarah Hansen of Okay Creations: Thank you for another beautiful cover. You captured exactly what I wanted.

Natalie Catalano of Love Between the Sheets: Thank you for your continued support for my work. From organizing my cover reveals to blog tours, you have been in my corner from day one, and all your efforts are so appreciated.

To the many blogs who have shown me much love and support, I am so thankful for you. I respect each and every one of you for taking the time to promote me. Your hard work and dedication is so appreciated, and I respect you so much. Thank you for loving Walker and Reese and believing in their story.

To Kathleen Vaughan Candelario: With all you have going on in your life, you still took time to read my book. I value your feedback and trust your opinions. You have been cheering my couple on from the beginning. Thank you for seeing it through with me and believing I can do it. I had days where I doubted myself, and you were right there to tell me to shut up and write my story. Sometimes a friend knows you better than you know yourself. I love you for that. Thank you, my sister.

To Joe Marron: Thank you for all of your time and energy spent on making *Our Forever Promise* perfect. You have such a talent at wielding words and have a keen eye for errors. I loved our editing sessions where we laughed the entire time. You made this arduous task seem effortless and constantly made me smile. You were there for me on the tougher days when I just wanted to give up. Your humor and words of encouragement got me through it, and for that, my friend, I am forever thankful.

To my readers and fans: Thank you so much for loving Walker and Reese. I know at times I put you through the ringer with their story, and you probably wanted to throw your e-reader once or twice. You have shown me unconditional love and support. Words cannot express how much I appreciate you loving my couple as much as I do. Thank you to Nancy Gennes Metsch. We finally got to meet in person! I thought *I* gave amazing hugs, but *you* knocked it out of the park with your Sparkle! Thank you to Florence Richards. Not a day goes by that I don't wake to a post from you supporting my work. I am Forever thankful to you ladies for your friendships and support.

About the Author

I AM A dreamer. I've always been a dreamer. Some may not have worked out the way I hoped they would, but I also believe that everything happens for a reason.

Writing has changed my entire life. It brings happiness and fulfillment to areas in my life that I didn't even know I was missing. It's also one of the hardest jobs I've ever done. It takes me away from my family, friends, and the little day-to-day tasks that once upon a time seemed normal. Sometimes I like to revisit my portfolio of old short stories, poems, and the inspirational quotes I have kept for many years. Reading through it all shows how far I've come and that the journey I am on now is exactly what I dreamed of many years ago. This makes me smile.

A long time ago, I used to write short stories and poems in journals and kept them privately to myself. It took quite some time and many sacrifices, but now I have three published books and have my very own writing cave. *What the heck is that?* Well, it's my second home where I laugh, dream, imagine, and write my heart out to hopefully produce something that will make other people smile.

Never one to dwell on what I don't have, I value what I do have. I couldn't do what I do without the love and support from my husband, Henry Wasowski. We have been happily married for twenty two years and still have the passion from when we were first dating.

Our love story created the family we have today, our three sons: Zachary, Christopher, and Cameron.

Family is everything to me. When I take a much needed time-out, I love to be with them, have friends over for wine night, and just talk and laugh for hours. Summer days in NJ are spent down the shore, and nights are spent at home around the fire pit toasting s'mores.

One of my most valued lessons that I've learned in this life was from my beloved mother-in-law, Julia Wasowski. She was an amazing woman, and I miss her every day. A role model for many, including myself, I don't believe there was anything she couldn't do. She taught me to never take one day God has given you for granted, because you never know what tomorrow will bring.

She had many words of wisdom that I carry with me and have passed along to my kids and friends, and now to you, dear readers. They come in handy on the hard days when life treats you harshly and you just want to give up:

Life is an incredible journey.

We are all an open book. Every day is a new chapter to write in our story. Lessons are to be learned and shared.

Keep moving forward.

Never give up on your dreams.

Smile, and make others smile.

Believe me…Your spirit will thank you for it.

Xoxo

I would love to hear from you. Please feel free to reach out to me:

EMAIL:
AuthorMaryAWasowski@gmail.com

FACEBOOK:
https://www.facebook.com/pages/Author-Mary-A-Wasowski

TWITTER:
https://twitter.com/wasow6